Post-War Dreams

by

Brenda Whiteside

Post-War Dreams

Cover Art by *Rae Monet, Inc. Design*

The Wild Rose Press, Inc.
PO Box 708
Adams Basin, NY 14410-0708
Visit us at www.thewildrosepress.com

Publishing History
First Vintage Rose Edition, 2015
Print ISBN 978-1-5092-0352-9
Digital ISBN 978-1-5092-0353-6

Published in the United States of America

"But...but you can't love Susan."

My voice, soft as a whisper, didn't betray the rising fear boiling up from the pit of my stomach.

He gripped my arms with emphasis. "No, I don't."

My stomach calmed a bit, the fear at a simmer. "Does she love you?" I had to convince him his thinking had clearly gotten off course.

"No. I mean I don't think so."

"Is she demanding you love her?" Love was everything. Without love, this wasn't our problem.

"No..."

His hesitation cheered me on. My panic churned barely below the surface as I led him down the path of reason. "Well, then, Benjamin, why—"

"Claire, she's pregnant. I'll have to marry her."

"Marry?" I choked on the word. Fear and panic erupted. "Oh, God, no. Benjamin!" The tears toppled and flooded my cheeks. "This is her problem."

"You know it isn't, Claire." His words were thick and strained. "I have to take responsibility."

"No, Benjamin, no!" I slapped my palms to his chest as if I could stop this madness with a physical barrier. "No, you don't."

He encircled my waist, gently caressed, but held me firm until my tantrum played out.

I folded into his chest, but my anger still had some steam. I balled one hand into a fist and hit his chest. "Why? Why do you always have to do the right thing? Why?" I swiped away tears so I could see his reaction when I glared into his face.

His chest heaved as he stared into my hostility with calmness. "You wouldn't love me if I didn't."

Praise for Brenda Whiteside

"Cheers to Whiteside for writing a heroine who exists outside of conventional romance novels in terms of age and marital status. [*SLEEPING WITH THE LIGHTS ON*] is written with a pleasantly light sense of humor…"

~RT Book Reviews

~*~

"Evocative and thought-provoking. *AMANDA IN THE SUMMER* exposes love's inexplicable complexities."

~Tamara Hogan, award winning author

~*~

"[*THE ART OF LOVE AND MURDER*'s] strength is in its characters and descriptions…The setting was a character in itself. I loved the town! The author really made it come to life, not stinting on details (but not boring the reader either)…the writing kept me turning pages and I never once thought about setting it down."

~Long and Short Reviews

~*~

"A plot that will give you turns that will blindside and twists that will leave you asking, 'what the…'[*SOUTHWEST OF LOVE AND MURDER*] is that dang good! Hard to put down once you start and had you on the edge of your seat needing more!"

~Undercover Book Reviews

Dedication

I grew up listening to my mother's stories of her colorful childhood, sitting with her on Saturday afternoons watching old black and white movies of the 1940s, and learning songs she sang from her teen years. No two eras intrigue me as much as the 1930s and 1940s because of her. My mother's storytelling formed the basis for *Post-War Dreams*. Her childhood memories enriched my life and led me to write. She still enriches my life.

Chapter One
A Day in the Life of…

Finally…a home.

The cheap chenille could've been angel hair as I smoothed the spread over the bed. For most of my life, I'd never had my own room. I'd slept in orange groves, hobo jungles, or beneath the pink ceiling of Aunt Grace's farmhouse.

Straightening, I glanced around, and my mood brightened sunnier than the faded yellow walls of the room. My room.

"Putting your eggs in, Claire. Get on out here."

The aroma of bacon fat and boiling coffee grounds followed my father's words. With the toe of my shoe, I shoved movie magazines under the bed; magazines left strewn beside the orange crate nightstand last night before I drifted off to sleep with visions of Clark Gable in my head.

In three steps, I entered the closet-sized bathroom and checked my hair in the cloudy mirror above the worn, porcelain sink. A tug at my blouse closed the gaps between the buttons, and I wondered fleetingly if I'd inherited my curves from my mother. With hands on my hips, mimicking a Betty Grable pose, I addressed an imaginary camera. "Another day in the life of Claire Flanagan, rising star." A flick of my head spilled waves of strawberry-blonde hair onto my face. "Thank you, thank you for being here." My personal silver screen reflected my image, but masked the thousands of ardent fans on the other side. Pulling the chain turned off the bare bulb over the mirror and brought down the curtain.

Humming, I scooped schoolbooks from the orange crate nightstand and strolled into the living room of the rented, wooden house in the Mulberry Shade Cabin Court. The hide-a-bed had been folded back into a sofa with Da's work shirt thrown over the arm. I tugged the coffee table to the front of the sofa with a free hand then straightened the green, latch hook rug. My father, Hamish Flanagan, stood in the kitchen, an extension of the living room. The scene sent a wave of contentment through me.

"Morning, Da."

"'Bout time you got out here. Don't want to end the week with a tardy mark."

His feigned gruffness as he cracked the shell of an egg got little more than a scoff. "They aren't so rigid with seniors. I have tons of time anyway."

Da shrugged as if his undershirt annoyed his shoulders. "Tons of time might be different from your point of view and mine."

The schoolbooks hit the kitchen table with a thud next to last night's newspaper. The block letters across the top stated *U.S. Forces Begin Japan Occupation.* But a lesser headline had my attention while folding the pages. "This is gobbledygook. It doesn't matter the war's over, they're going to keep rationing sugar."

"We still got some."

He sounded distracted. Normally, complaints on rationing would bring a lecture about patriotism or a story from his life during World War I.

"You didn't have to cook eggs this morning. Cereal would've been fine." Breakfast was his meal to prepare while dinner was mine, but bacon and eggs on a weekday was peculiar.

"Why not? Thought you might like some. We don't have to wait 'til Sunday for eggs."

I slipped an envelope from the stack of books. "Would you mail this today?" I fanned myself with the letter. Summer's heat throttled September even at an early hour.

"More requests for autographed movie star pictures?" He nodded for me to lay the envelope on the counter. "Ain't you got enough of them yet?"

"A new star is born every week." My collection filled a cardboard box stashed under my bed. Dreams of Hollywood stardom fueled my obsessive hobby.

With a tug of the door on the dinted, chest-high icebox, I took out the milk, and while shaking the jug, considered my father's ruddy face. Sweat beaded on his temple, a trickle finding a jagged path down his cheek. "What's on your mind, Da?"

He flipped the egg he cooked. "Your momma always said that. *What's on your mind, Ham?*" His mood popped like the grease in the skillet. "Always something on a man's mind."

The wooden legs of the kitchen chair screeched on the faded red linoleum as I scooted to the table and poured a glass of milk. Whatever was on his mind could come to a nice sizzle without my help, and I changed the subject. "I wish we had another picture of her." The only photo of my mother, on a horse, now faded and scratched, gave little more than an impression of what she must've looked like.

"The fire took most everything." He checked the toaster. "Not a one left of little Jimmy or Lois."

I ignored the mention of the brother and sister I couldn't remember. Evoking the memory was like stirring smoke. But, Da lingered in the past, his weathered face wrinkled in thought. My own thoughts drifted to the picture of my mother.

As if he read my mind, he continued. "Her shiny, black hair hung loose on her shoulders." His smile creased deep lines in his cheeks, and he repeated words I'd heard often over the years, when he cared to elaborate. "She was like an Indian princess with big brown eyes—you got those—and that long black hair. Yep, a Choctaw Indian princess." He touched my head. "But you got my hair, like it used to be. Your momma said your hair was strawberry-colored gold." He nodded, turning back to his skillet. "She'd think it right pretty."

Warmth spread across my chest, deep inside, and I didn't know if the pleasure resulted from the compliment or longing for the mother I'd never known. I flipped the hair from my neck. *How silly to miss something you've never had.* My mother existed only in my mind, created from my father's few memories and an old faded snapshot.

He set the plate of eggs and toast on the table.

"Thanks, Da." I cut into one of the fried eggs.

"Well, damn." He pulled the plate from under my fork. "I overcooked the yolk. That'll be my breakfast, and I'll cook you another. Won't take a second."

"Don't be silly. I can eat that one."

"You like runny yolk. Eat your toast and drink your milk." He spooned more bacon grease into the skillet.

I nibbled toast and picked at the flaking blue paint of the tabletop. Had Aunt Grace, my father's sister, been there, she'd have said Da spoiled me rotten. He would've told her to mind her own. *A dirt-poor girl without a mother can't be spoiled rotten.* Of course, if Aunt Grace, a proper lady, had been there, she'd have been cooking breakfast. Although I missed the sporadic stays with Aunt Grace and Uncle Eb, I didn't want to live on the farm like I did when I was a little girl. Feeding chickens and climbing in the hayloft had been fun as a child, but as a young woman, my future wouldn't be on a farm.

"I should write Aunt Grace a letter," I mused out loud.

"Funny you mention her. I talked to your Uncle Eb yesterday."

"Oh?" This sounded like a lead in to *the something* he had on his mind.

Da concentrated on preparing the skillet for his second try at fried eggs.

I thumped the table impatiently at his long pause. "And?" His obvious deliberation made me squirm with wariness.

"Looks like they're paying real good for the end of season green beans and okra. Eb says the raspberries are still coming ripe. A man can make a lot of money in a short time." He carefully cracked an egg over the skillet. "Then the walnuts will be ready."

I frowned and watched for some sign of the relevance of this news. Surely, this had nothing to do with us. "You've been making very steady money as a watchman, Da." And the steady factor had translated

5

into fewer days of drinking.

"True enough, honey, but that job ain't going anywhere. Them crops come and go. A man's got to grab easy dough when it's there for the taking."

I twisted slightly and clutched the back of the chair. "But, Da—"

"The watchman job will be there when I get back."

"You can't be sure." The talk at school brought news of fathers and brothers coming home every day. "There're lots of men looking for good, steady jobs now that the war's over."

"They'll let me take a leave." He darted a glance at me. "Wouldn't be like we was on the road since the picking's around Hemet. And Aunt Grace misses you something fierce. She says Cousin Bernice likes her high school. Knows you'd be right happy with her crowd of friends." He gently tested the eggs, making sure they weren't sticking to the pan. "Fit right back in."

"No!" I slammed a hand on the table. My father's shoulders flinched. "I've got my own friends. I'm not going."

"Now, I—"

"No, Da. I'm *not* going to change schools again." I had a good friend in Pauline Russell, the best I'd ever had. My last year in high school would be spent at one school—North High. "You promised when we moved here our days of following crops were over. We've only lived in Phoenix three months, and you're already breaking your promise." My voice quivered. The tears were close. Swallowing hard, I refused to cry like a little girl. He had to see the woman in his child and treat me as such.

My father rubbed a work-worn hand over his face, starting with his eyes, circling around his cheeks until he ended back at his eyes before he dragged his fingers through his faded red hair. I'd witnessed this gesture all of my life, a pause giving him a moment to think when perplexed. "This ain't like following the crops. It'll only be three months, six tops. We'll be able to come back with money in our pockets." He half-turned toward me with a smile and ignored the eggs frying.

His hopeful face tugged at my resolve, but only momentarily. "Then go. I'm not." I arched my brows the way I'd practiced in the mirror, which gave me a mature, haughty expression, and shook my hair. "You can send me rent and food money until I find a job after school and on weekends."

"Ah, honey—"

"I'm not a six year old you can drag all over the country like you used to do. I'm seventeen, and I have a life here."

"Now, Claire—"

"Are the eggs done?" I squared my shoulders on the chair back. My heart thumped against my chest. If I wanted to defy him, I couldn't look at his pleading eyes.

"You love Hemet. You always said it was your favorite place in California." Da spoke softly, imploring as he cooked.

"Yes, in California."

He lifted the skillet from the stove. "Listen to me, Claire."

"No, Da, I won't." Waving toast in the air punctuated my words. "I *don't* camp under trees, I *don't* follow crops, and as much as I love Aunt Grace, I

7

don't live on someone else's farm anymore. Not even for a few months."

"You know I can't leave you, Claire." A heavy sigh followed his words. "We ain't never lived separate, and we ain't starting now."

I met his gaze and set my jaw. The heat in my cheeks threatened to set my eyes watering, but I held steady and waited out the confusion in his faded green eyes. He'd never met my stubbornness with anger, but outright defiance, new to both of us, might be different.

He lifted my chin with his free hand. "Okay." His tobacco stained thumb rubbed my cheek. "*For now.*"

I clutched his fingers and brushed a kiss across his knuckles. "Of course we can't live separate." Words hung up in my throat for a moment. I blinked, took a deep breath, and threw on a bright, sassy smile. "Why, you'd never get to work on time if I didn't get you up to cook breakfast. And what would you do without me to make your dinner?"

He shook his head when he patted my cheek with his rough hand. Other than the love shining in his eyes, he didn't appear satisfied with our truce. He'd relented and given in to my challenge, but the resulting decision was tenuous at best.

Holding his work calloused hand, I massaged his stubby, scarred fingers with a delicate touch. "Staying here is better, Da. You have a good job. The men in the court would miss you in their Saturday night poker games."

"Maybe. But listen to me, young lady. Nothing saying come summer—"

I let his hand drop. "Summer is ages away. Might be time for a short visit, but goodness, we can't make summer plans this far ahead."

"What I was going to say—"

"I need to get some bobby pins and lanolin-enriched shampoo like Aunt Grace had last time we were there." The plate clinked against the skillet in his hand when I lifted it toward him. "I want to fix my hair like Betty Grable in her movie *Pin-Up Girl*."

He could suppose future plans all he wanted. I didn't know if the short protest from my father or the success of my first defiance convinced me, but he wouldn't break my heart and leave me behind. And he wouldn't break my heart and make me go.

With a submissive noise in his throat, he tipped the skillet and slid the eggs onto the plate.

****

Damn, I hurt. Ben Russell hung his arm over the edge of the bed, felt around for his pack of cigarettes, and the usual morning ache spread through his back and biceps. Lifting freight off trucks at the Sears and Roebuck warehouse strained even lean, twenty-year-old muscles.

He let the sheet slip from his chest. Barely sunrise and the stealth beast of September's heat invaded the house with a stifling breath. He struck a wooden match. The flame fused with dawn seeping in around the edges of the curtained window, dimly lighting the naked walls of the room he shared with his brother, Davie.

Tipping his chin upward, he exhaled. *Another day in the life of a working stiff.* The smoke drifted into semi darkness, giving substance to the invisible aroma of bacon, biscuits, and coffee. He could hear the muffled voices of his mother and sisters as they prepared breakfast.

"I wonder where the son of a bitch is waking up this morning," he muttered.

He rubbed his eyes and wondered why the hell he thought about his father. Years after the family moved from Kansas to Arizona, years after living in a tent on the banks of the canal along Grand Avenue, and sometime after his father built their house on Thomas Road in Phoenix; the love of drink overpowered the responsibilities of raising six children. The old man disappeared one day. Abandoned his family. A relative in Kansas sent a note a few years back about seeing him. *He could live anywhere he damned well pleased.* They got on without him.

Ben breathed deep; the smoke filled his lungs while the scent of bacon filled his nostrils. He pinched his shoulders together, rolled his head side to side, and worked out yesterday's kinks. What the hell. He didn't get such a raw deal when he quit school to find a job. School had been a damn waste of time anyway. He'd suffered through one year of high school, but marching around with a wooden rifle in ROTC, like a fool, had been the clincher.

At least the old man taught me how to shoot a real gun before he took a powder.

He took another drag off his cigarette.

"You're damn small," the beefy-faced foreman at Sears had said the day he went for a job five years earlier. He showed the big Kraut foreman a thing or two. Short and skinny, even for a fifteen year old, he had puffed his chest and declared, *"You can damn well try me, can't you?"* Then he'd pushed his chin into the big burly man's face. *"Got nothing to lose trying me."*

Ben smiled at the memory. He could show his son

of a bitch of a father how a *real* man took care of a family.

But taking orders from a pea-brained boss had grown old. Sure, he was next in line for a foreman job, but so what? Then he'd take orders from fat, smelly O'Ryan. Not much better. He didn't intend on spending the rest of his life pushing freight, or pushing men who pushed freight. His future lay in building houses, someday owning a construction company.

The creak of the oven door told him the biscuits were nearly done. His brother stirred in the bed across the room.

"Yeah, I'm awake," Davie's voice, muffled in his pillow, called out sleepily.

"If you aren't, you should be."

His brother yawned audibly and kicked at the sheet covering him. "Jesus, it's hot in here. When's it ever going to cool down? Should've put the mattress on the porch last night to sleep out there."

"Keep your eyes open for a good deal on a car," Ben said. "Time I got my own wheels. Maybe someone coming into the garage will be looking to sell." He swung his feet over the side of the bed and stubbed out his cigarette in the ashtray on the floor.

Another yawn from across the room. "You tired of begging to use mine or tired of double dating?"

"Both, you bastard." He raised his arms over his head, stretching. "You're so hot 'n' heavy with Barbara in the front seat, it gets damned embarrassing with a date in the back."

"You sound jealous."

"Hard to get to first base with your big brother in the front seat."

Davie snickered. "Kind of hard to get to home plate your first time when you can't even get to first base."

The pillow came hurtling through the air before the wise ass had finished his needling.

"You jealous, being hog-tied by a woman?" Ben guffawed.

"Engaged, you punk. And at least I don't spend my nights horny like you."

A knock at their door halted anymore bantering.

"David Leroy! Benjamin Willis! Are you boys up? Biscuits are nearly done, and I'm not keeping them warm this morning."

"Yeah, Mom," they answered in unison.

He scuttled out of bed and beat Davie to the only bathroom in the rambling house. The noise of the flush brought his brother in without knocking.

"You serious about me keeping my eyes open for a car?" he asked as he waited for his turn at the sink.

Ben nodded, toothpaste filled his mouth and bubbled out the corners. He leaned over and spit. "I'm going to see old man Mallory about a construction job. I'll need my own transportation. Can't ride the bus like I do to Sears every day."

"Construction, huh?"

"Hell, yes, Davie. With the war over, construction's going to take off. Mallory knows I got rid of the outhouse and built on this bathroom. Got all the material from his hardware store. Did those odd jobs for him last winter on weekends, too. Mallory Construction is getting busy, and I'm going to be in the right place at the right time. Hell, I'll own the place someday."

"Be a carpenter like the old man." His brother's words came low as if thinking out loud while he spread toothpaste on his brush.

Ben wet his comb, faced the mirror, and flung water as he raked through his thick waves. "Nothing like that son of a bitch."

"I didn't mean—"

"Never mind. I know." He dried his hands. "You know, Davie, I don't know why the hell Barbara would want you. You got Mom's nose and your feet stink."

"Yeah, well, you can't tell a book by the cover. She has the hots for me twenty-four hours a day. You, on the other hand, ain't nothing but a pretty boy with not enough in your jeans to satisfy—"

"Who the hell you calling a pretty boy? And my wanger makes yours look—"

One loud rap on the bathroom door interrupted them as their sister, Ruth, yelled, "Biscuits are on the table. Mom says to get your asses out here."

Davie erupted with laughter as Ben opened the door to the receding backside of his older sister. "Mom did *not* say asses."

Ruth wiggled her fanny in response. He flipped his towel back at his brother before shutting the bathroom door.

In his bedroom, Ben shrugged into clean jeans and a gray, long-sleeved shirt with Sears embroidered above the pocket. He ran a finger across his front teeth as if to polish them. With a side glance at the mirror, his slight overbite was visible. He never believed himself to be handsome, despite what his sisters told him. At least he didn't get Mom's hook of a nose like Davie did.

His brother came through the door, pushed him

aside, and rummaged in the dresser for his clothes. "When you going to talk to old man Mallory?"

Ben shoved him back as he turned to leave the room. While rolling the sleeves of his shirt to the middle of his biceps, he answered, "Soon." His stomach muscles tensed with the thought. "Got to be soon, before he gets his crews set. I got to get the job."

"You will, Ben." He nodded. "It's your future."

"Hell, yes." He finished the last roll of his shirt then flexed his biceps, feeling the material hug each arm. "Now, I'm going to eat all the damn bacon before you get your ass out there."

"Hey, Ben." Davie paused, forearms resting on the edge of the drawer.

He stopped in the doorway. "Yeah?"

"You're twice the man Dad was."

"Yeah, and twice the lover you are." Ben managed to get out the door before the shirt his brother threw hit him in the head.

****

Outside the window, Arnold loped toward the nearly full school bus, pushing his black hair from his forehead. I kept my face turned toward the melee of students on the sidewalk, watching for Paulie.

"Oh, good, there's an empty seat next to you." He'd made his way along the bus aisle to my row. With one hand on the seatback in front of me, and the other on the seat behind my back, he leaned down. "Scoot over so I can sit with you."

Three rows up, two girls ogled Arnold, giggling, dreamy-eyed in their appraisal. I smiled sweetly. "Sorry, but Paulie asked me to save a seat. You better grab the one up front or you'll be stuck on the next bus."

"Ah, Claire, can't Paulie sit there?" Bending his elbows, he brought his face in close, his green eyes appraising mine.

They were nice eyes, rimmed in black lashes set below thick, black brows. With his hair falling onto his forehead, he reminded me of Tyrone Power in *Crash Dive*.

"I wanted to talk about getting together this weekend," he continued.

Across the aisle, another girl, one of the seniors on the cheer squad, turned to look at Arnold. Keenly aware of the muscles beneath his shirt, I admired the broad shoulders invading my space. "That would be grand, but I promised Paulie." In spite of Arnold's dashing good looks, he didn't have the same effect on me he had on others. I kept my voice low, although with the noise in the bus, I needn't have worried about being overheard. "Be a good boy and sit up front." I brushed fingers against Arnold's hand. When his neck turned red, the guilt of teasing tainted my pleasure ever so slightly.

"I work the matinees on Saturday and Sunday. I thought...maybe...you know, if you come to the back door, I can let you in. I could...sit with you for a while."

See a movie? Perhaps Arnold deserved more consideration. I dipped my chin, glanced at him, and smiled with a cocked brow. "What's playing?"

"Does it matter?" He winked.

"Of course it matters." I checked the edge in my voice. The girls sitting three rows up and the cheerleader watched us intently.

15

"*Diamond Horseshoe.*" Arnold's hand brushed at my back.

"Oh! Betty Grable's new movie. Sure. Let's make it Sunday." I spied Paulie pushing her way toward us. "Now scoot. Looks like the seat up front is taken. You'll be on the next bus."

"Ah, that's okay." He stayed close even as I leaned away. "Seeing you for more than a few minutes in between classes was worth it."

"Why, hi, Arnold." My friend stood behind him, smiling, giving me a wide-eyed, aren't-you-lucky face.

"Hey, Paulie." He stepped back, politely. With obvious effort, he dragged his gaze from me to acknowledge her.

Sliding across to the window, I patted the aisle seat. "All yours, Paulie. 'Bout time."

She edged past Arnold, closer than needed to get to her seat, yet never took her gaze off his tanned face. "Hegelmeyer was yackety today. You have Heggie first hour don't you, Arnold?"

"Hey, mister," the bus driver called from the front. "Get on out of here. I'm full and leaving."

Hesitating a moment, he nodded in the direction of Mr. Jesper, but continued to stare at me. He caught the hair on his forehead between his fingers and brushed the strands back as he smiled.

"*Goodbye*, Arnold." My dismissal earned me an elbow in my side from Paulie.

His feet shuffled as if he couldn't get them in motion, but finally threw a hand up and made his way off the bus. Female heads turned to watch his exit.

"God, you're so mean," Paulie whined as the bus roared to life, jerking away from the curb.

I theatrically pushed the hair from my face and turned my head upward as if I needed to study the ceiling of the bus. "I don't know what you're talking about."

"Oh, pooh, you do so. Any girl on this bus, heck, any girl in school would love to take your place. They all say you're the luckiest to have Arnold for a boyfriend."

I knew all too well. I might've been poor Claire Flanagan of the Mulberry Shade Cabin Court, but as the object of Arnold Smith's affection, I had the envy of every girl in school. It didn't matter. High school crushes and giggly girls didn't interest me. His handsome good looks and popularity weren't enough to make me succumb to his pestering.

"I'm *not* his girlfriend. We're friends, that's all."

"Honestly, Claire!" Paulie swiveled her head to stare at Arnold, who waited on the walk for the next bus. She squared back around in her seat with a sigh. "He might not have asked you to be his girl, but it's perfectly obvious he's got a thing for you." She elbowed me again. "He's cute. He's popular. He's on the football team. What's not to like?"

I'd never had a serious boyfriend. We never stayed in one place long enough, and as my high school years were nearly over, now the boys seemed too young. Besides, if Arnold was the one, certainly the stars should shine brighter, and I'd hear bells or something. I enjoyed teasing him, and he made me laugh, but I didn't have the inclination to spend much time with him.

"I won't have time for a boyfriend."

"Why on earth not?" My friend looked as if I'd

gone crazy. "I've never considered time a factor when boys are involved. And for Arnold, I'd find the time."

I withdrew a yellow sheaf of paper from a book. "I'm thinking about this."

Paulie glanced at the flyer I offered her. "The talent contest?" Her brows lifted, and her nose crinkled with a smile. "Oh, perfect. Are you going to sing? You could win."

"That's what I think." I couldn't remember a time I didn't love to sing and had been complimented all my life on my voice.

"Maybe second semester you can get the lead in the school musical."

"A play?" I hadn't known about the play.

I gripped my books, considering the possibility. *The theater? I could be part of the theater.* There I stood, hands clasped to my breast, singing on stage, dancing to a musical number, the leading man following my every movement with adoration…

"Just like last year. You and Arnold are meant to be."

Paulie's words jarred me back to reality. "What?"

"His girlfriend last year—she had the lead in the play. Got so wrapped up in the idea, her parents took her to California and put her in some acting school. All the girls were glad when she left. Then you moved here…and pow!"

"Strange coincidence is all." An acting school. I'd give anything to go to an acting school. Maybe after graduation… "I'm not his girlfriend."

"He must be attracted to theatrical women, like you." Paulie laughed.

The bus slowed to a stop behind a city bus at the

end of my friend's street. She smiled as she waved out the window. My gaze followed her wave to a dark-haired man, lunch box in one hand, gray shirt thrown over his shoulder in the other. I admired a smile so bright the sun wilted.

"Who's *that*?" I asked.

"My brother, Benjamin." She stood. "Looks like he got home early today."

His gaze passed from his sister to me as he nodded his head. I'd been to Paulie's several times after school, but had yet to meet all of her siblings. *Benjamin.* I needed to spend a good deal more time at my friend's home.

"This bus is leaving with you on it, Pauline Russell, if you don't get off now," the driver called.

"Go, Paulie," I said without taking my gawk from her brother. "See you tomorrow." She'd asked me to spend the night with her the next day.

As she joined him, he said something, and when she answered they both looked up. Paulie waved. Benjamin smiled. Then she elbowed him, shoving him toward home. The muscles across his back rippled under the thin, white T-shirt, and a quivery sensation fluttered below my stomach.

Farther down the road, as Paulie and her brother walked along, I caught a glimpse of their mother standing on their front porch, waving. Mrs. Russell embodied the perfect momma; short, round, always smiling as she stood at the stove or bent over the washtub. I rested my head against the warm glass. Funny. I couldn't remember my mother, but I'd imagined her differently. A beautiful Indian princess would walk with grace, slender and tall, her voice lilting. She'd love her children fiercely, play with them all day long, and sing them to sleep at night. What kind of mother would a Hollywood starlet be?

Theatrical.

Arnold liked theatrical women.

The bus moved forward, and I glanced over my shoulder for another glimpse of Benjamin. Going to my friend's Saturday night now brought on a different sort of anticipation. Why didn't Arnold affect me the same way Paulie's brother had in a brief moment?

Arnold had undeniable potential. His Tyrone Power looks combined with broad shoulders would photograph well. Admittedly, there were times, when close, his dazzling smile and the mint scent of his breath were quite attractive. Aunt Grace might call me boy crazy like she did her oldest daughter Mae.

But Benjamin wasn't a boy. Boys' muscles don't show through their T-shirts and make my stomach quiver. The seriousness in his blue eyes intrigued me beyond any boy I'd ever met. Certainly more than Arnold.

Arnold's persistence had become seriously annoying, but other times, he made me laugh. And an actress needed a handsome leading man on her arm. Hollywood sent scouts all over searching out hidden talent in the most unlikely places. Phoenix, Arizona would be as likely a place to be discovered as any other. If Lana Turner could be discovered sitting on a soda fountain stool in a drugstore, then why not?

"This is your stop, Claire. Quit your daydreaming and get off my bus."

Blinking away glittery images of stardom, I lifted my head from the window and gathered the books from my lap. "Sorry, Mr. Jesper." I flashed a movie star smile before hopping down the steps. "What's a gal without her dreams?"

Chapter Two
Saturday Night at the Russells'

I kicked off the covers, exposing clammy skin to the breeze coming in the opened window of my bedroom. *God, I wish I had an electric fan.* I limited wishing to the fan, which seemed feasible, unlike wishing for an evap cooler. I lifted the nightgown from my legs, the breeze cooled my thighs, then I rolled closer to the window. With my eyes closed, I sighed contentedly and admonished myself for wishing for anything. Hadn't I already gotten what I most wished for—my own room, my own bed, and Da working a steady job so we didn't have to move around?

I hadn't heard him come in the night before. For a moment, no sounds came from the living room/bedroom of my father, but a short, snorting noise soon signaled he slept safely in his bed.

Swinging my legs to the floor, my toes landed on envelopes of autographed pictures of Victor Mature and Hedy Lamar. I pushed them under the bed with my foot.

After using the bathroom, I padded bare-footed to the kitchen, and slipped past the sleeping form of my father. I filled a glass with water, some splashing onto the dirty dishes he'd left in the sink. He'd found the leftover fried ham and collard greens I'd wrapped and stored in the icebox. I'd eaten dinner without him, but left a plate of food to eat cold whenever he came home. On payday Fridays, Da couldn't always make it past the Beckin' Inn Bar with his pay in his pocket.

Hopefully, the nosey old landlady, Mrs. Snyder, hadn't seen what time he got home.

Skinny, old, dried up prune. Always peeking out her curtains at the comings and goings of the Flanagans. Or she'd stand on her porch pretending to get fresh air so she could spy on us every time Da got home late.

I gulped another drink of water, as if washing a bad taste from my mouth. The old biddy had the nerve to knock on our door the first week of school. I remembered her words with disgust when the door opened to her sour old face. *"Are you home alone in the middle of a school day?"* she had asked me. Of course. When a person is sick they stay home in bed. *"You don't run around like that in front of your father, do you? A grown girl like you?"* Only an old biddy would find a flour sack nightgown indecent.

"I'll get breakfast." Da stirred, one arm coming up in the air waving. "You go get dressed."

I set the glass in the sink with the other dirty dishes. "Ha! Today's Saturday." At the back of the fold out bed, I put my hands on my hips, and narrowed my eyes. He would see my wrath, even if it had little effect on his behavior.

He raised his head from the pillow an inch, opening one eye as if he was Popeye. "I should of knowed."

"Why? Because you're hung over?"

He rubbed his face in a circular motion as he slid one leg then the other over the side of the bed to sit. "I'm no such thing." Again, he rubbed his face as he gathered his thoughts in search of justification to offer me.

I would've preferred he wasn't a drinking man, but had difficulty staying upset when his good-natured excuses were about as hard to see through as cellophane.

"Just normal cobwebs from a good night's sleep. A man's allowed to sleep in on a day off, ain't he?"

"Sleeping in, is it?"

"'Course, I should of knowed this wasn't a school day or I'd be getting you up."

"Umph!"

My father's payday habit didn't sit well with me, but I could do little about it. Truth of the matter, he made a stop at the Beckin' Inn once in a while between paydays. He always came home, never drank away the money we needed to get by. His fondness for drink, though, left me to take care of him at times. I didn't mind. No matter our circumstances, he'd always taken care of me like a protective, cuddly, loving, Irish Da should. Good men had their ways. Women worked around them.

"Then you go get in the shower and wash out those cobwebs while I make us some oatmeal. I'll get the coffee boiling, too." I patted his stubbly cheek. "After breakfast, maybe you'd like to take me to Lark's for shampoo, like Aunt Grace had, and bobby pins. I'm going to the Russells' tonight, so I want to try out a new hairstyle."

****

"I'm sorry our old clunker gave out this morning, or I'd take you to the Russells'." Da leaned against the kitchen counter, watching me gather my things into my arms.

I bent to see my reflection in the toaster. Bobby pins held the sides while the curls fluffed around my neck when I shook my head.

Smiling, I straightened. "That's okay, Da. At least we got nearly all the way home before it died. It's not far to the Russells', and the sun's down far enough so it's not hot." I hefted the small duffel bag over my shoulder, careful not to crease my dress in the process. "You be sure you get the clunker fixed before Monday morning. And as long as you're at it, fix the headlights 'cause you aren't going out again after work unless they're *both* working." I poked a finger into his chest.

He snatched my hand and kissed my fingertips. "You're a mother hen, Claire."

"The butter beans should be done shortly, and there's bread in the cupboard."

"I know where the bread is. Scoot on out of here. Your old man can feed himself."

"Someone's got to look out for you." I kissed his cheek. "I'll be home before lunch most likely. I think I'll go to a matinee in the afternoon." The screen door creaked as I opened it. "Don't lose the dollar you won from Mr. Ragsdale in last week's poker game."

"Don't you worry about your old Da none. Have fun with your party. Be sure to thank Mrs. Russell for letting you spend the night."

I cut across the grounds of the cabin court, a patchwork of water-starved Bermuda grass crisscrossed by dirt paths dotted with mulberry trees. As I walked between the square, wooden homes, a few of the tenants, sitting on their porch steps enjoying the oncoming evening, greeted me. A breeze, combined with fluffy clouds blocking the sun, had cooled down what started off as a warm September day.

The route to Paulie's didn't follow the roads as I skirted the properties of several large homes then crossed a field to enter a stance of cottonwood trees. Near the edge of the cottonwoods, her house with its porch became visible. The green paint had long ago faded and the white shutters and trim on the porch yellowed. Only the hardiest grass, surviving on infrequent summer showers, grew in patches around the house. A lone bougainvillea flourished at one corner of the porch, the red blooms twinkling like Christmas tree lights in the sunshine. The covered porch ran the length of the house. Two battered wooden porch chairs occupied one end, and a car seat commandeered from an unknown source stood beneath the kitchen window at the other end.

My friend sat on the steps waiting. She stood, dusting off the back of her skirt as I emerged from the trees.

"Hey, Claire."

I plopped the small duffel on the bottom step, but didn't sit, not wanting to take a chance of soiling the seat of my yellow dress. "Hi, Paulie. Am I too early?"

"Heck, no. I told Mom you'd be here for dinner." She looped her arm through mine. "Grab your bag, and we'll put it in my room."

At the kitchen door, I smiled at Mrs. Russell peeling potatoes at the kitchen sink. "Hi, Mrs. Russell. Thanks for having me over."

"You're welcome anytime, Claire, dear." At four feet ten inches, her elbows rested comfortably on the rim of the sink. "Glad you came in time for dinner."

A deep breath as we passed by the kitchen flooded my senses with the yeasty smell of bread baking. "This is so nice of your momma," I said to Paulie's back.

"She likes us all at home. The more the merrier. Shoot, there's always someone extra at the dinner table, especially Saturday night 'cause she makes a big pot of potato and egg drop dumpling soup. Although, there're a few less since Jack joined the Navy."

We entered the bedroom she shared with her older sister, Ruth.

"Throw your bag on the bed."

"Jack is your oldest brother?" I'd visited Paulie a few times after school, but never stayed long enough to meet her sister or brothers, except for the youngest, Richie.

"Yep. He's been gone nearly a year."

Passing back by the kitchen, I snickered to myself with the glimpse of Mrs. Russell at the stove. She sang, her head bobbed, and her round bottom wiggled while her foot tapped to her song.

"Ruth is next oldest." Paulie pushed the screen door open. "Then David, then Ben, then me, and then Richie. You know Richie."

"He's a cutie." We returned to the porch. "So, when are all your siblings getting home?" I brushed at my nails in an attempt at casualness. My thoughts had drifted to the brother I'd seen at the bus stop.

"All my siblings?" Paulie smirked.

"Yes, your brothers and—"

"I know what siblings means." She giggled. "Sometimes, you sound kind of hoity-toity." We leaned against the porch railing. "Ruth won't get home 'til after her shift at the restaurant around eight. Davie and

Ben had to work today, but should be home before too long. Richie is around here somewhere or over at the neighbors. You can bet the guys will all be home for dinner."

"Dinner is quite an affair here, with so many people." My heart tugged a little, thinking about my father sitting alone in the kitchen, eating the butterbeans.

"An *affair?*" Paulie laughed. "Chaotic mess is more like it."

I'm not sure why, maybe because Da recently mentioned the family I couldn't remember, or maybe because of Paulie's large family, but my thoughts wandered. I gazed down the dirt road, straining to recall a memory, before the fire, of what must've been meals with laughter and children's high-pitched voices, my father at one end and my mother at the other end of the table.

"I'm not going to have a big family," Paulie stated. "One or two kids will be plenty."

I shrugged, noncommittal. The imagined recollection of my family, too vague without the memory of the faces, eluded me and, as thoughts often do without our control, morphed into another vision. My mother's form faded as I took her place. Da became a handsome dark-haired man with a loving smile.

A silly, fanciful notion.

Closing my eyes for a moment dismissed the illusion of my future. The cottonwoods rustled, warning of the breeze about to invade the porch. I turned toward the trees so the wind caught my hair and lifted some strands from my neck.

"What about you?" Paulie pressed.

"That's a long ways off to think about." I fussed with a bobby pin.

"We're out of high school this year. Surely, Mr. Right will come along soon." She nudged me. "Mr. Right may be in front of your eyes right now."

I frowned and ignored the obvious reference to Arnold. "There's lots to consider, you know? Finding a man who will put family first and, well, risking…" I rearranged another bobby pin and flashed a smile. "He'd have to compete with Hollywood."

"Ah, Claire, you can't worry about how it'll turn out or you'll never get married." Paulie spoke quietly, her hand coming to rest on my arm. "I don't have a dad, and you don't have a momma, but we did once, and we do okay now."

My complicated, multi-layered past had been peeled away in a few sentences.

"Years away, dear, years away." I batted eyelashes at my friend's serious tone. "I'll have to see if I can fit marriage in around a Hollywood career."

"Really…" Paulie pursed her lips, her fingers tightening on my arm.

I patted her hand, moved away slightly, and dismissed a conversation I wouldn't even have with myself. "Speaking of Hollywood, I've given some thought to Arnold's qualifications in the leading man role."

Paulie rolled her eyes. "At least you're considering him for something." She squeezed my arm affectionately, shrugged her shoulders, and let her hand drop.

My friend could be silly at times and certainly over the top about Arnold, but her concern, although unnecessary, was sweet. I shook my head slightly to fluff my hair. "What do you think?"

"Your hair looks gorgeous, Claire. Gosh, you're a looker in that dress."

I glanced down, a bit self-conscious at the way my bust hinted at exposure. "Thanks."

Paulie straightened, smoothed her white blouse into her pink skirt, and glanced at her own modest chest. She sighed. "I'll never fill out a dress the way you do."

"Oh, you're so petite, so slender." I admired her features. She had an enviable button for a nose, unlike mine with a bit of a bump on the bridge; the result of a game of Kick the Can with cousin Mark years earlier.

She grimaced. "I doubt petite and slender will ever get me called sexy like you."

Rita Hayworth and Betty Grable were sexy. I pulled my tummy in and straightened my shoulders, flattered even if it was my best friend bestowing the compliment. "You're so cute. I wouldn't worry about the curves."

"I won't get the attention of guys like Arnold with cute." Paulie sighed. "Something tells me he prefers the curves." She leaned forward against the railing and rested her elbows. "I mentioned to him maybe stopping by tonight, since you two are practically going steady."

"Paulie!" I shot off the railing, hands on hips, glaring at her.

"You are..." She shrugged and avoided eye contact.

"But you should've asked me."

"Oh, pooh." Paulie moved to the gray car seat pushed against the wall at the end of the porch, her chin up defiantly. She whirled around and flounced onto the seat so her skirt fanned out on each side of her. "Saturday nights here are pretty much open to all our friends and friends of friends."

I strolled over to the car seat, and pushing Paulie's skirt aside, sat close to her.

She patted my arm. "F...U...N. Most popular boy in school, talent contest—the star of North High. Your father will be happy you're having fun, not wondering where his dinner is."

Paulie had scratched below my surface. I had no reason to be mad, but parties with a large group, much less knowing a guy long enough to consider him more than a friend, was new territory. Jitters skidded through my stomach. I countered nerves with theatrics. With my hand on the side of my face, I drawled, "Well, *dahling*, there is something to be said for stardom."

Paulie pursed her lips, nodding.

"You're way too serious. I think there's more here than you're admitting. 'Fess up."

"Like what?" She blinked, nervously.

"Like *you're* the one who wants Arnold here."

"I'm no different than any other girl in school. Don't look at me like that!"

I laughed. "Calm down, Paulie. I don't blame you. In fact, tomorrow when I go to the matinee, you're coming with me."

"I am?"

"You're my best friend. If he can get me in, he can get you in, too." Having her along might keep Arnold at a distance for now. Three friends seeing a movie together. "Betty Grable and Dick Hames." The latter name came out as a sigh.

"But isn't it a date?"

"Nah. He's sneaking us in the back door. If this was a date, he'd walk me in the front door."

Paulie's eyes glistened. I considered tamping down her enthusiasm. But maybe my doubts about Arnold had more to do with me than him. After all, I had only known him for a few months, and although he seemed more like a boy than a guy to be serious about, the girls at school had grown up with him.

"I've never snuck into a theater before. Sneaking into a dark theater with Arnold…" Paulie laughed. "Are you sure this isn't supposed to be a date?" She appeared at once timid and suspicious.

"I'm sure. He's getting me—us—in to see a movie for free." She narrowed her eyes, but I quickly recovered. "Dick Hames! He's *so* dreamy."

"Arnold's dreamy."

"Oh for Pete's sake, Paulie. Arnold is a *boy* and a friend, but not in combination."

"Oh, pooh, Claire." She batted at my skirt.

"Okay, okay, a good friend. We haven't made any promises to each other or anything. He's cute. He's fun…but…"

"But what?"

"Oh, I don't know." A hint of guilt over the difference between how I felt about Arnold compared to how he felt about me passed like the breeze drifting over the porch boards. His were childish whims of infatuation, pushy, uninvited. "It's kind of hard to explain…" I toyed with the folds of my skirt. If most of the girls at North High were stuck on Arnold, a great catch I didn't appreciate, then I wished my best friend could change places with me. *If only…*

"Hey, ladies." The blur of a male figure in jeans

had ascended the porch steps, not pausing to pass pleasantries. He opened the screen door and entered the house.

Benjamin.

My second encounter brought on an unexplained reaction. My heart pattered even though I'd barely caught a glimpse.

"Oh, hey, Ben," Paulie said. "You look tired, big brother."

Her words stopped him inside the doorway. "Little bit." He paused behind the screen.

"This is Claire."

When his head tipped in my direction, I'd swear my breath caught in my throat.

"Nice to meet you, Claire."

"Same here," I muttered as the screen door shut behind him.

"Now, where were we?" Paulie put a finger to her mouth.

I looped an arm through hers. "We were going to see if your momma could use some help. Come on." I pulled her from the seat. "Let's help, then freshen up before dinner."

We let the screen door slam behind us and turned into the kitchen in time to see Benjamin lift his mother from the floor and spin around twice.

"You stop that, Benjamin Willis. Man or no, I can take a hand to your hide, if I need to." Her hands flailed gently at his chest.

He laughed as he set her down, then steadied her before letting go. Taut muscles on the back of his arms flexed with the effort. His deep laugh filled the kitchen. I couldn't help being drawn into this entirely pleasant scene, comical and radiating love, inviting me to take part in their joy.

His mother snatched a dishtowel from the counter and swiped at his legs.

"Hold off now. I give, I give." He withdrew what appeared to be a check from his back pocket.

Mrs. Russell accepted the paper without comment and stuffed it into the frayed pocket of her red checked apron. He kissed her on the forehead, took the bottle of beer she offered, and left the kitchen with a nod in my direction.

I sniffed the sweat of hard work and the yeasty smell of beer as he passed by. My head reeled for a moment with the warmth of the kitchen and the people within, combined with the essence of what I labeled *man*.

****

Ben stood under the cool water and rinsed away the ache of work. His eyes closed, the water pummeled his head, and he smiled, proud of the plumbing. No more trips to the outhouse or heating water for the outdoor washtub. Tomorrow, he'd talk to Harold Mallory. If he could get on a crew with Mallory Construction, the first step of his plan—to own a construction company—would be in motion.

He took a deep breath as he stepped from the small, metal enclosure. The aroma of Mom's bread baking filled his senses; hope swelled his chest.

If Mallory hired him tomorrow, he'd give Sears a week's notice. With the higher salary, he'd be able to save more before contributing to the family expenses. He and Davie relinquished their pay to their mother, but not because of any rule of the house. Mom had never asked them to quit school and work. Ben thought of the system as an unspoken code of ethics. The checks were cashed then put into two tins. He and his brother took from the 'what is leftover' tin for their personal needs. They all played by the same code, except for Ruth. She shared, but she didn't hand over her check. Men were responsible. Women operated by another set of standards.

He smiled at his reflection as he shaved. The grin continued as he stood at the bureau in his room to put on a fresh, tan shirt.

Female voices drifted from the kitchen while he rolled the sleeves to the middle of his biceps. He took his last drink of beer, now room temperature, as an unfamiliar, ringing laugh rose above the chatter.

Young Claire sure is a pretty gal.

****

There were no introductions made when the dinner guests descended as soon as Paulie set the glasses and jug of iced tea in the middle of the table. She'd quickly given me a rundown of who sat where. David, with his fiancée, Barbara, sat across the rectangular, wooden table from me. Two guys I'd never seen before sat on the other side of Barbara. I deduced they were friends of David as they continually leaned across her to yell their comments—the amount of talking and commotion made yelling necessary to be heard. Mrs. Russell sat at the head of the table. Another girl, a friend of Barbara's, sat at the opposing end. Richie sat to the left of me, Paulie to my right, and on the other side of Paulie, sat Benjamin.

Richie chattered non-stop.

"My gosh, is dinner always like this?" I asked the

youngest Russell when he'd paused long enough to take a bite of a dumpling.

"Like what?"

"Like…" I looked around, unable to find a word to describe the group.

He tore a piece of bread from a loaf in front of him. "Can you reach me the butter?"

"Excuse me, Paulie." I leaned across her and touched the butter dish as another hand took hold from the other side. My gaze followed along a nicely muscled forearm to a bulging bicep in tan.

The face of Benjamin Russell leaned out from beside Paulie. "You want to fight me for it?"

Smiling eyes, so blue I thought of early spring skies and the morning glory flowers Aunt Grace grew, startled me. I froze, lulled by the intensity of his gaze as I gripped the butter dish.

"I'm only teasing."

His second comment jarred the words from my mouth. "You better be, because I have a mean right." I lifted the dish and ducked back beside Paulie.

"Thanks." Richie snatched the dish from my hand.

I sat, blind to the commotion around me, and wondered what had just happened.

"Time to get the rug rolled up." David's voice rose above the din.

The guys stood, chairs scuffing on the wooden floor. Benjamin darted between Richie and me; his knife swooped in for a slab of butter he slathered on his bread before dropping the knife on Richie's plate. He strode out of the kitchen, taking bites of his bread. My gaze followed him without my command.

"Are you done eating?"

Paulie's voice brought me back to the table. I took a deep breath, swallowed my thumping heart, and smiled. "I'm stuffed. Mrs. Russell, dinner was superb."

"Why thank you, dear. An old, Americanized German dish."

"Could I get your recipe? Da would love it." What fun, to cook something new for my father. "And German."

Mrs. Russell chuckled as she rose. "Not much of a recipe, but I can tell you what I put together." She picked up dishes from the table. "I doubt *Mutter* would consider this version very German."

I scraped some plates into a box Mrs. Russell had set on the table. "*Mutter*? Your mother was German?" My curiosity rose. The war and Germany had dominated the news for so many years. "Did your mother live in Germany?"

As we scraped dishes, washed and cleaned the kitchen, Paulie's mother told the story of her parents' arrival into the United States.

As she spoke, I marveled at how lucky it was they'd immigrated long before the rise of Hitler.

Marlene Schmitt, an only child, lived on a farm in Wichita, Kansas until marrying at the age of sixteen. I thought the story delightfully romantic, but Mrs. Russell soon decided she'd talked enough. The topic of Mr. Russell apparently not one she cared to elaborate.

"Old stories Pauline knows by heart." Her hands fluttered in the air. "Let's get the poker chips out, shall we girls, in case anyone wants to play cards later?"

While Paulie dug the red, white, and blue chips out of a drawer, I peeked into the living room. The two mismatched couches and tattered, overstuffed chair had been pushed against the walls. The threadbare, floral rug lay like a jellyroll against the other wall. A Kay Kyser band record played on the RCA Victrola, and the only person in the living room, one of David's friends, thumbed through the records.

"What happened to everyone?" I strolled across the empty room.

The wide-faced friend glanced up and smiled. "On the back stoop having a smoke or getting a beer out of the tub." He stuck his hand out awkwardly. "My name's Pete."

"Nice to meet you. I'm Claire. Any good records there?"

He ruffled the tight pile of curly hair atop his head and turned back to the stack of music. "Hell, yes." Clearing his throat, he muttered, "Sorry 'bout that."

"Oh, no need." I wanted to giggle at his unease. His flat face and curly, brown hair combined with his silly, crooked grin were comical. "Any Frank Sinatra or Benny Goodman?"

"Oh, sure." He tapped his foot, his head bobbing to the band tune playing.

"I love to dance, almost as much as sing. Do you?"

"Can't carry a tune." He grabbed my hand and twirled me around. "But I sure as hell don't have two left feet."

I laughed as he led me around the empty floor. His polished moves were in direct contrast to his unpolished social skills. Mrs. Russell appeared at the doorway of the kitchen and clapped her hands, moving the top half of her body in rhythm with the music. When the song ended, he twirled me a last time. I spun around as Paulie and our friend, Laura, walked into the living room.

"Why, Pete, I didn't know you could cut a rug like that," Paulie teased with her compliment.

"You ain't seen nothing yet. Flip the record over, will you?" He took my hand again and bowed from the waist. "One more time?"

Paulie skipped over to the phonograph with Laura in tow. She cranked the sound up, tempting more couples off the stoop and onto the floor. David and Barbara danced next to us. I had to laugh at Pete's goofy expression as he showed off his easy to follow dance skills.

On one spin, I caught sight of Benjamin, who stood against the far wall. His gaze drifted over me, appraising, and caught me mid-twirl, so when Pete went into a back bend, I stumbled. He recovered, popped up, and grabbed me around the waist. He danced close to me for a moment, apologizing for catching me off guard.

"No, my fault." I glanced to the wall again, but Benjamin had vanished. "That...that was cool. Please, do it again."

He swung me out. This time I paid attention and danced in place until he righted himself.

"You're one hip chick, Claire."

His goofy enthusiasm had me laughing as he twirled me then bent me over backward when the song ended. An upside down Arnold stood in the doorway. He ran his tongue along his bottom lip, half of a leering smile.

****

Ben flicked his cigarette into the dirt, hopped down the two steps of the back stoop, and ground the butt into the earth with his toe. Plunging his hand in the icy water, he pulled a beer from the tub of bottles.

"Oh, gosh, that's fun!" Barbara burst through the back door onto the stoop with Davie close behind. She fanned her hand in front of her face. "I didn't see you in there, Ben."

Davie threw his arm around her waist, scooped her from the stoop as he barreled down the steps, and stopped beside his brother. "Ben's got no rhythm. Poor boy can't dance."

"At least I'll admit it, unlike you, lumbering around in a circle."

"Ha!" His brother picked a pack of cigarettes from his pocket. "I'd guess if you saw some lovely young miss, you might risk looking like a fool."

Ben took a drink of his beer as he considered the lovely young Claire. She certainly knew how to light up a room. "You might be right, although tonight, they're either too young or too old." He winked at Barbara. "Or too taken." Even Claire apparently had a boyfriend in Arnold Smith.

"You should get out more, meet someone, or bring a gal from work," his brother said, offering him a cigarette. "Or join a monastery."

Ben shook his head to the smoke and laughed at Davie's needling.

Barbara's eyes sparkled. "I know a girl—"

"No!" They both interrupted in unison.

Davie kissed her nose. "Honey, you're as cute as a pussycat, but we've both seen enough of your girlfriends to decline your offer."

She spun away from him. "I have some very nice friends." A smile accompanied her protest. "I'm going to go powder my pussycat nose." Prancing up the stoop steps, she left them snickering.

"When are you two tying the knot?"

His brother took a drag, held the smoke, then released with an audible breath. "Not as soon as she'd like."

Ben narrowed his eyes. "Don't put her off, Davie." He didn't have to guess what held up setting the date. "I'm sure Mallory will hire me. And Jack's letter said he'd get a pay increase this month. I'll wager Ruth'll toss a bit more in the can, too."

"I've got some saved. Mom knows I've been pinching a few bucks here and there." Davie rubbed the back of his neck. "I don't want to move Barbara in here. We want our own place."

"So get it. Don't worry about this household. I'll take it on with ease." Ben's bravado rang true to his ears and brought a breath of excitement to his chest. "I got a feeling about construction. You give me a month. Set the date for the next."

"Davie," Barbara called from the doorway. "Perry Como. Slow song."

His love-struck brother dropped his cigarette and stomped on the ember. "An invitation I can't refuse."

"Tell her," Ben called as he took the steps in one stride.

Davie flashed a smile and thumbs up, then held the door for Arnold as he came out of the house.

"Hey, Ben." The kid swirled the bottles around the tub until he found two colas.

"How you doing, Arnold?"

"Couldn't be better." He squatted beside the tub to flip the cap from the bottles with the opener hanging on

41

a string. He took a drink. "Are you still working at Sears?"

"Yep."

"Do you know if they're hiring any part time help, and who I'd talk to?"

"Thought you worked at the Paramount Theater."

"I do, except that's a kid's job. I'm saving for a car. Need to make better money, and when I graduate, I think Sears would be a swell place to work full time. If I could get my foot in the door now, part time, I might have a shot at a decent job after graduation."

"Good thinking there, Arnold." Ben took a swallow of beer. "As a matter of fact, it's a possibility. Go in and talk to Maggie in HR. Say on…Wednesday. She's a good lady."

"Maggie, huh? Gee, thanks." The kid raised a brow. "If I mention you, do I get special treatment?" He snickered. "Just how good is she?"

"I have no pull there. Talk nice to the lady." *You twerp.*

"Oh sure. I'll turn the charm on." He winked. "Speaking of ladies, I better get back to Claire. She'll be missing me."

"Sure. Later."

Ben frowned at the little pissant's back. He didn't actually know Claire. She'd certainly held Pete's attention. Her laugh was so real you had to laugh with her. And her voice—when Paulie talked her into singing—she sang better than any of the Andrews Sisters. From what he'd seen of her today, she seemed too mature, too classy for a punk like Arnold.

What the hell does she see in that guy?

****

Paulie giggled for the umpteenth time as Pete unsuccessfully led her through a dance maneuver. He laughed, good-naturedly. I noticed a different scenario unfolded with Laura and David's other friend, Fred. He might not be a slick dance partner like Pete, but from the look on Laura's face, he had other attributes.

Arnold planted himself in front of me and blocked my view with his wide shoulders. "Here's your cola, cutie."

"Oh, Arnold, you're so suave," I cracked, taking the offered bottle.

He rested his free hand on the wall above me and leaned within a breath of my face. I backed up as far as possible, but he still loomed only inches away.

"You are, you know, awfully cute."

"You're very nice to say so." His closeness made me uncomfortable, and I glanced from side to side to see who might be watching. Perhaps if I'd been intent on securing Arnold's undying love, I might've been more receptive.

"I'm not trying to be nice."

His husky voice grated on my nerves like sandpaper. I shrugged off growing irritation and glanced up. His gaze didn't meet my eyes.

"Are you staring down my dress?"

He jerked, his hand falling from the wall. His neck went red. "No. Well, yes." He gawked at my chest again.

I erupted into laughter.

"Jesus, Claire. You drive me crazy." He licked his lips and finally brought his gaze to my face. His frown addressed his embarrassment, and he pouted like a little boy.

"I'm sorry, Arnold. Honestly, you looked like a kid in a candy store there for a minute."

His expression relaxed, although he didn't look amused. "Ah, Claire."

Frank Sinatra crooned from the Victrola, his voice soft and mellow in a slow melody.

Arnold touched my arm. "Dance with me." He didn't wait for an answer as his fingers found mine and drew me away from the wall.

I glanced around his shoulder, more interested in the social maneuvering in the room than his dancing steps. Paulie and Pete talked to Barbara's friend on the other side of the room. The glint in Pete's eyes when he stared at my friend struck me as fondness beyond friendship. Arnold sighed, nearly groaned as he hugged me closer, and his hand dipped a few inches lower to my waist. Pliant, I didn't much care which way he pulled me until his hips made contact. A hard bulge massaged my flat stomach. I caught my breath, shivered, and pushed back from him.

He leaned his head so his mouth tickled my ear. "You want to take a walk?"

"No." I tried to yank my hand from his, but he held tight. "Arnold!"

"I'm sorry," he whispered. "Don't walk away from me."

My heart pounded. And not from mutual ecstasy. Most young women would've been shocked at Arnold's condition, but sporadic stays with Aunt Grace had lent much to my education in carnal matters. Between the farm animals and older cousin Mae's activities in the hayloft, I'd become well acquainted with the physical attributes of the male species.

Knowledge aside, the only emotional response I experienced was irritation. The protest didn't make it to my lips. When I looked into his face, another more exhilarating notion sprang to mind—the little boy's fascination with my cleavage, his pleading face, and imploring tone granted me power I'd not known existed.

He moved his hips against me again, and heat spread over me. I glared, yanked my hand from his, and took a step back.

"Please, Claire. Don't walk away from me right now."

"Then stop, or I'll leave you dancing alone!"

His eyelids drooped. "Do you know what you do to me?" He pouted.

"I'm pretty sure I do."

"What do you want me to do?"

He relinquished control with a deep-throated whine, and became mine to wrap around my finger anyway I chose. "I want you to play nice." In spite of his most manly reaction to me, I glimpsed the kid in the candy store again. He pouted, appropriately reprimanded as I scolded. "I mean it. The song is nearly over. Back up a bit and calm down or we'll never dance again."

He obeyed, clutching my hand.

When the song ended, "Cow-Cow Boogie," with the volume turned up a notch, played out. I spun away from him. "Well?" I asked, ready for a fast dance.

"I'm sitting this one out." He skulked toward the back door.

Paulie appeared beside me. "Where's he off to?"

"To get a cola, I think."

45

As he walked away, shoulders stooped, I felt a pang of guilt. Like a young rooster, his first attempt at strutting his stuff for a hen had gone badly. My ability to take advantage of his childish infatuation with me gave me power, but rang a bit shallow.

I shrugged and glanced around. "So, where's your shadow?" She met the question with a blank stare. "Pete, Paulie, Pete."

"Ben waved at him to play a hand of cards." She gestured toward the kitchen. "And what do you mean my shadow?"

I edged over to peer into the kitchen. A portion of the back of Benjamin with Pete next to him was visible. "He's been by your side most of the evening," I sang in a teasing lilt, still gazing at what I could see of him.

"Oh, pooh." Paulie waved me off. "I've known Pete for…well, a long time."

"So?" I brought my attention back to her. "I think he's kind of sweet, maybe sweet on you."

We peered into the kitchen as he slammed down his cards and punched Benjamin's shoulder. Benjamin's deep laugh resonated beyond the kitchen walls, impassioned me for reasons I didn't understand or take time to consider.

"You think?" She tipped her head and considered the possibility.

"I do. He fancies you, and Fred seems really smitten with Laura." Now, if I could shake Arnold and find someone more to my liking…

I glanced into the kitchen again.

"And Laura's hot for Fred." Paulie giggled.

"Where's Laura anyway?"

"I think she slipped out to the porch with Fred, but

they won't be there for long. Momma keeps her eye on everyone. She has her ten minute rule."

"Her ten minute rule?"

"Momma seems to know where everyone is at all times, and if a couple sneaks out to be alone, she manages to find them within ten minutes." Paulie shook her head in wonderment. "She'll pretend she's out for some air or looking for someone else, but she makes sure the couple isn't alone for more than ten minutes. When she finds you, you know to hightail it. Momma doesn't miss a thing around here. Hard to even have a secret."

I laughed. A glance in the direction of the back door brought a sigh, and I thought of Arnold outside pouting. He'd come to the party because of me, his infatuation a compliment in spite of his unwanted advances. "I guess I better see about Arnold."

"See about him. Why?" Paulie narrowed her eyes. "What did you do?"

"Nothing really." Although the moment had been at his expense, my chest swelled with a sense of empowerment. "I scolded him a little for being too fresh." He'd get over it.

Her eyes sparkled. "Tell me what he did."

"Later," I whispered conspiratorially in her ear. "Right now, I need to *soothe* my leading man's ego."

I found him standing by the tub of bottles with Richie. The ice had melted, and only a few bottles remained in the cold water. Richie talked while Arnold listened, nodded his head, and tipped his bottle for a swig. I lifted the skirt of my dress in one hand, fanned out the folds, and stepped down as if descending a grand staircase.

47

"Hello, fellas." I seemed to remember Betty Grable saying that in one of her movies.

Arnold merely nodded his head. The faint light from the doorway fell weakly across the boys, but the brightness of the moon allowed me to see that his eyes held much more welcome than he let on.

"Hi, Claire." Richie's smile shone. "If you're after a cola, they might be all gone." He bent over the tub.

"No, I don't want one. Thanks, anyway." I stood next to Arnold, but not close enough to make physical contact.

No one spoke. A lone cicada sang while I considered what to say to him. Although I didn't like his pushiness, his friendship meant enough to me that I didn't want to hurt him.

"Did you know you can eat cicadas?" Richie asked. A repulsive fact that wrinkled my nose. "Yeah, they taste like asparagus."

"Oh, Richie." I laughed and looked at Arnold to draw him in. He appeared fidgety and lost in his own thoughts.

"They live for four years, mostly underground. In Mississippi they get really old—like seventeen years."

"Richie," Paulie called from the back door. "Momma wants you in the kitchen."

"Shucks." He shuffled toward the house. "See you guys."

"It's rather late in the season for cicadas to be singing," I said after he'd gone inside.

Arnold tossed his empty bottle in the box beyond the tub. "I hoped I'd hear you sing again tonight."

"You did?"

"Sure." He shoved his hands into his pockets, his

voice still somber. "You have a swell voice, Claire."

"I'm going to enter the talent contest." I dipped my chin and looked at him. "Do you think I have a chance?"

"You'll win." The enthusiasm in his voice nearly matched the lust in his eyes.

I clasped my hands behind me and rocked side to side. His passion might speak for something other than his belief in my talent, but still sounded sweet to my ears.

If only he wasn't so pushy.

"I absolutely love the movie theater. What time should I be at the back door tomorrow?"

He inched closer to me. "Two." His arm flinched as if he might reach for me.

"I could go to the movies every week," I gushed. "You're so lucky."

"I'm working, but yeah, seeing the movies—or as much as I see of them—is swell." He cocked a brow. "I can get you in all the time."

"Really?" His green eyes sparkled at my enthusiasm. "Although, sneaking me in…"

"Not always. I get a discount, so we can do it on the up and up. Doesn't always have to be on the sly." His voice cheered, eager to please.

"A discount? Oh, that would be grand!"

Our minor dust up had settled. Things were coming together. A handsome leading man with open access to the theater, and the talent contest—the first venture into taking my aspirations public. Add to that a good friend I didn't have to say goodbye to at the whim of my father and who had an interesting brother. I truly was home. The moonlight glowed like the spotlight of a stage, shining on me.

His hand touched my waist then jerked back as Mrs. Russell's voice drifted out to us. "I'll check the tub of drinks."

The door opened and the small, round lady toddled down the steps. "I thought I should check on the drinks."

I snickered. Mrs. Russell's ten minute rule had been invoked.

"It's getting rather late, don't you think?" I asked. "I doubt we need any more."

"I think you're right, dear. And that's a good thing, because I think we're out of ice and drinks anyway." She smiled, eyes wide. "I suppose we'll be cleaning up shortly." Peering into the sky, she mused, "What a lovely moon tonight."

I followed her gaze and agreed. "I think the man in the moon is smiling at us."

Beside me, Arnold fidgeted and glanced upward then at me. He shuffled his feet, but apparently had trouble conversing in Mrs. Russell's presence.

"Well, then." The short lady clapped her hands. "Why don't you grab those last two bottles of beer, Claire, and Arnold, you can take the tub toward the back of the yard. Dump the water so it runs over to the cottonwoods."

"Sure, ma'am." He grabbed the edge of the tub to drag it away.

I followed Paulie's mother to the back stoop.

"Not much of a conversationalist, is he?" Mrs. Russell commented as we entered the house. "Handsome young man. Paulie does have that right."

"He's leading man material," I told her. "Engaging

conversation may not be in his repertoire as of yet, due to his youth."

She laughed. "You may be right there, my dear."

No music played as we walked into the living room. The rug in place, David and Pete moved the furniture back. A few others called their goodbyes as they left through the front door.

In the kitchen, Barbara stacked dishes into the dishwater. I joined her and dried, glancing out the kitchen window. Benjamin talked to friends as they climbed into cars or drifted onto the road to go home. He laughed and waved to a departing car then turned toward the house. I drew out of sight, not sure why I needed to avoid being seen watching him. When he came into the house, he didn't pause in the kitchen, but continued on to his room, I assumed.

"Hey, Barb, hon. About done there so I can take you home?" David came behind her and wrapped his arms around her waist. "We have to drop Laura home, too, and she has a curfew."

"You go, Barbara," I said. "I'm spending the night. We can finish."

"Thanks." She dried her hands on the flour cloth, patted David's arm, and turned her head for a kiss before she stepped away from the sink.

"Have you seen Laura?" he asked Paulie when she walked into the kitchen with Arnold.

"She went out front."

My friend walked outside with the couple to find Laura. I went back to drying dishes.

"I guess I'll take off now."

Arnold's voice startled me. I'd forgotten he'd come in with Paulie.

"I had a swell time tonight." He moved next to me and brought the length of his body in contact with mine.

I leaned slightly away from him. No sense sending him out the door with his man parts at alert. I tilted my head and folded the dishtowel. "See you tomorrow at two o'clock. Bye, Arnold."

His face edged close, but when the screen door slammed, he jumped.

"Looks like everyone's gone," Mrs. Russell called out as she came indoors.

Reluctantly, he moved to leave.

"Oh, Arnold, I didn't know you were still here," she said.

I suppressed a smile. Somehow, I didn't believe her.

He strode to the front door. "Thank you, Mrs. Russell." With a quick wave, he ducked out the door as Paulie came back in.

"Do-ta do-ta-do." Mrs. Russell sang a nonsensical tune and did a tap-dance step all her own as she set the clean glasses on the shelf. "Fun tonight, huh, girls? Do-ta do-ta-do. Go on now to your room. Ruth's in the shower, so get some gab time in before she climbs into bed."

Paulie threw her arms around her mother and kissed her cheek. "Night, Momma. Sleep tight."

"Good night, Mrs. Russell."

We headed into the hall and shut the bedroom door behind us.

"Oh my God, I'm tired," I said and threw myself on Paulie's bed.

My friend flopped next to me, laughing. "Did you see the serious spit swapping between Laura and Fred before he took off?"

"No, really?"

"Yep. She's found herself an older man."

"Like Pete," I said.

"Pete?"

"Yeah, what does Pete kiss like?" I propped my head on my hand.

"How would I know?" Paulie shrugged her shoulders, gesturing with her hands in the air.

"You could find out, if you want."

She toyed with a strand of her hair. "Mmm, Pete…nah. Pete?"

"He's definitely sweet on you." I held up a hand when she opened her mouth to protest. "And don't tell me he's a good friend you've known forever. I've heard it said good friends make good lovers."

She hit me on the head with a pillow. "Speaking of lovers…"

I shoved the pillow back, and waited for the expectant request.

"Tell me about Arnold's freshness with every tiny detail."

"Oh, child," I drawled and folded my hands on my chest. "I don't know if you're ready for such information."

"C…laire." Paulie scooted closer. "Spill before Ruth comes in and shuts us up."

I told her every lurid detail as requested, perhaps embellishing with a little extra drama. The performance was the important aspect of any good story.

Chapter Three
Leading Men Are Made Not Born

"No car possibilities come through the garage yet, huh?" Ben asked on the drive to Mallory Hardware.

"Might be a black Ford, 1933," Davie answered. "A guy came in last week and said he'd let me know this week. The car's been parked for a while, but I'd help you work on it."

Ben flipped his cigarette butt out the window. "I guess I could try the place down on Grand, but doubt I got enough for a lot sticker price. I know you'll tire of getting up early every damn morning to drop me off at some construction site."

His brother pulled to the curb in front of the hardware store. Resting his arm over the top of the steering wheel, he smiled broadly. "You know, old man Mallory's daughter always had a thing for you in grade school."

Ben cocked an eyebrow. "I remember." He slid out of the car, shut the door, and leaned in the open window. "It's the whole reason I'm going after this job. I heard she never got over me."

Davie laughed heartily.

"I'll find a ride home. You and Barbara have fun today."

Ben strolled around the side of the building to the back door. Even though the hardware store closed on

Sundays, Joseph Mallory would be in the back office working on the books. As he rounded the corner, a shiny blue car with gleaming white walls came into view. He stopped to admire the Ford. In the window, on the passenger side, a cardboard sign read: For Sale $225. Ben made one trip around the vehicle, and as he reached the front bumper again released his breath in a whoosh.

He studied the sign again. "Son of a bitch." There were only a couple of small dints on the driver side door. Ben leaned in the window, his heart thumping, as he gazed at an interior obviously well cared for.

"Is that you, Ben Russell?"

He glanced over his shoulder at Joseph Mallory who stood in the doorway of the office at the back of the store. His quizzical expression erupted into a wide smile as he recognized Ben. Mallory, in his mid-sixties looked the picture of health. He'd taken on a stoutness in the last few years, yet his arms were muscled and his eyes bright. He ambled into the sunshine.

"Good afternoon, Mr. Mallory." Ben stuck his hand out to the calloused handshake offered.

"Now, Ben. I told you to call me Joe, if I remember correctly."

"You're right, you did." He gestured toward the car. "I was admiring this Ford. Are you selling her?"

"My sister, Betty, is."

Ben opened the driver side door. "You mind?" He slid in the seat when he got the nod from Mallory. He relaxed, ran his hands around the wheel, and skimmed his fingers over the flawless seat as he imagined the fanny of a young lady seated there. A fanny that would scoot over close while she put her hand on his shoulder or leaned her chest against his arm as he gripped the wheel, the engine roaring as they cruised Grand.

Whoa, boy.

He pulled at his pant leg and cleared his throat as he climbed out.

"Why the hell does your sister want to get rid of this beauty?" He couldn't keep his gaze off a vision sent to him by divine intervention.

"Her husband died last year. The car's been sitting in the garage and mocking her, she says. She asked if I could, in her words, 'Get rid of the damn thing.' Betty doesn't want it in the family 'cause it was like his lover, and she can't stand the sight of her." He shook his head. "Hell, she isn't even asking enough. I told her I'd park it out front on Monday and maybe someone would buy it."

"A thirty-nine?" Ben admired the rear fender skirts and white wall tires.

Mallory nodded. "Yep. Deluxe."

"Got some extras on her."

"Yep." Mallory hooked his thumbs in his pockets. "A four door sedan with grille and bumper guards is worth more than two hundred, I can tell you."

Ben ran his hand along the hood. "Hell, yes," he all but sighed out loud. "Can I look under the hood real quick?" When the hood was lifted, he leaned over the clean engine, unable to believe his eyes, then rubbed the back of his neck. "Sure would like for my brother to take a look at her. He's a mechanic."

"You want to take her home? Bring the cash in the morning, if you're interested?"

"Hell, yes. That okay with your sister? Me taking her home?"

"Why, Ben, it's not like I'm handing her over to a stranger." He patted him on the back and chuckled.

Ben stuck out his hand to offer Joe a handshake. "You got it." He gazed at the car, not believing the good fortune of finding her before Joseph Mallory parked her in front of the store tomorrow.

"Were you just walking by when you spotted the car? Ride the bus here or what?"

The questions broke into Ben's thoughts. So lost in the excitement of probable ownership of the blue Ford, he'd forgotten his true mission.

"I'm here to see you, actually." His palms went sweaty, and his excitement quelled by a slight hint of nerves. "Unless you're too busy, I'd like to talk to you."

"I could use a break. Come on in."

Ben followed his future employer through the scarred metal door of the back office.

****

"This feels very sneaky." Paulie's glance darted side to side.

We stood outside the back entrance to the Paramount Theater. "I wish he'd just open the door. The movie starts in ten minutes." I stamped my feet with impatience. Following my friend's lead, I scanned side to side.

"What if someone comes out to dump trash?" She giggled.

"What?"

"Well, what would we say? Why are we hanging around the back door?"

I recognized more excitement in her voice than nervousness. "Ignore them, I guess. None of their business." I glared at the back entrance for the tenth time. "Where is—"

The door swung open. Arnold grabbed my arm and pulled me in. I managed to grasp Paulie, dragging her along before the door closed shut. His arm went around my waist, but he stopped, mouth open, when he saw the unexpected companion behind me. We stood in a narrow space, cordoned off by a black curtain. I could hear the cartoons that preceded the movie. The floor sloped upward, putting Paulie below and behind me. I hoped the dim lighting combined with her vantage point hid Arnold's surprise at her presence. He blinked and his nostrils flared.

"We were wondering where you were," I whispered. "I thought Paulie would have kittens before you let us in."

He frowned and seemed totally lost for words. Even in the dim light, his green eyes darkened with disappointment, or maybe anger.

Paulie stepped forward, so I inched closer to him and brushed at his arm still clinging to my waist. "Arnold." Touching him did the trick. His frown relaxed. "Are you going to keep us standing here, or do we get to sit down?"

"Wait here while I see if the other usher's in the lobby." He stuck his head out the black curtain.

Paulie wiggled beside me, cupped a hand to her mouth, and whispered in my ear. "I feel perfectly wicked!"

Arnold reached back and took my hand. "Come on. Follow me."

We followed the narrow passageway a bit farther to the end of the black curtain where it met the wall. He slowly edged the curtain back, glanced around, and when the scene on the screen changed, throwing a veil of darkness across the theater, we emerged. He quickened his pace so, as the light from the screen brought some visibility, we stood in the aisle by a row mid-theater. With his flashlight, he guided us to the three seats closest to the aisle.

Tightening his grip on my hand, he nodded at my friend. "Go on, Paulie. Have a seat."

Once she moved forward, he nudged me to follow. He sat next to me on the aisle. "Don't let anyone sit here. I'll come sit with you as much as possible."

"That would be nice." I nodded, though my attention was already taken in by the screen as the credits scrolled down.

His hand clutched my jean-clad knee with a warm, firm grip. I clenched my legs together, not objecting so much to the touch but his presumption in doing so. If I could hear bells ringing or get goose bumps, he could presume all he wanted. It wasn't happening for me.

The credits faded as the movie began.

"I'll talk to you later," I whispered in his direction without a glance. He leaned close, but I put a hand up. "Shush. I don't want to miss the beginning."

He paused; still I continued to stare straight ahead until he gave up with a sigh. As he rose, I wiggled fingers and relaxed in the seat.

Paulie whispered, "What did he say?"

"He'd sit with us when he could."

"I think he looked surprised or something, that I'm with you."

"No, I don't think so. Shush for now." I settled back in the velvet chair, inhaled the smell of popcorn and relished the plush cushion as the light from the screen danced over the bold gold and red décor of the theater in my peripheral vision. Not counting being with my father, I'd rather have been at the theater than anywhere else.

Totally ensconced in the movie, I jumped when Paulie tapped me on the shoulder.

"I have to pee. You need to go?"

"No." My gaze remained on the screen.

"Want to split a cola?"

"Sure."

She slipped out of her seat with barely a notice from me. Moments later, Arnold plopped into the aisle seat, surprising me with his hand on my knee once again.

"Hi, Claire," he whispered, leaning in close. My ear dampened with his breath. "I brought you some popcorn." He sat the treat in my lap with pressure, his hand remaining on the box. "I'll bring you a drink next time."

"You…you don't have to." I took hold of the box, lifted, and wrenched it out of his grasp. "Paulie's bringing us one to share. Thanks for the popcorn."

I jiggled my knee, but his hand remained. He must've thought I responded favorably to his touch because he moved his fingers in a caress. I still didn't hear bells.

"Why did you bring her with you?"

I canted away from him so I could look into his face. In the glow of the screen, flickering with the change of scenes, his handsome features took on a theatrical effect. For a moment, I could understand why all the girls in school went weak-kneed around him.

"You didn't say I couldn't bring someone with

me." I smiled, playing stupid, knowing well enough he'd intended on sitting with me in the dark like a movie date. But I'd meant my words to Paulie—if this was a real date, we'd have walked through the front door together. "You like her, don't you?"

"Sure, Claire, but I wanted to be alone with you."

"Oh, really, Arnold. We're in a theater full of people." I gestured with my hands. The woman behind us made a noise to quiet us, so I leaned a bit closer to whisper, "It's not like we're—"

Without warning, he pressed his mouth against mine, bumping noses in the process. His hand left my knee and grasped my waist. I froze. His lips worked at mine for a moment before I pushed him away.

"*Arnold!*" I hissed.

"Oh, Claire," he moaned. He made a movement to kiss me again.

I slapped a hand against his chest and stopped his advance. "You can't push yourself on me like this."

The heat beneath his shirt warmed my palm. I swallowed hard, and my stomach fluttered in spite of my protestations. My body's response puzzled me. As soft and inviting as his lips were, I didn't want Arnold reacting to me in this way. Or me to him.

"Push myself?" He licked his lips. "You know how I feel, and I see it in your eyes when you look at me." His hand massaged my waist, then dropped a few inches to my hip.

The lady behind us made another shushing noise.

I squirmed and shook my head. The dark theater lulled, the face of gorgeous Dick Hames filled the screen, and the most popular boy in school doused me with his desire. Arousal and repulsion came at once.

"Was my kiss so bad?"

"No. It's…I don't know what you see in my eyes when I look at you. I don't mean to…" *Lead you on. Did I?*

He had dropped his chin, and his gaze ran over my body. I cleared my throat. He licked his lips.

Beside Arnold's head, Paulie's face appeared out of the darkness. "Pssst. Let me in, guys."

He jerked and stood as I sat back, swishing my knees to one side. Once Paulie sat, I glanced at him, but he'd already headed back to the lobby. I heaved a thankful sigh and faced the screen. Arnold as my leading man, yet only a friend at the same time, wasn't working.

My friend tugged my sleeve.

"He brought us popcorn," I whispered.

"He brought more than popcorn." She bumped me with her elbow.

"What?"

"Why do you think I took so long? I had to wait until you two quit necking."

"We weren't necking."

The woman behind us leaned close to our shoulders. "Girls, please."

"Sorry." I brought my mouth next to Paulie's ear. "We were *not* necking." I punched her arm when she snickered. "Watch the movie, and I'll tell you after. Give me a drink of the cola."

Two hours later, after I'd insisted on sitting through the end credits, the lights came up. I blinked, gazed around the opulent movie theater, and waited while the heavy, red velvet curtains closed across the screen.

"All right. We can leave now."

"Finally," Paulie said. "You sure like to get your money's worth. Or you would, if you'd paid." She followed me up the aisle. "I wonder why Arnold never came back."

"Maybe he got busy." Or maybe having someone with me took the fun away. That suited me fine.

Once in the lobby, Paulie stood on tiptoes and scanned over the people milling about. "We really should thank him."

A hand came from behind and wrapped around my fingers.

"I want to talk to you a minute before you leave." Arnold dragged me a step before I responded to his sudden appearance.

"Wait." I jerked my hand, but he held fast.

Paulie smiled and indulgently dismissed us with a wave of her hand. "I'll wait right here."

He squeezed my fingers and guided me through the theater patrons to the side of the snack bar and around a corner into what looked like a storage area tucked behind a curtain. Lugging me around so my back was against the wall, he took my other hand, and moved so close I felt his breath on my face.

"It was swell seeing you today, Claire. I wish we'd had more time, and you'd come alone."

My chin nearly touched the opening of his white, collared shirt where the heat from his body channeled. A spicy fragrance on his skin mixed with the aroma of popcorn on his shirt and produced an intoxicating balm. I swallowed, dizzy with his scent.

"Thank you for sneaking us in. I really need to get back to Paulie so we can catch the bus home."

His body shifted, and his thigh brushed against my leg. In one fluid motion, his hands brought mine above my head, pinning me to the wall, and his mouth muffled my gasp with a kiss.

In an endless moment, I tasted him, the texture of his tongue licking mine, his warm, wet lips. I squirmed, wrenched at my hands, and twisted my face away with a gasp. "Arnold, stop."

He levered his full weight against me, his hardness rendering me speechless. With his body leaning into me, the size of his manhood became more apparent than on the dance floor last night. My mind wandered to some of the larger animals I'd seen on Uncle Eb's farm. I nearly snickered at the thought when he shifted against me. His eyelids drooped dreamily. My irritation spiked.

"Stop!"

"Claire," he moaned soft and husky. He let my arms go, but ran his fingers down my sides, gently. His weight held me in place, but not so forceful to be considered rough.

"I don't like this, Arnold. Stop," I hissed through clenched teeth.

He backed up; one hand still rested on my waist. "Why?" Though he frowned, the longing in his eyes didn't cease.

"*Why?* For Pete's sake, Arnold." I pushed him farther away then smoothed my blouse. "I'm not going to put up with this kind of behavior from you."

"Don't be mad at me, Claire." He ran a hand through his hair. "You drive me crazy." His other hand massaged my waist, and short snorts of breath showered my forehead as he made the effort to calm down. "I just have to *touch* you."

"A girl likes to be courted, not manhandled every time you get close." I shoved at his chest, but his body sprang back as if made of rubber.

"Courted?"

"Yes, courted. I've never said we're anything more than friends, but you insist on taking liberties I haven't given you permission to take."

"I don't want to be your friend."

And what did I want? When would I go all mushy over him like the rest of the girls? "If you can learn how to treat me properly, well then, kissing *might* come along in due time." Maybe if he took it slower... "Watch the leading men in the movies. You'll see what I mean." I shoved off from the wall and turned out of his embrace. "I need to get back to Paulie." I stomped from behind the curtain and glanced back. It occurred to me how clueless he was.

Paulie rocked on her heels. "My gosh, about time."

I looped an arm through hers, and we headed out the door and onto the sidewalk. "Arnold needs to watch more of the movies he ushers for."

"What's that supposed to mean?"

"He's got the looks, but he doesn't have the style."

"Sure didn't look that way to me, and everyone else in the theater, while I cooled my heels with the cola, waiting to get back to my seat."

We'd arrived at the bus stop.

"Really, Paulie. *He* kissed *me*. I didn't kiss him."

"You didn't look to be fighting him off too hard."

Fight him off? No, I hadn't fought too hard. I hadn't kissed many boys, especially big, handsome boys other girls swooned over. Boys who teetered on manhood, who opened their mouths and stroked my tongue with theirs. Boys with bulging appreciation, curious and hard.

My cheeks heated. "I'm awful. I should have slapped his face. But—"

"What were you doing just now?" She narrowed her eyes at me.

"Kissing again. Yes, again," I answered the excitement in her face as she grabbed my arm. "The man is getting a bit carried away, and if he doesn't learn some style—"

"But it was good, wasn't it? Don't tell me you didn't like it."

"Well…"

"'Fess up, Claire!" My friend's eyes were as sparkly as the evening star. "Tell me. What are his lips like?"

"Oh, really, Paulie."

The bus wheezed along the curb, gushed hot air over my calves, and the doors whooshed open. I pushed her ahead of me. Once we scooted onto the gray vinyl seats, Paulie persisted.

"All right." I relented. Until I could make up my mind exactly what Arnold meant to me, there didn't seem to be any harm in feeding my friend's vicarious thrills. "Let's see, he's more of a Van Heflin than a Cary Grant. We'll have to work on his style…" I lowered my voice and brought my forehead to nearly touch hers. "He leaves me a bit breathless in ways I find rather exotic."

"Uh-oh." She moaned. "Is it love, Claire?"

"Love?"

I sat back. The last word I associated with Arnold

was love. Horny impulses fueled his childish infatuation. Love was between a man and a woman. His boyish pursuit might be flattering and certainly provided some experience I'd not had, but love was an entirely different issue. Was I being unfair? He was my age.

A moment of reality washed over me, which I quickly shook off like a wet puppy. "No, silly girl. It's totally unacceptable to fall in love with your leading man."

****

Ben settled against the bus seat, his lunch pail trapped between his feet on the dirty floor. He kicked a cigarette butt aside with the toe of his work boot.

One day down. Four to go.

His last week at Sears had begun. Tomorrow morning, he'd pick up his car.

I'll call her Lady Blue.

He and Davie had dropped the car back at the hardware store this morning, along with the money. Tomorrow morning, they'd go back by for the title and Lady Blue.

He pushed open the window next to him and lit a cigarette.

Two things he needed to become a real man—a job that paid enough to support a family, and a car.

Almost twenty-one and he hadn't had the opportunity to be with a woman the way a man would. The fooling around he did with Elsie two years ago out behind her old man's garage felt good, but getting his hands down her pants didn't qualify him for manhood. Then Betty last year...*oh God, Betty last year*. So close. Her gaze looked up from his lap, those wet lips...

67

He squirmed in his seat and glanced around before he rearranged himself. She held on to her virginity like an old lady clutched her bag of money for a rainy day. If he'd had his own car, with a spacious backseat, he would've been able to ease her into a good time for both of them.

Now, he had the car and the job. With Jack away and Davie getting married, the new job secured an easier time for his mom and sisters.

Yesterday's meeting with Joseph Mallory had gone better than he could've hoped. For over an hour, he and Mallory poured out their future plans while they poured coffee until the pot was empty. Although he'd always gotten on with the man, the ease of the meeting went like a sit down with a favorite uncle. Ben's enthusiasm about the construction business flowed naturally. Mallory, on the other hand, was geared up for the expected after-war business, yet confessed to Ben his desire to retire in eight to ten years. He'd sell both his hardware store and his construction company—because he didn't have a son to take over.

An idea had taken form immediately. He'd quietly acknowledged the sense of the older man's reasoning, and his pulse quickened at what the possibilities Joe's decision held for his future. What exactly Mallory said that led him to believe he had a similar vision, he couldn't say. It may've been the slap on the back when he left, or the firm, friendly handshake, or the way he'd said, *"Ben, my boy,"* when he spoke to him.

He'd work for Mallory Construction in one week, and his chest swelled with anticipation, not only for the new job, but also for a certainty he divined for his future. Somehow, some way, he would own Mallory

Construction one day.

The bus jerked to a stop. He lifted his pail from the floor, headed to the door, and hopped down the steps, the end of the day fatigue less of an issue tonight. The cottonwoods rustled happily with a long overdue cool down. Whistling, he walked the dusty road, looking forward to a hot shower and Mom's Monday night ham and beans.

As he approached the bottom of the steps, music sifted through the mesh of the screen door. He recognized the song, "It Had To Be You," but not the voice. He paused on the porch to listen.

Claire.

The last few notes drifted out followed by his sister's voice as he stepped inside. Momma stood at the kitchen sink in her blue flowered housedress, the ever-present apron around her waist. With short swipes on the counter top with a wet rag, she wiped up whatever she'd left behind from making dinner. Her sewing machine stood uncovered in a corner of the kitchen, a dress for some customer held by the needle of the machine. Silently, Ben sniffed the delicious scent of ham and butter beans.

He set his lunch pail on the table as if handling glass, tiptoed behind her, and kissed her on the cheek.

"Oh! Benjamin Willis, you gave me a fright." She slapped at his chest. "A nice fright, though. Those girls have had the music so loud, I can't hear a thing. I guess they tried to drown out the sound of my work at the machine." She smiled, unfazed over the battle of Victrola verses Singer.

"Dinner smells good." He peered into the pot steaming on the stove. "Is Claire staying for dinner?"

"No, I imagine she'll leave soon." She went back to her cleaning. "They chose music for the talent contest at the school on Friday. Claire has quite a nice voice."

"Yes, she does."

Mom smiled. "Indeed. She's a young lady with stars in her eyes, I'd say." She turned, hands on hips. "Did you give your notice?"

"This is officially my last week at Sears." He lifted her hands from her hips, swung them side to side as he twirled her around, then gave her a hug.

"My, Benjamin, I didn't know you hated working there so."

"It was okay, Mom. This will be better." He kissed her cheek again. "Better for all of us."

Without spelling out the truth of his statement in detail, his spirits soared with the implications. Davie could plunge into marriage, Mom could relax her sewing efforts some, and he didn't have to feel guilty about buying the car.

His mother grinned and nodded acknowledgement as if reading his thoughts, which he believed she could do most of the time. "Well, just so you're happy." She patted his cheek before turning back to the sink.

He glanced at the material on her sewing machine. "Looks like you're working on something there."

"The Mallorys provided work for me, too. Or referred it my way. Making dresses for the cutest little twin girls who live on the other side of them." She lifted the lid and stirred the pot.

His stomach reacted to the aroma released. "I'll get washed up for dinner."

"You've got about an hour."

He strolled into the living room. Claire stood by the record player, putting albums back into their covers. She hummed, and her brown pleated skirt swayed with her hips.

Nicely rounded hips.

"Did you get your music chosen?" he asked as he approached her.

She snatched an album from the table and held up the cover. "It Had To Be You." Her cheeks colored.

How pretty she looks with the excitement of the contest.

"It's…it's a great song and easy to sing." Her lips curved in a smile.

"Easy for you anyway." Her smile pulled him closer like an invisible rope. "I assume you're the one entering the contest, not Paulie."

Claire laughed as sweet as the music. "Yes, you assume correctly."

"Where is the pip squeak?"

"Finding something in her room." She gestured toward the back of the house then fussed with the stack of albums. "I'm just cleaning up."

Her strawberry-blonde waves touched lovely pale collarbones. Taller than his sister, she held herself in a manner that begged to be admired. Her voice wasn't the only pretty thing about her.

"Is this talent contest for fun or something more?"

Claire shook her hair back and lifted tresses the color of a summer sunset from her neck with a flourish. "I'd definitely like to pursue a career in the movies."

The word theatrical came to mind while her smile dazzled him.

"This contest should be a lot of fun." She stared

directly into his eyes, the dark brown of hers simmered. "Do you go to the movies?"

"Now and then."

She dipped her chin and gave him a beguiling upwards glance. "I bet you're a Rita Hayworth man." When he only shrugged, she continued, surprising him with her flirtatious tone. "Come on, now. We all have our favorites."

"Yeah, she's...okay." The words he could use for the sexy, red-haired actress he'd leave unspoken to the young Claire. "Do you dance and act in addition to singing?"

"I will." She nodded, quite serious. "I think it's best to be well-rounded, if you're going to have a chance in Hollywood. I don't exactly have any credits to my name yet, still, I'm pretty sure I could act, if given the chance. As far as dancing, yes, a few lessons will be in order, eventually."

"So, it'll be off to Hollywood for you after graduation?" Unusually confident for a high school girl, he could imagine her hopping on a bus to follow her ambitions. *Pity.* "Not interested in hanging around Phoenix to raise a family?"

"Oh goodness, lots of time." Once again, she pushed the hair from her silky smooth neck with a flip of her fingers. "Following your heart should be first."

And who will steal your lovely heart?

Apparently, Arnold hadn't quite become the master of Claire's affection. But then, she was young.

Too young for him to think in terms of heart-stealing.

Her dark eyes regarded him with maturity beyond her seventeen years. Her peach lips turned up in a smile as she batted her lashes. Didn't much matter what he thought he read in her eyes. *Seventeen, and still in high school.*

"I finally found the necklace." Paulie, holding a pendant on a gold chain in front of her, burst into the living room. "Oh, hey, Ben."

"Hey, pip squeak."

His sister gave him a playful punch on his arm. He nodded at Claire, her smile tender like a child and womanly sensuous in the same moment.

"I better get my shower before dinner. See you around, Claire. Good luck on the contest."

"Thank you, Benjamin."

She gazed at him, so open, as if inviting him to share her thoughts. He had more to learn about this young woman.

****

I gulped as Benjamin retreated to the back of the house. Why on earth did I get so nervous around him? My stomach muscles relaxed, and I hadn't even realized they'd tightened until then.

"Don't you like it?"

Paulie's voice jarred me. "What?"

"The necklace." She scanned my face. "Are you okay, Claire?"

"Sorry, Paulie. I…uhh…I'm still thinking about the lyrics to the song." I took the necklace she dangled in front of me, glad to focus on something other than her brother. "Why, it's grand." An oval topaz stone glittered from the pendant, suspended on a fine, gold chain. "Are you sure? If your grandmother gave this to you…"

"If Granny was alive, she'd say it's perfect for your

yellow dress. And you look so good in your yellow dress. You have to wear it for the contest." Her button of a nose crinkled with a smile.

Her generosity left me speechless. Heirlooms impressed me as daunting possessions, none of which I owned. The smooth stone and delicate chain in my palm connected me to the Russell family beyond the here and now.

For a brief moment, we stood in silence. Mrs. Russell turned on the water in the kitchen, Benjamin closed a door in the hall, and my friend smiled. The magnitude of the moment impressed itself upon me.

I belonged there.

"Are you going to come back to practice some more on Thursday?" Paulie asked.

My heart beat double-time for a moment. "Would you mind if I came back tomorrow?" I blurted out while staring at the necklace, not meeting her eyes.

"Heck, no. Why don't you stay for dinner tonight?"

I hesitated briefly. "No, I can't really on a school night. Da would miss me." I opened a compartment on my purse to gingerly drop the necklace in. "I better get going so I can get dinner on the stove before he gets home. I've got some homework in Latin, too." I lifted books from the sofa.

"I *hate* Latin."

She followed me to the front door, and we hugged.

"Thanks, Paulie."

"Oh pooh, no thanks needed. See you at school tomorrow."

I descended the steps as gracefully as possible in case someone might be watching me. Before I entered the stance of cottonwoods, I turned and waved at my friend. She waved and disappeared into the house.

I heard a car stirring up dust on the approach to the Russells'. Beyond the trees, along the road, David headed for home.

I breathed the air scented with decaying leaves, while glancing at the clear blue sky through the limbs above. Benjamin's blue eyes had looked right through me. He made me so nervous I babbled on and on about being an actress. He must've considered me a silly twit. Conversation with a boy like Arnold put me in control, but with a man like Benjamin, I'd floundered. My chest had deflated, left me breathless, robbing my brain of oxygen, so I'd sounded like a witless child.

It wasn't as if he cared one way or the other about me or what I did. Perhaps he had a sincere interest in my pursuit of a movie career, which made sense. After all, the world of Hollywood's silver screen was interesting to everyone.

I huffed with impatience—I'd never even once asked him about himself. *Honestly, why did I go all quivery around him?* Arnold stood taller and certainly had a more theatrical nature. Plus, he adored me. Unfortunately, unless I was with him, keeping in mind his leading man potential, and with his hands on me, well…I didn't actually *feel* anything at all. With Benjamin, merely the thought of him aroused emotions I had difficulty quelling. Arnold was a boy, dull and childish, compared to Benjamin. A boy caused flutters; a man caused quakes.

Benjamin…

I shook my head.

A mouse skittered through the leaves in front of me. I glanced at my watch. Forcing my feet to move faster, I hummed a few notes of "It Had to be You." I really needed to concentrate on the contest for the next few days. I skirted the property line of the houses on the other side of the trees. No real reason existed to go to Paulie's tomorrow. I knew the words of the song and didn't need the practice. But it wouldn't hurt.

I kicked at a branch in my path. So, Paulie has a handsome brother who's mildly interesting. *So what?* He might've watched me sing at the party, but then, most everyone stopped to watch. *He's polite, that's all. Look at the way he treats his momma.* The fact he handed over his paycheck spoke volumes about him.

He's a man.

And I was nothing more than his little sister's friend.

I stepped onto the stoop of my home, shifted the books in my arms, and rummaged in my purse for the house key. With a glance over my shoulder, I caught a shiver of the nosy old landlady's curtains as the door to my house opened. I walked in, kicked it shut with my foot, and muttered, "Mind your own business, you old biddy."

****

"Here, let me have your books." Arnold came up behind me at the end of the math class we had together. "You have Latin next, right?" He swept the books from my arms, and we walked out into the crowded hall.

Two younger girls looked perfectly moony as we passed them. Another senior I didn't know smiled at Arnold, ignoring me.

"Do you need to go to your locker?" he asked.

"No. I have my Latin book." We dodged a cluster of students as they made their way toward the stairs.

"Are you sure you have time to walk with me?"

"Study hall is next. Sandberg doesn't give a hoot what time we walk in." He guffawed. "How did practice go yesterday at Paulie's?"

"Fine. I picked a song."

As we approached the stairs, Arnold leaned into me, actually herding me to the alcove under the stairway.

"What are you—?"

He laughed and nudged in front of me, blocking any exit I might have. "I want to talk to you. In private."

"Mr. Sinclair isn't as lenient as Miss Sandberg, Arnold." I peeked around him. The halls still teemed with students.

"But I have something to say." His voice rasped with emotion. "I want you to wear my ring. Be my girl. Make it official."

"Your ring? Oh, Arnold, I—"

"You know I'm crazy for you, Claire."

He'd told me in one way or another enough times, so I paid little attention to his imploring tone. "I've got so much to think about with the contest and all right now." After the movie encounter, I'd pondered what to do about him without any definite decision.

"Who better to celebrate your win with than your steady?" His breath heated my face. "You can sing to me anytime you want, Claire. I'll help you practice."

"Thank you, but I've got that under control." I darted a glance behind him again. The hall had nearly emptied. "I've really got to get to class." I lifted my books out of his arms.

Taking his gaze off me, he removed the ring from

his finger. "Here, Claire."

I used the opportunity to duck around him as the final bell rang. "I'll think about it, Arnold. I have to go now."

"Claire—"

"I'll talk to you later." I rounded the corner as his arm shot toward me and clutched my wrist. With a jerk and a twist, he hauled me back into the alcove; my books spilled onto the floor, and I gasped. "*Arnold.*" He loosened his grip and dropped my hand as I glared.

He continued to loom over me. Shoving the ring in his pocket, he released a ragged sigh. "Why do you do this to me?"

His whiny question made me want to gag. When he ran his fingers along my arms, stopping so his thumbs poked at the sides of my breasts, the pulse in my ears pounded with anger.

"I thought we were friends," I hissed. "Get out of the way or else." I flung his hands from my arms. Stooping to pick up my books, I elbowed his hip on the way down.

"Ow!"

"You are an oaf. A stupid, clueless oaf," I muttered, gathering my things into my arms. *Leading man material? He hardly even qualified as* man *material.*

He squatted next to me and picked up a paper that fell from one of the books. I snatched the sheet from his hand.

"Claire, don't be mad."

I stopped, staring into his bewildered face. "I don't know what to say to you, Arnold. We're not boyfriend and girlfriend. Not kissing friends or dating friends. I hardly think we're even friends. Now, stay out of my way."

I stood, leaving him on his haunches staring after me as I wheeled around and raced up the steps.

Chapter Four
It Had To Be You

"Honestly, Paulie. I don't see what you and the rest of the North High females see in Arnold." We rode the school bus to her house as I related the incident before Latin class. "Yes, yes, I know, he's a *dreamboat*." She turned on me with wide-eyed dismay, but I continued. "You've known him longer than I have, and I can't believe his creepy side hasn't revealed itself in all those years."

"Creepy? My gosh, he's crazy for you, not *creepy*."

"He's too...pushy."

"He's *passionate*."

"Has he always been so *passionate*?" I rolled my eyes. Paulie was blind to anything besides praise of Arnold.

"I don't know." She shrugged. "No one took much notice of him until last year. He went to Minnesota for the summer to work on a relative's farm. When he came back, he'd grown at least three inches and, well, you've seen his body." She slumped forward as if melted from some inner heat.

"Seen it. Felt it." I waved off my friend's lovesick smile. "Yes, he's handsome, he's built, and he *used* to be fun." *Why can't I like him the way he likes me?*

Paulie sat up, heaving her shoulders against the bus seat. "So, throw him over! Break his heart!"

"I did."

Her eyes grew as round as records as she squeaked a surprised gasp.

Once my anger had cooled, I'd experienced some empathy for him. I couldn't keep trying to make something more of my feelings. "It's better I set him straight now before he thinks there's something between us." I'd grown tired of playing dodge ball with him, fighting off his awkward advances. "Arnold isn't in love with me, he's in lust. I don't feel the same way he does." It was time to stop dangling myself like a carrot in front of a rabbit too short to make the leap.

"It's too bad for you, Claire Flanagan. He's the perfect partner for you, what with your singing and acting. *And* he can get you into the theater."

All the reasons I'd used to convince myself. Paulie's conviction couldn't succeed any better than I had. Romance with Arnold, no matter how good looking he was or what his connections were, wasn't going to happen. "All that makes him the perfect friend, too."

"Oh, pooh!"

"That's what he is."

She crossed her arms, smugly pinched her lips together with an upturned chin. "You've made all the girls at North High very happy."

All the *girls*, yes, and they could have a *boy* like Arnold. "And you." I gave her a sideways glance.

Her cheeks pinked immediately. "Claire!"

I laughed. "Here's your stop."

We stood, books in hand, as the bus came to a halt.

The bus driver glared at us in the mirror as we stumbled a bit. "You girls keep your rear ends in your seats until the bus stops," he barked.

I paused next to him, Paulie close on my heels. "Why Mr. Jesper, you glide this old bus to a stop so skillfully, we didn't realize it was still moving. Thank you for the great job you do."

He opened the door without looking up. "Hmph. Move on, move on."

"Someday, I'm going to get that man to smile," I told a snickering Paulie as Mr. Jesper slowly drove the bus back onto the road.

Mrs. Russell greeted us, pointing to the kitchen table laden with glasses and sugar cookies not long from the oven. "I had just enough ice left for a jug of tea. Thought you two could use a cold one." She winked at me as we dropped our books at one end of the table. "This kitchen's heated up a bit." She plucked her dress away from her thighs.

The house was warm, not stuffy. A breeze floated in the open window, carrying the cookie-sweet aroma around the kitchen. Paulie's momma sat with us, eating cookies, asking about our day, enthusiastic and smiling, which rendered her face all nose and teeth. I mused that my friend must look like her father.

"You should've brought Laura home with you two," Mrs. Russell commented in between bites of cookie.

"She can't usually go anywhere after school during the week." Paulie wet her finger, pressed the damp tip into the cookie crumbs, and licked them off.

"Laura will be here Saturday night for sure," I volunteered. "She *loves* Saturday night at the Russells' like everyone else does."

My words brought the wide smile back to the older

woman's face as she tapped her fingers on the table. "I think I've had enough, girls. Don't want to spoil my dinner." She dusted cookie crumbs from her hands with her apron. "I finished sewing early today, so the machine won't compete with the music."

My stomach rolled a bit. "I didn't mean to cause you any inconvenience." I swallowed the embarrassment of disrupting Mrs. Russell's routine on top of being drawn to her home for some strange desire to see Benjamin again. The latter thought was so ridiculous I glanced at my books and considered leaving.

"No, no, honey. None at all. I didn't mean I finished *because* of you girls. I'm done, because I'm done. More for my benefit, I can enjoy the music while I get dinner."

"We won't be at it for long," I apologized nervously, deciding I would be gone before Benjamin came home. I puzzled over why the thought of him made me so jittery. "Now that I know the song, I'm going to run through it a couple of times, and I'll be out of here."

"Stay as long as you want, dear." Mrs. Russell rose and carried glasses to the sink. "Stay for dinner if you like."

"Thank you, I can't. Lots of homework tonight." I stood and tugged on Paulie's sleeve. "Come on. You have to be my judge," I told her as we headed for the record player.

"I'm going to be your director." She slipped the record from its sleeve. "You have a great voice, but you have to use your body movements, too."

I laughed. "Why, you sound rather theatrical."

She put her hands on her hips. "I think you're rubbing off on me." She lifted the needle onto the record. "And be sure you make eye contact. Make each judge think you're singing to him."

I smirked. There was no need to give me stage presence advice, but she looked so excited by her self-proclaimed role that I nodded, pretending to be directed. Twice through, she was satisfied with my performance.

"You're an easy one to direct. Friday night, you'll wow them." She balanced the needle over the record. "One more time?"

"No, I think I've got it." Better to leave before Benjamin got home. There was no reason to see him, no reason to linger. Heaven knows why I even thought about him, but when I did, I got a fluttery sensation from my tummy on down.

"Want a cookie for the road?" Mrs. Russell asked when I retrieved my books from the table.

"No, thank you, but they're really good. Thank you for the snack, and thanks for putting up with my practicing." I wanted to hug her.

"I enjoyed it." She wiped her wet hands on her yellow checked apron. "I think I might come cheer you on Friday night."

"Really?" Delight warmed me. "That would be swell."

I was still smiling when I hugged Paulie, then bounded down the porch stairs humming. With the words to the song repeating in my head, I didn't notice Benjamin's blue car on the road until his voice found me at the edge of the cottonwoods.

He'd stopped. The dusty road settled to the ground

behind his car. "Hey, Hollywood. Going home already?" He leaned across the passenger side, speaking to me through the open window.

"Hi, Benjamin." My shortness of breath couldn't be from walking such a short distance.

I haltingly stepped over to the car and bent to see him better. His shirt was unbuttoned, his muscled chest barely disguised under a thin, white T-shirt. "You can't call me Hollywood yet." *Was he mocking me, his little sister's friend?* "I haven't even won my first talent contest."

"I've heard you sing." His blue eyes regarded me. Seriousness with a touch of something else. "Hollywood can't be far off."

"Thank you, Benjamin." I dipped my chin, but couldn't break away from the scrutiny of his gaze. I wondered for a moment if he could see into my heart through my eyes. Could he see the sparks his stare ignited? There would soon be a full-fledged fire, if I didn't move out of range.

"Are you ready to travel the world?" A slight frown crossed his forehead.

"Travel the world?"

"Or at least all over the states. If you plan to be an actress, you'll be on the road a lot, I'd imagine." He shifted his hand on the seat beside him. "Making movies."

"I've done a lot of traveling already, so I don't suppose that would be a roadblock to success." Da could go with me.

I focused on his half-smile, flattered by his interest in my future. But right then, leaving Phoenix didn't sound like such a hot idea.

Benjamin nodded and glanced at his home.

Oh, God, he's just making polite conversation again.

"Have you traveled much?" I blurted.

"Can't say I have." He shifted his arm again, and a bird sang overhead. He dipped his head lower to gaze beyond me, above my head.

Let him go, Claire, he's bored. "I better get home. Your momma will have dinner on the table before long."

His smile ignited his morning glory eyes and casted such a light my face warmed from the glow. Words stuck on my tongue. I simply stared back.

"Okay, then." He cleared his throat, nodded, and sat up in front of the steering wheel again. "See you around."

"Yes." My cheeks flamed. "See you…sometime." As I whirled around, the leaves crunched under my feet, and I practically charged into the cover of the trees.

****

Yeah, you're slick as molasses, Ben. Can't even hold the attention of a high school girl.

He parked to the side of his house, shut off the engine, and stepped onto hard, packed dirt. Claire might be a high school girl, but with her lofty ambitions and talent, she could make it happen. Paulie had told him she'd moved around with her father for years. He glanced toward her departing figure. Experienced beyond her age.

Probably thinks I'm pretty rough around the edges.

Claire was self-assured, feisty.

Flirty, the way she tilts her head and smokes you with those brown eyes, strawberry-blonde hair framing her perfect chin and peach cheeks.

He climbed the stairs, stopped by the porch railing, and gazed toward the cottonwoods. *What the hell am I thinking? Claire's future is a whole lot more than getting involved with some working stiff.*

She'd disappeared into the trees.

As if she would've given me a second thought anyway.

****

"What time did you say we got to leave?" Da called from the living room.

"Six forty-five. It hasn't changed from the last time you asked me." *You'd think* he's *the one who has to get up in front of the whole school.* "We've got half an hour, so cool your heels. Your jitters are going to make me nervous." My shortness was uncalled for, and I darted out to the living room, stopping in the doorway.

My father, dressed in his best khaki pants and blue poplin shirt, sat at the kitchen table rolling a cigarette and muttering. His fingers, usually adept at the chore, fidgeted, and spilled half the tobacco out of the paper on the way to his tongue. He cursed inaudibly.

"Da?" I stifled a snicker, loped over to encircle his shoulders from behind, and kissed his fresh shaven cheek. "Don't worry. This should be fun."

He patted my hand and leaned his head into me. "I ain't worried. I'm excited. Going to be something seeing you up on a stage all by yourself."

"Oh." I kissed him again. "Thank you."

"For what?"

"For being my father."

He chuckled. "Don't have much choice about that, now do I?"

"Da!" I slapped his shoulder. "Now, I'm going to fix my hair. You didn't eat much for dinner, so have something more, if you want, while I finish dressing."

"I'm fine, gal. Go on with you."

Back in the bathroom, I finished taking the bobby pins out of my hair, the ones I'd hurriedly used to refresh some curls after school. Da wouldn't be the only friendly face outside of my school chums in the audience. Paulie had told me Mrs. Russell and Richie would be there, too.

I hadn't been able to practice at the Russells' on Thursday as planned. Miss Finley, the music teacher and organizer of the contest, had called a walk-through practice of all participants. Disappointment bit at me, not because I couldn't practice again—because I had looked forward to seeing Benjamin. Once I'd allowed myself that, he crept into my thoughts, uninvited, every day since.

I sang to myself to crowd thoughts of him out of my head, practicing the talent song. Even that didn't work, because the words to the song brought him to mind. I'd call up those serious blue eyes and the muscles beneath the thin, white T-shirt, and get hopelessly lost in daydreaming. No matter how many times I told myself the chances of Benjamin seeing me as anything besides his sister's little friend were slim, I couldn't stop my imagination. Arnold didn't help the situation. We called a truce, although his continued pestering only enhanced Benjamin's maturity and attractiveness in my mind.

"You sure Paulie will bring the record to school?" There was no calming my father.

I took two deep breaths to fend off the nerves his

incessant questions sparked. "Everything is under control."

If I won the contest with three of the Russells there to see me, I was certain to be the talk of their household. How pathetic I got pleasure Benjamin might at least hear my name.

I slipped into my shoes. *He would be sure to listen to the chatter, since he thinks I have talent. He thinks I'll end up in Hollywood.* I ran the comb through my hair one last time. *Hollywood starlet.* That would certainly get his attention.

"I think we better hit the road, Claire."

"Coming!" I got as far as the door to my bedroom. "Oh, wait." Running back to my nightstand, I snatched up Paulie's necklace and put it on. "I nearly forgot," I explained to my impatient father who waited with the front door open.

"Is that all you need? Nothing more?" He tapped his foot.

"I'm all set." I patted the chain against my bare skin.

"Are you sure now?" His smile crinkled his face.

I breezed past him. "Come on. I'm tired of waiting on you, Da."

****

Paulie met me by the side entrance to the auditorium, and gave me the record.

"You were right. This necklace looks great, don't you think?"

"Perfect." She squeezed my arm. "You look like a star."

I opened the heavy, metal door, but paused to remind her, "Make sure Da finds you, okay?"

"I will. Break a leg!" She waved as I entered the hall leading to the stage.

The door silently clicked behind me.

Walking up the steps, muffled chatter grew louder. There were fifteen contestants with at least as many stagehands running every which way.

The door that had closed behind me flew open, and Martha Donovan and a flute case came barreling in, shoving me to the side as her ample girth took the stairs.

"Sorry, Claire. I'm first up and I…" Her voice merged with the noise at the top of the stairs.

As the sixth contestant to take the stage, I was in no great hurry to jump into the fray of the backstage ruckus. On the last few steps, the low roar of the voices engulfed me. Miss Finley's lilac perfume lingered on the backstage odors of rubber matting and body heat, seducing me. I breathed deeply as my heart rose a few inches in my chest and gently tapped double time.

"Quiet, quiet!" She was on her tiptoes, waving her hands wildly in the air. A few of us made shushing noises and eventually got everyone to silence, although the fidgeting remained. "You all know where you should be so get there, and stay there. Good luck to all."

Everyone scattered. She checked her watch as she took her position center stage.

I trotted over to the kid who operated the sound. Kevin was a tall, skinny boy with glasses perched on a pointed nose, the lenses so thick his eyes appeared beady. He reminded me of the moles Uncle Eb cursed on his farm. The teenage stagehand maintained an air of theatrical importance in contrast to his appearance. He had anything mechanical or electrical under his control.

"Here's my music," I whispered and handed him my record.

"Roger that, Claire."

"I'm up after—"

"Martin playing the piano. I know. "It Had To Be You." Good choice."

"Thanks." I moved off to stage left to wait. I wanted so badly to peek out the curtains and find my father sitting with Paulie, Mrs. Russell, and Richie.

Miss Finley stood stage center, like an imposing guard at Buckingham Palace no one dared to cross. She nodded, and slowly the curtains drew back.

From my vantage point, I couldn't see the audience. My patience grew thinner. My foot tapped faster as she thanked the parents, families, teachers, and students. On and on.

We each had a number. Even numbers waited in the wings stage left while odd numbers were across the stage in the other wing. Martha waddled out with her flute from stage right. I stood third in line on my end of the stage. Peeking around the two students gave me a view of Martha, and once the two contestants in front of me performed, my view would improve. I'd be able to see at least part of the audience at that point.

"Carmen!" I whispered as loud as I dared to the girl at the front. "Do you see Paulie?"

She rose up on tiptoes to scan the audience then leaned around the boy between us and nodded.

"Is there an older man with red hair sitting close to her?"

One of the student stagehands motioned me to shush.

Carmen spied again and turned to give me another

nod. I relaxed back. Da was with people he knew. Maybe Paulie could calm his nerves. Most likely, she'd have him even more excited.

Martha's flute caused the same reaction as bringing my teeth together on tin. I thought she must've chosen a most un-flute-like piece, or she needed a few more lessons. Thankfully, her instrument finally silenced, and Carmen stepped out onto the stage.

A lovely Mexican girl, who wore very red lipstick, did a dance called the Flamenco. Her bright turquoise dress had numerous ruffles. She stomped her tap shoes so loudly, I'm sure the first row wanted to put their hands over their ears. I found her exotic performance exciting, and hoped the judges didn't agree with me.

Between the Flamenco and Martin's piano before me were a duet and a soloist. John sang with me in choral and had a decent voice. I had no idea if he pulled off a good performance or not because, as he stepped onto the stage, I moved up to stand in his position. The audience became visible. Within moments, I located my father in the second row, center stage, seated next to Richie. As John launched into his rendition of "Swinging On a Star," my gaze along the row spied Mrs. Russell, Paulie, Arnold, Laura, and…Benjamin.

****

When the kid on stage belted his song, Ben questioned why he'd decided to come to the high school talent contest. How many of these lame performances would he have to sit through before Claire lit up the stage? He'd wanted to sit farther back in the auditorium, but Paulie and Mom had other ideas. Watching Claire without being noticed was his preference, though she'd probably pay him no mind anyway.

"Poor Martha," Laura whispered in his direction. "John is better than she was. She hasn't got a chance."

Poor Martha, hell. "Not a chance," he agreed. "How many 'poor Marthas' are in this thing?"

Laura giggled. "I think around fifteen or twenty."

He groaned.

"Claire is sixth up." If more of them were like the Mexican girl, he might stay entertained. The lovely, dark-haired beauty had flounced around the stage on nicely shaped legs. The guy on stage was the third act and tolerable. Two more to go.

Laura had a different opinion. "He's good, isn't he?"

Ben turned to her. The smile on her face spoke more to the guy's looks than to his talent, although he did have a so-so voice. "He's okay."

"Hmmm. Not as good as Claire." Loyalty trumped attraction.

He silently agreed. Claire had style, grace, and a good voice. Add to that her strawberry-blonde hair begging to be mussed gracing collarbones begging to be…

Ah, hell, get that out of your head.

He cleared his throat and glanced around. Arnold, sitting next to his sister, leaned in close and whispered in her ear. He wondered if the little bastard had had the good fortune to lay lips on Claire's lovely collarbones. His sister certainly acted as if he was God's gift.

Nothing but a pretty boy. About as useful as tits on a boar.

Would Claire allow him to place his hands on her narrow waist and bring her soft, full chest against his?

Hopefully, she's focused on Hollywood and can see a life beyond a little jerk like that.

She was a smart young lady.

Young.

He'd worked, helped support a family, and been out of school for years. She was still a high school student.

He cleared his throat again and focused on the act on stage. The duet was no match for Claire.

By the time the skinny kid sat down at the piano, Ben slumped low in his seat. Piano music bored him. Staring straight ahead, his mind drifted. His job with Mallory Construction got better every day. He'd learned to carry hod, and he'd taken easily to working the plaster on walls. Joseph Mallory told him he was a natural. He wasn't any less tired at the end of a workday, but he was a whole hell of a lot more satisfied.

Only when the last piano chords died down and Laura tapped him on the shoulder, did he bring his attention back to the auditorium stage. When prim Miss Whoever She Was, announced Claire Flanagan, he sat up straight.

Claire glided out onto the lacquered wooden floor of the stage, her yellow dress creating a glow around her. As soft waves of hair undulated on her shoulders, dark eyes sparkled beneath thick lashes. She smiled at each of the four judges then began to sing.

****

To say my heart was in my throat was so cliché and didn't come close to how I actually felt anyway. I smiled at each of the judges and made Paulie proud, I was sure. In fact, I could look at the judges yet still see her family and Da because they sat directly behind the teachers, two rows back. When my friend gave me a thumbs up, I responded with a smile and a nod. One of the judges returned the smile. The judges were merely camouflage, for each time my gaze graced them, my real target was Benjamin. Once I began, my heart did the singing.

It had to be you...

Hollywood dreams were silenced as the fantasy of a home, a family, and Benjamin came alive with my song.

And as the last note trailed off, the applause startled me. So caught up in singing to Benjamin, I'd nearly lost sight of my surroundings. Then Da smiled so broadly the lines in his weathered face were like fissures. He turned to the parent on the other side of him then the people behind him, undoubtedly claiming me as his talented daughter. My friends clapped wildly. Mrs. Russell's wide grin practically disappeared under her nose. Arnold threw his arm around Paulie's waist, winked at me, and pursed his lips in a kiss. My stomach muscles tightened with the urge to smack that kiss off his face. He couldn't get it through his thick head we were only friends.

Then there was Benjamin.

Benjamin.

His smile was tepid, his blue eyes veiled, as he politely applauded. The only one I cared about pleasing gave me nothing.

I briefly curtsied for the judges, flashed my Hollywood smile at each of them, and strolled off the stage. With a glance over my shoulder before sliding behind the curtain, I noted Benjamin's crooked smile.

And he still watched me. Perhaps I made something of nothing. Yet, hope swelled in my chest.

Gliding past the remainder of the contestants, I took congratulations from some, quiet daggers from others. Their faces and voices barely registered. Benjamin was *here*, for me, and now waited for the results. Did he come because he wanted to be here? Was it possible he saw me as someone other than his sister's little friend? What had he called her? Pipsqueak. Was I just a friend of the pipsqueak?

I grabbed a folding chair next to the soundman.

"You knocked their socks off, Claire."

"Thanks, Kevin."

"I'll watch you in the movies some day."

That's what I wanted, wasn't it? I felt at home on the stage. There were no nerves, and I liked to wow the judges.

Doubt loomed.

Could I compare the thrill of being a Hollywood star with the thrill of a future with Benjamin Russell as my real life leading man? The bright lights of Hollywood paled in comparison to his blue eyes. I leaned elbows on my knees with my chin in my hands.

"Don't be nervous," Kevin leaned down to whisper in my ear. "I have a feeling you have them all in the palm of your hand."

All? Benjamin was barely at my fingertips. Hollywood fame seemed more attainable. *Maybe I don't have to choose.* I sat up. The decision to choose between Benjamin and a career didn't need to be made right then, if at all. The solution appeared to be easy enough, and a calm came over me with the rationale.

I shot off the chair, paced, and ticked off the

contestants as they each performed. One student was in tears and nearly bailed, but Miss Finley got her under control. Another piano piece went sour when the guy hit a wrong key and couldn't get it together after that, and a nicely played violin solo pleased the audience.

When at last we all gathered in the wings, waiting for the judge's decision, my destiny lay before me with all the glory of a babe newly born into the world.

Hollywood could walk hand in hand with love.

****

Damn, she was beautiful. It was like she sang to me, only me.

Ben took a deep breath to calm his beating heart. Maybe she wouldn't win. *Bring her head back to earth and Arizona.*

Guilt edged in between admiration and desire. *Why the hell does she have to be so young, still a girl, not yet a woman?* If she was out of high school, he could get those fanciful ideas out of her head, settle her down. The hell of it was, she'd probably be able to make a man out of him.

He cleared his throat and rubbed the back of his neck.

"Did you say something, Ben?" Laura leaned toward him.

"Ah, no." He shifted in his chair. "It's getting awful stuffy in here."

"The winners are about to be announced, so it's nearly over." She giggled. "It was awful nice of you to come, even if you're bored."

He smiled, yet offered no explanation for his agitation. Watching Claire was anything but boring. Well, she wouldn't go anywhere for a while anyway.

Sometime this year, she'd be eighteen and, in a few months, out of high school. Not long. In the meantime, with his sister as her best friend, she'd be around enough. He'd have to keep his ears open, get to know her better. Keep his eye on her.

I sure as hell don't mind doing that.

****

The tension among my fellow contestants was palpable. Girls clung to each other in anticipation, tittering under their breaths. Boys punched each other. I had stopped pacing, and stood behind the others when Miss Finley announced the winners. Third place went to the violin solo. The senior who sang "Swinging on a Star*"* was awarded second place.

My heart pattered while I held my breath.

"Claire Flanagan is this year's talent contest winner," Miss Finley announced.

Air whooshed from my mouth. Although I'd been slightly concerned about a couple of the contestants, and felt I had a good shot at winning, my surprise and joy had me lightheaded. My feet didn't touch the ground as I glided over to accept the coveted contest cup.

I bowed. My row of fans continued to clap. Da's eyes glistened. Arnold winked even while his hand moved from Paulie's shoulder to her waist. This gave me pause, but with the excitement of the moment, only a shadow of a question passed over me before the sunshine of Benjamin's smile blinded me. The cup I held, the applause I heard, didn't compare with the acknowledgement on his face.

Miss Finley had the last word, sending parents, friends, families, and faculty to migrate en masse out the two auditorium doors. Paulie pointed to the side of the building. The noise from the audience combined with the students behind stage ricocheted around me. I weaved through the bodies, grabbed the record, and darted to the side door, chattering with my fellow thespians. The stairway reeked of nervous bodies, Palmolive soap, and Old Spice cologne, so when the first breath of fresh air reached me, I wanted to vault over the heads of those in the front to reach the outdoors.

My three friends assaulted me when I cleared the doorway. The two girls hugged me first with Paulie singing, "I told you so. I told you so!"

Arnold managed to poke in between them with a caress on my arm. "That's my girl. You were grand."

Once Paulie calmed down, Mrs. Russell let go of Richie to congratulate me. My father, with Benjamin, hung back. Da would save his gushing until we were alone, but I wouldn't have minded a hug from Benjamin. He nodded to something my father said, all the time staring at me with a neutral expression. I had the presence of mind to not react. He was there. I'd made some sort of impression, if only as a theatrical persona. I was more than pipsqueak's little friend. All of this ran through my head as I kept an uninterested expression on my face. Or so I hoped.

A girl can't be too easy. A man likes a certain mystique.

"You have to come to dinner tomorrow." Paulie tugged my arm. "I've already asked your father if you can spend the night. A bunch of people are coming over again, and Laura is going to spend the night, too."

"Will you, Claire?" Richie elbowed his way

between the girls.

"Hey, twerp, back off!" his sister barked.

I took his hand. "I will. Thanks for coming tonight."

A smile overtook his face; his long lashes batted at me. He looked to his sister with a wicked grin then snubbed his nose.

"Yes, Paulie. I'll come for dinner and the night. Now, I need to get Da home."

Arnold ran a hand down my arm. "I'm sorry I won't be there. I have to work at the theater."

"Oh, too bad." With a jerk, I put distance between us. "I really need to get going. Da is waiting." I gave my two friends one more hug. "Thank you, all of you, for coming." I smiled at Mrs. Russell, then let my gaze drift over to Benjamin. His eyes smiled back more than his mouth. I might not've picked up on the subtlety a week ago, before the brief encounters of the last few days. Tonight, I did, and the goose bumps tingled down my neck and arms.

When he shook my father's hand, I nearly got tears in my eyes. Bewildered by my reaction, I stopped mid-stride.

Da walked toward me. "You ready, gal?"

Benjamin fished keys out of his pocket as he turned toward the parking lot. I welcomed Da's presence beside me, and the thought of going home. I looped my arm through his and waved to my friends.

Paulie loped beside us for a bit. "Are you sure you can find time to fit us in tomorrow night?"

"Oh, *dahling*, I'll make time." I drew my hair up from my neck as I jutted out a hip, one hand to my breast in a pose.

She giggled. "Oh, good. We'll look forward to your presence."

Ahead of me, Benjamin stopped to light a cigarette. Muscled biceps flexed, and dark hair fell onto his forehead. Match extinguished, he returned my scrutinizing stare. Frozen in my starlet pose, his gaze swept over me, and came to rest on my eyes. My hand slowly fell from my breast. A corner of his mouth came up as he glanced away.

I melted. "Oh, no, Paulie. The pleasure will be mine."

And now my mind was made up, the pleasure would be Benjamin's, too.

Chapter Five
Rita Hayworth is a Harlot

"Here's to Claire." Paulie raised her iced tea glass in the air. "Quiet, everyone! I want to make a toast."

I elbowed her, but she jutted her chin out and ignored me. Her nose crinkled with a smile. The dinner table noise fell off as everyone looked at her.

"I said, here's to Claire, the most talented person at North High School."

"Here, here!" David cheered.

I half-stood, bowed, and cast a glance at Benjamin seated at one end of the table. My intention to sit closer had been thwarted by Richie who'd been adamant about sitting next to me, with a friend of his on the other side, which put me too far from Benjamin. The corner of his mouth ticked up as he raised his glass in my honor. Once my rump hit the chair again, the talk and food passing resumed. I stole another glance, but he'd been distracted by David.

Unable to engage Benjamin in conversation from where I sat, dinner ended in disappointment. With a family this large, conversation was loud with the diners in constant motion. No one lingered over empty plates when there were dishes to wash and furniture to move. The guys retreated to the living room to attend to the furniture while the women busied themselves in the kitchen. After I dried the last dish, Benjamin was nowhere to be found.

While Paulie changed her blouse due to a mishap scraping a plate, I stepped out on the front porch, hoping to see him.

Several people congregated in the front yard next to three cars parked side by side. Benjamin wasn't among them. David leaned against one of the cars, like a court jester spinning tales for his subjects who fanned around him in a semi-circle. They laughed at his stories, which were punctuated with his hands. Barely a year older than Benjamin, the only feature they had in common was dark, curly hair that refused to stay combed back. David's frame was stockier and shorter. Benjamin's good looks, along with his quiet, serious nature were the opposite of his brother's.

The sounds of Bing Crosby on the Victrola drifted out through the screen door. I lingered a moment to enjoy the last sliver of sun dipping behind the cottonwoods. The ground below the corner of the porch was littered with flower petals the bougainvillea had discarded.

Richie barreled around from the back of the house on a bicycle, scattering the faded red petals, and screeched to a stop when he saw me above him on the porch.

"Hey, Claire. Want to play a game of Kick the Can?"

Mrs. Russell appeared at the screen door. "Richard Ellis! Didn't I ask you to bring me a box from out back? I meant now, not next week."

"Ah, shucks." His lips formed a pout, and he kicked at the dirt.

"I couldn't play right now anyway, Richie. I'm

dressed for the party."

"It ain't no party. Just a bunch of people here like always." He brushed sandy-colored hair off his forehead and comically rolled his brown eyes.

"Okay, maybe not exactly a party, but I have on a dress, so I can't play a game like Kick the Can." The disappointment in Richie's eyes was sweet. "I think I see some fellas up the street playing football, though. Maybe you could join them after you get the box for your momma."

"Naw, I don't much like football." He shifted his delicate frame, sitting back on his bicycle seat. His nose crinkled like Paulie's when he smiled.

"Then maybe you can join some people in a card game later."

"Richard Ellis Russell, don't make me ask you again," his momma called out with more seriousness.

"Aw, shucks!" He jerked his bicycle around in a huff and disappeared behind the house.

I turned to go back in as David's group broke up and clomped up the stairs.

He grabbed his girlfriend, her short, dark hair bobbing as he danced her through the doorway. "Let's cut a rug, Barbara." The slight, pretty girl laughed as she was swept away to the living room.

After the group passed, I paused inside the door. A picture hanging on the wall caught my attention. A piece of white paper glued to a piece of cardboard hung on a single silver thumbtack from a string attached to the back. The subject of the pencil sketch was easily recognizable; the old Mallory house with pillars, gables, and the huge shade tree in the front. Two children played on the well-manicured lawn under a sky threatening a summer storm. In the right hand corner the initials B.R. were printed.

"There you are." Paulie hooked her arm through mine to usher me toward the living room. "Come on in."

My mind worked on an idea and couldn't be distracted. "This is new." I stood my ground, motioning to Benjamin's drawing.

"Yeah, Momma hung it. Ben drew it." She waved, as if to dismiss the art as an insignificant pastime of her brother's. "He's always drawing."

"He's really good."

"I suppose. Come on. Laura slipped in the back door a bit ago." Paulie snickered. "She's having trouble cooling her heels 'til Fred gets here."

I tucked my idea away as she hauled me into the next room. The living room undulated with music, voices, and laughter. My gaze flicked over the commotion to locate Benjamin, who leaned against the far wall, beer in hand, and talked to Laura.

"There she is," I said, yanking my friend forward.

We darted between two couples dancing and came to a stop in front of her brother. I barely acknowledged Laura, conscious of keeping my head turned toward him. I didn't consider my profile particularly becoming because of the bump on my nose.

"Hello, Benjamin." I smiled and flipped the hair from my neck.

"Hey, Hollywood."

I swore he said it seriously this time, not teasingly like a couple of days ago. Dinner churned in my stomach. His gaze was steady, creating a roadblock between my mind and mouth until Paulie tugged my arm.

"Let's get a cola."

I ignored her directive, looking to Laura for a reason to stay in breathing distance of Benjamin. "Why, Laura, your dress looks quite stunning. I do think brown is your color." I spoke to her, keeping my face slanted toward Benjamin, obsessively avoiding giving him a profile view.

"Uh, thanks. Your blue dress is…lovely."

I tipped my chin in acknowledgement of her attempt to match my mature manner.

"It looks great with your hair." She ended on a high note, pleased with her social banter.

Paulie elbowed me as she rolled her eyes. "'Scuse us, Ben." She shook her head and gave Laura a nudge. "Let's go get a cola, you guys."

"You two go ahead." I waved them off. "I'll join you in a moment."

"What do you mean you'll *join* us in a *moment*?" Paulie set her hands to her hips.

I whirled around. "I have something to discuss with *Benjamin.* Go get colas and bring me back one. Please." I kept my voice low, dismissive.

Paulie clutched Laura's elbow. "Oh, for Pete's sake. Let's go. Claire wants to shoot the breeze with my brother."

With my hands clasped behind me, I studied the toes of my oxfords for a moment before lifting my chin to Benjamin. When I did gaze into his face, he smiled as if he might say something.

"What?"

"I was thinking." His glance skimmed me briefly from head to toe. "You do look nice in blue."

My breath caught; his assessment was a visual caress. Shaking tresses of curls from my face, I blinked to regain my composure, and managed a reply. "Why, thank you, Benjamin." I dipped my chin and peered into his dark-lashed, blue eyes.

He nodded his head and took a drink from his beer. His other hand was casually tucked into his jean pocket, and he stood with one leg crossed over his ankle. My gaze wandered along his arm, watching the muscle flex above the roll of his shirtsleeve as he brought the bottle to his lips. I struggled to breathe in a normal fashion, while my pounding heartbeat was anything but normal.

Can he hear my heart? See the heat flaring across my chest and neck?

He glanced beyond me to the couples dancing. "So, now what?"

"Excuse me?"

"What's the next step for your singing career?" He brought his focus back to me.

"Actually, I'd rather act than sing. Oh, I suppose I could do musicals, if the script was right for me." I batted my eyelashes. Levity helped the jitters his attention brought on.

"If you need a manager, I think Paulie would be happy to accompany you to Hollywood." He chuckled.

I joined in his laughter. "I'll take that under advisement."

He continued to study my face as our laughter died off. "You won't go taking off before you graduate, will you?"

A dizzy sensation passed over me. His tone, his serious expression, or perhaps I read minds—I didn't know what gave me the impression his question was more than idle conversation.

I shook my head in answer. When a corner of his mouth turned up, like I'd seen him do before, a pleasant quiver crossed my chest. His mouth took on a sexy smirk, yet I inwardly gasped. *Is he mocking me—still the little sister's friend he could toy with?* Or was he pleased I wouldn't be going off soon?

Again, he looked over my shoulder to the activity in the room behind me.

"Would you notice if I left?" My voice came out small, timid to my ears. *Notice me now.*

An eternity passed between the time Benjamin took a long pull on his beer and turned his head back in my direction, his blue gaze right at me. "I'm certain I would."

I caught my breath a moment, and purposely released the air slowly to still my fluttering heart. Warm, as if I'd exerted myself, I was sure my Irish cheeks were flushed red. I thought he might speak again, but instead, his gaze shifted to my mouth, his lips slightly parted.

Ripples spread from my heart to lower regions, and I swayed.

"Are you okay?" His hand lightly clasped my shoulder.

Mrs. Russell happened to walk by at that precise moment. "Is something wrong?"

Regretfully, Benjamin released me.

"No, no." I waved a hand in front of my face like a fan. "I'm just a bit warm. Paulie's bringing me a cold cola."

One thick brow quirked over twinkling eyes as his mother said, "Okay, dear." She moved on to the back stoop.

I cleared my throat and went back to studying my oxfords for a moment when the idea I had earlier came to me, inspiring a wonderful notion.

"I wonder if…" I stumbled as I met his gaze. "Do you think you could maybe help me with some drawings I have to do for school?" He looked quizzical, so I forged ahead. "In science, we have to do some diagrams and illustrations for extra credit. God knows I need extra credit in science. I'm just not an artist. You are, so maybe I could get some help from you."

"An artist?" He shrugged with a slight smile of pleasure. "I don't know about that. I draw a little."

"Oh, my gosh!" I clasped hands to my chest. "Your drawing of the old Mallory house is wonderful. Do you think you might be a professional artist someday?"

"Hell, that's no profession. I'm going to build houses—design them, too." He tipped his bottle, making his point. "Not like the cheap boxes going up on the other side of town since the war ended either. I'll design custom homes for professional people."

"That sounds grand." His future plans were all well and good, but I needed to stay focused on the promise of his time with me in the months to come. "You'd be doing some drawing when you design, right?"

"You're right, Claire." His smile came slowly.

I took his reaction as an indication I scored points with insightful conversation. My throat went dry, yet I couldn't shut up for fear of losing his attention. If I could get Benjamin to volunteer to help me with some fantasy extra credit, I foresaw hours of time spent with him.

I rubbed sweaty palms together and hoped I didn't

109

look eager. "I like to draw, although, I'm not very good at it."

"Since when do you like to draw?" Paulie's voice came from behind me

I whirled around. "Since always. There's lots you don't know about me, silly."

Her retort was left on her tongue as her sister, Ruth, and another woman popped into our group and interrupted the exchange.

"Susan, I'd like you to meet my little sister, Paulie, her friends, Claire and Laura, and my brother, Ben." Ruth pointed to each of us. "Say hi to my friend, Susan."

We murmured hello in unison.

"Nice to meet all of you." She barely noticed us, turning her smile immediately on Benjamin, and offered him her hand. "I've heard so much about Ruth's family, I've been dying to meet you."

I had no doubt by *you* she meant Benjamin. She stepped forward, successfully nudging me to the side, and planted herself directly between us.

"Ben, honey, that beer looks mighty good. Do you think we could find another?"

His glance flicked over her. "Sure, Susan. This way."

She clutched his arm, leaned into him, and she nodded at the rest of us. "'Scuse us, girls?" She sashayed off, Benjamin in tow.

Ruth laughed. "Catch you later!" She turned toward the couples dancing and waved at a friend to join her on the floor.

I slumped against the wall, and absorbed the residual heat from Benjamin's body. Relaxing, I closed my eyes and leaned my head on his imaginary shoulder.

"Claire, did you hear me?" Paulie's voice called to me as if from the bottom of a well.

"Mmm?" My eyes remained closed while memorizing his smile and words moments before.

"I said, don't you wish you hadn't broken up with Arnold and he was here?" She jabbed the toe of her shoe against my foot.

"No, I don't. You do. He's working anyway." I turned a cheek against the wall to capture more of the warmth Benjamin had left behind.

She jabbed my foot harder with the toe of her shoe. "What are you doing?"

I opened my eyes and sighed. "Why did Susan have to come tonight, anyway?"

"Who cares?" Paulie asked.

Laura's eyes widened. "Claire cares!"

I righted from the wall, denial sticking in my throat.

"Claire has a thing for your brother. You do, don't you?"

"My brother?" My friend's words reeked with incredulity. "Ben?" She sounded as if no one could ever consider her brother worthy of attraction.

Laura smiled, all-knowing. "I've had some thoughts about him myself, but—"

"You, too?" She glanced from me to Laura and back again. "Benjamin?"

"Be *quiet*!" I snapped. "It's not like he knows I exist, so I don't need you blabbing your mouth."

With a shake of her head, the light of understanding spread across her face like the sun came from behind the clouds. "That's why...now it makes sense…why you—"

"This has *nothing* to do with Arnold." I cut her off before she could start in on me about him. "Contrary to what you think, the world does not revolve around that kid."

"Oh, really, Claire?"

Certainly, in the week since I first laid eyes on Benjamin, Arnold had fallen out of favor with me. But the boy had been fully responsible for his ineptness. Paulie of course would not see that, so I let her think what she would.

"Susan looks like Rita Hayworth," I lamented.

"Oh, pooh! She thinks she's a glamour-puss." She spat the words as if she rid her mouth of a foul taste. "Did you see the way she swung her be-hind?"

"She's so mature, so sexy," I agonized, and ran a hand down my hips, every bit as curvaceous as Susan, I reasoned, but not as evident in a full-skirted dress.

"Who cares? She isn't *that* special." My friend's words, meant to be consoling, fell flat.

"She does look like Rita Hayworth." Laura sighed.

"Laura! Just because her hair is red and she wears her skirt too tight, doesn't mean she's any Rita Hayworth." Paulie's voice was full of contempt for her brother's apparent seductress. "Besides, Claire looks like Betty Grable except her hair isn't the same shade of blonde."

"Betty Grable?" She gawked at me, doubt evidenced by her wrinkled forehead and nose.

I half-smiled at Paulie's thin attempt. "Thanks, anyway, but I don't think too many would share your opinion." I sighed, shoulders drooping with the weight of disappointment. "Rita…Hayworth!"

"Oh, pooh. It doesn't matter, because she's too old for Ben. I bet she's at least twenty-five, and he's not even twenty-one. He wouldn't like an old woman like her." Paulie gestured with her hands in the direction they had walked. "I mean, what would he want with an old woman like her anyway?"

"Ha! I can tell you what he'd want," Laura volunteered. "He'd want to get her in the hay just like my brothers would, that's what he'd want. And I bet she'd do it, too."

"Shut up, Laura." She poked her shoulder. "Just because your brothers act like animals, doesn't mean mine would."

I nodded. "Paulie's probably right." Then why did I have the dull ache of disappointment heavy within? "No offense, Laura, your brothers are playboys. Benjamin is a working man."

"Man is the key word," she smirked.

"Benjamin's too serious to fall for her cheap antics," I continued, talking over Laura's snickering. "He's more sensitive about life and love…and…he may be…distracted momentarily, but he'll see through her." I hardly sounded convincing, even to my own ears.

"Really, Claire." Laura scoffed and waved a hand in the air. "Ben is no different than any other guy."

"She's *throwing* herself at him!" I poked the air with indignation.

"Well, that makes it easy, doesn't it?" Her argument smacked of reality.

I resumed my slumped position against the wall and ran my tongue over the lipstick I so carefully applied less than an hour ago. "Damn."

Paulie looped her arm through Laura's and jerked

113

her around a little harder than necessary so we formed a tight circle. "Shut your trap a minute, Laura." Her eyes narrowed, but when she turned her head to me, she relaxed her face and her voice took on a gentle note. "My gosh, Claire. Ben is...is...so not special like Arnold. You could've had Arnold, who wasn't good enough for you. Why on earth is my brother's flirtation with the red-headed hot pants such a big deal?"

"Ah, Paulie. Arnold is a *friend*. And a *boy*."

"He didn't see it that way. What do you mean a boy? He's our age."

"I won't be a high school student forever, and your brother is a *man*."

Paulie's expression remained clueless. Explaining would be useless. My feelings were deep, complicated, and impossible to relate to the sister of my desire.

"Oh, never mind." I stood straight, smoothed my dress, and wiggled toes inside my shoes. "Please keep this to yourself. You, too, Laura." *Susan be damned.* I vowed to find a way to get Benjamin in spite of the Rita Hayworth look alike. "Let's pick out some records now and do some dancing."

****

Ben tipped his bottle to his lips and swallowed the first cold drink of his second beer. He glanced around the living room as he waited for Susan to use the bathroom.

Why the hell do women take so long?

Across the room, his mother stood in the kitchen doorway, tapped her foot and smiled as she watched the couples dancing. Behind her, at the kitchen table, a foursome played cards.

Claire and Paulie danced side by side, each with

one of Davie's friends. Claire's skirt flared below her butt as she twirled, exposing attractive knees and half her thighs. The dress settled and hugged her butt before the fullness righted again. She caught his gaze as she came out of the turn, batted her eyelashes, and flashed an infectious grin.

Why hadn't he noticed the curve of her ass before? He took a deep breath. *Because she's too damned young right now, you idiot.*

Susan was another story. He checked the roll of his sleeve, flexed his biceps, and breathed deeply when her scent drifted up from the shoulder of his shirt. His breath released a bit jagged with the sensation her musky perfume brought on. She certainly didn't mind a little physical contact. He took another long drink of beer.

Claire's laughter drifted over the heads between them, drawing him back. She peeked from behind her dance partner, as if she knew he would be looking in her direction.

Interesting.

Could be Arnold wasn't really part of the picture? The guy she danced with looked pretty damned captivated by young Claire. He was too old for her, too. Her age, coupled with the fact she was still in high school, melted away when she spoke. Her flirting, raw and straightforward, could unnerve a guy. Hell, he told her he'd miss her when she asked. In spite of knowing damn well he should treat her like one of his sister's little friends, he'd tipped his hand in that admission. She had a way about her all right. Plus her figure and hair—she qualified way above high school. He knew exactly how her dance partner felt. Ben rolled his shoulders.

Damn, better to get my mind back on Susan.

"Why, Ben, hon, you look like a wallflower ready for picking," Susan purred as she slid beside him. Her breasts nudged at his arm when she whispered in his ear.

His senses went on overload; the heady, musky scent, wet, red lips and sexuality exuding from the soft flesh she pushed against him. "Are you the gardener?" He didn't recognize his own raspy voice.

She laughed.

Frank Sinatra crooned, and Susan stepped away from the wall, held on to his arm and towed him forward. She took the bottle from his hand and set it on the floor. Swinging into him, her hand around his neck, she said, "Let's rub bellies."

His face grew hot; his laugh uncontained.

"Now, don't let me embarrass you, Benny." Susan's throaty laugh delighted him. "I pretty much say what I'm feeling."

They swayed, Susan's body maintaining contact with his.

"I've always said honesty is the best policy." He rested his fingers in the small of her back; the heat radiated well beyond his hand as her hips firmly pressed against his.

****

As the evening wore on, I rarely lost sight of Benjamin. He danced twice with Susan, and although the songs were slow, I was comforted in that she pulled Benjamin onto the dance floor, not the other way round. At one point, the couple slipped out to the porch but, to my relief, Mrs. Russell's ten minute rule kicked in.

Egged on by Paulie to sing with Doris Day, my performance slowed the dancers to watch. Benjamin and Susan stood in the kitchen doorway, listening, and I imagined myself with the smile and legs of Betty Grable.

As the evening drew near eleven, Mrs. Russell made cleaning up motions. The guys got the clue to move the furniture back into place. Most everyone migrated to the front porch for a few minutes of conversation, some climbed into cars, others walked onto the dirt road in the direction they lived. Paulie and I made sure to take up a position at the kitchen window when Laura walked Fred to his car. He sure knew how to get in as much contact as possible within ten minutes. Laura looked perfectly moonstruck as she helped us gather dishes and deposit them in the sink of dishwater.

David clasped his arm around Barbara. "Taking Barbara home," he called to whoever cared to know.

Benjamin and Susan disappeared out the front door.

Laura and I followed Paulie to her bedroom. She flopped down on her bed. Laura flipped her shoes off and settled on the round rug on the floor at the foot of the bed while I stood by the window.

"So, where was Pete tonight, Paulie?" I asked the question.

"How would I know?"

"Fred wants to date." Laura blurted. She sounded anything but excited over the new development.

"Don't suppose your dad would go along with that," Paulie said.

"No, he won't. Shit!"

We laughed spontaneously at her uncharacteristic language. We didn't mean to be cruel, but Laura groaned.

Paulie rolled to the foot of the bed and tapped her on the shoulder. "You can see him here whenever you want. He comes over quite a bit. In a few months, you'll be out of high school."

"Sneak?"

"Yeah, sneak." Paulie was chipper. The idea obviously appealed to her. She rolled over to her back. "Did you see David and Barbara dancing?"

"Mmm," I answered from my stance by the window, my back to the room.

"They're so cute together, aren't they?"

"They are," Laura agreed. "They're like boyfriend and girlfriend twins. Same dark hair, almost the same height. I think they even laugh alike."

"Mmm," I muttered.

The bed squeaked behind me. "What are you *doing*?" Paulie asked.

I stood at the corner of the bedroom window, the curtain in my fingers tucked back an inch. Peeking out, I could see Benjamin and Susan. The light from the kitchen window strained to reach the couple at the bottom of the porch where they stood in purple shadows. Their voices hung at the edge of the dimly lit steps, so I gleaned meaning from their body language like a silent movie without subtitles.

"I'm watching everyone leave," I whispered with a glance back at my friends.

Paulie hopped from the bed. Anticipating her action, I held fast to the curtain when she snatched at the material.

"What're they doing out there?"

I didn't have to ask whom she meant by 'they.'

Laura crawled onto the bed. "I bet their swapping spit." She giggled.

"They are not," I hissed. "Shut up! Glamour-puss is hanging on him and wiggling around, rubbing her knockers on his chest."

She erupted into laughter, but covered her mouth when I shot her a mean glare.

"What are they doing now?" Paulie shuffled around by my elbow to try to catch a glimpse of the front yard scene.

"Oh, man, Benjamin's hand is practically on her butt." My stomach roiled with distress. "She's such a tart!" Anger boiled over. The heat of my breath collected between the curtain and my face. "Oh, I think she's leaving. She kissed him on the neck! No, wait. Benjamin still has his arm around her. Yep, she's leaving." My grip on the curtain relaxed, my knees weak. "Yeah, she's gone."

I fell back across Paulie's bed, bouncing Laura beside me. The image of Benjamin's hand low on Susan's waist, his fingers touching the curve of her buttocks, filled my mind. A quake welled up deep from inside my body, the intensity of the lusty sensation enjoyable, until it collided with the recognizable sensation of despair in my chest. Grabbing a pillow, I covered my head and groaned.

The bed jarred, and Paulie joined us. She pushed the pillow off my face. "It isn't any big deal, you know. She's a harlot."

"Who's a harlot?" Ruth came in, unbuttoning her blouse as she kicked the door closed.

Brenda Whiteside

"Susan, your so-called friend," her sister answered.

"A harlot?" Ruth snorted. "She's not a harlot, little girl. She's a woman who does what she pleases."

"Only a harlot would act the way she acted around Ben." My friend declared. Laura murmured agreement.

"What? Come on, girls. It's 1945. Women can be just as forward as men can." Paulie's older sister walked around in her bra and slip, which caused Laura to take an interest in the pattern on the bedspread. "She works side by side with men at the plant. She's nearly twenty-five and can take care of herself. Why shouldn't she be able to make the first move on a guy?" She turned her back and slipped out of her bra. She lifted a shiny, red nightgown from a drawer and glided it over her head and shimmered down her body.

Laura found the opposite wall more interesting to look at the minute Ruth reached for her bra hook. I followed her every movement, intrigued with the way the light danced off the silk from clinging hips to bouncing breasts. The silk had to be Chinese. She brushed her bleached blonde hair, cropped short to the bottom of her neck.

Defending the gospel, Paulie said, "Guys don't marry gals like her."

"Ha! That's gobbledygook." Ruth turned the covers back on her bed. "Even if that's true, so what? Who says Susan wants to get married? Maybe she'd rather have a career."

"Keep working at the plant?" Her younger sister's eyes grew wide. "Isn't she going to quit, now that the war's over?"

"Hell, she may get promoted to foreman one of these days."

"I'd like to be an actress or even a singer." I broke in. "I suppose someday I might get married." Career or marriage? I wanted both. "I guess we'll all get married."

Ruth sat cross-legged on her bed, faced us, and lit a cigarette. "Good luck, kiddo. You better get the career out of the way first. Once you're married, you'll give it up."

How wise and worldly she appeared in her Chinese silk nightgown, exhaling smoke, while picking tobacco flakes off her tongue. I was compelled to agree with her.

"That's the way men are. They want you at home, having babies, and cooking. So you better be all dolled up with dinner on the table when they walk through the door." We were speechless as Ruth stubbed out her cigarette and slid the ashtray over to her nightstand. Climbing under the covers, she rolled over, and put her back to us. "I know what I'm talking about."

Paulie finally stirred and made a gesture with her hands as if pushing her sister over a cliff. "Oh, pooh!"

Laura got up to pull her pajamas out of a cloth knapsack beside the bed. "I get the bathroom first," she declared.

"You girls don't giggle all night," Ruth ordered. "And turn off the light. You don't need it."

Paulie complied, and she and I changed into our nightclothes by the light of the curtain's filtered moonlight. After, we knocked quietly on the bathroom door, and once Laura let us in, we gently closed it behind us.

"Where'd your sister get her nightgown?" I asked between brush strokes on my teeth.

Paulie sat on the toilet, waiting her turn. "She said some guy who comes in the restaurant gave it to her. She claims he liked her service. He got it in Europe."

I rinsed my mouth. "She must be a really good waitress," I snickered.

"She knows how to flirt, that's for sure." Paulie stepped up and spread toothpaste on her brush. "She thinks she's the best waitress in town, too. Says she'll own her own restaurant someday."

Laura sat on the edge of the tub. "Wow. You think she could?"

Paulie snorted, sending a dribble of toothpaste down her chin. "She says if she works her ass off." She spit before continuing. "Her words, not mine. She says if she works her ass off, she can do anything a man can do, like own a business."

After a quick session of Eenie, Meenie, Minie, Moe to determine who would sleep in the middle, we turned off the light and tiptoed out of the bathroom to bed.

I lay in the middle with my eyes wide open. Benjamin slept under the same roof, only a room a way, and miles away from Susan.

"What're you going to do about Susan and Ben?" Laura whispered.

Paulie rolled toward me. "There *is* no Susan and Ben," she hissed across me.

"I don't have to do anything," I whispered. "You heard Ruth. Susan's older and wants a career. We probably won't even see her again." And soon enough, I could put my plan into action. I'd use my science class to create the needed chemistry between us. I'd merely have to fabricate some extra credit assignments. "All I have to do is be patient. Benjamin will notice me, and he doesn't need any childish help from you two."

After we whispered our goodnights, I stared at the ceiling, and listened to the soft breathing around me. The different rhythms fused together then the ringing in my ears chimed in. Bells. I smiled. If I looked out the window, the stars would be twinkling brighter.

I closed my eyes, and imagined Benjamin's hands. The tips of his fingers touched the blue cloth of my dress covering my backside. I shivered at the thought as goose bumps spread down my thighs. Someday, his hands would rest on my hips, and anywhere else they cared to wander. I squirmed, disturbing a sound asleep Paulie beside me. Then I lifted his thin white T-shirt over his head and my hands caressed taut muscles, as I blissfully drifted off to sleep.

Chapter Six
Goodbye Hollywood, Hello Full Growed Woman

Paulie leaned on her elbow and peeked over me when I woke up.

"What?" I whispered, careful not to wake her sister in the other bed.

She fell back beside me. "No need to whisper. Ruth's gone." She kicked off the covers yawned, and reached across me to poke Laura. "Wake up, sleepy head."

Our friend rolled over, covered her head with the pillow, and let out a muffled "No."

"Why not? Are you dreaming about Fred?"

Laura lifted her face, the pillow still wrapped around the back of her head. "Shut up." She plopped back down, face into the mattress. "You're thinking about Pete." She lifted her head a few inches. "Make that Arnold."

I ignored my two friends as they bantered around me. My thoughts were also of the prior night and a male, but certainly more mature than my friends' silly teasing. Sunday morning could prove to be much more fun than last night, if I didn't let nerves tongue-tie me. Since there'd be no sexy Susan hanging on Benjamin, we could sit on the front steps and talk. I'd engage him in conversation about his art and his future plans again. My heart palpitated as I sprang into a sitting position.

"Can it, you two." I yanked the pillow off Laura's head. "Let's get up. I can't stay all day. Da and I have to go grocery shopping."

I vaulted over Laura, grabbed my bag of clean clothes, and loped to the bathroom. Paulie joined me while Laura stayed in the bedroom to dress. Paulie banded her hair in a ponytail, but I carefully brushed and fluffed. I applied lipstick, which drew an eye roll from her, although she politely refrained from commenting.

I expected this Sunday would be as good as any Saturday night at the Russells'.

"What shall we have for breakfast?" Paulie asked as we all headed for the kitchen. "We can eat anything we want on Sundays. Mom cooks on Saturday. We're on our own on Sunday. I'm thinking peanut butter and mayonnaise sandwiches."

"With lettuce," Laura agreed.

I didn't care what we ate. I scanned the hall for signs of Benjamin. Then the living room. No Benjamin in the kitchen either. Mrs. Russell sat at her sewing machine in the space between the kitchen and the living room. She smiled without looking up.

"Claire, get the bread," Paulie said.

I opened the door to the oversized, wooden breadbox and lifted out the loaf of heavy, white, homemade bread.

"Good morning, Mrs. Russell." I plopped the loaf on the breadboard to slice off six pieces. "It's so quiet around here. Where is everyone?"

The sewing machine whirred. Wire rim glasses perched on the end of her beak-like nose, her thick brows nearly met in the middle of her forehead wrinkled in concentration. She tied off a knot of thread and removed the blue flowered material from the machine.

Leaning back in her chair, she smiled at me. "Richard headed off on his bike with his fishing pole long before you girls got up. Ruth Anne left a few minutes ago. I think her eventual destination is Seven Springs for a picnic. Which is what David would have liked to do." She chuckled. "Barbara talked him into taking her to church. And as for Benjamin? I don't know where he went. Ever since he got a car, he's not around here much." Her voice trailed off as she held up her creation for inspection.

One of my favorite things to eat, peanut butter and mayo on white bread washed down with hot tea, was tasteless. Maybe he had a morning date with Susan. Maybe they were parked somewhere in broad daylight necking. The peanut butter was a clump below my ribs that even the hot tea couldn't dissolve.

"What does the most talented girl—woman, no person—at North High have planned next for her Hollywood career?" Paulie asked as mayo oozed down her thumb from her sandwich.

I sighed, considering the question.

Why didn't I know? The contest win had been the affirmation for future plans. Yet, now, the familiar excitement that thoughts of the theater always brought didn't come. Time spent thinking about Benjamin trumped thoughts of a singing career. "I'm not sure."

"I've heard some local people sing on the radio after the Godfrey's Talent Scouts show Sunday night. You could do that." Laura scooted from the table to get another cup of tea. "Maybe some Hollywood scout would hear you and whisk you off to stardom."

Would Benjamin follow me?

My imagination burned for a moment, but fizzled soon enough. I meant nothing to him. Yet.

"Yeah, maybe." I wiped my mouth. "But today is grocery shopping day, and even stars have to eat. Especially fathers of stars."

The girls followed me to the sink, Laura gulping the last of her tea as she walked.

"My mom should be here any minute to pick me up. You want a ride?" she asked.

There was no sense in hanging around. "Sure." Benjamin might be gone all day. Da would wait for me anyway to do the afternoon shopping followed by Sunday dinner. This would be my first time to make potato and egg drop dumpling soup like Mrs. Russell had taught me. Da would get a side of fried bologna, and I'd have pickled beets. After dinner, we'd listen to *The Adventures of Ozzie and Harriet*.

A car horn sounded out front. Mrs. Russell rose from her chair at the sewing machine, walked to the screen door, and opened it while we gathered our things. "Looks like one of your brothers, Laura. Tell your momma hello for me."

"I will. Thanks for having me."

"Anytime."

I stopped next to the little woman. "Thank you, Mrs. Russell." She smelled like the fabric aisle of the department store and lilac soap.

She patted my arm. "Anytime, dear girl."

I embraced her invitation, and intended on taking her up on it frequently.

****

Two days later, I invited myself home with Paulie. Latin lessons gave her trouble, and I was more than happy to go home with her for some tutoring. If I lingered long enough, I could ask Benjamin for help with the extra credit drawing of amoeba for science. I flipped through my science book while I sat on the bus waiting for my friend.

"I suppose that seat is saved for Paulie." Arnold's voice interrupted the search for my drummed up extra credit project.

I met his dark stare from the seat in front of me. "As always."

Other than the talent show encounter, he had kept his distance as I'd instructed him. My hope was the time away from me would bring him out of lust and back to being a friend. We'd seen each other around school, but he'd refrained from approaching me.

"What's new, Claire?" He hung his arms over the back of the seat. His fingers grazed my knees.

I swished my legs sideways. "Nothing much."

Two girls took the seat across the aisle and nearly tripped over each other to catch Arnold's attention. I probably gave them a look. I'd grown tired of the North High female attraction to him.

"My job at Sears is working out swell."

"You're not at the Paramount anymore?"

"Nah. Kid's job." He smiled self-satisfied and puffed his chest out. "I'll be getting a car soon."

I glanced out the window. *Where is Paulie?* "That's nice."

"Maybe you'd like me to pick you up for a movie when I have wheels."

I rolled my eyes. "Arnold—"

"Have you missed me at all, Claire?"

I fidgeted with the pages of my book. "I've missed my friend Arnold." Truth was, I'd hardly given him a thought. He seemed happy enough in the audience at the contest. I'd been meaning to ask Paulie about the attention he bestowed upon her that evening, but quite frankly, I'd been so caught up in my own dramas, the thought had gotten lost.

"Shit," he muttered under his breath. "I don't need another damn friend, Claire."

"There's no need to be abusive, you know." My comment brought his jaw tight as he ran a hand through his straight black hair. "Everyone needs friends, of all kinds," I added.

"Friends aren't supposed to affect you the way you affect me."

He smiled rather lopsidedly, and I nearly found myself enchanted by his childish grin. Until his grin morphed into a leer.

"And a good friend might be more accommodating," he added.

The hair on my neck stood up, and I balled a fist on my book. I considered slapping the sneer off his face when Paulie's cheery smile popped up above us.

"Hey, guys!" She hadn't actually acknowledged me with her greeting as she leaned toward Arnold. "I thought you had football practice."

His gaze lingered on me a moment before turning on the charm that blinded my friend. "I sure do, Paulie." He stood. "They can't start without me now, can they?" He rubbed her shoulder as he passed. "Claire and I were shooting the breeze, wondering where you were."

"I'm here now." She beamed.

"And I have to get going." He flicked her chin with his thumb. "Such timing."

Her nose crinkled with her smile. "See you tomorrow then?"

He winked. "For sure."

She followed his departure off the bus before plopping down beside me. Her sigh lifted and released with so much gusto, desire bounced off the bus walls.

"What's going on with you two?"

"Nothing. At least not as much as I'd like." She pursed her lips and batted her lashes. "He's getting over *you*, Claire. I've been there to listen, that's all."

"He's been confiding in you?"

"Yes, and he knows you two are friends…only. He really does." Her eyes were wide with sympathy.

"He does?" The impression Arnold gave me and Paulie's take were mismatched like the last two socks in the laundry basket. "I'm not so sure he's giving you the whole story."

"What's that supposed to mean?"

"He considers us just friends, Paulie?" My words came out harsh. How could she be so naïve? "I'm not so sure…"

"Oh, pooh, Claire." She stuck her turned up nose in my face. "Don't keep hanging on to this. You didn't *want* him. He can have *any* girl he wants, so don't go regretting you let him go and think he's still pining over *you*."

"I'm not hanging on." I lowered my voice in an effort to calm her down. "I'm just saying, don't let him use you to—"

"*Use* me? So, you don't think someone like Arnold

could possibly find *me* worth his time without *you* around?" Her bottom lip came out as she hugged her books to her chest.

"No, Paulie. I don't mean anything like that at all." I touched her arm. Prickles of regret ran across my shoulders. "He's a flirt, but if he's been confiding in you, well then, there must be more to it than mere flirting." I gave in to her, even as wariness spread through me.

How could I warn her off him without hurt feelings and damage to our friendship? For the time being, I'd have to let her have her joy, but vowed to keep my eye on the situation.

He'll have hell to pay with me if he breaks her heart.

"I meant to ask you after the talent contest…he seemed pretty cozy with you." She frowned at me, perhaps thinking I mocked her. "Like he thoroughly enjoyed your company."

She dropped her books to her lap and relaxed her face. "Like I said, we've been hanging out a little together around school. He says I'm easy to talk to."

"That sounds…nice." I smiled in an effort to soothe her. "Well, just be careful, I mean of your feelings…your heart…if—"

"Am I going to have to escort you off my bus, or will you go peaceably?" Mr. Jesper called out as he peered in his rearview mirror.

We hadn't noticed the bus stopped. I followed Paulie to the door and down the stairs. I didn't have the stomach for teasing Mr. Jesper.

Paulie chose to drop the bus ride topic. "Momma bakes bread on Tuesdays, so I'm sure we can get a warm slice with honey."

While we labored over Latin at the kitchen table, sipping tea, and eating bread and honey, I kept an eye on the clock. The hands moved agonizingly slow. Since I was in no mood to gab, we managed to stick to task, and Paulie's momma sat close by at her Singer.

"I think that's enough for today, Paulie." I calculated Benjamin would drive up the road from work soon. My hope was to casually run into him on the way out of the yard.

The whirring of Mrs. Russell's sewing stopped. "You know girls, this Saturday is Benjamin's birthday. My young man will be twenty-one. Seeing as it's Benjamin, I think we'll have a nice family-style dinner and cake. A few close friends. No big gathering. We do that all the time anyway. What do you think?" She looked from her daughter to me and back again.

While Paulie agreed that would be a good idea, I had to bite back excitement. *Good* idea? *Fabulous* idea. A vision of a more intimate dinner with the Russells, garnering a seat next to Benjamin, and wishing him a happy birthday—what could be more perfect?

Perfect.

I smiled and nodded in agreement as I collected my books.

Paulie walked out to the porch with me. I immediately searched the road and was rewarded with a blue car in the distance.

Glancing up at the sky as if Benjamin's car had not come into view, and to stall until he drew nearer, I said, "Gosh, look at those dark clouds. We might get some rain."

"Looks like Ben is home," she said. "Guess you

know that, don't you?"

I flipped the hair from my neck and pretended to notice his arrival at that moment. "Oh, I do believe you're right."

My friend laughed. "Don't work your dramatics on me. I'll stand here until he gets out of his car then you can have him all to yourself. Although, it's beyond me why you would." She laughed again.

"You're wicked, Paulie."

"Oh, I suppose he's kind of handsome, in a brother kind of way…"

"Luckily, he's not my brother." By then, my heart beat a rapid rhythm. I tightened my stomach muscles. *Flat tummy and chest out for a womanly pose.* I positioned my body so Benjamin would not catch a profile view the moment he got out of his car. "You can disappear as soon as he hits the steps. Got it?"

His car wheeled onto the property and stopped beside the house. Benjamin stepped out carrying a lunch pail, his dark hair dulled with white plaster dust.

Ruggedly handsome.

"Hey, Ben," Paulie called.

"Hey, Paulie." He smiled at me.

His smile nearly undid me. My ears had a ringing sensation, and my eyes developed tunnel vision. I barely heard Paulie make some excuse to go inside.

Benjamin stopped on the second step down so we were eye to eye. He rested an arm on the railing in front of me. His forearms were caked with the same white dust as his head, giving form to normally unseen waves of hair.

"Good afternoon, Benjamin." I melted into his morning glory blue eyes.

"Hi, Claire. Practicing for another contest?"

He set his lunch pail down and pulled a pack of cigarettes from his pocket. The gesture gave me a sense of languidness; he was in no hurry to leave my company.

"No, not this time. I helped Paulie grasp the linguistics of Latin."

"That sounds like a pretty tall order." He lowered down onto the top step, far enough away he had to look up, but also perhaps to leave room for me to sit.

I sat next to him, as close as I dared so as not to be too brazen. "She does have trouble, although I believe she's teachable." We laughed.

There was a moment of silence when the laughter died. The rustling of the cottonwood leaves filled the space. The dirt below us gave off a damp smell while the air, heavy with unseasonable warmth, foretold the impending storm. The waistband of my skirt, already damp from sweat in the short time I'd been on the porch, cooled me each time the light breeze passed over us.

"I'm probably not very pleasant to sit next to," he commented with a small chuckle.

Highly pleasant!

"Plastering is a messy job." He flicked half a smoked cigarette into the dirt at the bottom of the stairs. "I'm covered in it."

My head swam, but my plunge was a result of more than Benjamin's aroma. He embodied the complete man—dedication to family, hard work, and a visual manliness, which piqued my womanly desires. The air in the few inches separating us, heavy with his scent, so filled my senses, I could taste him.

"There's certainly nothing wrong with hard work. I rather like the smell of…plaster."

He flicked some caked clumps from his arm. "Not as much as the smell of greasepaint." It wasn't a question.

I didn't want to talk about theater aspirations at that moment. "I guess certain smells go with every trade. What is it you do exactly? With plaster?" I rested an elbow on my knee, propped my chin on a fist, and gazed at his face, hoping he would appreciate my interest. Smiling eyes rewarded me.

"Plaster is what you see on walls, inside a house or building." His enthusiasm spilled out. "You mix it from a powder then spread the plaster—which is thick, sort of like a paste—with a trowel on the wall in sweeping motions."

"Sounds rather artful."

"Yeah, I guess it is. Takes a certain skill, which Joe says I have." His voice was soft, proud not boastful.

"How wonderful, Benjamin." With elbows on my knees, I brought both hands to cradle my face.

He gazed into my eyes for a moment. A storm raged between us, more intense than the one brewing above. When he cleared his throat and sat up a bit straighter, I did the same.

"Your artfulness is what I'm hoping you will lend me." I fussed with the folds of my skirt before looking into his face again.

"How's that?"

"Remember the extra credit we talked about last Saturday? If I do some drawings of things like amoeba, then I can boost my grade." Not even a small twinge of guilt colored my fantasy assignment. "That is, if you're still willing."

"Well, if you have some pictures to give me a clue what they are, I might be able to help."

"I don't know much about science stuff either, but there're pictures in the science book. Are you sure you wouldn't mind? Maybe you're too tired after work."

"Nah, I think you'll have to hang around longer though. I'd need to shower before we set to it. Maybe you could stay for dinner."

Ache of regret that I couldn't stay filled my chest. "I have to get home tonight 'cause I didn't warn Da. Another night would work."

"I've got something to do tomorrow after work, so how 'bout Thursday? Would it be too late to get the credit?"

"Oh, no. This is an ongoing thing all year." Best to keep it open-ended, set the scene for months to come if I needed.

"So, we'll have you around the rest of the year? No high-tailing it to California and stardom? With your voice…"

"I'm considering my options." Although, until that moment, I'd never considered *not* becoming the next big star in Hollywood, I wasn't at all surprised by my spontaneous decision. Not when faced with Benjamin. "I've gotten rather attached to Phoenix. I'd hate to uproot Da now that he's accustomed to his job." My dramatic embellishments poured from me. Had Da been there, he'd have given a big hoot at this one. "I'll graduate, then consider what to do." At that moment, all I cared about was not being far from Benjamin. A light twinkled in his eyes, hopefully from his feelings and not a reflection of the dimming sun.

"Thursday then?"

We stood. "Thursday," I agreed nearly giddy.

Benjamin looked beyond me over my shoulder and concern etched his face. "Those clouds really moved in fast while we talked. You plan to walk home?"

I followed his gaze. "Yes. I guess I better hurry."

"No. I better take you."

My heart jumped into my throat. "I hate to make you late for your dinner."

"Not like you live in the next city. Won't take long." He picked up his lunch pail, set it by the door, and walked to the kitchen window. "Mom. Going to take Claire home so she doesn't get caught in the rain."

Mrs. Russell came to the screen door, wiping her hands on her apron. "Good idea, Benjamin. Now, drive careful, and I'll put the fire on low. Goodbye, Claire dear."

"Let's get going, Claire. If it starts raining before I get in the car, I'll have plaster instead of just dust all over me."

We hopped quickly down the stairs, and as we slid onto the seats, the first sprinkles of rain spattered the windshield.

"Ho, just in time." Benjamin laughed.

I joined in, winded, not from our quick dash to the car, but breathless from his closeness.

He started the car, clicked on the wipers, and smiled before backing out of the yard. He proved to be a very cautious driver. I could nearly have walked home quicker than he made the drive. He took his mother's advice to heart to drive careful, and I was again touched by his sense of family, his respect for her.

It was several moments before I could find my

voice. The car wrapped us in our own private world. The rain pattered on the roof, the wipers thumped rhythmically on the window, and my heart tapped happily. His scent of hard work and plaster aroused a passion that tightened my chest and sent goose bumps from my tummy to between my thighs. I squirmed a bit, delighted with the sensation. The intimacy overwhelmed me with feelings I'd never experienced. My mouth watered, and the ringing in my ears was back. Hearing bells seemed entirely appropriate.

"I really appreciate the ride, Benjamin. I dare say I'd be fairly wet by now."

"I'm sorry I didn't shower first. Don't breathe too deep or you'll probably get plaster dust up your nose." He laughed. "Is this where I turn?"

"Oh, yes, sorry."

"I think I know the court. Had a friend who lived there." He cleared his throat, glanced at me, then back to the road. He scanned his dashboard as if checking the vehicle for proper functioning.

I couldn't take my gaze from him, devouring his every move. There was no one around to distract him or see my inappropriate staring. He seemed so consumed with the working of his car, I doubted he noticed my adoration. I wanted to memorize his every move, his every word to replay later as I lay in bed.

He cleared his throat again. "How's Arnold doing at Sears and Roebuck?"

His question baffled me. "I…I guess okay."

"Hasn't he mentioned it? I helped him get on there."

"Oh. I know he likes it. I don't see Arnold much. Paulie sees him more than I do, so she could probably tell you."

"I thought…" He glanced at me quickly. "I thought you and Arnold, well, were…I thought you saw him often."

"Ah, well, no. I don't. Arnold would perhaps like it if I saw him often. He's a fun enough…boy…no, we're not dating." We had arrived at the court, and I pointed him in the direction of home as I talked. "This one."

"Good." He smiled, brought his car to a halt in front of our house, and shifted into park. He threw an arm across the back of the seat, his hand grazing my hair as he did. "Good," he said again.

I didn't know if he was pleased I wasn't Arnold's girlfriend or that we'd found my home. The notion he cared one way or the other about a boyfriend thrilled me. I clung to the idea and my heart fluttered with this development. Could there be more? Would he expand on his thoughts?

I stared into seductive eyes that caressed my face. His gaze slid to my mouth, down my neck, and back to my eyes. His appraisal had my head reeling. Nothing existed outside the car. Instead of a leer like Arnold's, Benjamin's gaze sought to know me and me him. It was as if we communicated without speaking.

He blinked, a crooked smile came to his mouth, then he glanced away. "We seem to be of interest to someone." I pried my stare away to look out the front car window. Mrs. Snyder strolled in front of the car, her beady eyes peering at us.

Nosy old biddy.

I waved gaily, which caused her to shake her head and pick up speed. Benjamin laughed.

"That's the nosy old landlady. She takes a big

interest in what I do."

He put the car in gear and both hands on the wheel. "I better get back home. Mom's holding dinner."

The rain had slowed to a drizzle. I opened the door. "This was so nice of you, Benjamin. I'll see you on Thursday?"

"Thursday, it is. Hope I don't disappoint you, er, and your teacher."

"Oh!" I threw a hand in the air. "Impossible."

****

So much for keeping my distance from her.

Ben shook his head as he eased out onto the road. No harm could come from helping her with school assignments, as long as he kept in mind that was as far as their friendship would go. Now that she'd decided to stay in Phoenix to pursue other paths, maybe he could pursue her path. Eventually.

How lame was it to drive like a little old lady, to drag out the time he could spend with her in the close confines of his car? He wanted to breathe her in, revel in her ringing laugh, and feast on her lips. Damn good thing he was a filthy mess from work. It was all he could do to keep his hands off her.

She likes me. Her eyes had spoken volumes. *Arnold, the little jerk, isn't in the picture.* The young lady had taste and class.

They could take it slow; let her grow up a few more months. Couldn't be long until she'd be eighteen. Wouldn't be all that many months until she'd be out of high school. Then they could do some serious courting. Until then, he'd have to keep his zipper zipped and his feelings on hold.

Why the hell, now, when he had a car and the

possibilities for some action, did he fall for a high school student?

Ain't that a pisser?

****

After dinner, I lounged across the bed, supposedly working on math homework, but instead, scribbling Benjamin's initials across the page. I practiced writing Claire Russell, Mrs. Benjamin Russell, Mrs. Claire Russell.

My father tapped on the doorframe. "I'm home." He'd not come home for dinner. Probably a stop at the Beckin' Inn Bar had waylaid him.

I didn't look up. "Dinner's in the fridge."

"Might eat a little later." His speech was a bit slow, which meant he was only mildly intoxicated. "I'm going to step outside and have a smoke with Clarence." He shuffled into my room as I continued daydreaming. "Give a holler out the window if I'm not back in here by nine, would you? Don't want to miss my radio program."

"Mmm, sure."

His foot scraped on the floor. "What's that you working on there?" His leg nudged my foot as he leaned to see my notebook paper.

"Nothing, Da."

"Sure don't look like homework to me."

"Da, please. Can't a woman have some privacy?" I scooped up the notebook, slammed it shut, and sat on the edge of my bed.

"Benjamin Russell, huh?" He crossed his arms over his chest. "What's going on, Claire?"

"What are you talking about?" His accusatory tone of voice annoyed me.

"You're too young."

"Too young for what?"

"For much of anything with Benjamin. He's a growed man, young 'un, and you can't be messing around with full growed men."

"Da! I've not been messing around with anyone. And I am not a *young 'un*! You know damn good and well I'm a woman, young yes, but still a woman." I stood and held my arms out from my sides. "You can't look at me and see I'm not a woman."

"Don't you go using cuss words with me, young lady."

I glared, my lips pursed so tight my face lost blood flow.

"I can see all right you *look* like a woman, but you're still in high school, and Benjamin is a working man." He cleared his throat. "Do we need to have a talk, Claire?"

His neck seared red, and it was all I could do not to laugh. He'd neutralized all my anger.

"Oh, Da." I patted his cheek. "I'm a good girl, and I know everything I need to know. Benjamin is a friend right now. That's all."

"You're too young, you know."

"Too young for what, Da?"

"Too young to get serious about a man."

I took a deep breath. "All I've done is to write my name."

He tilted his head to the side, and rubbed his face in a circular motion. His eyes were misty.

"A person can't help feelings popping into her head and heart," I told him.

"Guess I knowed that. Still important you listen to

your ol' Da. You ain't getting married until you're eighteen."

"All I did was to write our name a few times." I raised my hands in exasperation. "Besides, Aunt Grace was married when she was fifteen."

"That's another story, and you is not your Aunt Grace." He ran a hand over his face again to clear the tears from his faded green eyes. Apparently, he'd had enough alcohol to settle him into the sentimental stage. "You're my little girl, and you're going to be a full growed woman before you get married." He pointed a finger at me. "That is that!"

I snatched his rough, stubby finger into my hand. "Oh, Da." I held his hand with both of mine.

"What about your singing career? I thought you was going to be a star someday?"

"I want more." Would my father understand? "I feel like I've stepped off the stage and into real life. Being a star has lost the shine for me. I'm happy here, with you, and...my friends." I stared at his big, rough hands. "What I want more than anything is to be a wife and a mother. To be a mother, always there for my little girl, and to make a nice home for my family is a lofty ambition which would bring me so much joy." I peered into his face. "Don't you think I should do that?"

Da absent-mindedly turned my hand over and rubbed the back of it. His eyes glazed over. "Like your momma would have done if she'd lived."

My eyes burned. Ending the evening crying with my father was not what I'd wanted to do. I pulled my hand from him and slapped the nightstand. He jumped. "I don't intend on getting married tomorrow anyway. You won't get rid of me all that easy." I wrapped my arms around his shoulders. "You like Benjamin, don't you?" I wanted my father to feel at least a little of what I did.

"Yeah, well, all them Russell kids is nice."

He liked him. Like. Not a deep enough emotion to describe what dwelt within me. My heart seemed to swell and fill my chest.

"I love him, Da."

His watery eyes opened wide.

"There, I said it out loud." I giggled at the joy bubbling inside as much as from Da's expression. "I do. I love him. Except…" A few of the bubbles burst. "He doesn't love me. Yet." But he would. He just *had* to. "So nothing is going to happen for a while." I took him by the shoulders and a half-smile creased his ruddy cheeks. "How about a deal? You agree I'm no longer a little girl, and I won't get married until I'm eighteen."

His smile widened.

"Deal?"

"Deal," he agreed.

Chapter Seven
A Birthday To Remember, A Birthday To Forget

Benjamin brought Lady Blue to a stop beside the house. He glanced to his right, through the passenger side window, at the dark clouds above the cottonwoods.

Could get rain tonight.

He stepped from the car, leaned in to get his lunch pail, and as he straightened, the aroma of cake baking in the oven filled the heavy air.

Today was his twenty-first birthday, and by the time he climbed the porch steps, he walked taller and livelier.

Mom greeted him with a kiss. "Happy birthday, Benjamin Willis."

He put his arms around her, hugged her tighter and longer than usual.

She slapped him on his backside. "Should I give you your birthday whoopin' now or after the guests arrive?"

"No more whoopin' me, Mom. Your boy is a man, and it just ain't right." He spun her around twice and lifted her off her feet.

"You stop that, Benjamin Willis. Man or no, I can take my hand to your hide, if I've a mind to."

They both laughed as she grabbed the dishtowel from the kitchen counter and swiped at his legs. Snatching the towel from her, he wrapped it around his

145

hand, and reached behind her to lift the lid on the large iron kettle.

"Damn, Mom, this smells great!" The moist, white steam held the fragrance of beef simmering. He leaned over the pot of carrots, beans, and potatoes bubbling amongst hunks of brown beef, which rarely graced the table. "Beef stew! I can't remember the last time." He kissed her on the forehead, pleased by her wide smile. "You sure know how to spoil a man."

"This is a special birthday, which justifies the expense." She nudged him aside with her hip. "Now, put the lid down or you'll let all that good simmering go to waste. Go get yourself cleaned up and presentable for your birthday dinner."

****

I moved the flour container to grab the glass jar containing the money. Da had cashed his check on Friday, but had neglected to stop and pay the rent. I'd have to face the old biddy.

After checking my teeth by the reflection in the side of the toaster, I applied lipstick. With my bag slung over a shoulder, I opened the front door and kicked open the screen. No need to close the door since Da would be back from the neighbor's in a bit, and he never took a key. I crossed the undernourished grass in front of our home to the road separating our yard from Mrs. Snyder's equally sparse lawn. She opened the door before I could knock.

"Hello, dear." Her voice was raspy, which is why most of the younger children in the court called her a witch and were afraid of her. "Are you okay?"

Thin lips covered yellowed teeth. Her dull brown hair, streaked with gray was wadded into a bun at the back of her head. A few of the grays had escaped and corkscrewed out from the top and sides, giving her a look of insanity.

I blinked. "Why wouldn't I be?" My neck tingled with nerves. The woman could intimidate me.

She shrugged, giving me a forced smile.

I held out my hand, anxious to pay the rent and leave for Paulie's. "I brought you the rent money."

She glanced at the money without moving. "It was due yesterday, dear. Your father might have brought it over instead of carousing last night." She shook her head and took the money from me. "You poor, dear child."

Nerves snapped with anger. "I'm not a *poor* child. And I don't know what you'd know about my father's activities."

"Well! I can see you're not being properly taught in regards to respecting your elders. I do understand how a poor, motherless child like yourself needs direction."

I clutched my bag hard enough to feel the strap cut into my palm. I imagined slapping the tight-lipped face with an open palm, and how good the sting would feel. Instead, I stepped back and glared at the old biddy.

Pushing the hair back from my face, I jutted my chin out. "I don't suppose you do understand." *Pitiful, lonely, old biddy.* "What would you...you know? At least I have a father who cares." I stopped myself before adding, *which is probably more than you have.*

I whirled around on the ball of my foot and promised myself next time I'd really let her have it. Lonely or not, she deserved a tongue-lashing.

Adrenaline spurred me forward at a good clip to

Paulie's. At the edge of the cottonwoods, I adjusted my peasant blouse off my shoulders. Ahead, the scene on the Russell front porch grabbed my attention. From the way Paulie leaned toward her sister, and Ruth's fervent puffing of cigarette smoke, I guessed they were arguing. Nothing new. She flicked her cigarette into the yard and went inside as I reached the steps.

"Hey, Paulie."

"Wow, Claire! You're a looker in that blouse." My friend looped her arm through mine and took the duffle bag from me.

"You look pretty cute yourself with your jeans rolled up. Just like we saw in the magazine at the drugstore. Did your momma say anything?"

"She doesn't really like it. I told her it's the newest teen style." Paulie snickered. "She doesn't get it."

We started for the door. "What's the latest beef with you and Ruth?"

"Oh, gosh, Claire." Paulie stopped, her hand on the door. "I'm glad you got here before the harlot."

I totally had the wind knocked out of me as I herded Paulie to the far corner of the porch, away from the screen door, kitchen window, and any unseen ears. "You mean Benjamin invited Susan?"

"No. My dumb…dumb…full of shit sister did. She arranged a surprise double date thing after dinner. This totally goes against what Momma had planned, if you ask me. This was supposed to be a nice, family-type birthday dinner. Each of us could invite someone close. Well, my dumb full of shit sister invited her boyfriend *and* Susan. She thinks Ben works too much and needs to go out more for fun. I guess the harlot can supply plenty of that." Paulie's nose wrinkled like the idea stunk something awful.

It did.

"So, you got mad? Crap, Paulie! She'll figure out you're sticking up for me and tell Benjamin. She's a blabbermouth." My stomach roiled with the notion Ruth would tell him his little sister's friend had a crush on him. "On Thursday, when Benjamin helped me with my drawing, Ruth gave me a weird look. She'll guess I'm stuck on him. I'll just die!"

"No, she won't. She thinks I just don't like Susan." Paulie patted my arm. "Don't worry, Claire." Her bottom lip came out in a pout as she crossed her arms on her chest. "I'm on your side, and she made me mad."

"I know." I shook my hair in an effort to throw off the disappointment. "Maybe he won't be as welcoming to Susan as Ruth thinks he'll be."

I didn't believe my own words.

****

Ben glanced out the kitchen window and paused. Claire looked concerned about something while his sister appeared hurt. Paulie's arms were folded across her chest. With her bottom lip in a pout, she looked even more like the cute little girl everyone said she was. Claire, on the other hand, her arms wouldn't fold so neatly on her full chest. Her dark lashed, brown eyes smoldered. He'd felt the heat, admired the high cheekbones and full lips, when he'd spent time with her on Thursday. The temptation had been there; to gather a lock of fluffy curls that now bounced off her shoulders in an animated exchange with his sister. The contrast between strawberry-blonde hair framing a fair complexion and dark eyes rimmed in black lashes were like night and day; opposites that needed each other to

149

be complete.

The hour he'd spent with her on Thursday had done nothing to quell the desire that kicked up a notch every time she came near. He couldn't take his gaze off her. The jeans, rolled to her knees, exposed shapely calves. His gaze drifted to her denim-clad hips.

Damn, I'd love to lay my hands right there, on the curve of her ass.

He turned from the window. "Mom, you could use some help. Ruth is still painting her face. I'll get Paulie in here." Opening the screen door, he said, "Hey, if it isn't double trouble."

"Oh." Claire startled. "Hello, Benjamin."

"Paulie, Mom is looking for some help. Give her a hand, would you?"

She cocked an eyebrow at Claire and elbowed him as she passed by to go into the house.

"Should I go in to help your momma, too?"

"Nah, they can handle it." Ben gestured toward the old car seat and waited for Claire to be seated before he lowered down close. "What's that you got?" he asked teasingly about the small, white box in her hands.

"A little gift."

She tilted her head, fluttered her eyelashes, and he was tempted to touch her chin and lift her face toward his. He rubbed his hand on his leg and fought the desire.

"For later. It's yours, but maybe you should wait until you get all of your gifts. Unless…unless you want it now." Her cheeks flushed.

"I think I'd like to open it now." He took the box, brushing her hand as he did. He wondered how so minor a touch created a volume of sensation like the smallest spark of heat warms you on a cold day.

She folded her hands under her chin and gazed intently on the gift.

The gold elastic tie dropped to his lap as he slid it off and opened the box. "Claire, it's grand." He held the cigarette lighter high above them to examine it. The late day sun caught the gold colored metal. "I can really use this."

"Go ahead and try it." Her smile spread across her face. Dark simmering eyes lit up with sparkling enthusiasm. "I had Da put fluid in it last night."

Ben opened the lid and flicked the small wheel, lighting the flame. Together, they stared at the bright yellow and blue fire in silence.

Would a quick kiss on the cheek be inappropriate?

He longed to feel her softness against his face, his mouth. He closed the lid and tucked the lighter into his pants pocket and patted the weight of his first birthday present.

Claire released a small sigh and dropped her hands to her lap. "I'm glad you like it."

The corners of her mouth lifted in a sensuous smile that pulled at him. He saw his reflection in eyes so dark brown he couldn't distinguish the black center from the outer rim. The cottonwood trees and the porch disappeared as she pushed a stray curl of hair from her cheek; her hand grazed a long slender neck, then paused on a perfectly formed collarbone before continuing across an expanse of creamy skin. Her fingers touched the blue trim of her blouse that exposed her shoulders, the first hint of cleavage, and finally came to rest in a jean-clad lap.

"Happy Birthday, Benjamin." Her voice was low,

sweet.

Oh, God, how much longer could he go without touching her, or trace his finger along each collarbone, and kiss the soft skin of her neck so guarded by her strawberry curls? His heart thumped against his chest, and the heat rose within his jeans. He needed to move away from her. He cursed the timing of a desire he knew would haunt him. Would she still be there when he decided it appropriate to approach her? *Can I wait…?*

He didn't hear the car drive into the yard until the horn sounded. They both jerked, bringing the porch and the day back.

"Hey, birthday boy. Let the fun begin," Susan's voice called out as the motor shut off.

Hesitating, but thankful for the distraction, Ben stood to greet her as she climbed the steps.

****

The woman negotiated the slats of the steps and avoided the spaces so as not to catch the pointy heels. Black pants hugged her hips, and moved fluidly around her legs. Each swinging step revealed delicate straps encircling slender ankles. Susan's deep red mane was piled on top of her head with an air of sophistication. I was caught between anger and intimidation.

She held out a small, wrapped package. "Now, this is for you, hon, except you're not to open it until all your guests have arrived." She clasped her hands behind Benjamin's neck and leaned her hips into his. "The rest of your birthday present I'll save for later, to unwrap when we're all alone."

I was trapped. I didn't want to witness her shameless flirting, but if I moved, I'd draw attention.

My stomach churned at Benjamin, thinking how he was enwrapped in sensations I could only imagine. Susan had him.

I'd felt so close to him only moments earlier; my heart still thumped from his compliments. His gaze, now locked on Susan, was all I needed to realize a challenge I wasn't sure I could meet. My eyes burned.

Statue-like, I waited, hardly breathing, praying they would move inside so I could disappear.

Benjamin gave a small, dry laugh and turned his head toward me. "Susan. Uh, you remember Claire, don't you?"

Her hands dropped to his arm when she looked down at me still seated on the car seat. "Ah, yes. One of your sister's little friends."

Heat rose up my chest and prickled the hair on the nape of my neck. Only Benjamin's smile kept my mouth shut.

"Isn't this fun, Claire?" she cooed and moved her hips against him. "Don't you just love a birthday party?"

I found my tongue trapped in clenched teeth, and it took super human strength to speak. "I better see if Mrs. Russell needs any help." My comment was directed at Benjamin, as I rose slowly, purposely ignoring Susan.

Back inside, I moved around the Russell kitchen, as familiar with the space as I was with my own home. With effort, I avoided glancing out the window at the couple on the front porch. Although I laughed and talked to Paulie and her momma, my thoughts didn't leave the porch. I struggled to not peer out the kitchen window, but the urge eventually overcame me. Why had the harlot showed up to spoil this day?

David and Barbara arrived, and a friend of Richie's. Ruth's boyfriend, Edward, stopped on the porch to chat with Benjamin and Susan. Laughter and conversation swirled around me, yet I moved as if in a nightmare—their joy surreal in my misery.

Unable to think of any way to recapture Benjamin's attention, I decided to stay out of sight from the shameless flirting. I busied myself in the kitchen until everyone sat down for his birthday stew.

Mrs. Russell called everyone to eat as I set the bowl of stew in the middle of the table. She took her seat at one end, Benjamin at the other. Susan sat to his right. I sat next to Richie, too far from Benjamin for personal conversation.

Mrs. Russell gave a touching speech about how she was glad we were all there and how they all missed her oldest son, Jack Murphy, who would hopefully be home soon. She finished with, "Now dig in."

The loud, multiple conversations at a typical dinner in this house allowed me to avoid any exchange which might have involved the couple at the other end of the table. Richie talked incessantly to his friend and me. Giving them all my attention, I was able to avert my gaze from Benjamin and Susan. Richie had my visual attention, but in fact, I kept an ear trained on the two people at the end of the table. Benjamin's voice was low, and his words never discernible, although Susan's laugh and an occasional, "Oh, Benny," caused the knot in my stomach to twist ever tighter.

As the forks rested on plates, the food mostly gone, I helped clear the dishes. Only then did I venture a glance at Benjamin, and nearly dropped the plate in my hand when he returned my gaze while Susan chatted in his ear. My heart jumped to my throat when I fleetingly thought he might've meant to look at me and not just in my direction.

Maybe he thought about me even with Susan pushing her breasts into his arm.

A flush of heat raced up my neck, and I quickly turned toward the kitchen.

As Paulie and I set dishes in the sink, her momma instructed us in a hushed tone, "Leave washing until after cake, girls. I know these young people want to get on with their evening. Some big barn dance in Glendale." She lowered her voice further, and whispered disparagingly, "Although, I wouldn't mind them staying here. I think the dance was Susan's idea."

Paulie smirked at her mother's words. Ruth had been the instigator of these plans, but in Mrs. Russell's world, family members could do no wrong. Some outsider could always be blamed.

Benjamin blew out the candles in one giant breath while everyone cheered then sang. I joined in as cheerfully as if all were right in my world. The pain in my chest gave me firsthand knowledge of what the term heartache meant, while what little I'd eaten wedged above the knot of disappointment and anger in my stomach.

He opened a box of handkerchiefs from Barbara, socks from Ruth, and a tool belt from David. Richie gave him a new comb and a package of chewing gum. Susan told him to open her present last. He tore bright blue paper from the small square box. When he removed the lid, his face was unreadable. He glanced directly at me for a brief moment before Susan grabbed his arm.

155

"Take it out of the box, silly. Show everyone what I got you."

Benjamin held up a two-tone cigarette lighter. The gold colored cap topped a base of silver. Only not shiny silver, more buffed, most likely pewter. I'd seen some like it when I shopped for the lighter I gave him. On the bottom corner, there was something in gold, although I couldn't distinguish what from that distance.

"See your initials?" Susan pointed. "In gold. BWR. Benjamin Willis Russell," she announced.

"Isn't that grand?" Ruth asked no one in particular.

Barbara and David agreed and asked to see it closer. Mrs. Russell gave a polite smile, and glanced at me. I smiled back, my bottom lip trembling.

"Well, it looks kind of fancy to be of any real use," Paulie blurted out with a glance in my direction.

Her momma shook her head. "Pauline Louise, don't be rude."

"You have no taste, little girl," Ruth reprimanded her. "It's a very classy lighter for a man. A man who's changed his profession with big plans." She laughed. "I think Ben is so impressed he's lost his tongue."

"Oh…well…Susan, thank you," he finally stammered. "It's…great. Really great."

The harlot leaned into him. "I want to be the first one you light with it."

David snickered, and Mrs. Russell adjusted the fork beside her plate.

Overwhelmed with pity for me, I wished, with all my might, I could take back the cheap gold-colored lighter. If I could go back in time, I wouldn't give the package to Benjamin when we were on the porch. I'd hold it in my hand until everyone had left and not give him anything at all. Why had I thought it so special? Why hadn't I left when I found out Susan was his date for the night? How did I ever think I could compete with her, a workingwoman—all sexy and Rita Hayworth looking? I swallowed so hard, a pain shot up my throat.

I clutched my hands in my lap and stared somewhere in the middle of the table as Benjamin cut the small chocolate cake. There was enough for each of us to have one piece. I took a bite, and the first sweet taste gagged me. Everyone chattered at once so no one noticed when I whispered to Richie, "You want mine? I'm too full from dinner."

He reveled in my pretended attention while the cake was consumed. I managed to swallow tears so deep there was no risk of them finding their way out. Not here, not now. Vicious thoughts helped to dull the hurt.

Harlot.

I wished she would either choke on the cake or spill sugary frosting down the front of her blouse. She could reach over to molest Benjamin and put her elbow into her plate of sticky cake. Maybe her hand would jerk, and she'd stab herself in the tongue.

Sadly, nothing like that happened, and as the last bite was taken, Mrs. Russell rose. "Why don't all of you going to the dance, go ahead and leave? No need to help with the dishes. I have plenty of help, and I'm sure you'd like to get on your way." She seemed to rush them. "Happy birthday, Benjamin Willis." She walked over and gave him a quick kiss on his cheek. "Now, get on out of here."

"Okay, okay. I'm sure Ruth doesn't mind getting

out of a little work."

"Hey, watch it. What do you think it is? Your birthday?"

The three couples scooted their chairs from the table, and in a screech of wood on wood, rose and headed for the door.

Benjamin turned back before leaving the room. "Thanks for a very nice birthday party." His gaze fell on me for a brief moment. "I really liked all my presents. I…uh—"

"Come on, big boy." Susan pulled him out the door. "My feet want to dance."

Mrs. Russell clapped her hands as the door closed behind them. "Well, now, Pauline Louise, put on some snappy music to help us get through this supper mess."

Her peppiness rang hollow to me.

"I'm just glad to have you girls helping me. Richard, get me a box off the back porch for the trash then you can go on over to Kenny's house, but you be back in an hour. You hear?"

The stout little woman danced around the table, picked up dishes, and carried them to the sink. I feared tears would flow if I broke my silence, so I stuck to task, immersing myself in holding a plate and carefully scraping food.

Paulie had no trouble vocalizing. "What a dumb bunny Susan is."

"Pauline, that's no way to talk. Don't you think Benjamin appreciated the socks and belt he got?"

"Momma, she's absolutely—"

"Enough, Pauline Louise."

She didn't think I noticed, I'm sure, but I saw her glance at me. Paulie was right. There were no secrets from her momma.

"Susan is a forward young woman. Perhaps, we don't approve of her...her mannerisms. She seems to find the company of a younger man, your brother, quite interesting right now."

"Momma—"

"A young man like your brother will no doubt find the attention of an experienced young woman like Susan very...interesting...himself. These things just have to run their course." She waved a cake-coated fork in the air. "And run its course, it will. Then we'll be done with it and on to more...likeable circumstances. Now, go on to bed. I'd just as soon wash and dry by myself tonight."

Paulie's mouth gaped open.

The knot in my stomach caused me further problems, and I excused myself to the bathroom. By the time I joined Paulie, sprawled across her bed, Mrs. Russell's words had actually brought me some comfort. However, my total mortification over the present I gave him colored my mood like the cheap gold of the lighter. I couldn't shake my embarrassment. Every time I thought of the moment Susan spoiled, I boiled with anger. How could I face Benjamin? I couldn't.

****

Ben rolled over and buried his face in his pillow. That didn't help. He could still see, still feel Susan's welcoming, naked body. He pressed his early morning arousal against the mattress.

Jesus, what a night.

How more perfect could the night've been? Beef stew, chocolate cake, and sex. Hell, chocolate cake and sex should go together all the time. He could taste the chocolate, taste Susan. His mouth watered as his loins responded, ever hardening with the thought.

There were voices on the other side of his door. Whose voice?

Claire.

Her smile sprang to mind, her hair wavy on bare shoulders, and the rise of her breasts beneath her cotton blouse.

Ben groaned and pushed his hips harder against the mattress.

****

"You have to have some breakfast before you leave." Paulie nudged me toward the kitchen.

I pushed back and headed for the back door. The likelihood of running into Benjamin was less if I avoided the kitchen and the living room. "No, I don't. I'm not hungry, and there's a ton of homework waiting for me at home." Escaping out of the Russell household without running into Benjamin drove my insistence. I sat the duffle bag by the back door. "Where's your momma. I need to thank her."

"She's out back, hanging clothes on the line." My friend grabbed my arm. "My brother is a ninny, Claire. Don't run. He couldn't help the date set up thing anyway."

My eyes burned as I fought back tears. "The whole evening couldn't be helped. Especially not now."

"It's the lighter, isn't it? I'm sure he liked yours better."

"Oh, God, Paulie." I huffed a mirthless laugh.

She pinched her lips together. "Maybe he had a shitty time last night."

"Paulie, I can't face him. Back me on this for now,

okay?" My lip quivered.

"I'm always behind you." She gave me a much-needed hug. Picking up the duffle, she pushed open the back door.

Mrs. Russell stretched to pin a sheet on the line, then came back flatfooted. She picked up the empty laundry basket as we approached. "Now, where are you off to so early?"

"I really need to get home. With shopping and the party yesterday, I didn't get any of my chores or homework done." I stepped close to her. "Thank you so much for a wonderful dinner."

She dropped the basket and took me by my shoulders. Her touch was cool from handling wet sheets, but her eyes were soft and loving. "You're welcome here, always. Like one of the family." She kissed me quickly on the cheek. "Now, off with you to get your chores done. Don't want Hamish upset 'cause you were here too long. Say hi to him for me, will you?"

"I will." My smile started on the inside and spread outward.

Her daughter transferred the duffle bag to my shoulder.

"Bye, Paulie. See you tomorrow."

I set my gaze on the cottonwoods, my heart a touch lighter from Mrs. Russell's embrace. She was the sweetest woman I knew, and her fondness wrapped around me like the early morning sun on that Sunday morning.

My feet dragged the deeper I got into the trees. I wasn't sure how long before I would see her again, or her son.

Chapter Eight
Good Shepherd's Home for Wayward Girls

Sunday afternoon blurred into evening until I shuffled to bed, awash in misery. Da tucked me in like I was ten again.

"There now, all tucked tight." He patted the covers around me. "Let me feel your head again." His rough hand touched my forehead.

"I'm not sick, Da. Must've stayed up too late with Paulie." My words hardly qualified as a protest. In my despair, I welcomed the attention he lavished.

"Well, you got no fever, gal, so I'd say it's another case of the epizooty."

I had no idea what he meant, however, whenever an unknown ailment plagued me, he'd pronounce me sick with this affliction.

He stood next to my bed. "If you wake up in the morning still feeling puny, then stay in bed." He stopped by my door. "Nothing else going on I need to know about?"

I hesitated a moment. This kind of gloom wasn't the kind I could discuss with my father, even as close as we were. I shook my head.

"Then get some sleep. Everything looks better in the morning with the sun shining on it." He closed my door.

The sun did shine the next morning with little

effect. I functioned through the week as if sleep walking, listening in class, following instructions, and interacting with schoolmates. As the last bell rang on Friday, I wondered where the week had gone.

"Why don't you come home with me tonight?" Paulie asked for the third time that week as we settled into our seats on the bus. "Arnold might stop by."

As if that would entice me.

"Really?" I asked.

"He could." She fidgeted with her books. "I told him he could."

"Paulie?"

"What?" Her books still had all her attention.

"Is there something going on with you two?" As much as that would make her happy, my gut said she'd end up miserable. Any attempt at warning her off would be futile.

"Probably not." She heaved a sigh and thumped her books on her lap. "Apparently, we're friends." Her bottom lip came out as she batted her eyes at me.

I decided I could let the subject rest. "Has Susan been around?" I'd managed to go the week without asking about her, but now the school week was over, and my dam of emotions had a crack. I had the weekend to drown in the flood.

"No. Not exactly." Paulie averted her gaze, but not before I saw the grimace.

"What does that mean?"

"He's seen her." She squinted in sympathy. "Just not at the house."

My heart winced from the implication. "I really hate your sister."

"Maybe if you came over—"

"God, no! I can't face him." My palms sweated at the thought.

"He...sort of asked about you." She bobbed her head side to side, which only emphasized the 'sort of.'

"How?" I couldn't help the glimmer of hope.

"He asked me about school and what was new." She smiled, her voice cheery. "Then he asked how science was going."

The hopeful tremor in my chest stilled. I rolled my eyes. "How the heck is that asking about me?"

"He never asks me about school. He was fishing for information. He was obviously asking about *your* grade, which is really like asking about *you*."

"Oh, Paulie, really." I laughed sarcastically. "Now you're making things up."

"I am not. Honestly, Claire. He doesn't give a diggety dang what I do at school."

I huffed. "Then why didn't he come right out and ask you about me?"

"How the heck would I know? I can't figure out guys." Her forehead wrinkled with concern. "He's wondering what happened to you, I know it. Why you didn't come around this week."

My chest tightened. "I can't." I slumped and leaned against her.

We sat in silence for a while. I replayed the front porch scene in my head and tortured myself once again.

"David and Barbara announced their wedding plans."

Paulie's words broke into my thoughts, cheeriness back in her voice.

Although actually happy for them, I had to pretend a cheerful attitude with my sullen mood. "Wonderful. I bet your momma is excited." I could imagine Mrs. Russell dancing around her kitchen, planning a celebration dinner. "When's the wedding?"

"They're going over all the plans this Saturday. No big party this weekend. Well, unless some people wander in, it's mostly a family dinner to discuss it." She nudged my arm. "You want to come?"

Her invitation touched me. *If only the clock could be turned back.* "No. That kind of talk, wedding talk, is too…family. No one should come wandering into the gathering."

"You know you're as good as family." She bumped me with her shoulder.

"Paulie…" I closed my eyes a moment.

"Oh, pooh, all right."

I glanced out the window. "Here's your stop."

The bus tires crunched on the side of the road at her street. Paulie stood.

I squeezed her arm. "You could come over on Sunday after Da and I go grocery shopping and stay for dinner. Da could take you home after."

"Okay, sounds like fun. I can't cook very good, but I could help you out."

"Yeah, right." I laughed. Being the youngest female in the Russell clan, she'd managed to avoid culinary instruction beyond peanut butter and mayonnaise sandwiches. "It'll be fun." The bus driver had his gaze on the mirror. "Get going before Jesper starts yelling."

****

My dishes clinked against each other and disturbed the quiet as I set them in the sink. Da hadn't come home after work. Since it was Friday and pay day, The

Beckin' Inn Bar must have beckoned.

The quiet, and being alone, suited me. Half-expecting Da to be late, I had changed from my dress to a nightgown as soon as I got home from school. I unfolded his bed and turned back the covers for whenever he decided to wander home. Retreating to my room, I curled up with a movie magazine until hunger drove me to fix a sandwich for an early dinner.

I plugged the sink and ran the water to wash dishes. A knock at the door surprised me. Cinching the robe tighter around my waist, I plodded the few feet to open the door a crack. Arnold stood inside the screen with his shoulder against the doorframe. The sun touched the tops of the mulberry trees at the edge of the cabin court and nearly blinded me.

"What are you doing here?" He was the last person I expected to see at my door.

"Claire." He shuffled his feet and gazed at me with glistening eyes. "Claire."

Even with the sun in my eyes, I could see his demeanor was a bit disheveled. He ran a hand through his black hair before wiping his arm over his face. His eyes glistened as he shook his head.

"I need to talk to you," he whispered, his words slightly slurred.

"What's the matter with you?" My glance darted over his shoulder to Mrs. Snyder's. He leaned in closer, and with his next words, the evidence bathed me in fumes. "You're drunk. Go away!" I closed the door then leaned my ear against the wood. Angry tremors played across my chest.

He twisted the knob and banged, jarring my head.

"I'm not leaving, Claire, until you talk to me."

"Arnold, go home." I pleaded through the barrier. "No!"

I opened the door a sliver. "*Please*. My nosey landlady will be over here any minute. I don't need her to see a drunk boy hanging around my door."

"I'm not drunk." His eyelids drooped a moment before a lazy smile lit up his face. He brought his cheek against the door jam. "I have a bottle in the car, if you'd like a little nip with me."

Please let Mrs. Snyder not be home watching my house. "Go-a-way!"

He crooked the side of his mouth. "Hey, Claire…Paulie…she had a nip. And then…"

"What about Paulie?" I opened the door another inch.

He waggled a finger. "I'm not saying more unless you let me in."

"You've been drinking…I'm not sure I should trust you." I didn't trust him, but I'd always been able to wrap him around my finger any which way I chose. And I'd seen Da drunk enough times. Arnold posed no threat. Except, he was going to get me into trouble with the stupid landlady.

He blinked, his lips pouting. "How long have we been friends, Claire?" He ran a hand through his hair again. "I've had a little drink with Paulie is all."

"Paulie doesn't drink."

"Maybe you don't know everything about Paulie." His voice teased. He scuffed his toe against the doorjamb and peered at me with sad eyes. "Oh, Claire. I have to talk to you. About Paulie. About you."

Praying the nosey biddy across the street wasn't watching, I stuck my hand through the opening, gathered the front of his shirt in my fist, and hauled him inside. I pushed him against the door and released his shirt. "What about Paulie?" I glared, hands on hips. "Make it quick."

He smoothed his shirt down and stood straighter. "I got my car."

"Arnold! *What about Paulie?*"

"I got my car." He smiled. "You want to take a ride?"

I pulled the curtain back a bit on the window next to the door and peeked out. Sure enough, an unknown car was parked in front of my house. "Oh, hell, Arnold. Mrs. Snyder will know you're here." I thumped his chest with my fist. "Damn you, Arnold. What happened to Paulie?"

The smile dropped from his face as he glared. "Paulie got a ride in my car and a whole lot more."

My heart skipped a beat. Anxiety sent pricks of heat up my neck to burst like fire on my cheeks. "What? What do you mean?"

"Little hot pants got what she wanted." He sneered. "I gave it to her good."

"Oh my God." I clutched the robe to my chest as if to hold down my wildly thumping heart. My words flung sharply across the space separating us. "Did you…did you hurt Paulie?"

"Hurt her?" His laugh mocked my fear. "She came out of her panties the minute she hit the back seat. Spread her legs so fast, I couldn't get my dick in quick enough."

"Shut up!" I gasped.

He slumped against the door, his cockiness gone as fast as it had risen. "She wasn't you. She should've been you. Shit. Even with my eyes closed those little tits can't pass for yours." He wiped his mouth on his arm and muttered, "I pretended, but it wasn't you."

"You're lying," I hissed in his face. I wanted to make him take it all back.

He didn't appear to hear me. "Then she figured it out. Figured out I didn't want her. Too late," he said, as if talking to himself.

"What?" I stomped my foot. "Arnold!" I raised my voice. "What did you say?"

Peering up, a smile came to his face. "I wasn't going to get off then. Gave it to her good."

"What did you do, you bastard?" I huffed; hot air snorted from my nostrils. My eyes watered.

"I gave hot pants what she wanted." His lip quivered. "Her moaning and crying, *"Oh Arnold, oh Arnold, tell me you love me."* I didn't say it. She got my prick, but she didn't get the words." He put his hands to his face. "Oh, God, Claire. It wasn't you. I wanted you."

I slapped at his face, knocked his hands to the side, and shoved a palm against his shoulder. "What have you done?" I shrieked so loud the neighbor two doors down probably heard me. I didn't care. I slapped him again, this time making contact with his cheek.

He barely flinched. His green eyes, red rimmed and smoldering, glared. "Let me show you what I did. You know you'd like it."

I reached behind him, grabbed the doorknob, and turned. The door opened a few inches, but when he felt the pressure on his back, he held his ground. I'd gotten too close. He grabbed the edge of my robe and yanked down as his other hand grappled at my breast. I drove my fist into his stomach. Immediately, he released me and slumped against the door. I was poised to land another blow when his sob surprised me.

"Oh, Claire." He hung his head; his arms limp at his sides.

"Get out of here. Now!" When I grabbed for the doorknob again, he caught my hand and brought it to his swollen crotch.

"Make me feel good, Claire."

"Aghhh…" I groaned, wrenched my hand from his grasp, and lunged for the doorknob. This time, I powered past him as he struggled to regain hold of me. Throwing open the door, intending on pushing him out, didn't work the way I envisioned. We both fell onto the bodies of two police officers.

As strong hands caught me by the shoulders and righted me, a giant of an overweight man in blue grabbed Arnold by his neck.

"Now, what have we here?" Arnold's restrainer asked with a gravelly voice. His eyes squinted at me. "Got yourself in a bit of a mess, have you, missy?"

I grabbed my robe around me and shook the hands from my shoulders. Repulsion and anger at coming into contact with Arnold's erection melted into fear. What were two policemen doing right outside my door?

"What…why are you here?" I glanced behind me.

The smaller, thin policeman eyed me with a cocked brow. "Well, missy, you can't be having these kinds of goings on without drawing attention."

The large one still had his hand on Arnold, who had remained still as if his neck was captured in a vice. The hefty cop towered over him at least three times his girth. His stomach spilled over the top of his trousers, causing the waist of his pants to curl down. A trickle of sweat inched down his temple, and large circles of dark dampness spread from under the arms of his navy shirt.

"Let's say we take a little ride and talk about this." The skinny officer behind me finally spoke.

"I was just leaving," Arnold croaked out. The officer pinched tighter, and he winced, hunching his shoulders up as he did.

I inched to the left so I could see both men. "I…I'm fine, really. This boy…was…we were…"

A black sedan pulled up behind the police car and brought my stumbling to a halt. I wasn't sure I could come up with any acceptable explanation anyway while the intimidating stares of the officers bore down on me. The skinny one kept his eyebrow cocked. Tubby rocked on his heels with a smirk on his face. Even though I hadn't done anything wrong, I had the impression I was under scrutiny.

I pursed my lips and glared at Arnold before turning my attention to the latest arrival. Arnold didn't so much as shrug.

A woman dressed in a tailored, brown suit and white gloves exited the passenger side of the vehicle. A man remained at the driver's wheel. My peripheral vision took in the scene these visitors caused. Skinny-old-dried-up-prune Mrs. Snyder stood on her front stoop. Two neighbors peeked from their doorways.

The woman from the car walked authoritatively to stand between the two policemen. A round, felt hat rested on the top of her tightly curled brown hair. "Hello, officers."

"Ma'am," they answered in unison.

She unlatched her handbag and brought out a card

she held in front of each officer's face. The big man nodded without expression, but a shadow crossed the thin policeman's face.

Her bare lips disappeared in a thin smile. "Are you Claire Flanagan?"

When I opened my mouth to answer, her face struck me dumb. She was a finer version of Mrs. Snyder. The real Mrs. Snyder gawked from her doorstep over the left shoulder of this refined edition.

Arnold stood silent, two policemen glared, and the shock at hearing my name from this doppelganger left me confused and speechless.

The skinny officer touched my shoulder. "It's okay, miss. Answer the woman."

My heart thumped and competed with space for air in my throat. "Yes, yes I am."

She nodded curtly. "Is your father at home?"

"No, he's…he's not returned from work yet."

She clasped her hands at her waist. "Do you think you could change into something more appropriate? You'll need to come with me."

"Why? Where?" I gulped. "Who are you?"

"Forgive my manners." She unclasped and clasped her white-gloved hands. "My name is Emma Banks. I work for Social Welfare, dear. I've come to escort you downtown. We need to get some information from you."

I gasped for air in an ever-tightening chest. Something terribly wrong was happening. I couldn't organize the events of the last half-hour to make any sense of this request.

"It won't take long, dear. Could you get anything you might need for the next couple of hours?"

I furtively glanced from Arnold to his captor and to the kinder, skinny policeman next to me. Arnold squirmed a bit under the neck clasp, but continued to stare at the ground.

"We'll be taking care of your friend, missy." Tubby officer shook him a bit. "Miss Banks here is a fine woman to be taking care of you."

My mind darted from one thought to the next. *What did they think happened? Did the old biddy call the cops on us? Could this have anything to do with what happened to Paulie? Where is Da?*

"Miss," the small policeman quietly said. "Go get dressed. Everything will be okay."

"What about me?" Arnold whined.

"You're coming with me, lad." The big officer walked him toward the police car.

I stepped up onto the stoop, in a daze, and opened the door. Emma Banks followed me into my home. Skinny cop hung back at the doorway, looking ill at ease. Without hesitation, the woman walked in and stopped next to the fold out couch now in bed position. Her straight, pointy nose wrinkled as she sniffed.

I continued on into my bedroom, changed into jeans, and grabbed my purse. How could I put this evening on hold? I needed to find out how Paulie was. How could I stall until my father got home? What if he came home liquored up?

"I don't think I should go anywhere until my father comes home." I hung back in the doorway of my room. My stomach hurt. Grasping the doorframe, dizzy, I blinked, my vision hampered as if peering through a picket fence.

"Your father will be along later. I'll explain

everything when we get downtown," she stated firmly, leaving no room for questions.

The officer shuffled behind her. "We need to get going, ma'am."

She nodded. "Do you have what you need, Claire?"

I checked my purse for the house key and lipstick. "I…I guess so."

Her elbows remained tight against her sides as one gloved hand unfolded and fingers motioned toward the door.

I put one foot in front of the other, with difficulty. Skinny cop stepped back as he held the screen door open. A few more neighbors had joined the others to watch and whisper.

The officer guided me into the backseat of the black Ford. I sat as close to the door as possible with my face nearly touching the window. Tiny, icy pricks stabbed at my neck and scalp. Emma Banks and her driver were silent. The squad car with the big policeman drove around us. Arnold's car followed them, the skinny cop behind the wheel. They turned left out of the cabin court while we turned right. Why weren't they going to the same place as I was being taken? My heart pounded in my chest, and each thump reverberated in my temples.

How will Da know where to find me?

"When did you speak to my father?" My voice sounded weak.

Miss Banks didn't move. "Don't worry about the details. I told you I'd explain everything when we get downtown."

I bit my lower lip; my eyes burned as the scenery flew by the window. I stared unseeing until we reached an ugly, colorless building in the heart of Phoenix.

The inside of the building loomed gray and stuffy, and still I shivered with cold. Nothing improved for me once inside. My questions were unanswered or met with total indifference. I perched on a black metal chair beside a scarred, wooden desk and clutched my purse in my lap. It seemed hours droned on until Miss Banks returned with papers in hand.

She set a cup of black coffee next to me. "Here."

"Thank you, but—"

"Now, let's take care of this." She drew a pen from a drawer.

I answered a few questions, sipped some coffee, and she left me again. Other than a slight buzzing in my temples, I was numb, confused.

When she appeared again, her thin smile pricked through my numbness.

"Am I going home now?"

"No, dear, not yet. We have one more stop. Come."

She didn't wait, but stiffly turned, and I had no choice but to follow. Again, I sat in the backseat of her car. We left the downtown, but not in the direction of my home. I could've been on another planet. The buzzing in my temples now competed with the hum of the car wheels on the pavement.

When the car stopped, my captor finally spoke as she opened my door. "Get out."

"Where are we?"

She didn't answer but applied pressure on my elbow as she led me toward the building.

Hours now since I'd been taken from my home, the sun long gone, Emma Banks introduced me to an unsmiling nun halfway up the steps of the imposing building.

Slow panic crept up my shoulders like a migrating sunburn and brought tears to my eyes. "Why are you leaving me here?" Tears toppled down my cheeks. "Where's Da? You said he'd come."

The nun's arm rested heavily around my shoulders as my deliverer turned away. At the bottom of the stairs, stopping beside the car, Miss Banks clasped her hands at her waist. Through a smile that wasn't a smile she said, "This is best for you. Your father doesn't have the ability to care for you properly." She slid into the black car, leaving the words to drift up the steps and slam into me.

My eyes blurred over with tears as I choked a sob. The nun offered no explanation or words of comfort as she led me up the last dozen steps. I wiped at my eyes with the sleeve of my blouse, staring up at a white stucco building illuminated by a bright, full moon. This vision could've been out of a western movie at a Sunday matinee. Arches and trim painted in bright turquoise, a bell tower on the roof and massive ten-foot high double, dark wooden doors mimicked a Spanish bastion. A small, metallic sign lit by an elaborate, bronze lamp hung eye level by the door. I blinked away a lingering tear to read, *Good Shepherd's Home for Wayward Girls.*

Wayward girls.

The words swirled around my head. Wayward girls sounded wrong, bad. Home for wayward girls? I didn't need a home. I was Claire Flanagan, daughter of Hamish Flanagan. We had each other and a home. More tears fell as the nun opened the giant doors.

By contrast, the stark interior lacked any

descriptive style. My tears silently tracked down my cheeks as the nun urged me along through an empty, circular vestibule, her arm around my shoulders, heavy without comfort, and down a short, wide hall of white walls with four dark, wooden doors.

The end of the hall opened into a larger room with at least thirty beds lining opposite sides, symmetrically arranged with headboards against the walls. Two small, stained glass windows, located close to the ceiling, provided the only illumination. Squares of red, green, and yellow from the moonlight filtering through the colored glass sprinkled the gray-blanketed beds on the opposite side of the room.

Once we stepped inside, the nun flipped a switch and dim, overhead lights erased the patterns on the blankets. One painting hung on each wall, halfway between the windows and the headboards. The nun guided me to a bed below one of the paintings. Jesus, wearing a crown of thorns upon his head and a single tear on his cheek, looked down on me.

She opened a rough, wood cabinet beside the bed to take out a tan, linen nightgown and white underpants from a shelf. "Everyone will return from evening prayer shortly." She held the garments out. "Remove your clothing after I have gone and change into these." Leave your soiled clothing on the floor at the foot of your bed. Someone will see to them."

I gasped. "My things?"

"Nothing will happen to them. They will be kept safe until you leave us, when they will be returned to you."

A small sob escaped. "When will that be?"

She clasped my shoulder, the touch lighter this

time with soothing warmth. "I do not know why you're here, child, only that you need to be here." She pointed to what looked like a gray dress on the shelf. "This is your dress for tomorrow. There is a toothbrush, washrag, and comb in the drawer. The bathroom is the door at the end of the beds. When you are changed and have completed your toilet needs, go to bed." She turned from me.

"But..." My one word was a plea.

"Tomorrow will be soon enough. Sleep now."

After changing, I laid on the narrow cot, staring at the ceiling and wondered why I let myself be led so easily. Why had I followed the sharp-faced Emma Banks up the cement stairs into the building in an area of downtown Phoenix I'd never been? Why did I sit in the windowless room sipping coffee, alone and docile? Why, after merely confirming my name, my father's name, my lack of a mother, and my current address as Miss Banks referred to my home, did I get in the woman's car again and allow them to drive me to an unknown destination?

And where was Da?

****

"Momma, oh, Momma, Momma, Momma!" Paulie ran heavy-footed past Ben and threw open the screen door as he sat on the porch Sunday afternoon. Her face was red, and she was winded. He jumped to follow her, concerned. Their mother whirled around as they entered the kitchen.

Paulie grabbed their mother's arm, pulling her toward the door. "We have to go. We have to do something!"

She tugged back. "Slow down, Pauline Louise, and

tell me what's wrong." She ran her hands down his sister's arms and turned her around. "Are you hurt? Who's hurt, child?"

"No, Momma, not me." She batted their mother's hands away. "It's Claire. *They took Claire*."

His heart skipped a beat. "Who took Claire? What the hell are you babbling about, Paulie?"

"The welfare people!" She stomped her feet. "We have to go get her." Clutching their mother's arm with one hand and his shirtsleeve with the other, she stomped toward the door.

He yanked from her grasp, took her shoulders in each of his hands, and held her fast. "*Stop*. We can't know where to go or what to do if you don't calm down and tell us what's going on."

Paulie took two deep breaths, and he released her. "When I got to Claire's, her father was sitting at the table, crying. I could see him through the screen, and he didn't even hear me knock. He cried saying, "Oh Claire." So I charged on in." She touched their mother's arm. "I know it wasn't polite, but there was something awful wrong, and I couldn't wait for a proper invitation."

She waved a hand for her to continue.

Ben balled his fingers into fists at his side. "Go on, damn it, Paulie."

"Seems Friday when he got home, Claire wasn't there. There was an envelope with some government documents addressed to him. Mr. Flanagan says he doesn't know what to make of them except they say Claire has been put in the custody of Social Welfare."

"Oh, my!" Mom pulled a chair from the table and sat down.

"Custody of Social Welfare? What the hell does that mean?" Ben's face grew hot.

His mother shook her head. "It's not good, Benjamin."

He rubbed his hands together. "Where is this Social Welfare place?"

"Mr. Flanagan got in his car Friday night, drove to the address on the envelope, and the place was shut up tight. He went back Saturday morning, but still no luck. He banged on the door until a janitor answered. He told him to come back Monday morning at eight. Mr. Flanagan went down there today anyway. No one was there."

"She won't be there." Mom rubbed her chin, staring at the table. She raised her head, meeting his gaze. "That's a government office. Claire will have been placed somewhere, a foster home or perhaps with a religious institution."

"Oh, God, Mom. I don't like the sound of that." His stomach turned. A vision of Claire, alone, probably crying, came to mind. "She's too old to be taken like this, isn't she?"

"She's a mature, young lady with lots of responsibility...but she's not yet eighteen."

He took a deep, ragged breath. "Why would this happen?"

"Mr. Flanagan said it's the battle-ax landlady. Claire told me she's snoopy and doesn't think it's proper for a girl to live with her father. Can you imagine?" Paulie stomped around the kitchen, gesturing with her hands. "Claire's father is the nicest man in the world and always taking good care of her and treating her good, and Claire loves him and—"

"Shut up, Paulie." Ben couldn't stand the thought of Claire in trouble, and his sister's incessant ranting ramped up the tension in his head to the point of bursting. "What can we do, Mom?"

"Well…" She stood and untied her apron. "The first thing we do is go see Hamish. The poor man needs some support. Go get my purse from my bedroom, Pauline." She ran a hand through the back of her hair and patted the sides down. "We'll look at those papers. Figure out what needs to be done."

Ben took his mother's hand. "Can we get her back, Mom?"

She patted his arm. "She's special, isn't she?"

He nodded.

"She's special to all of us." Mom took her purse from Paulie. "Come hell or high water, we'll get her back. No government flunkies had better mess with the Russells and the Flanagans!"

****

At every opportunity, for the first three mornings, I timidly asked questions of every nun I saw. Having never come in contact with nuns before, I was at first intimidated by their severe black attire and their quiet demeanor. But it was as if they were deaf. Either a gentle shake of the head or a solemn stare that wilted me met my persistent inquisition. Frustration and fear quelled my timidity soon enough. The angry approach didn't fare any better. They seemed to grow gentler as I grew angrier. I quit asking.

The girls who populated my dorm were of no help. The few my age strove to scare me or impress me with their hardened views of life. Most were pregnant. The younger girls, some of them pregnant, were either happy to be there away from abusive homes or existed as silent little creatures.

Each night, I told myself Da would be there to pick me up the next day. I never believed he wouldn't come, only that he couldn't come. Somehow, outside those eight-foot high, wooden doors, he'd been barred from entry.

I prayed. Instead of the standard nightly prayer to bless the ones close to me, I petitioned God for myself. Surely, God could hear me clearly in this place steeped in religious rituals.

After several days of unanswered prayer, I knew He'd abandoned this building, which only masqueraded as a home.

Days blurred together. I grew accustomed to the scratchy gray dress all the girls wore, the monotonous routine, and the bland food. My lessons in math and English offered some relief. An automaton, I fell to my knees a half a dozen times a day at specified devout moments. At night, in the dark, my loneliness penetrated every cell of my body, and the tears flowed. My last memories before disappearing from my own life with the people I most cared about haunted me. Da, drinking and unaware of what happened, would be frightened and lonely; we'd never lived apart. Paulie, her rude transition, losing her virginity, was my fault. I'd allowed her to continue her infatuation with Arnold when I could've done something to shield her.

And Benjamin.

If only I hadn't been so timid, had declared my feelings, perhaps he would've responded in kind. Now, leaving him to become totally beguiled by Susan, I'd lost him forever. How would I ever get my life back?

****

"Hey, Benny, baby you aren't much fun tonight." Susan ran her hand along the inner thigh of his leg. "You still have your pants on."

Ben took another swig from her bottle of whiskey.

"Is that all we're going to do tonight, drink?" she asked. Her hand continued up his leg, applying a slight pressure as she rubbed over the zipper on his pants.

He swished his hips to the side, dislodging her aim. "We could try talking." He sat up straighter and glanced around her apartment. "Why don't we pour this into glasses? We're not in the back seat of my car."

"You know, you've avoided me all week, and now when I finally get you where I want you, you want to talk?" She snatched the bottle from his hand. "I like it this way." She tipped whiskey to her mouth and sipped. Licking her lips she said, "It's oh so sexy, passing a bottle back and forth, watching your lips cup the hole." Her laugh was deep in her chest.

The familiar rise of heat from Susan's words bothered him tonight. And not in the normal way. *What the hell?* He didn't want to feel the rush of desire. "How long have you lived here?"

Susan nudged him with her elbow. "Have another drink, sweetie."

Ben took the bottle, but didn't drink. "It's a good size apartment. Davie and Barbara could start out in something like this."

She glanced around as her hand continued up to his chest and fingers darted in between the buttons to rub his skin. "About a year." She kissed his neck. "Have we talked enough yet?"

He turned his head, met her lips, and kissed, except

the sensation that should've driven him forward couldn't be generated. He groaned and leaned away from her. "Ah, hell." Scooting forward on the couch, he set the bottle of whiskey on the coffee table.

"What the hell is up with you tonight?" When he didn't answer, she poked his shoulder. "What do you want to talk about? There's only one thing we have in common, Benny, and you're wasting time."

Ben shook his head and looked over his shoulder. Her eyes, wide open with the question, shot darts. He scrutinized her face, glanced at the ample cleavage she displayed, and tipped his head down to her legs where the skirt had ridden above the garter clips. Nothing more than a slight carnal interest spiked below the belt. His heart was dead.

She followed his slow assessment and ran her fingertips across the exposed skin of her breast. Her other hand went to her skirt, hiking the material higher. "I have some particularly fun things planned for tonight, Benny."

He stood. "Not tonight, Susan."

"What do you mean, not tonight?"

"I'm sorry." He shook his head and rubbed the back of his neck. "Look, I'm just not in the mood."

She stood with her hands on hips. "You're a little young to not be in the mood."

"Then maybe you should find someone older, someone you don't feel the need to teach."

Susan moved closer and rubbed her breasts against his chest. Her hand grazed his crotch, which brought a smile to her face. "Not in the mood, huh?"

Ben stepped back. "No, not tonight." He strode to the door.

"Maybe not any night again." She tossed the words.

"Goodnight, Susan," he muttered, closing the door behind him.

He felt for the keys in his pocket as he strolled to Lady Blue. When he slid the key into the ignition, he paused a moment and stared at the empty passenger seat, remembering the last time Claire had sat next to him. How could he miss her so much? His stomach churned with worry.

Ben turned the key, gunned the engine, and accelerated away from Susan's apartment. He'd probably not see her again. He lit a cigarette and blew the smoke out the window into the cool air. He didn't care. The next woman he wanted his arms around was Claire. He took a deep breath to calm the nerves tightening his chest. Mom would go through another round of papers with the courts tomorrow. Would Hamish agree to the temporary custody arrangement? And a bigger question—would the courts? Mom considered Claire family, but the courts might see it differently.

Chapter Nine
There's No Place Like Home

Before sitting down to lunch at the beginning of the second week at the Good Shepherd's Home, the nun who oversaw our noon meal sent me to retrieve our newest addition from the dorm. My feet dragged as I made my way through the maze of halls. I didn't relish meeting another smart-mouthed, pregnant teenager.

Relief and sadness flooded through me when I entered the quiet dorm hall. A waif of a child perched on the edge of the bunk next to mine. Thin and pale, no more than four years old, she sat in silence and stared at the stained glass reflections. A green ribbon held her brown hair at the nape of her neck. A few stray strands brushed her sallow cheeks and high forehead. She glanced up, not smiling or frowning.

"Hi." I sat beside her. "My name is Claire. What's yours?"

She blinked without expression. "Amy."

A worn, yellow dress obviously in need of washing lay on the floor at the foot of the bed. A doll, missing an eye, snuggled down in the folds of the dress.

"Is she your doll?"

Amy's lip quivered. "She said I can't keep her."

"We'll ask about that after lunch." I patted her hand. The required gray dress hung on her small frame and the buttoned front was askew. "Let me see if I can fix this for you. Looks like you might have missed a button."

I studied her face as I fixed her dress. Her cheeks were still damp from washing, and some dirt smudges remained on her chin and forehead. The washrag was crumpled on her shelf. She allowed me to do another cleaning of her face and hands. Together, we walked to the lunchroom, her small hand in mine.

That night, after lights were out, Amy's tears concerned me more than my own.

I tiptoed the three steps to the child's bed and knelt. "Amy, are you okay?"

"I want my doll," she whispered and sniffed.

I gripped the side of her bed. Why the hell did the nuns have to take her doll? What did it hurt for a young child to hang on to the one thing she had for comfort?

"Was it a special doll?"

She sniffed again. "She's all I have." A tiny sob followed her words. "I always have her no matter where I am. I can't s…sleep with…without her. She'll be s…scared." Amy barely got the last word out before her crying renewed with more emotion.

"What's her name?"

"A…Amy. Just like me."

"I happen to know where they keep dolls they take from little girls." I waited as she choked in a sob then quieted to listen. "It's a very special place. She'll have lots of other dolls to keep her company. Amy has her own bed and her own doll pillow."

"She does?" Her wet eyes opened wide.

"Yes, and when you leave here, she'll be so happy to see you again. They tell all the dolls that, too, you know."

"Really?" She sniffed and her tears slowed.

"Really. I'm not very sleepy right now, so I think I'll just stay here for a few minutes. I bet you're tired."

She shook her head even as her eyes drooped, and she pulled the sheet up to dry her face. She didn't exactly smile, but the stress in her expression softened across her brow. Sighing, Amy put her hand in mine and drifted off to sleep.

I woke the next day like I did every day, thinking of my life outside the walls of the Good Shepherd. Had Paulie recovered from what must have been a frightful experience with Arnold? Did Mrs. Russell and Benjamin know what he'd done? I could only imagine what Benjamin would've done to Arnold if he'd found out. My stomach churned every time I pictured my friend in her compromised predicament. Once I escaped from confinement, I'd make amends to Paulie in some way. Most of my vengeful thoughts ran to acts of massive embarrassment for Arnold, so no girl at North High would ever find him even mildly attractive again.

I fretted constantly if Da was eating right, not drinking too much, and keeping his old jalopy in safe running condition. He needed me to take care of him.

As for Benjamin, regret tore at my heart. Susan must be firmly planted in his life by now. I'd been too timid, too patient when I'd had the chance to boldly win his affection.

I would acquiesce and go with Da to California, if he still wanted to work the crops there. My season in Phoenix passed me by, so I might as well be replanted somewhere new and start again.

These thoughts raked across my mind every morning before I even opened my eyes.

A feather light touch skimmed my arm. I opened my eyes to a small face peering inches from mine.

"Oh, Amy. Good morning."

"Can you help me with my buttons?"

My day took a new turn from all the others before. Amy presented me with a welcomed, although pitiful, distraction from my pain. My nods and smiles helped her navigate through her day. When my head hit the pillow that night, my chest hadn't tightened with the normal daylong worrying. But the night folded around me as the whispering of others in the dorm quieted, and I was drawn into my worrisome thoughts once again.

Before my endless supply of tears emerged, Amy's soft whimpers cut through the darkness.

Approaching the nuns about Amy would be useless. When certain all our dorm mates were sleeping, I gently opened my drawer and removed my extra pair of white socks. Stuffing one sock into the toe of the other, I tied it off using a lace from my shoe. Out of the box of paper and crayons we used during our free time between lunch and afternoon bible class, I grabbed a handful of crayons. I took my booty to the bathroom and locked myself in a stall. With the crayons, my stuffed sock became a doll with blue eyes and red lips. After putting the things away, I knelt beside the little girl's bed.

"Amy, I have a special doll for you until you get your real doll back. Would you like to have her?"

She lifted her head from her pillow and rested on her elbows. Green and yellow moonlight, filtering through stained glass, glistened on her wet cheeks. I held the sock doll up for her inspection. Her mouth twitched toward smiling.

"The thing is; this is our secret. You have to hide her in the back of your drawer, way back under your extra blanket, each morning." I had no idea how the nuns would view my creativity, but I wasn't going to chance another heartbreak for Amy. "You can take her out only after the lights are off when the nuns are gone. Can you do that?"

That was the end of nighttime tears for Amy and me. The doll gave her a sense of physical comfort until the time her real best friend would return. During the day, she looked to me, and helped me see my path more clearly.

They, whoever *they* were, couldn't keep me from my life forever. When I finally got back home, Da and I would go to California. We needed a new start, away from the cabin court and the likes of Mrs. Snyder. I couldn't go back to North High and see Arnold day in and day out without always remembering how I'd been instrumental in the harm he'd done to Paulie. I loved Paulie and would do what I could to make it up to her; however, my staying wouldn't make the injustice right. Arnold's lustful ways toward me would only bring more pain to my friend.

And Benjamin.

My chest ached and my eyes burned when my heart ignored better judgment and slipped his serious, blue eyes into my thoughts. Try as I might, I couldn't keep away the vision of his chest behind the thin, white T-shirt or his bicep flexing below his rolled sleeve. Memories of Benjamin lifting his momma, twirling her in the kitchen, handing over his paycheck, teasing Paulie, sitting behind the wheel of Lady Blue flooded my thoughts. I swallowed hard and fought tears of regret and loss for something I'd never had.

At the end of the third week, early Friday morning, a nun approached Amy. We sat on our beds, putting on our socks and shoes when she smiled at my young companion.

"Child, we have a new home for you."

Amy's eyes grew wide, but her bottom stayed glued to the bed until her gaze drifted to the nun's hands. Her eyes crinkled and her mouth opened in a doughnut hole smile when she saw her doll.

"Come on, we'll get you on your way."

Amy popped off the bed, followed the nun a few feet, then stopped and reeled around. She charged back and studied me while pinching her lips together in thought.

My sadness for her joy brought tears to my eyes. "I'll miss you, Amy, but I'm happy you're going home." She'd become my anchor, a reason to be there. How could I stay without her?

After darting a glance at the cabinet where the sock doll was hidden, her arms encircled my neck. "Are you going to have a little girl some day?" she whispered.

I kissed her cheek and whispered my answer. "Yes, I am."

"She can have my doll."

"Oh, thank you."

With a smile, she hopped off to follow the nun out of the dorm.

I slumped back on the bed, rubbed hands over the rough wool blanket, and wondered. *Would* I have a little girl some day? I'd answered Amy without thinking.

A calm resolve settled over me. Family mattered;

what little I had, and what more I wanted. My singing voice would be saved for my children's lullabies. My theatrics would entertain my husband with animated conversation and flirtations behind closed doors. What I most craved could be found with family. I just needed to get out of Good Shepherd.

"Claire."

So lost in daydreams, I didn't see the nun standing at the foot of the bed until she said my name. In her arms, she held my belongings.

"Change and gather yourself to Mother Superior's office."

For several minutes, I stared at my clothes like foreign objects invading space on the wool-blanketed bed. Only when the remembered comfort of my jeans wrapped around me like an old friend did I dare guess at the implications.

I walked the long hallway, each breath quicker as I neared the Mother's door. By the time I knocked on the ornately carved wood, my heart pounded louder than my rapping knuckles.

Mother Superior rose to greet me, her large body, draped in yards of black, rustled from behind her massive mahogany desk. "You have been a good and dutiful girl." She took my hand and patted me. "Mrs. Russell, you may take the child now."

I'd stopped behind a mammoth, leather chair facing the Mother's desk and hadn't realized anyone else was in the room. My arms went all tingly like when you lay on them too long. Mrs. Russell's petite frame was dwarfed in the armchair, hidden from me until she popped up.

With outstretched arms, she blithely circumvented

the prodigious Mother Superior. Undaunted by the grave atmosphere of the ruling woman in her chambers, Mrs. Russell smiled broadly and hugged me. "Oh, my dear girl, you're going home." She physically turned me toward the door, which she needed to do because I was rooted to the floor in shock.

Exiting through the same dark, wooden doors I'd seen for the first time a three-week lifetime ago, I clutched her hand so hard the poor woman probably lost circulation. As we made our descent down the mountain of steps, I slowed when my gaze fell on the blue car waiting for us below.

Benjamin.

****

Ben's pulse quickened when the massive doors finally parted to release Claire and his mother into the bright sunlight. As they descended the steps, holding hands, he smiled, declaring them his two favorite women. The three weeks since they'd gotten the news of Claire's disappearance into the welfare system had seemed more like three months.

Unable to wait quietly behind the wheel, he jumped from the car as their feet touched the last step. "Good to see you, Claire," he called across the short distance. His body twitched with the urge to dash out and take her in his arms. He hesitated, finally trotting to the passenger side to open the door. "Welcome back to the real world." He settled for resting his hand on her shoulder.

Her eyes glistened, and her cheeks blushed peach. "Thank you, Benjamin. I'm happier than you can possibly know to be back in the real world."

"No problem with the paperwork, then, Mom?" he asked as they climbed into the car. He said a silent thank you to his mother as she guided Claire to slide in between them.

"Not at all. They were very accommodating." She closed the door and glanced across at him. "We'd have called in the troops, if they hadn't."

He barely glanced at his mother, his gaze taking in Claire. Her touch against his arm, the golden, strawberry hair cascading over her shoulders, and her naked lips filled him with desire. He ached to hold her, comfort her, protect her from ever again being taken from the people she loved.

People she loved. *God, let me be the one she loves.*

Mom patted Claire's knee, drawing her slowly away from his virtual embrace. "Let's get on the road, Benjamin."

Claire's brow wrinkled. "Where's my father, Mrs. Russell?"

"He wanted to come, dear, but we decided it best if he didn't."

"Why? What happened to cause all of this?"

As he eased onto the road, Ben glanced at his beloved passenger. He'd kiss away her frown, if he could. Then he'd flatten the punk who had caused her trouble.

"We weren't sure right away. When the dust settled, we figured out your landlady had put in a complaint to the welfare people at some time, so there was a file, although never acted on. She had inside help." Mom sounded agitated. "I did some digging and found out the woman who came so quick to your door was her sister. She had her on alert for the first sign of any reason to take you away from Hamish. She's a dirty-minded old biddy, dear, who wanted to make trouble."

"Why would anyone want to do that to me?"

Yeah, why? Ben's chest ached with her plea.

"Who knows? You aren't the first to come to trouble by her. A neighbor told me…never you mind. But the noise, when Arnold visited you—"

Claire threw her hand to her mouth.

He clutched the steering wheel. *It figures the little ass-wipe had something to do with it.*

He'd been waiting three weeks to hear Claire's side of this. Paulie had an attitude every time he asked her what she knew about that visit. He could tell she was hiding something from him.

"Was there a problem when Arnold visited you, Claire?" Mom asked.

She let her hand drop to her lap. "We argued. I made him leave." Claire's gaze locked on the road ahead.

"An argument?" His mother kept her voice low, her tone affectionate. "Nothing more, dear?"

Ben held his breath. If there *was* more, he wouldn't be able to sit quietly. He clenched his teeth and flared his nostrils to take in enough air. He couldn't see Claire's face as she inclined her head toward his mother.

"I yelled a lot. We had broken up, and I didn't want him coming around." The scene out the window drew her gaze again. "I think he'd been drinking. He was rude, but all we did was shout at each other."

Mom exhaled, sounding relieved. "It was enough for the landlady to get welfare out there."

Ben's tension wouldn't let go. Claire clutched her hands together, still visibly upset. It was all he could do to keep enough attention on the road to drive.

"Where's Paulie?" she asked

"At school." His mother's voice took on a perkier tone. "You can see her tomorrow."

"At school?" Claire fidgeted beside him. "How is she?"

"She's fine, why?"

"She…she's been fine? All along?"

He darted a glance at her. Why was she so concerned for his sister?

"I don't know what you mean, dear." His mother sounded as confused as he felt uneasy. "She's missed you and has been very worried, if that's what you mean."

"Oh." Her voice was small, timid.

Ben could be quiet no longer. Gripping the wheel, he slowed a bit and glanced at her. "Did he hurt you, Claire?"

She whipped her head around to stare at him and bit her bottom lip.

"Did he? Tell me, because if he did—"

"No, Benjamin." She released her hands and wiped her palms on her jean-covered thighs. "It was stupid of me to let him in. He was…being loud…I was scared nosey Mrs. Snyder would do what she ended up doing anyway. So, I let him come in. He'd been drinking…I think…and…when I figured out he…didn't really need anything in particular…well, I…guess I yelled pretty loud at him…for drinking."

Some of the tension drained from Ben's shoulders, his fingers loosened, and the building heat of anger cooled. Claire and his sister were tight friends. Her concern for Paulie's feelings must have something to do with the punk, but at least there'd been no harm done to Claire.

"Well, it's over with now." His mother declared a finale to the ordeal. "Turn here, Benjamin."

Claire moved forward on the seat and scanned the scenery out the window. "Where are we going?"

"To your new home." Mom's perky voice was back.

The tension in her body translated through her upright posture and the jerk of her shoulder against his arm. "New home? Where's my father?"

"He's waiting for you there. It's best not to be under the eye of the old biddy."

Claire twisted toward his mom. "What…what all happened while I was…cloistered away?"

She chuckled. "That's a good way to put it. Well, let's see, where to begin. When Paulie went to your home on that Sunday, she found out from Hamish the welfare people had picked you up. Monday morning, I marched down to that office with him. The red tape is ridiculous. Poor Hamish was beside himself."

Ben wanted to let go of the steering wheel and take Claire's hands in his. She entwined her fingers, twirled a ring around and around, and clutched them together. He shot his mother a look over her and shook his head. Telling her about how upset her father had been served no purpose now.

Mom cleared her throat. "Never you mind, we got it all figured out. We took care of those bureaucrats together. The whole misunderstanding was silly, especially since you'll be eighteen soon when they would've released you anyway. The whole thing was perfectly stupid. In no way would we let you stay there until your birthday! Stupid bureaucrats. So, to speed the process up and get you out of there today, Hamish agreed to hand you over to my custody. It's just a bunch of ballyhoo on paper. Turn here, Benjamin."

"But how can this work? If they find out, they'll take me away again."

He cleared his throat, not sure what to say to quell the panic he could hear in her voice.

"No such thing will happen. Remember, you're nearly eighteen. And to keep it all between us, he moved you two into a nice little duplex, the other direction from us, but still within walking distance. Such a nice place."

"O...kay. So, as far as the state is concerned, you're my guardian now...we've moved." Claire sighed, relaxing against the seat, her shoulder softening against his arm. "It's over. Everything can go back to normal?"

"Back to normal. We can pick up right where we left off." The words left his mouth before he thought about them. His neck grew hot as he glanced at Claire. She studied her hands, tipping her chin down. Ben flicked a peek at his mother, who had taken an interest in the scenery. "You know. Back to working on some extra credit for science." His hands sweated on the steering wheel.

"You must have more to do after work and on the weekends than to help me with science. Maybe more fun things."

"Nah. I wouldn't mind at all, helping you out." What more could he say with his mother sitting on the other side of Claire? "I'll have time." He glanced at her, wishing he could convey all he felt with his eyes.

"I…I'm not sure." She batted her lashes, glancing at him briefly.

He hadn't realized how much he'd missed her smoldering, dark eyes. "Okay, then. I'm there. Anytime next week, if you need the help." He didn't want to wait that long to see her again. "I bet Paulie would like to see you tomorrow." Leaning forward, he shot a glance and hoped his mother would take the suggestion. "Mom, don't you think Claire should come over tomorrow before Paulie drives us all insane?"

"That depends on Claire. Here's the street," his mother directed him.

"How about coming over for dinner, Claire. I, uh, know Paulie wants to see you as soon as possible."

"I'd love to…to see Paulie…"

"Now, Benjamin, Claire can come over tomorrow, if she wants. She's always welcome. We'll expect you when we see you, dear."

He was pushing her too fast. She needed to see her father, get her feet back on normal ground. He'd have to bide his time, be patient. A moment of silence, and he had an idea.

Ben picked a cigarette from his pocket, put it between his lips and dug in his pants for the lighter Claire gave him for his birthday. Holding it farther from him than necessary, he flipped the wheel to light his cigarette. With a smile directed at Claire, he closed the lighter and tucked it back in his pants pocket. He blew his first puff out the window, gave a sideways glance, and was rewarded with a hint of a smile.

His mother leaned forward and pointed. "The green house, Benjamin."

A let down settled on him. He didn't want to

relinquish Claire to her father. Reluctantly, he pulled onto the gravel drive of the green duplex, his joy not matching Hamish Flanagan's face when he opened the door. She scooted forward on the seat before Ben brought Lady Blue to a stop. He'd lost her for the time being.

Mom opened the door with Claire nearly pushing her out. Hamish stepped out on his stoop as the car crunched on the gravel drive. His arms went up in the air as if celebrating an athletic triumph and came down in time to catch his daughter's forceful embrace.

"Da!"

His mother stood at the end of the drive, keeping a respectful distance. Ben opened his door to get out, but changed his mind and closed it softly. Claire's intense reunion with her father left him feeling like an intruder. The joyful scene unfolded out the window. In spite of missing her warmth beside him, witnessing her joy brought an equally satisfying feeling. Now, there would be tomorrow, many tomorrows to spend with her. He'd like to go thank the nosey, old biddy landlady for showing him what life could be like without Claire. Soon he'd wrap his arms around her slim waist, press into her full chest, and taste her peach-colored lips.

He wouldn't allow himself to hold back any longer.

****

After the farewells to Mrs. Russell and Benjamin, Da proudly showed me around. As happy and thrilled as I was about our new home with two bedrooms, my mind kept wandering away from my father's words to Benjamin's words moments before.

"We can pick up right where we left off."

Those were pre-Susan times. And he had used the

lighter I gave him, not the fancy one from her. I wanted to draw only one conclusion, and the thought so consumed me, I barely listened to Da.

Was she out of the picture?

Or did he merely want to welcome me back? Benjamin, always polite and thoughtful, wanted his little sister's friend to be comfortable and welcomed. He offered to help me with schoolwork like a big brother would.

"You like it okay, Claire?" Da's brows pinched together. "You're pretty quiet, gal."

I looped an arm through his as we walked over to the couch. I needed to get my mind off Benjamin and back to the moment. "Yes, Da. I must be a little tired."

My father rubbed his eyes. "This is all your old man's fault. If I hadn't stopped on the way home, if I'd been more responsible…"

He'd aged in the last three weeks, or maybe I'd forgotten some of the wrinkles on his weathered face. His eyes watered, pitifully. Sitting beside me on the couch, he slumped over, his body resigned to his guilt.

Guilt I hadn't considered. I'd placed blame on Mrs. Snyder, on Arnold, even myself—never on my father. Da stopped after work sometimes. I was alone sometimes. The ordinary routine of our life hadn't been cause for blame. "It's nobody's fault."

"Yes, it is. Mine. None of this would've happened if I'd been home."

"You can't be with me every minute, Da. It could've happened at four o'clock as easy as later in the night."

Da's head bowed so low his chin nearly touched his chest. He closed his eyes for a moment. "I should've come home." His voice was a whisper.

My eyes filled with tears. As lonely as I'd been over the last three weeks, my father's loneliness had been wrought with guilt. Two tears dribbled down his ruddy face to meet at his chin. I wrapped arms around his shoulders. A few of my tears spilled on his shirt. We sat like that in silence, with the only sound our breathing as salty tears rimmed my mouth. At last, I sat up and wiped my face.

"I'm okay, and we have this new home. With two bedrooms. How grand is that?"

Da's tears had stopped, but he continued to hang his head low and rub his knuckles.

"Do you remember the time we were waiting to hop a freight train while we spent the night in a hobo jungle?" I tapped on his hand. "We were somewhere around Yuma, I think. Some old guy sat down next to me and called me missy, while you were building a fire to cook our dinner. Remember how you walked right up and punched him in the nose?"

Da dragged a rough hand across his face. "You remember that? You was probably only five or six years old."

"Of course, I remember. I remember lots of times you've taken care of me. I remember none of the other men wanted to say a word to you, and I know that guy wouldn't have sat down next to me, if he'd known who you were. I heard them talking later, when we were eating. They told him you don't get near the kid of Fightin' Flanagan."

Da chuckled in spite of his despair. "Those was some lean times, but we managed right fine, I guess."

"Lean, yes, still, you've always managed to take

care of me. How about the time an eagle swooped down and grabbed the rabbit you had killed for our dinner? I can't remember if we were in California or Oklahoma. You chased the eagle until I thought you were going to fly, too, throwing rocks at him. He dropped our dinner right at your feet."

"Lordy, I was mad at that bird."

"One time, when we were spending the night in an orange orchard on our way to Hemet to stay with Uncle Eb and Aunt Grace, I heard you when you thought I was asleep. I was snug and contented in my sleeping bag, the smell of sweet orange blossoms all around us. Stars overhead. You touched my head and told me I was pretty and strong like my mother. I doubt you slept much, watching over me. No one's perfect, but you've been close enough."

He sat straighter. "Now, you're nearly eighteen. My, my, how time does go." He patted my leg. "I guess we better get dinner cooking. I didn't kill no rabbit, but I got some sausage you might like. And no critters around to take it off our plates." He studied me a moment. "You sure you're okay?"

"I am now."

He stood and brought me with him. "Them Russells are nice people. I don't know what I'd have done without them."

"They are, aren't they?"

"Yep, you could do a whole lot worse than Ben Russell."

Da hadn't forgotten our pact.

"What about California?" I asked the question to his back as he headed for the kitchen.

"What about California?" he called back.

"I did a good deal of thinking in the last three weeks." I followed him. "If you still want to go to California to work around Uncle Eb's, I'm ready to go."

He turned, leaving the icebox door open behind him. "What in tarnation are you talking about, Claire?"

"I've missed three weeks of school anyway. It would be a good time to start over at a new school. It's plain selfish of me to keep you here."

Da bent to take the package of sausage off the shelf. "I thought you liked it here in Phoenix."

I flipped hair from my neck then crossed my arms on my chest. Phoenix meant more than I would ever let on. And I didn't want to think about how much. My chest ached a little. "Well, I do, but that isn't the issue."

He closed the icebox, leaned against the counter, and rubbed his face in the familiar circular motion. "Three weeks ago, I might've jumped at this, Claire. Maybe, anyway. You're happy here, and I think that damn place got you all confused. Besides, now you're under the custody of Mrs. Russell. I can't be taking you out of state. We'd be runaways or something."

I pulled a chair from the table and sat down, head in hands. Arnold, Paulie, Benjamin—their faces flashed through my thoughts. I had to see Paulie no matter what I did. Arnold, I'd like to grind into the dirt, and my temperature rose with anger when I thought about him.

Benjamin.

Even though I'd been consumed with relief on the ride home, nearly numb to all else, his nearness had tugged at my heart. But he wasn't mine to have, not after all this time, I was sure of that much.

Da walked over, grasped my wrists to stand me up.

He gave me a kiss on the top of the head. "My poor baby."

"I'm nearly eighteen. We could leave right after my birthday."

"You listen to me, gal." He hugged me close. "Once you're back at school and running over to Paulie's all the time, you'll feel at home again. You're all discombobbled right now, and this ain't no time to be making decisions." He patted my back. "Now, that's the final word. Let's get dinner."

Too emotionally exhausted to argue, I gave him a quick hug. I knew what I had to do, and a few more days until my birthday wouldn't matter. Once I made amends to Paulie, there would be nothing keeping us in Phoenix.

****

Day gave way to night. There wasn't enough light coming in the window to read. Ben glanced at the lamp, not compelled to turn it on. Lying perfectly still, he relaxed; his chest barely rose with his shallow breathing.

"Too full to move?" Davie came into the darkened bedroom.

"Yeah, maybe. Mom cooks a good pot of beans." He rose to his elbows. "You heading over to Barbara's?"

"Yep. Why don't you come with me? I'm sure Allison will be there hoping you'll show up. She's got the hots for you."

"Shit, I doubt that."

"She does. Allison's no Susan, but she might swap a little spit with you."

The mention of Susan brought a rise of sensation

below his waist. He shook his head and chuckled. "Ah, Susan."

"Why'd you dump her?"

"Is that what you think?" He sat up. "Hell, I'm not sure who dumped who. I think I was a friggin' project, and once she brought me to term, the interest was gone. I got tired of her game."

"Sure was a short courtship." Davie glanced at him as he changed shirts.

"Courtship, hell. Susan isn't the courting kind of woman. Not that I pushed the issue." He picked up the book lying on the floor next to his bed. "*Nothing* except sex. And she always wanted to be in charge...of *every* damn thing."

"Too much sex? Who the hell would complain about that?" His brother snickered. "She seemed kind of bossy. Sort of like a sister of ours." He picked his car keys from the bureau. "You coming with me or not?"

"Nah." Ben fell back onto the pillow. "Think I'll read." The truth was he wanted to think about Claire for a while.

"You'll break Allison's heart."

"She'll live."

He lay in the ensuing darkness. Lighting a cigarette, he took a long drag and looked at the lighter in his hand. Claire's lighter. He was reminded of the night on the porch. Dark, smoldering eyes, red-blonde curls lit with fire, shoulders so smooth gleaming like the surface of pearls. She had a habit of reaching under the length of her hair and flipping it back which exposed her neck and made him feel as if he'd seen more of her than he should. He yearned to run his fingers along the nape of her neck, brush his lips into the hollow of her collarbone.

He flicked his lighter open, spun the wheel and watched the flame match the fire in his groin.

****

I couldn't believe it was nearly ten o'clock when I woke. After a hot shower, I removed the bobby pins from my hair, brushed out the curls, and dressed. I smelled coffee as I left my room. The living room and kitchen, one large room, were much like the arrangement at the cabin court, except my father now had a bedroom on the other side of the kitchen. I practically skipped out to the living room like a ten year old on a holiday from school.

Da sat at the kitchen table drinking coffee from a chipped mug and reading a newspaper. Oatmeal, ribbons of steam rising from it, and buttered toast were set at the seat across from him.

"Would this be for me?"

He smiled over a page of his paper. His ruffled red hair was only a shade darker than the rims of his eyes. "I timed it pretty good." Contrary to his jovial voice, he looked sleep deprived.

"My gosh, Da. You certainly did." I sat down. "Didn't you get any sleep?"

The paper rustled as he scrunched it down to lean on the table. "I did. More than I've had in three weeks. Feels like I got too dang much sleep."

I squinted my eyes in disbelief. "Really?"

"I'm not kidding you, Claire." He leaned back and rubbed tobacco stained fingers over the rough knuckles of his other hand. "I may look and feel like a freight train hit me, but I'm finally sleeping."

I opened the sugar bowl and tipped it to load my

spoon. "Did they lift the rationing while I was away?"

Da chuckled. "No, gal, they didn't."

"Maybe I should write the President a letter." I wasn't serious. In fact, there'd been enough changes while I was away. Even continued sugar rationing gave me a grounded sense of home.

"You do that, honey."

"Would you mind if I go over to Paulie's tonight?" Before falling off to sleep, I'd made the decision to see her right away. Regardless of how the rest of the week played out, Paulie had to take top priority. She'd obviously kept her experience with Arnold a secret from her family. I would be her shoulder. I'd go from there.

"That's a good idea. I bet she's as anxious as a horse at the gate to see you again."

"Do you have anything to do?"

"I'll check my calendar."

"Da!"

"Actually, RJ is getting up a poker game tonight. Think I'll mosey on over there, if you ain't going to be home."

My spoon stopped halfway to my mouth.

Da let go his paper and held both palms up. "Ain't going to be no drinking."

"And how's that going to happen?"

"RJ's on the wagon. Can you imagine? He had a choice between liquor and Thelma May walking out, or dry days with her staying. So, he says, let's try poker with lots of food and tea." Da laughed so hard his eyes teared.

I laughed, too, but from the joy of seeing him happy. The oatmeal and black coffee weren't the only things warming me.

"You go on to see Paulie. I better pick you up. What time you want me there?"

I didn't know how long to plan for my talk with my friend. "They'll bring me home."

I tore off a piece of toast and envisioned sitting next to Benjamin. The toast went dry in my mouth. I screamed at myself in my head. I wouldn't be able to avoid him, but I had to stop thinking of him romantically. David had a car, too. As soon as Paulie poured her heart out and forgave me, I'd ask David to bring me home.

"Okay, don't be too late. I'll be here waiting for you."

My toe tapped as nerves channeled through my body. I played with my toast. My appetite had left me. Thoughts of Benjamin would not be driven out. My heart was already doing double time.

****

Da insisted on driving me. Without the benefit of the walk and fresh air, my nerves spiked. I'd changed clothes three times, finally settling on jeans and a peasant blouse, all the time wondering how Benjamin would see me. As we approached the house, I wished I'd worn my brown fitted skirt. I didn't have anything in my closet to compare with Susan's wardrobe; however, the skirt would've been more mature.

What does it matter? I asked myself the question more than once.

My palms were sweaty as I grabbed the door handle. "You want to come in? I'm sure you'd be welcomed."

"Nah, hon. Don't want to be late for my tea party

card game."

I stepped out, closed the door, and leaned in the window. "The lights are working on this jalopy, aren't they?"

"Yes, Miss Worry Wart."

"You have gas money? You can't even tell if you're out of gas in this heap."

"Your Da ain't no dummy. Now get!"

"I'll see you." I blew him a kiss as he backed the wretched old car out of the drive and drove back the way we came.

I took a deep breath and cursed the turn of events that had landed me in the Russell front yard for possibly the last time. Gazing on the porch and faded green house, sadness settled on me and tugged my mouth and brows downward. The urge to leave, write Paulie a letter begging her forgiveness, and steal off to California played across my mind. I'd never have to face Benjamin again, face his happiness without being a part of his life…

I couldn't do it. I had to see them one more time.

With a tap on the door, I let myself into the Russell home. The familiarity immediately soothed my nerves. I paused a moment and let the smells and voices in the kitchen fill me with comfort.

A shrill scream and arms tightening around me like a straight jacket abruptly interrupted my musings.

Chapter Ten
First Kiss

I turned within the circle of my friend's arms. "I'm glad to see you, too, Paulie."

"Oh, Claire. Are you a sight for sore eyes! My God, I've missed you."

Holding her at arm's distance, I searched her face for the sorrow and pain I'd imagined she'd lived with for the past three weeks. "I've missed you more." I hugged her again. "Are you okay?" My tears were close as I patted her back.

"Isn't that just like you?" She pursed her lips. "You're the one everyone's been worried about. I've been so afraid for you. I've had the most awful thoughts of why they took you away."

"Paulie…are you…" I ran my hands over her arms and leaned closer. "Arnold—"

She grabbed my hand, wheeled around, and towed me to the porch and down the steps. She paused to look around then hauled me over to the bougainvillea bush. With the bush between the house and us, she drew close.

"Don't say that little bastard's name," Paulie hissed.

Her words shocked me momentarily.

"I know it's his fault, all his fault, and what he did, well, you're not to blame."

"Not to blame? But I am. I've been so worried about you." I touched her hair, smoothed some stray strands back from her face. "I'm sorry I wasn't here for you. I'm surprised you're even talking to me."

"Why? Because he went to see you?" She huffed as if exasperated. "I could give a damn! You're the only one who matters. Don't say it's your fault. That little prick!"

Her vocabulary had certainly changed when it came to Arnold. I touched her shoulder. "Paulie—"

She batted at my hand. "Stop fussing over me and tell me what happened, Claire. I've heard Mom's account, but her story is a sketchy, second hand version." Her brow furrowed. Our faces nearly met as she leaned in and clutched my arm. "What did he do to you?"

"To me? Nothing, except make me hate him." I touched my forehead to hers and whispered, nearly choking with dammed up tears. "You tell *me* what happened, Paulie. I have Arnold's account, except his story is...is—"

Paulie jerked upright. "He *told* you?"

"That's why he came to see me. He wanted to brag about...about getting in your pants, for God's sake!"

Her reaction, merely a frown, wasn't what I expected.

"You mean you two didn't...?"

I gasped. The implied question sent uncomfortable shivers down my spine. "No. He told me you did."

"What an ass." She paced a few steps away, muttered under her breath, and stomped back again. "All this time, I thought the welfare people caught you two, you know...or he pushed himself on you so you

212

screamed, or the nosey old biddy walked in on you making—"

"Oh God." Prickly waves of anxiety heated my neck. "Not only did you have to deal with what he did to you, but you thought I had suffered the same result?" I brushed my fingers across my forehead, checking for fever. "Paulie, did he hurt you?" My voice cracked. "He said he…forced himself on you."

She rolled her eyes. "Forced?"

"He told me you were drinking then…you…he said you were…more than willing then changed your mind and…he…he wouldn't stop so he got you good." My words affected me much more than Paulie; she had a smirk on her face. "Those were *his* words," I added.

"Why on earth…" She forced a laugh and looked up at the sky with a shake of her head. "You want the truth, Claire?"

I took her hands. "I've been so worried. All I could think about when I was in that place was how I should've protected you from him. If he hurt you—"

"He didn't hurt me, Claire. Well, the sex did hurt a little, but not like you think." She squeezed my hands. "Why on earth would you blame yourself for my stupidity?"

"Because I knew how aggressive he could get, and you were so blind to him. I should've made you listen."

"As if I would've listened. Come on, Claire." She stood on tiptoes to glance up at the porch and around the bush. Satisfied, she peered into my face again, her voice softer. "Did you think I had a little school girl crush? You know I had the hots for him." She sighed and the smirk came back to her mouth. "I thought about him plenty in all the ways I could dream up. I wanted to make him react to me the way he reacted to you, you know? Nothing you could've said would have changed that."

"But—"

"But nothing! I'm curious why he would tell you such a cockeyed story. Speaking of cocks—that's what rules him, for sure." Paulie glanced around, making sure we were still alone. "Okay." She wet her lips. "He came over. Remember, I had asked you to come over, although I knew you'd refuse what with being so miserable about the cigarette lighter incident at Ben's birthday dinner. I knew Momma had to go into town shopping and everyone else would be gone. I *counted* on it.

"He had his stupid car and wanted me to go for a ride. Well, you can imagine I jumped at that. And yes, he had a bottle of something, and yes I could smell it on his breath. I didn't care." She snickered, sarcastically. "In fact, getting in his car, liquor on his breath—I got so excited, I was dizzy." She let go of my hands and rubbed her temples. "So *stupid.* I didn't drink, and he didn't either when I was in the car. Anyway, we drove over behind the Kleeson warehouse and parked. I couldn't believe he was actually flirting with me. He didn't mention you, not even once. I thought, *wow he's finally noticed me.* He put his hand on my leg, so I scooted closer to him. He kissed me, Claire. You know how crazy I was for him? His kiss sent me over the edge. I wanted him to love me, really *love* me. His lips, hands…Christ! I wanted it all." She made a noise, half-laugh, half-disgusted sigh. "Every inch of him. *Make love to me, Arnold, please make love to me* was all I could think. Stopping him never came to mind."

My friend's admission only made me hate him more. Arnold had intended on hurting me with his version of the story. He knew how much Paulie meant to me.

She shrugged. "When it was over, and he lay on me, limp and sweaty, I asked him if he loved me." Paulie swallowed as if to choke down any residual hurt he'd caused her. "Bastard! He didn't even look at me. *"No, I don't love you, but I'll screw you anytime you want,"* he said."

My hand flew over my mouth.

Paulie waved her fingers in the air, dismissing the brutality of his statement like a bothersome gnat. "So, what did he say to you? What really happened after he left here?"

My throat closed with choked down tears. All my worry and guilt, my assumption Paulie had been molested or violated, collapsed. The void created slowly filled with relief while anger beat a drum on the inside of my chest.

She gripped my shoulders. "Claire, I had sex. That's all. He didn't hurt me."

"Maybe not physically—"

"I got what I wanted. Period." A cloud drifted across the sun, softening her features with the shadow. "I've had enough time to get over him. *You* had to deal with it, alone, surrounded by strangers. Now, take your hand off your mouth, and tell me what the hell happened when he got to your house before Ben comes looking for you."

"Ben?" The mention of Benjamin brought me out of my shock.

She waved a hand in my face. "Not until I hear

215

what happened."

I couldn't tell her everything he'd said. His proclamation of love for me; his pretending he'd held me instead of her could only make things worse. No telling what other words I'd hear Paulie had added to her vocabulary if my story angered her further. "I guess he drank more after he left you. He told me about you two to make me jealous. When I didn't get jealous, only mad, I think he wanted to hurt me. Which is why he told me he'd hurt *you.* I screamed and yelled, and we ended up outside. Miserable, bitchy landlady had her excuse to get rid of me. That's all that happened. I *hate* him. If I ever see him again—"

"Thankfully, that's not an issue. When the cops took him home liquored up with a complaint of disturbing the peace, his parents shipped him off to his uncle's farm."

"Good!" I thought better of that. "Oh, Paulie." I squeezed her hands.

"I don't care, Claire. Honestly. I cried for a couple of days, more for you than the hurt feelings I had. When he rolled off me, and I looked at him, it was like the first time I ever really saw him. A weasel, a wimp, a stupid little boy."

"He was. All of those things!" The flush of anxiety receded so I could breathe normally again.

"By the way, making love seems to be highly over-rated."

Her levity drained the last of my nerves. "Oh, Paulie!" Relief left me feeling weak kneed.

"Really." She laughed. "It was so disappointing. I can't believe that's all there is to it, or people wouldn't be doing it all the time, would they?"

I hugged her and whispered into her hair. "We're going to be okay, aren't we?"

"Mom's wondering where all her kitchen help got off to." Benjamin's voice floated down from the porch. "Not like you're much help in the kitchen, pipsqueak."

"Oh, can it," Paulie tossed the crack up at her brother and patted my back. "We sure as hell are going to be okay."

She turned toward the steps, but I clung to her. She glanced over her shoulder with a puzzled expression.

"I should help, too," I offered.

"Don't be silly." She winked and hopped up onto the step, breaking my hold.

Bright blue eyes looked down on me. "Hello, Claire."

"Hello, Benjamin." I moved to follow Paulie up the steps, but he stopped me.

"No. Stay there."

I froze. "Why?"

He waited for the door to close behind his sister. "I kind of like looking at you standing next to Mom's flowers."

I caught my breath. Benjamin was openly flirting with me. "Why, Benjamin, that's almost poetic of you." I flipped the hair from my neck with a nervous laugh.

He clambered down the steps and stopped mere inches from me. "Up close is so much better."

Walk away, I told myself, although surely my knees would buckle if I did. We stared into each other's eyes for a warm moment until the heat between us was palpable. With a deep sigh, Benjamin transferred his gaze to the flowers.

"Mom's flowers are doing great."

I followed his lead and admired the bush. "They're bougainvillea. They are quite lovely, aren't they?"

I knew without looking, he no longer stared at the flowers. The dusty smell of the yard along with the woodsy scent of Benjamin's after-shave filled my head. His morning glory eyes swept over me and set my heart racing. I wanted to swoon into his arms. Why did he have to be so sociable, so nice to his little sister's friend? His affable nature tortured me.

"I really should go help with dinner." My shoulders leaned, but my feet wouldn't follow.

"You're the guest tonight, and guests shouldn't have to help in the kitchen."

I glanced around to anywhere except in his eyes, frantic to break the hold he had on me.

His voice went husky as he briefly touched my arm. "I missed you, Claire."

My head swam. I risked dizzily falling into him when I turned to meet his gaze. "You did?"

"I did." The serious Benjamin stared deeply at me.

The ache in my chest when I stared into his face overpowered my voice. "I thought…the last time I saw you…you were—"

"I was stupid not to tell you how much I enjoyed spending time with you."

"You were helpful with my drawings. Especially when you had other things you could've been doing." I touched the bougainvillea, avoiding his gaze. "You're clearly a very clever artist, and you seem to enjoy—"

"You, Claire. I enjoy you."

"That's so nice of you to say, although, I won't need any more help because…because, well, we've decided to move to California as soon as I turn eighteen." I continued to finger the flowers as if they needed my close inspection. My fingers trembled.

"What?" He shifted closer. "When did you decide this? Why?"

The surprise in his voice startled me. My attention went to his face, clearly dismayed at my revelation. "This morning." My shaky hands knocked loose flowers from the bush. "This is a good time to leave."

"It isn't." He shook his head. A shadow covered his face as if the clouds had covered the sun. "I thought you liked it here. I thought this was home for you, Claire."

"It is." I stepped back from him. "It was." My lip quivered. The burning in my eyes would soon turn to tears.

He closed the gap between us. "I don't understand."

"Why do you care?"

"I care for you."

"Benjamin." I breathed a ragged sigh. "I appreciate your friendship, but—"

"Ah." His laugh sounded bitter. "This is the way it is then. I'm a fool." He took a step back and his chin dropped.

"Oh, Benjamin…"

"Christ, Claire." He ran a hand on the back of his neck. "I'm sorry. I'm a damn fool."

I opened my hands in a questioning gesture, my mouth gaping and closing again. Confusion draped over me like an opaque curtain.

His smile lacked joy. "You're so sweet, so open, and easy to talk to. We got on so well. I guess I thought you felt the same way. My mistake." He rubbed a hand along his chin and moved farther away. "You must think me an idiot."

The veil of confusion lifted, and my heart leapt at the light. He turned toward the stairs. "Wait!" I dared to step closer and touch his shoulder. "I thought you and Susan…"

"Oh, hell, no." He faced me. "Not Susan, or anyone else."

"No one?"

"There's no one else, Claire."

The words danced in the air between us. I repeated them in my head, not sure if the confusion or my mind was unraveling. Thoughts of California evaporated as the cloud released the sun and threw beams of happiness on us. My arms fought me to throw themselves around his neck. "Oh. I…I'm not seeing anyone either."

"Works out pretty good then." He laughed. "Did I tell you I'm happy you're home?"

My lips joined the battle, fighting me to taste his smile. "You might have mentioned that, in a way." We laughed quietly.

"Don't go to California."

I couldn't speak. He came so close I could share the air he breathed.

"I've just gotten you back."

Gotten me back? I had misunderstood his meaning yesterday. But of course, because I assumed Susan had won his heart.

I closed my eyes, counted to three, and opened them again. He hadn't disappeared. Maybe Benjamin was entirely right. We *could* take up right where we had left off, before Susan and Mrs. Snyder had ruined it all.

"I suppose you have to talk to Hamish before you can—"

"Not really." I found my voice at last. "I didn't really want to go to California. The separation from all of you made me think I needed to…make a change."

"What was it like? Were you lonely, Claire?"

"It was a strange three weeks, Benjamin. Yes, I was lonely, but not alone. I fretted something awful, worrying about Da and Paulie. I thought about you. I thought about you a lot." My heart pounded fiercely with this admission.

His eyes, sad and watery, drank me in with emotion.

I gulped. "There was the sweetest little girl and we helped each other. While I moved through my days, home and all of you stood still for me. Then I came home, and things hadn't stood still. Nothing stood still, and I'd lost three weeks."

"It was my loss, too."

His stare pierced my soul. Fingertips grazed my bare arm, left a trail of goose bumps, and I begged them to come back. He read my eyes and brought the palm of his hand to rest on my forearm. His touch was the portal to a new existence.

I moved into him. My thighs brushed his legs. His chest caressed my breasts. The waning day cocooned us, and our shallow breaths synchronized. We entered our own dimension where nothing existed outside the space we shared.

I'd never wanted anything so much as to feel every inch of his body against mine.

As if hearing my thoughts, he drew me in, his arms wrapped around my waist, and my arms embraced his shoulders. His lips parted, beckoning me. I closed my eyes and swooned with the heat when his mouth took control. His lips, soft yet firm, played gently on mine. I pressed, my lips parted, and craved all of his attention.

He tasted me and shivered.

The warm, wet, deliciousness of his tongue, the heat of his breath, sent shock waves the length of my body so my hips rocked into his. His growing desire pressed against me. I silently gasped with no notion to move away. My heart pulsed in time to the throb of my body against his manhood.

His arms lifted me up to my toes as my fingers laced around his neck. My head filled with his scent of smoke, aftershave, and musky desire. My tongue relished the texture of his, tasted the sweetness of his promise. When I thought I could take no more, when I thought I might burst from a want I'd never known, Mrs. Russell's voice called from within the house.

Chapter Eleven
Honey On White Bread

Ben let the apple crisp and whipped cream rest on his tongue. Maybe he could block out the taste of Claire and the heat building as he gazed across the table. Mom had called them to dinner, but not before Claire's sweet lips left an imprint on his memory forever. Now, sitting across from her, dinner winding down with dessert, he longed to get his arms around her once more. The apple crisp, although good and a rare treat, was not nearly as tasty as Claire.

"You're taking longer to eat dessert than you did all of dinner," his mother said, laughing.

Ben winked at her. "Damn, Mom, this is good."

Davie leaned back, patted his stomach, and agreed with Ben. "The whole dinner was great, Mom. Good thing you don't make dessert every day or we'd have trouble getting our buffalo butts out of our chairs."

Richie found the remark incredibly funny and laughed so animatedly he nearly fell off his chair.

"Oh, stop it, Richie. It ain't that funny." Ruth grabbed his arm to set him up straight. "By the way, I did help a little with dinner, you know."

"Why, you helped more than a little, Ruth Anne." Their mother reached across Davie to pat her oldest daughter's hand. "You're a wonderful cook. You'll make a good wife someday."

His sister made a noise like spitting a piece of cotton from her tongue. "I'll be a good restaurant owner someday. I'm not interested in doing duty for some ungrateful man."

Mom sighed. "Ruth Anne…"

"Ah, Mom, leave her be," Ben chimed in and winked at Claire. "She'll never find a man to put up with her anyway."

"A lot you know. There are more than a few men holding their hearts in their hands right now." Ruth raised her eyebrows and a spoon in the air. "I have to choose carefully. I want a man who's not afraid of a woman who can think for herself. One who can own her own business and be his equal."

He shook his head as he put down his fork. "A man wants a woman who he can provide for; who will take care of the home and the kids." His sister's eyes narrowed, while Claire's interest in his speech emboldened his words. "I'm not saying she shouldn't have a mind of her own. A real man likes a strong woman with a head on her shoulders." He glanced at Claire who smiled sweetly, encouraging him to continue. "No wife of mine will ever have to work. I'll always be there, *always*."

Ruth darted a glance at their mother then flattened her mouth in an evil stare at him.

Mom fidgeted with her fork. His bold words wilted in the air, and he silently chided himself. She never spoke of their father to complain about him leaving her to care for six children. The man might never have existed, if the proof of their union didn't surround her every day. He'd have to take her aside later to make amends for his careless tongue while trying to impress

Claire.

"Well, I don't want a wife at all," Richie declared. "Girls just want to kiss you!"

Ben chuckled in relief when his younger brother broke the tension.

"You're such a scrawny thing, I don't think you have anything to worry about," Davie guffawed.

"Well, you have a big nose and you got Barbara!"

"Hey, twerp." Davie tossed a wadded napkin.

Their mother rose. "Now, boys. Take it to the living room while we clean up."

"I'm heading over to Barbara's." Davie jangled his car keys. "Good to see you, Claire."

"Come on, Richie," Ben scooted his chair back. "I'll beat you at a game of checkers." He glanced at Claire as he rose. He could bide his time with his little brother until the women finished the dishes. And then he'd find a way to spend some time with her, alone.

****

I rose slowly and caught Ben's attention once more before he moved off to the living room. My chest swelled with admiration from his declaration of family values. His big brother kindness further sweetened my opinion. And of course, the memory of the brief kiss before dinner colored my vision. I was certainly glad he expressed his appreciation of women who knew their own mind. There might not have been a kiss without my brazenness. I took a quick, deep breath to relieve the flutters in my thighs the memory of his kiss brought on.

I picked up dishes and followed Paulie to the sink. We stood hip-to-hip washing and drying dishes.

"I wonder who the passionate speech was intended

for?" She quirked a half-smile.

I took extra care in getting a glass dry. "Whatever do you mean?"

"You two got this under control?" Ruth appeared behind us. "I need to go see Susan."

Paulie didn't look up from her dishwashing. "Oh, sure, get out of the work part of dinner."

The mention of Susan shot a nervous twitch up my spine. I glanced at Ruth whose brows were pinched together. "Are you and Susan going out?" I asked.

"I doubt it." She walked away as she explained. "She's got some problem or something she needs help with. Mom, I'll see you later."

"What do you suppose that's about?" I asked.

"Who knows? Who cares?" Paulie finished the last plate.

Leaning closer to her ear, I whispered, "I care."

"Don't worry about Susan. She's out of Ben's life." She dried her hands and smiled. "I've seen how he looks at you."

"Hey, Claire!" Richie called from the living room. "I beat Ben, so I challenge you."

"Go on, girls," Mrs. Russell said from behind us. "You did the hard part. I'll wipe up the counters."

Benjamin's face lit up when I entered the living room. His smile had changed. He openly looked at my lips, gazed across my shoulders, lingered at my hips. While sitting next to him, I made an effort to concentrate on checkers, but there was a flow of unspoken communication between us. His knee brushed against me now and then as if by accident. I shivered when his fingers touched my arm with a suggestion of a checker's move. Richie laughed at my ineptness. I had no idea what moves either of us made. My breath would stop between Benjamin's touches. My brain became oxygen starved. Richie so enjoyed beating me, we had two more matches before Benjamin declared the games over.

"Do you need a ride home, Claire?" he asked.

"Not already!" Richie protested.

Paulie rescued me. "I'll play you, squirt, and I'll beat the pants off you."

Her little brother's nose wrinkled, and his mouth pouted in resignation. "Oh, okay."

My friend laughed as she took my seat. "The work I picked up for you from school is on the cupboard in the corner of the kitchen. You'll be busy tomorrow."

"Ugh! Thanks a bunch, Paulie." I bent over and gave her a hug. "See you on Monday. Thanks, Mrs. Russell. Dinner was grand."

"You come over here and give me a hug, Claire Flanagan."

I practically floated over to the petite woman curled up in the tattered overstuffed chair. "Mmm." I hugged her tightly. "Thank you for everything."

She patted my back. "No need, no need." She shooed me with a wave of her hands. "Now, you work hard on your school work tomorrow."

"I will."

Tomorrow could never come as long as this evening lasted forever. I followed Benjamin out the door into the cool air, to the porch dimly lit by the porch light, and into the darkness at the bottom of the steps. The anticipation of the ride home so filled me with joy I wanted to sing.

Ben slowed so I came beside him. My books filled

his arms. Even in the dim light of the moon, I could appreciate the biceps beneath his rolled sleeves. I couldn't help myself as I lay a hand on his arm, my fingers tracing the bulge. He took a ragged breath at my touch.

He walked me to the passenger's side, put the books in the back seat, and stood beside the opened door—barely a body width away. I brushed against him to slide into my seat and scooted across, nearly in the middle. When he sat at the wheel, he didn't exactly hug the door. His elbow nudged my arm as he started the car.

We were quiet as he drove at a leisurely speed. My mind flitted from one thought to the next.

I'm crazy for you, Benjamin. Tell me again you missed me. Should I scoot closer? Will you kiss me when we get to my house? Can I stand a day not being near you? Touch me, kiss me.

At the far edge of the cottonwoods, he glanced at me as if he could hear the words hammering in my head, and veered off the road. He stopped the car, and immediately doused the lights. The silent darkness came like a curtain dropping abruptly on a lit stage. Benjamin rested his hands on the wheel and faced forward, his only movement the rise and fall of his chest with each breath.

I brought my knee onto the seat to turn toward him. My heart beat hard enough to take my breath away. I wanted him to make the first move, so I waited nervously.

"You're a good student, aren't you, Claire?" He stared at the dashboard.

"Why, yes, I am. But why on earth do you ask?" I

had no idea what fostered this line of conversation.

"You have good grades in all your subjects?"

"Yes. Does it matter for some reason?" I was baffled.

"Pretty much duck soup, piece of cake?"

"Pretty much."

He tipped his head toward me and a slight smile creased his face. "So, I was helping you with extra credit for what reason?"

"Oh!" I laughed. "Should I be embarrassed at getting caught?" I ran my hand along my neck and flipped the hair from my neck.

He smiled. "Do that again." The moon shining in the window caught a slight glint in his eyes. Eyes I knew were blue and inviting.

"What?"

He cleared his throat. "Push your hair up like that again."

"Like this?" I repeated my habit.

He groaned and rubbed his chin like an itch he couldn't relieve.

Why the movement brought on such a reaction, I had no idea. His groan had the precise effect on me my hair flipping movement apparently had on him.

"Mmm." I slowly slid my hand under my hair once more, languidly flipping the tresses from my neck.

His groan came deeper this time as his hand nudged mine to slide along the back of my neck. He massaged gently and tangled hair in his fingers. My head relaxed back with the shock waves his caress sent down my spine. His other hand touched my knee.

"Claire, I want you to know…how I feel."

My eyelids fluttered, the caress bringing me to near

unconsciousness even as my body climbed a slow ascent to arousal. Heat spread across my chest, my breasts tightened, sending goose bumps to tickle my lower abdomen. I thought of his kiss before dinner, his body against mine, and my thighs shivered. "About me? How you feel about me?"

His hand slipped down my neck, grazed my collarbone, and came to rest next to his other hand. As if a magic spell had released me, my head slowly righted, and with a sigh, I opened my eyes fully to his serious face.

"You're different, Claire…special." His fingertips burned through my jeans. "You're like honey on white bread."

"Honey? What?" I tilted my head and leaned closer. I didn't understand his meaning, although his whispery, serious voice drew me in.

He lifted the hair from my shoulder and fingered the strands as he spoke. His hand gripped my knee firmer. Bringing his face next to mine, he spoke into my ear. "You know what honey does to plain white bread?" He kissed my cheek softly, his lips like the touch of a butterfly wing. "You dribble it on, slow…and…thick. The bread soaks the honey in and changes." His lips caressed my earlobe. "I'm white bread to your honey."

The warm breath of each word disturbed the cool air and swirled around me, wrapping me in a gentle whirlwind of desire. A tremble ran the length of my body as I leaned into him and yearned for him to feel the very essence of my desire. Surprising shivers came in waves, and I clutched my thighs together. I'd never known such heat low in my hips. I needed him to press against me, to hold me tight, and quench the fire building deep inside.

His lips trailed down my neck, and with each kiss, a small moan escaped my lips. My arms, limp at my sides until then, came to life. While I brought an open palm to his beating heart, the other hand inched up his arm, my fingertips electrified by the downy hair of his forearm. As his mouth reached my shoulder, my hand massaged his chest with the rhythm of each heartbeat, and my other hand gripped his tense, hard bicep.

He moaned, and with a startling jerk, pulled away from me. "I need to take you home, Claire."

I blinked and refocused on a scene that had changed before my brain could catch up with my sight. My short breaths and racing heart couldn't return to normal so fast. I tugged on his arm to bring him back close, and he didn't fight me. "Kiss me, Benjamin."

His mouth fit mine perfectly. My lips parted slightly and the sweetness of his tongue sent the most delicious quivers between my legs. With my arms around his neck, I straightened my leg and scooted closer. My breasts, tight and achy, pushed against his chest. We couldn't taste each other enough. He took my lower lip between his, ran his tongue around my mouth, kissed me deep as if drinking me in. My breath came faster with every dart of his tongue. His hands on my waist inched down and sent a tremor which rocked my hips; I arched my body against him.

But with my movement, he broke the embrace. "Claire." His voice was thick with emotion. "Claire." He touched my cheek. "I'm going to take you home." He clasped my wrists, set my hands in my lap, and grasped the steering wheel with one hand. His other hand trailed off my cheek, through my hair, then slowly to his own face. He rubbed his eyes and took a deep breath.

I clasped my hands in my lap as I wrestled with what I should say. His caution disappointed me, but his maturity was so decisive, my desire intensified. I couldn't find any words.

"You know why I'm taking you home now, don't you?"

My breath wouldn't come back to me. My lungs seemed to be crowded by my heart beating high in my chest. I understood, but couldn't stop the throb between my thighs. I didn't know how to handle emotions brought on by physical desire I'd never before experienced. His seriousness gave me pause. My breath steadied as I breathed deep and searched his blue eyes for direction.

"I'm going to court you, Claire Flanagan, proper like."

"Court me?"

"Yes. Take you on dates. Go to movies. Get to know you inside and out."

"We know each other, Benjamin."

"And when you turn eighteen, I'll court you a little bit longer."

"Benjamin, I turn eighteen in a week."

His mouth crooked sideways in a devious smile. "You don't say?" He turned the key in the ignition and the car engine hummed. "Hell, won't be much courting until then, I guess. I'll be out of town all week."

We bumped back onto the road.

"Out of town?" I couldn't survive not seeing him for even a day. "Why?"

"Work. Joe is sending me to Yuma for a job." A

broad smile lit his face. "He's making me a foreman and says I'm the only one he can trust on an out of town job."

I let my head fall to his shoulder in overwhelming disappointment.

"I'll be back for your birthday, promise." He kissed the top of my head. "This is a great opportunity for me, Claire."

"I know." I rubbed my cheek against his shirtsleeve. "I'm anxious to get the courting started." I walked my fingertips along his arm to his hand and back again. He shifted in his seat, and my heart thumped knowing what I was doing to him. I dropped my hand to his knee. "Do you think you could pull over and give me a kiss for each day you'll be gone?"

He laughed. "No, I can*not*."

"Don't you want to, Benjamin?"

His sigh came. "More than anything."

I soaked up the desire in his voice, let his words wet me with pleasure as I closed my eyes and fell limp against his side.

"I'll be back for your birthday. Or the weekend right after actually. We can...talk...about...about us, then I'll kiss you until you're sick of being kissed...then I'll kiss you some more."

When he turned the steering wheel, his arm jarred my head, and the street where I lived came into view. We rode in silence until my home came into sight and parked behind my father's old jalopy. I sat straight and moved away from him when he stopped the car.

"Do you mind if I don't walk you to your door?"

It took me a moment to understand the meaning behind his question, and I snuck a glance at his lap. My face heated with brashness. I bit my lip to hide a smile. "I don't suppose we're officially courting yet, so that won't be necessary." I glanced at the house, but no one peeked from the window. "I do expect a goodnight kiss." I gripped his thigh above his knee and leaned in.

"Oh, hell yes." He turned only his head while he clutched the steering wheel.

The kiss was hard and short, cramming as much as we could into a few moments. I broke away with a ragged breath.

His nostrils flared as he licked his lips. "Goodnight, Claire, honey."

****

Ben lit a cigarette with a shaky hand as he turned off Claire's street. After rolling down his window, he slowed and reached across the passenger side to roll down that window, too. He needed some damned air.

The cigarette hung from his lips. He had one hand on the wheel, and with the other he rearranged himself to relieve some of the throbbing.

"Son of a bitch," he muttered and inhaled the smoke deeply. Hell of a good thing he'd be out of town this week. By the time he got back, she'd be eighteen. Then…

Could life get any better? A beautiful, young woman, sweet and passionate to spend his time with waited for him; another raise coming with the promotion to foreman. No, life couldn't get any better.

Someday, he'd own the business.

And Claire? He'd marry her.

Chapter Twelve
One Last Kiss

Concentration battled daydreaming all my waking hours. The week without Benjamin dragged on like months. This afternoon, as I reclined on my bed next to the open window, the curtains lifted up with a stiff breeze. Daydreaming won out. Thoughts of Benjamin consumed me.

"Claire." Da tapped at the bedroom door.

I continued staring at the curtains reaching for the ceiling, literature book on my chest. "Yeah, Da. Come in."

"Look what I brought home."

I peeked over the book. "That's a healthy looking bird."

He proudly held up a whole chicken by the legs. "He's for your birthday dinner." His eyes twinkled.

"My birthday dinner?" I sat up and the book fell to the side.

"For tomorrow. *I'm* going to fix *you* a birthday dinner." I must've had a rather blank look. Da laughed. "Did you forget it's your birthday, gal?"

I yawned and rubbed my eyes. "I guess I did." A birthday seemed an inconsequential event in the timeframe of the weekend. Only Benjamin's arrival mattered.

Two more days.

Paulie mentioned Benjamin was due home on Saturday, one day after my birthday as promised.

Excitement swept over me, and I jumped off the bed. Da didn't need to know my excitement stemmed from Benjamin's return from his out of town job. Let him think the chicken dinner sent me dancing.

"Tomorrow is my *birthday*!" I did a pirouette. "I'll be eighteen."

I grabbed the wings of the bird, now Fred Astaire, and did my best impression of Ginger Rogers. My father erupted into a fit of laughter.

****

"Aahhh!" Paulie's mouth opened wide in a noisy yawn. "I could kill my brother." With her elbow on the school cafeteria table, she rested her cheek in the palm of her hand while slowly lifting a spoon of macaroni to her mouth with the other.

"Richie got you up early?" I buttered bread.

"No, Ben woke me up last night when he got in, and I couldn't get back to sleep."

I dropped the knife. "Benjamin's home?"

"Oh, yes, thrilling, I know." She chewed her macaroni with equal enthusiasm.

"I didn't think he'd be home until tomorrow."

"Well, new love of his life, he rushed to get the job done so he'd be home a day early." She took another bite and talked around her chewing. "Said he had some special shopping to do. I suppose you can guess for who."

My appetite instantly vanished. I tossed the bread on top of the macaroni and pushed the tray aside. "Honestly? What did he say?"

Paulie rubbed her eyes as she yawned again.

"That's about it."

We'd never had a telephone. I'd never cared, but right then, I wished we had one. "Do you think he'll come over tonight?"

She shrugged, took a drink from her milk carton, pushed her chair from the table, and picked up her tray before smiling with droopy eyes. "I've got to get some books before class. You'll see him tomorrow at dinner, Claire."

The afternoon droned on. I stared out the streaked windows of my classrooms more than I looked at the teachers or the blackboard. If Da hadn't planned a special birthday dinner for me, I'd have invited myself to Paulie's after school. Would Benjamin be as anxious to see me, as I was to see him? Could he wait until I went for dinner on Saturday? I imagined time after time our first embrace, his arms wrapped around me and his lips on mine, until the last bell rang me back to the classroom.

Paulie stood over me. "Come on, birthday girl. Or I suppose birthday woman."

I gathered books from the desk.

"Why won't you let me throw you a party? I could still put one together by tomorrow night," she commented as we entered the busy hall. "Coming over for a dinner with my family is hardly a celebration in honor of such a milestone birthday."

"Da's dinner tonight will be celebration enough. I know he's baking a cake, too, which should be amusing." I smiled at the thought. "He thinks it's a surprise, but I heard him ask our neighbor if she could give him *directions* for *building* a cake."

Paulie laughed as we walked down the stairs

outside. "You could've asked Momma for something better than potato and egg dumpling soup for dinner. We have that all the time."

An ordinary dinner with the special people in my life would be the best celebration. If I had to share Benjamin with all his friends, I'd have gone crazy. Dinner would be hard enough to endure, then maybe some games in the living room, which might allow for talking along with some discreet touching. Finally, he could drive me home, and we could have some time alone.

An excited shiver ran through me. "I love your momma's—"

Surprise whipped the words from my mouth. Lady Blue sat in a parking space at the bottom of the steps.

"Hey, double trouble," Benjamin called to us from the cement bench under the olive tree in the courtyard next to the building.

I shaded my eyes as he rose to his feet and walked toward us. My stomach tightened as fingers of pleasure tickled across my chest. His blue shirt, the sleeves rolled to his biceps as always, mirrored the sky— neither of which could compare with his eyes. Complete joy flooded me with the notion he couldn't wait until Saturday to see me. I nearly laughed out loud.

"Why, Benjamin, whatever are you doing here?" I asked as he stopped in front of me.

"I thought you two might like a ride home for a change." He gazed steadily at me as he lifted the books from my arms.

"Since you haven't taken my books or even said hello, I'll take it you don't really care if I'm along for the ride or not." Paulie thumped him on the shoulder.

"I'm still peeved at you anyway, which means I really ought to intrude on this homecoming, but I'm too tired to mess with you." She turned her back on us and sauntered over to the bus.

I heard her, but Benjamin's nearness had voided any ability to respond. Vaguely aware she'd left to board the school bus, I fell in step beside him. "I didn't think I'd see you until tomorrow."

He freed one hand to take my fingers into his. "I couldn't wait that long." Squeezing my hand, he led me to the passenger side of his car, opened the back door, and tossed the books on the seat. I grabbed the door handle. He quickly nudged my hand aside. "My pleasure, Miss Flanagan."

I scooted onto the seat. "Why thank you, Mr. Russell."

He leaned down, his face mere inches from me. When I inhaled, I could taste him. My stomach fluttered with the manly aroma, and my mouth watered.

"Happy birthday, Claire." He softly kissed me. When our mouths parted, he stayed close, his breath hot on my mouth.

My hand went around his neck to bring his lips back to mine, eliciting a deep, throaty moan from him. I hungrily took as much of him as he could give. He returned the kiss, my heat growing with each discovery our tongues made.

When he broke away, his breath came in short bursts. "Christ, Claire. Let's get out of the school parking lot."

While he walked around the car and got in, I needlessly smoothed my blouse more to still a racing heart than to straighten clothing. Tight breasts strained against my bra and made me smile with the sensation.

The engine came to life, and he gazed down on me. "Do you have to go straight home?" His voice, smoky with emotion, fogged my senses.

Desire surged through me—the same desire mirrored in his eyes. Da wouldn't be home for another hour and a half. Stomach flutters rippled through me with the meaning behind Benjamin's question.

"Mostly." I dropped my gaze. "But maybe a short detour would be okay." A slight embarrassment over the brashness of my motive for approving the detour quickened my breath.

"I'll take whatever time you can give me." He backed out of the parking space and darted a glance at me as we left the parking lot. "I missed you."

"I'm glad." I scooted closer. "All I could think about all week was you, and if you hadn't missed me, well, I'd be an awful mess."

"I did think of you all week, and I'm an awful mess anyway."

I laughed. "Good."

He made a left off the road onto a wide dirt path leading to the canal bank. We bumped to a stop and sat staring at each other. I could hear my heart above the engine idle when his hand left the wheel, grazed my knee, and he turned the engine off. Ben angled toward me, took a deep breath, and slipped his hand under my hair to caress my neck.

The goose bumps prickled beneath his fingers. I shivered. My eyelids fluttered. "Are we officially courting? Does this count?"

"It counts," he answered, the hint of a smile at one corner of his tantalizing lips.

"Aren't you going to kiss me some more?"

"Kissing is part of it." His words were throaty, as if fighting for room with his breath. "We have to get to know each other."

His hand continued to heat up my neck while his smile taunted. He obviously enjoyed teasing me.

"We need to take this slow. You're not yet eighteen."

"I am. Today."

"Well, then, that's why we start the courting today. But slow like."

His fingers tickled into my hair, inched along my neck, and sent jolts down my body. A small gasp escaped when my heart skipped a beat.

"And tomorrow?"

He brought his other hand to my cheek. "We'll see what we know by then." His fingers trailed along to my chin while he studied my face as if memorizing every pore.

My pulse raced. My mouth went dry. I longed to know him without delay. My eyes closed as I rushed in, took his hand from my chin, spread his fingers, and pressed his palm to my breast. "Then feel my pounding heart." I laid my other hand on his chest. "While I feel the beating of yours." Willing my nerves to still, I opened my eyes and stared into his. "All we need to know is this."

His teasing smile faded as his lips parted, and he drew closer. His hand burned through my blouse while his other hand inched up into my hair and cradled my head. I nudged his hand, repositioning his palm to cup my breast. His breath rushed from his lips in a moan; all the while, his gaze was riveted to mine.

"Your heart is beating very fast," I whispered, caressing his chest.

He responded with his fingers and gently massaged my breast. His thumb found my nipple and pressed into the hardness.

When his lips brushed across my mouth on the way to my ear and he nibbled on my lobe, a tremor traveled my body.

With his mouth hot against me, he whispered, "I'm going to kiss you. Once. Then I'm going to take you home."

I didn't know if he tried to convince himself or me that we could stop the heat building between us. In the few seconds he took to make the journey from my ear to my mouth, the anticipation of the expectant kiss built such a crescendo of passion another tremor stole my breath. His lips, soft against mine, revealed restraint, although, his hand on my breast told me he felt otherwise. My desire didn't know such willpower as his, and I pressed my mouth hard against his, wanting the kiss to be more.

My surge must have alarmed him, and he broke the embrace and gripped my shoulders.

He cleared his throat, took a deep breath, and shook his head as if to clear his thoughts. "If I get you home late, your father will tear me a new one."

I closed my eyes a moment, gasped twice, and finally took a ragged breath. How could he stop so easily? I wondered if he didn't feel as strongly as I did. Clasping my hands in my lap, I opened my eyes. "Are you sure that's why?"

"Why what, Claire?"

"Why you want to take me home?"

"I don't *want* to take you home." One hand slid from my shoulder and came dangerously close to my breast as his other hand tipped up my chin. "You have no idea how difficult it is for me to let you go. No idea."

His fingers slid over my breast on the way to my waist, and I shivered.

"Your father has a special dinner planned. I have too much respect for him to steal his time away from you." He kissed me quickly and ran a finger over my bottom lip before taking hold of the steering wheel.

I longed for more, would have stolen the day for us if he'd not been so level-headed. "He likes you, too."

"Damn good thing 'cause he's going to be seeing a lot of me." He backed the car onto the main road. "Starting with tomorrow night."

I wrapped my arms around his bicep and rested my head on his shoulder. "Will you drive me home after dinner?" My thoughts ran to coming back to the canal bank in the dark.

"I'll pick you up." He kissed the top of my head. "We'll have dinner, and after, I'm taking you for ice cream and coffee at Buddy's On Grand."

I squeezed his arm as I settled in against him with a contented sign. My eyes drowsily closed with comfort.

He bumped his arm, jarring my head. "I thought you might be a little more enthusiastic with my plans."

"Benjamin—"

"This is the first time when I've asked a girl out she's fallen asleep on me." He snickered.

"Benjamin Willis! You know perfectly well...I'm perfectly...well—"

"Perfect." His smile melted me. "You're that,

Claire. Perfect."

****

"Da, that was a superb meal." I patted his hand on the table across from me.

He shrugged. "Chicken might have been a little tough."

"Oh, no. It was delicious. Now I know you're such a good cook, I think I'll hand over cooking dinner every night to you."

"Don't think your compliments can fool me into that one." He laughed and pushed back from the table as he scooped up our plates. "Besides, you ain't had the cake yet." He left the dishes on the kitchen counter then picked up a plate with a bowl turned upside down to hide the dessert underneath. A wide smile creased his face. His eyes brightened to shamrock green as he made a production of placing the plate in front of me. "Chocolate frosting on yellow cake. Your favorite." With a flourish he lifted the bowl.

"Oh!" My hand flew to my mouth in surprise. Four fissures in a spidery pattern branched out from the center, two of them deep enough for chunks of the cake to fall outward revealing the yellow center.

Da muttered, "Ah, hell," but quickly recovered. "Well, I guess I built an earthquake cake."

Laughter burst from behind my hand. "I think we may as well both eat right off the plate since it's already neatly divided into pieces."

We dove in, laughing as we ate.

"You know, I'm going over to the Russells' tomorrow night," I said between bites.

He nodded. "I do, and I can take you."

"That won't be necessary. Benjamin will be

picking me up." I nearly giggled. "And after dinner, we're going to Buddy's for dessert. He'll bring me home after."

Da's fork stopped on the cake plate. "Sounds like a date."

"It is." I smiled.

"He's courting you?" His tone deepened to his serious discussion voice.

I nodded and matched the seriousness he projected. "Yes, Da, he is."

His brow furrowed in an obvious attempt to give me pause. But he couldn't hold the smile back for long. "You know I think he's a fine young man."

I licked the last of the frosting from the fork. "Good, because you're going to be seeing a lot of him."

"Hey, Hamish," the voice of our neighbor called out as he rapped on the door.

Da hesitated and took another bite of cake.

"Aren't you going to answer?" I looked toward the door and back to my father.

He ran a hand across his mouth. "I suppose." As he rose, he called out, "Coming, Al."

His reluctance struck me as strange, but I considered he must not want to interrupt our father-daughter time. Yelling for Al to come in for a piece of cake would've been more like him.

He opened the door wide enough to stick his face out and kept his voice low. Al didn't see the need for subtlety. The disturbing reason for his visit came across from his half of the brief conversation. My father looked like a whipped puppy dog when he came back to the table, avoiding my eyes. He carried our forks to the sink.

"You lost your job?"

He took hold of the cake plate.

I held fast onto the plate to keep him facing me. "Da?"

He rubbed his face in the habitual circular motion and wouldn't meet my gaze. "It's, well, it's like this…"

"Yes? Like what?"

"I, uh, well, I…" He glanced at me and grimaced. "Got my hours cut back."

"When?"

He cleared his throat. "Last week."

"Da!" I hopped up. "Why didn't you tell me?"

"Ah, honey. You been so happy since you got back, and it was nearly your birthday. I didn't want to worry you, gal."

As much as my heart tugged with the thoughtfulness of his concern for my feelings, I wanted to scold him for not including me in what, ultimately, affected both of us. "Surely, you didn't think you could keep it from me forever?" When my reprimand was met with another circular rub to his face, I continued. "Never mind now. Sounds like Al has a possible job for you?"

"They're hiring where he works. I'll get down there on Monday and check it out." He stood. "We're not going to worry about that now, not on your birthday." He squared his shoulders. "Okay?"

"I suppose." This day had been as much for him as me. I sighed and took on a hopeful attitude for the new job Al could secure.

He lifted the cake plate as he winked. "Let's get these dishes out of the way before we miss *Inner Sanctum*. In fact, turn on the radio to warm it up."

"Okay, but you know that show frightens me."
Actually, the scary radio shows my father preferred had
stopped sending my head under a blanket years before,
although I hadn't let on to my father. He got a kick out
of holding my hand and pumping up my nerves for the
eerie parts.

Da snickered. "Well, you just curl up in a ball at
the corner of the couch and hold my hand, gal."

And I did. My life would be changing with
Benjamin the center of my world. These evenings with
my father would be fewer and fewer until they were a
memory. So, I played the squeals more dramatic,
gripped Da's hand firmer, and relished his attention on
my eighteenth birthday.

****

Ben opened the back door to throw some cans into
the trash bin. He carried a beer in one hand. He wanted
to sit on the back stoop and watch the sun sink behind
the cottonwoods. Apparently, Ruth had the same idea.

"Hey, Ruth." The cans noisily settled to the bottom
of the bin. "No work tonight?" He sat beside her and
took out his cigarettes from a pocket.

"No, thank God. Friday nights are the worst with
all the teenagers piling in." She sipped from her bottle
of beer. "Give me one of those," she said, reaching for
his pack of cigarettes.

Ben lit both of them. They stared silently at the
tops of the trees, their smoke making lazy swirls above
their heads.

"Lucky you're the manager and can call your own
hours."

"Luck has nothing to do with it, bucko," Ruth
cracked. "Same as with you. You think luck got you

247

promoted to foreman?"

"You're testy." He flicked ashes into the dirt beyond the step.

"Ignore me." She moved to the bottom step and leaned her back against the one behind her. "I don't mean to be."

"What's on your mind?"

"Nothing much. You don't want to hear anyway."

He moved to sit next to her. "Sure I do, sis. Problems at the restaurant or your love life?"

"Neither. It's Susan."

He tipped his beer for a swallow, wiped his mouth, and leaned back. "I can't imagine there's anything wrong with *her* love life."

"Nice." She smirked. "She's not as promiscuous as you think."

He blew smoke over their heads. "What makes you think I think she's promiscuous?"

"Because that's how it sounded." His sister narrowed her eyes. "But she's strictly a one man lady."

He shrugged. Susan was fast and forward, but he had no reason to label her anything else. "I wouldn't know any different."

"She liked you, you know. Thought you were a lot of fun."

He didn't respond. Susan obviously hadn't given his sister the whole story. No sense going into the how and why of their former relationship. Her need for a strictly physical relationship and his need for more was ass backwards. "So, what's the problem?"

His sister stared at him for a moment as if considering her answer. "She's pregnant."

"Preg…pregnant?" A prickly heat spread across his

neck and face.

"Now we're talking luck, only not the good kind. She was in line for foreman, you know? Or at least under consideration. This will ruin her whole career. You know how hard it is for a woman to get that kind of promotion? Damned hard. She deserved every bit of recognition she got at the plant. Now this. Even if she keeps her mouth shut and gets the promotion, she'll get knocked down the minute she's showing. That's luck for you."

His head throbbed. "What's she…what are her plans?"

"I don't know if she has any yet. She's still reeling from the news."

Susan must not have discussed who the potential father could be with his sister or Ruth wouldn't talk so calmly with him. Maybe their friendship didn't extend to bedroom stories. Hard to believe Ruth didn't know about them.

"Has she told you, I mean, uhh, are you the only one who knows? Besides me?"

Ruth took a sip of beer. "I don't know, Ben." She gave him a sideways glance. "I probably shouldn't have said anything. You haven't seen her lately, have you?"

"No. I haven't."

She took a drag off her cigarette, letting the smoke sneak from her open mouth, drawing it up into her nose before it escaped into the air. "I hear you only have eyes for Claire."

With the mention of her name, his chest ached.

Oh, Claire. Susan is pregnant.

He dropped his cigarette at his feet and ground the ember out with his toe. "Yeah, Claire." As if he'd spun in a circle fifty times, the steps beneath him moved and his stomach was loose. He swallowed hard.

"Okay, don't confide in your big sister." She rose. "Just be careful, okay. No screw ups like Susan."

His head jerked, his throat tightened. "What do you mean?"

"Hell, Ben, you aren't that inexperienced are you?" She bent at the waist and poked a finger into his face. "You're too young to be a daddy, so take care, brother, with the young Claire. Got it?"

He slapped her finger out of his face. "Christ, Ruth."

She chuckled, mirthlessly. "See you later." The door slammed behind her.

He tossed his beer bottle into the trash bin. The glass clanged loud against the metal can, rousting a black bird from a mesquite bush on the edge of the property. Ben rubbed his hands together, studying the nicks on his knuckles from work. Maybe it wasn't his baby. Not like he was Susan's first. He could tell that much about her.

Yet, Ruth said she was a one-man lady, and she was damned serious on the point. But how much did she know? Ruth didn't let on if she knew about his relationship with Susan. Or maybe that's why she told him—gave him the chance to make the decision. He did the math in his head from the time they were first together.

"Hell," Ben sighed. *Susan's pregnant.* "Son of a bitch."

"What's the matter, Benjamin?" His mother's voice came from behind him.

He rubbed his eyes, taking a deep breath before

turning around. "Nothing, Mom."

She stepped onto the stoop, untying her apron and pulling the water spotted cloth from her waist. "Something's wrong or you wouldn't be sitting here swearing to yourself." She sat next to him, wadding her apron into her lap.

His emotions choked him. Wouldn't he love to spill his problems on his mother? She'd been able to fix nearly everything gone wrong in his life up until now, but there would be no easy fix to this.

They sat in silence until she wrapped her arm around his, nudging closer. "Whatever's troubling you, you'll figure it out."

"Don't know about that, Mom." He cleared his throat. He couldn't remember the last time he cried, however, the urge was strong. Maybe if he folded himself into her arms and cried out his misery, she could find a way to right this situation. She'd have to work magic. "Sometimes, it's real hard knowing what to do when the decision is between listening to your heart or your head."

She patted him. "That is a tough one. Guess you have some heavy thinking to do."

"I guess I do."

"Nothing I can do to help?"

He squeezed her hand and kissed her cheek. "No, Mom, but thanks. This one's all on me."

"Well, then, I'll leave you to it." She stood. "Benjamin." Her hand cupped his chin and tilted his face upward. "You'll do what's right."

He nodded with a heavy sigh. The back door closed quietly behind her.

Gazing out across the scrubby grass and dirt yard,

he scanned the cottonwoods and the darkened sky above. The sun, no longer visible, remained as only a bit of light securing the trees to the blue of the sky. Purple shadows fell along the ground beneath. As the shadows grew heavier and darker, so did his mood.

Chapter Thirteen
What Might Have Been

Ben's hand rested on the telephone receiver for the third time that day. Every time he tried to call Susan, Claire's smoldering eyes came to mind. He remembered the way she tasted; the heat of her skin beneath her dress against his hand; the fullness of her young, unexplored breasts. The receiver became a twenty-pound weight he couldn't lift with one hand. His throat tightened, and he doubted he could force the words into his dry mouth.

He sat back on the couch, his hands in fists, and stared at the phone. Susan wouldn't come to him. She was headstrong and independent. She was also a woman alone, and he knew what he had to do.

Later.

Claire came first. She would be the first to know his intentions because he loved her. Loved her and could never have her. She wouldn't share his name, his bed, his life. Their life. He wouldn't hear her singing in the next room of the house he would build for his family. She wouldn't have his children.

His chest heaved as he swallowed down the remorse of his fate.

****

From my room, I heard the exchange when Da answered the door. The small talk pleasantries sounded normal enough. I checked my hair in the mirror one more time before practically bounding out the door of my bedroom. I entered the room, all smiles with eyelashes fluttering. They stood beside the couch, Da leaning on the back, Benjamin appearing stiff in his stance. His head jerked up with my entrance. His cornflower blue eyes were shadowed.

My giddiness nearly blinded me to his somber mood.

"Here she is, the birthday gal," my father said, waving at me.

"That's old news, Da." I kissed him on the cheek, my eyes still focused on Benjamin's serious face. My chest tightened. Something was wrong. "How are you today?"

"Fine." His gaze swept over my face. "You're beautiful," he murmured. His tone belied the fact my father stood between us.

I wanted to thank him with a kiss, the thought of which both excited and embarrassed me. He may have forgotten my father was in the room, but I certainly hadn't. Da fidgeted, looking from me to my date and back, finally clearing his throat.

Benjamin blinked, holding his hand out to me. "Ready to go?"

The anxiety in my chest didn't subside with his touch or the suggestion to leave. His voice was uncharacteristically flat.

He switched my hand to his left, sticking his right out to my father. "Sir, it was good seeing you again. I won't have her home late."

Da pumped his hand and patted him on the back. "Thank you, Ben. Appreciate your thoughtfulness." He winked at me.

Benjamin's tension translated through his grasp. His silence heightened my worry as we walked across the yard to his car parked on the street. I told myself I'd misread his mood. He should be excited about our first real date and the time we'd be alone at the end of the evening. I longed for him to touch me, his lips to kiss me, and most certainly he desired me as much. At least, that's what I told myself.

"I'm glad you picked me up," I said, hoping for conversation.

He responded with a silent squeeze of my hand.

"Will there be anyone besides family at dinner tonight?" I didn't care who else showed up, but I needed to start a dialogue to quell my nerves.

By then, we'd reached his car. He opened my door, but blocked my entrance, still holding firmly to me. "I don't know." He peered at the gravel strip between the yard and the asphalt instead of me. "We…we need to talk before we get to dinner."

I played with his fingers in mine. Maybe the idea of some alone time before we went to his house had him distracted. The sun had dipped low behind his head, and I shaded my eyes. "I wouldn't mind a little side trip first." I wet my lips. "The canal bank road?"

He closed his eyes for a moment. When he opened them, no joy sparkled. He stepped back, leaving me to get in the car.

My heart contracted. I waited to speak until we had driven from the house. "Benjamin, what's wrong? What's happened?"

He gripped the steering wheel tighter than necessary. "We need to talk." He stared ahead.

I closed my mouth, clamping my lips tight as we rode in silence. He meant to park somewhere before he would explain, and there was nothing I could do except wait. Had someone died?

When we finally reached the road along the canal, he drove farther than our last visit. I gazed out the window and wondered if he was stalling for more time and why. The weak sun danced across the slight ripples of the water, skimming the surface without getting wet. A black bird hung on a branch protruding from the downward slope of the bank and cocked his head side to side as it checked its reflection.

The car at last glided to a stop, and he killed the engine. Still, he gripped the wheel and scanned my face. I waited, ticking off the seconds with each beat in my chest.

"I love you, Claire."

This was it? Good news, not bad.

I threw my arms around his neck. "Oh, Ben, I love you more than anything."

His eyes closed and his chin dropped, coming to rest on my arm. He continued his hold on the wheel, shoulders tense.

The dark cloud of his mood threw a heavy shadow on my joy. We should've kissed and hugged in celebration.

"For Pete's sake, Benjamin. I love you should be followed with a kiss." I released him, but shoved against his shoulder. "Is loving me going to be a bad thing?"

His hands dropped from the wheel. "I can't love you, but I want you to know I did." The muscles in his temples flexed as he clenched his jaw tightly.

Prickly tentacles crept across my chest and quickly closed in on my throat. "Whatever do you mean by that?" I gasped and touched his arm.

He opened his eyes and faced me with watery blue pools. "Susan is pregnant."

The words assaulted my ears like some foreign language and had nothing to do with our conversation. "I don't understand."

"Oh, honey." He took both my hands into his. "I was seeing Susan before…" He gulped and shook his head.

"Well, yes, but how did this happen?" I still needed a translator, a meaning for words totally incongruous to our situation. Benjamin had just told me he loved me, and I responded in kind.

"Susan and I—"

"I know *how*!" I jerked away from him. "I mean, *why*?"

"Why? I don't know why. I don't know anything except you." He drew me into his arms, hugged me, and buried his face in my hair. He breathed deep, one hand on the back of my head while the other held tight to my waist. His breath escaped raggedly.

I succumbed to his desperate caress while my mind raced. This had nothing to do with us. Susan's life was her problem, not his. Not ours.

"Benjamin." I wrapped my arms tightly around him. He kissed my neck through my hair. "Benjamin, why can't this be Susan's problem?"

He gave me one last hug, loosened his grip, and brought his face mere inches from mine. His eyes were watery, and once he'd lifted his face from my neck, I felt dampness in the hair against my skin. "Because I

Brenda Whiteside

was there. Susan didn't do this alone."

"But…but you can't love Susan." My voice, soft as a whisper, didn't betray the rising fear boiling up from the pit of my stomach.

He gripped my arms with emphasis. "No, I don't."

My stomach calmed a bit, the fear at a simmer. "Does she love you?" I had to convince him his thinking had clearly gotten off course.

"No. I mean I don't think so."

"Is she demanding you love her?" Love was everything. Without love, this wasn't our problem.

"No…"

His hesitation cheered me on. My panic churned barely below the surface as I led him down the path of reason. "Well, then, Benjamin, why—"

"Claire, I'll have to marry her."

"Marry?" I choked on the word. Fear and panic erupted. "Oh, God, no. Benjamin!" The tears toppled and flooded my cheeks.

"It's the only thing to do." His voice shook and his eyes were pools of darkness.

"No, it's not!" As more tears flowed, Benjamin's mournful face grew sadder. "This is *her* problem."

"You know it isn't, Claire." His words were thick and strained. "I have to take responsibility."

"No, Benjamin, no!" I slapped my palms to his chest as if I could stop this madness with a physical barrier. "No, you don't."

He encircled my waist, gently caressed, but held me firm until my tantrum played out.

I folded into his chest, but my anger still had some steam. I balled one hand into a fist and hit his chest. "Why? Why do you always have to do the right thing?

258

Why?" I swiped away tears so I could see his reaction when I glared into his face.

His chest heaved as he stared into my hostility with calmness. "You wouldn't love me if I didn't."

A sob broke free, and I collapsed back onto his chest.

"I'm sorry, Claire. I'm so sorry." He rubbed my back and spoke softly into my hair. "I'm sorry." He repeated it over and over, until my sobs subsided and I rested, spent.

When at last I found the strength to leave the comfort of his arms, I moved to sit up, but he held me close.

"I want you to know, honey, I will forever be sorry I've hurt you." He kissed the top of my head. "Know I will always hurt, *always*, when I think of what might've been." He let go of me, took my arms and righted me against the seat. He took the wheel, face rigid, then turned the engine key with shaking hands.

My arms hung limp at my sides. My legs ached as if I'd run for miles in circles. I had an overwhelming urge to go to sleep and my head bobbed with the effort to stay upright. "Take me home."

He didn't argue.

Exhausted, cried out, I rode quietly beside him, and stared blindly out the window. Numbness stilled my heart, and my mind went blank. My world stood silent, my life empty. Like looking out a small, round porthole, only a portion of the landscape was visible from my small, dark space...*tree, street, house*.

When he stopped the car in the drive, I opened the door without glancing at him. As I walked away, his voice sounded like a distant echo behind me.

"Goodbye, Claire."

****

"I'll get another job, Claire."

I ignored Da as I hauled in boxes I'd found behind the corner grocery store. I let the screen door slam behind me and kicked the front door shut with a foot.

He followed me to the kitchen cupboard. "I told you the place Al works is hiring." He tried to get me to look at him by edging in beside me.

I dropped the boxes and faced him, dusted my hands on each other, and knuckled fists on my hips. "And do you want to clean hallways and bathrooms?"

He opened his mouth and closed it with a shrug.

"Well, do you?" I snapped.

"It's temporary like, gal."

"Like everything else here." My hands swept the air. "No, we need to get back to California. We'll both be happier." I lifted a box, but Da grabbed the other side and stopped me.

"What in tarnation happened last night?" He yanked the box out of my grip, chucked it in with the others, then pointed a finger at me. "When you going to tell me about dinner?"

"You were at your poker game when I got home." Keeping my emotions in tact strained my voice. "I didn't go to dinner." My arms hung limp in resignation.

"But you left with...do I need to go take care of some business with Ben Russell?" His fingers curled into his hand, making a fist.

The sink counter steadied me as I leaned against the hard wood. "Nothing like that, Da."

His face wrinkled in concern. "Then what is it like? You don't just up and leave the state when you're all in love with someone."

"I'm not." I studied the metal button on his khaki shirt, not meeting his eyes.

"You said you was."

I turned my back to fuss with some dishes in the sink. "Benjamin and I...well, we...decided we aren't suited for each other."

His fingertips grazed my back. "Maybe you ought to stick around, make sure."

"Da! For Pete's sake." I whirled around, and he jumped back. "We're *going* to California. There's no reason for us to stay here."

He closed in on me again. My sudden outburst had startled him, but it hadn't convinced him. "You're nearly graduated, Claire. And what about your friends? Have you told Paulie?"

At the mention of Paulie, the front I'd put up for him crumbled. I sucked air to choke off tears and held my breath for a moment. I wouldn't be able to say goodbye. She'd only try to stop me, and I couldn't run the risk of seeing Benjamin again. Saying goodbye to Mrs. Russell would be as hard as seeing my best friend for the last time. The tears came in spite of my efforts. I buried my face in my hands and released hot breath into my palms.

Da draped an arm around my shoulders. "I didn't think you really wanted to leave."

"I changed my mind." I wiped a hand across my face. "Nothing is the same now. I can't stay here."

The lines in his face etched deeper with worry. "Ah, Claire—"

"We can stay at Aunt Grace's. Even if Uncle Eb doesn't need any help, I'm certain you can find work on one of the farms without having to go too far. With the way things seem to be coming back to life since the war ended, there might be a job in town for you, too. At least we'll have family to stay with until we can save a little and get a good place in town to live. As soon as I graduate, I'll get a job."

He rubbed his hand in a circular motion over his face; rough skin against a two-day old beard sounded like sandpaper. "I don't know, gal."

"I do." I patted his shoulder and left the shelter of his arm to pick up a plate. "My plan is solid."

He sighed; the wrinkles in his forehead relaxed. "Don't guess there's much sense fighting you when you have your mind made up." His mouth turned up at the corners. "Looks like you got it all worked out."

"Not entirely, but it's a start." Words were my beginning. If I had a plan, if we made a new start, maybe eventually the pain would go away. I doubted I'd ever be truly happy on the inside, so for now, I'd work on appearances.

He patted my shoulder and tipped his head into mine. "Are you sure, gal?"

I merely nodded at his rhetorical question. His face relaxed. His worry lessened with the thought of moving back to California.

I bent for a box. "Here, get started on your bedroom."

"Aye, aye, captain."

"Da," I called before he disappeared into his room. "I know you should give notice at your job, but I'd really like to hit the road tomorrow. Is there anyway…?"

He studied his shoes for a moment and rubbed the

toe of his scuffed, brown lace-ups on the back of his pants leg. "I think, sure, that's not a problem." He shifted the box from one hand to the other without meeting my eyes.

"What?" My father couldn't keep anything secret for long. His behavior told me if I pressed him, he would cave. "Da?"

He backed up a few steps. "I'll just get on with packing."

"You got your hours cut, right?"

The neck rub expanded to include his face, but eventually he met my gaze. "Oh, I got them cut all right. Cut to none." My mouth dropped open, so he quickly continued before I could scold him for his previous half-truth. "Now, don't go getting all excited. I told you before, you was too happy for me to spoil it with that kind of news. I figured Monday I'd have another job and none would be the harm."

We stood in silence for a moment. Being angry with him was senseless at this point. "All right, Da." There were no longer any obstacles to our quick retreat. "Looks like our move is meant to be." If only wrenching out my heart was as easy as pulling up roots.

I turned back to packing the kitchen as he scurried off to his room, obviously glad to avoid any further reprimands I might dish out.

Packing didn't take long. Our belongings easily fit in our car. Normally, I would've been singing while emptying things from the painted white cupboards and drawers. However, the lump in my throat had lodged itself tight and choked off any musical notes threatening escape.

The hardest thing to pack, to remove from once

comfortable surroundings and whisk off to neutral territory, was my heart.

****

Ben sat on the front steps and smoked while a pair of quail pecked in the dirt beneath the bougainvillea.

"Benjamin?" His mother called out the open kitchen window. "Wouldn't you like something to eat?"

He exhaled smoke and shook his head. "No thanks, Mom."

Even though he hadn't eaten dinner and then stayed in bed for breakfast, the knots filling his stomach didn't leave room for food.

The screen door slammed, sending the quail off in a flutter.

"Ben, I think it's time you told me what happened with Claire last night." The pipsqueak clomped up behind him.

"Damn it, Paulie." The flurry of gray wings disappeared over the eaves of the roof. "Do you have to be such a frigging bull all the time?" His little sister was the last person he wanted to talk to right now. She and Claire were so close; his chest grew heavier just having her near.

"Bull?" She sat heavily beside him, arms crossed on her chest, and rested her elbows on jean-clad knees. "Excuse me, buster! What's your problem?"

"You, maybe." He flicked his cigarette into the dirt at the bottom of the steps.

"Ben—"

"I'm in no mood for talking. Leave me alone." He picked a splinter from the edge of the step. His voice trailed off with emotion choking his words. He'd never hurt like this before. The pain in his gut overwhelmed him.

She touched his shoulder and lowered her voice. "Tell me, Ben."

"Sorry, pipsqueak." He patted her arm. "I'm not ready to talk."

His little sister gave an exaggerated sigh. "Well, okay, but you know I'll get the whole story tomorrow from Claire at school."

"I suppose you will."

At the sound of a car coming up the road, Paulie stood. "Okay, I'll leave you alone. There's Laura. You get off easy."

Ben waved at Laura's brother as he U-turned in the road and headed back the way he came once he'd deposited her in the front yard.

"Hey, Ben."

"Hey, Laura."

She paused beside him. He didn't glance up, and thankfully she continued up the steps. "I hope you have your science book, Paulie, because I need help and I forgot mine."

"I've got it, but you won't get much help from me."

The girls' exchange was as if from a mile away as he stared into the bougainvillea and thought of the first time he'd kissed Claire beside the flowering bush. His gaze wandered over the flowers to the stand of cottonwoods. More than once he'd watched her appear or disappear into the trees from and to her home when she'd lived in the cabin court, before her stay at the Good Shepherd's...before he admitted to himself he loved her. He'd hated the short time away from her.

Claire, oh Claire. How am I going to get through

the rest of my life without you?

He buried his face in his hands, ignoring the creek of the porch slats beside him.

"You want to come over to Barbara's with me. Get out of here for a while?" Davie's voice intruded on his self-pity.

Ben cleared his throat and swallowed. "Nah."

His brother sat beside him. "Pretty bad row with Claire?"

He rubbed his face, propped his elbows on his knees, and stared straight ahead. The urge to cry jarred him. His brother's voice smacked of sympathy.

"I've got a little experience with woman problems, if there's anything I can—"

"Not these woman problems, you don't."

"Claire—"

"It isn't Claire."

"Now you've got me curious. If it ain't Claire, then who? And why didn't she come to dinner last night? In fact, why didn't you come to dinner last night?"

Ben coughed and rubbed his sweaty palms on his jeans.

"Let me help, Ben."

He hung his head, absent-mindedly rubbing a scrape on his knuckle. "Not a damn thing you can do, Davie."

"I can listen. That sometimes helps."

Ben looked over his shoulder at the kitchen window. Not seeing his mother, he turned back, and squinted at Davie. His brother stared back, his normally smiling face serious with concern.

He did need to lift some weight off his chest and his brother might be strong enough to carry a little.

"Susan's pregnant."

Davie blew a low whistle. "That clears up last night's mystery."

They sat in silence. His brother mimicked him, elbows on knees, staring down at the ground below them.

His heart wouldn't ease, the pain in his core wouldn't cease. If only there was a solution. He sighed. "Hell, Davie."

His brother shifted, cleared his throat. "When did Susan tell you?"

"She didn't. Ruth did."

He sat straighter and stared at Ben. "Ruth? I'm surprised the whole damn family doesn't know."

He met his brother's gaze. "I haven't been named yet."

"So, you *haven't* talked to Susan?"

"I know I need to, but…" Ben ran fingers through his hair.

"Claire." Davie's face softened in compassion.

"Yeah, she knows now. I'll go see Susan after work tomorrow." He couldn't do it today. His head pounded, and his heart was far from throwing in for his fated future.

"If Susan hasn't called you, maybe she doesn't want you to have anything to do with it."

He shook his head. "You know I can't sit still for that."

"I know. Wouldn't be right."

"Wouldn't be right."

The quail was back, pecking in the dirt under the flowering bush. Ben watched, not seeing while lost in his thoughts. Life had been perfect. But no one gets perfect in life, not really, not forever. If he didn't love Claire, his fate with Susan wouldn't be all bad. But to know what he could've had. Davie couldn't help. No one could. This was his life now.

"Son of a bitch, Ben. I don't know what to say."

"Nothing you can say." The birds ducked under the bush. Somewhere in the distance, a hound howled. He gazed into his brother's face. "Sure appreciate you listening. It did help."

Davie stepped onto the bottom step. "I need to get over to Barbara's. You sure you wouldn't—"

"No, thanks. I'm going to sit and feel sorry for myself a bit longer before I get my ass up and settle my mind on this."

"You know, if there's anything I can do…you know."

A strong hand gripped Ben's shoulder.

"Thanks, Davie."

With a last squeeze, his brother stepped away onto the dirt below the steps.

Ben stared down the road until the dust settled and Davie's car drove out of sight. The sun, directly overhead, flattened the landscape, dulling the colors, and stealing the shadows. Flat and dull like the life ahead of him. Claire could provide the color of enjoyment in any day.

"Let it go."

He rubbed away the burn in his eyes. Maybe he and Susan could find a life together. The pain would never go away, yet he had to learn to live with it. There was still the construction company to grow and build on. He'd have a child.

"I made you a sandwich." His momma sat a plate

and glass beside him. "And a glass of tea." She patted his shoulder. "Don't tell me you don't want to eat. Just eat. You can't solve problems on an empty stomach."

"Thanks, Mom."

The door closed behind her as he picked up his lunch. He broke off a corner of crust and tossed the morsel to the quail. The bread could have been cardboard and the ham salad paste for all the appetite he had, his taste buds as dead as his heart.

Tomorrow after work, he'd stop by Susan's. Set things right. His child would come into this world respectfully.

Chapter Fourteen
Retreat

Gazing again at Susan's front door, Ben flicked plaster from the hair on his forearm and muttered, "Ah, hell."

He'd sat in front of her apartment, engine off, for the last few minutes, half-hoping her old Ford wouldn't be parked in the driveway. He would've welcomed an excuse to put off seeing her another day. There'd be no turning back once he confronted the issue.

But the inevitable could no longer be stalled.

The one story, U-shaped building looked more like a trap than an apartment complex. Susan's unit was in the corner of the back portion of the U—in a corner, like he found himself. A picnic table stood in the center. A child's red tricycle turned on its side lay abandoned next to the bench. He loved kids, he reasoned. Susan wasn't a bad woman, just not his kind of woman.

Claire's sweet smile clouded his vision. He rubbed his chest to ease an ache for which there was no cure. An ache he'd have to own.

"Get on with it, Ben." He opened his car door and headed to her apartment.

"Well, look who the cat dragged in." Susan gave him a once over after opening the door to his knock. "Do you always clean up so nicely when you go visiting?"

"I'm not too bad today." He brushed at his pants. "At least you can see my face."

"And still as cute as ever." With one hand on the door, the other hand on her hip, she gave him a sideways appraisal. "What brings you to my neck of the woods?" Her hair was off her neck, tied in a kerchief, her white shirt and navy slacks uncharacteristic of her normal attire.

"Doesn't look like you've gotten out of your work clothes either."

She put a hand to her head and yanked off the blue scarf, her deep red hair exploding to her shoulders. "I haven't been home long."

"Can I come in?"

She frowned and hesitated, but opened the door wider and left him to close it behind them. "You want a beer?"

"Sure." He rubbed sweaty palms together while he waited. If only… "Ah, hell," he muttered and rubbed at his chest again.

A few minutes later, she returned with two bottles, one beer and the other a cola. Not the Susan he dated, although a positive sign. He took the beer without comment and sat on the edge of the sofa. A long pull of liquid further stalled his half-practiced speech.

"So, Benny." She flopped into the corner, brought a leg up, and gave him a quizzical stare. "What the hell brings you to me on a Monday night after work?"

"I should be asking you why the hell *you* haven't come to see *me*."

"If I remember right, you were the one to walk out of this very room. You didn't give me the impression we'd be getting together again." She tipped her chin and smirked. "Was I supposed to come crawling after the young Ben Russell?"

His neck grew hot with her mocking. "I'm not talking about that."

"What are you talking about?"

"Your condition."

"My con—" Susan's mouth hung open. She snapped it shut and chopped the word off with the click of her teeth. "Apparently, Ruth likes to blab to her younger brother."

"We talk." Ben clunked his beer down on the coffee table, irritation with the overly independent woman eased into his nervousness. "But that's not the point. You should've come to me first."

She took a sip of cola and gazed off into space.

He rubbed his palms together, cracked a knuckle, and stared at her. "Did you think I wouldn't find out? Did you think I wouldn't be there for you?"

"That's sweet." She met his stare. "Really."

"It's fact." He didn't care about sweet. A man met his responsibilities head on regardless of what his heart might argue.

"Yeah, I knew you'd be that way. I thought about telling you." She bit her bottom lip and shrugged. "I had a plan, but...totally unlike myself...couldn't go through with it."

"We can make a plan together."

Susan took another sip from her bottle. "It wasn't that kind of plan."

"It doesn't matter now. I appreciate you not telling Ruth all of it. This is news I should take care of with my family." He'd need them. As much as he knew he was doing the right thing, the regret of losing Claire could eat him alive without their love and support. "We can get married right away. I don't know what kind of wedding you've had in mind all of your life, but with the circumstances, I think we better make it a quick civil ceremony."

The corner of Susan's mouth turned up. "Oh, you do, do you?"

"The sooner the better." He glanced at her abdomen.

"Do you expect me to move in with your mother?"

Ben heard the sarcasm in her voice. "If you want, we can stay here. It's a nice place. I'll build us a house someday, more of a place for a kid to grow up." He searched her face. Surely, she wouldn't turn him down. It was his child, too. "You know Mom will still depend on some help from me, but you don't have to worry. I have a good job. You can quit work right away."

Susan laughed. "Hold on, hot shot." She sat her half-empty bottle on the coffee table. "Who the hell gave you the power of attorney over my life?"

He sat straighter and matched her smirk with seriousness. *Damn her independence.* Her attitude angered him, but at the same time her control over his future ramped up his nerves. "As your husband and the father of your child, I—"

"Step back, buster." She sat forward. "No one tells me if I can or can't work."

Her stubbornness couldn't change the facts. "They'll make you quit anyway."

Susan snatched her cola from the table. She tapped it against her leg in irritation.

He put his fingertips on her knee to calm her, but his own trembling within wouldn't still. "Look, no wife of mine needs to work. I can provide for you, take care of you and the baby. You don't need to worry about anything."

Her head fell back against the yellow-flowered sofa. "Oh, hell, Ben." She tilted her chin toward him. Her hair fanned out, her eyes softened, saddened. The soft, sad expression was quickly replaced by the more common acerbic smirk. "*Just Benny and me and the baby makes three. We're happy in our blue heaven.*" She chanted the line from an old song, inserting Ben's name instead of the song's subject. "You almost make that sound good. No worries."

"Why *almost*, Susan?" Ben lifted her hand from her lap. "I'll make a good father, and if you let me, a good husband." He'd made his proposal. Relief of getting the words out flooded over him as determination to accept a new future set his shoulders firm.

She pulled her hand from his and caressed his cheek. "Yes, Benny baby, you would. *If* you were the father."

****

"Ain't that the shits?" Da kicked the tire of our old jalopy.

I crooked my arm around his elbow and hauled him out of the garage. "Come on, Da. It's time we stopped for food anyway. Perfect timing."

"Ain't never perfect timing for a break down," he grumbled, following me across the street.

"They said it wouldn't take more than an hour then we'll be on our way." I didn't have an appetite, but had to get him to relax and eat. "We'll drive longer, but you can't do it without food." We'd been nursing the car along for the last fifty miles. Our one-day trip would easily take two, and we'd have to find some place to stay along the way.

"You're right, you're right." He patted my arm. "Just part of our adventure." He lifted his shoulders, picking his feet up in a peppy fashion. I wondered how long it would be before he grew tired of trying to cheer me up.

The café door jingled when we entered. One lone customer sat at the counter drinking coffee from a huge, white mug. We settled into a booth by the window. A matronly waitress in a pink skirt and blouse took our order. Da's cheery manner while probing me to find something good on the menu amused her. Her flirting with my father amused me. I ordered soup to appease him then mostly stirred the chunks around in circles, bringing bits of carrots and chicken to the surface. I gazed out the window. My chest ached with shallow breaths, and I wondered if Benjamin had thought about me today.

****

"Why the hell don't you have a phone, Claire? Why the hell!" Ben spat out as he sped from Susan's house to hers. He couldn't catch his breath with his heart hammering his chest.

Not caring how dirty he was from work or if his mother would wonder why he hadn't come home for dinner, he raced to tell Claire. Would she still have him? Oh certainly, she had to have known the relationship he'd had with Susan before he dropped the baby bombshell. Surely, that wouldn't be an issue. That he'd chosen Susan, if only briefly, had hurt her, but he'd had no choice. He meant only to do the right thing. His chest heaved, and he cursed himself for not talking to Susan first. Why the hell had he made the decision to talk to Claire before Susan? This all could've been avoided if only he'd gone to Susan first. If he'd known she'd slept with some other guy when they met…that never occurred to him. Her break up with the other guy was the only reason they'd hooked up at all.

"Son of a bitch!" He dodged a dog running out in the road.

None of it mattered now. Joy settled on him, and he practically bounced on his seat as Claire's road came into sight. He could already taste her lips and feel her warm body against his.

He jerked to a stop in front of her house, happy to see Hamish's car not there. Flinging his door open, he jogged to the door and pounded. It was quiet within. He pounded again.

"Claire!"

****

The sun had slipped behind the orange grove by the time we drove into Aunt Grace and Uncle Eb's yard. Da edged the car alongside the white picket fence. I warned him off parking too close to the wooden slats surrounding the house and yard. Aunt Grace always planted sweet peas at each post, and in the darkness, we couldn't see where the plants might be. With barely a glimmer of sun left in the sky, bright lights beckoned behind yellowed lace curtains, and the big, white farmhouse mimicked an oil painting find at the city farmers' market.

As we left the stuffy confines of the jalopy for the cool California air, Aunt Grace opened the front door with a rush of lamplight that spilled down the wooden steps and illuminated the flower-lined walk. She reached behind her back to untie her apron, set it on a table by the door, and patted at the sides of her hair as she scurried down the walk. Her steps were light for a tall woman in sturdy, square lace-ups. Uncle Eb followed in his slow, lanky gait.

"Oh, heavens. There you are." She waved both arms in the air. Her gray checked housedress danced around her legs in the breeze.

Da opened the gate. She paused only briefly to pat him on the cheek, then passed him by to envelope me in an enthusiastic hug.

"I expected you yesterday." She turned her head to her brother, still smothering me with her welcome.

"Had trouble between Blythe and Indio. Damned old clunker kept overheating. Ended up spending the night in Chiriaco Summit."

"There's nothing there but a one room market with a gas station. Where did you sleep?" Her eyes opened wide with worry. "Not outside, I hope. Chiriaco's the middle of the desert with snakes and coyotes and—"

"Calm yourself, Gracie," Da chuckled. "Not like we haven't slept outside before."

"Your daughter is a young woman now." Her eyes narrowed at her brother in reprimand.

"Don't you think I know?" He shook his head, mischief in the way he rubbed his face and dragged out the explanation to his sister.

"The wife of the owner of the general store invited me to sleep in their guest room," I said to assure my aunt. "Da slept in the car. It was a perfectly acceptable night."

She pursed her lips at my father's chuckle. "Look at you." She held me at arm's length then quickly drew me back into her embrace, my body like a rag doll. "You're a beautiful woman. Oh, I've missed you so." Releasing me, she stuck one arm out and hauled Da closer. "Hamish, I'm happy to see you, too."

My father snorted. "Yeah, I can see that all right, Grace."

She kissed my forehead and released me. Both her arms went around Da. "I'm always happy to see my little brother."

"I know, I know. Don't go getting all mushy on me."

"Oh, you." She pushed him back and addressed Uncle Eb who had been leaning against the gatepost, twirling a toothpick around in his mouth. "Eb, don't just stand there. Come help with the luggage and boxes."

My father stuck a hand out at his brother-in-law. "Good to see you, Eb. We don't need to get it all out. Don't need everything we own tonight."

A barking dog came loping out of the darkness beside the barn. "Enough, Jack." Uncle Eb scratched his head. "Some watchdog you are, you old hound. You're a mite late on the get go."

Da laughed. "Your hound hasn't improved any with age."

"Get out what you need then put the car into the barn for the night," Aunt Grace directed the men. "Eb, put Claire's things in the den and Ham's in Little Eb's room. You come with me, Claire. Bernice and Little Eb are up in their rooms and don't even know you're here. They'll be so happy to see you." She slipped her arm around my waist and kissed my cheek. "Oh, sweetie, I've missed you. Look how pretty and grown up you are. Are you tired?"

"Maybe a little."

I gratefully leaned into her loving embrace, taking comfort where I hadn't realized I needed. My head rested on her shoulder. Aunt Grace, taller than me and sturdily built, had the same broad shoulders and hair as red as my father's.

"I'm going to warm up some dinner while you visit with the kids. We'll get you tucked in with a full tummy. We cleared out the den and moved one of the twin beds out of Bernice's room. A lady should always have her own room. Hamish will bunk in with little Eb. The child sleeps like a rock so my brother's snoring will go unnoticed."

"Thanks, Aunt Grace." I raised my head from her shoulder to gaze into her soft gray eyes twinkling with the lamplight. "We hate to put you to so much trouble."

"Trouble?" She opened the front door and paused. "Lordy, child, I'm happy to have you back. I have to say, this is sudden, but that don't bother me none. Hamish was sketchy on the details. Although, he assured me he wasn't uprooting you without cause. Made it sound like your idea."

I sighed deeply. My eyes threatened to burn with tears at the thought of Benjamin.

"Never you mind right now. We'll have plenty of time to sort out whatever needs sorting out." She squeezed my waist, stepped away from me, and yelled up the stairs. "Bernice, Eb, get on down here. Your cousin Claire is here."

Bernice and Eb came barreling down the stairs, and we gathered around the large kitchen table while Aunt Grace reheated our dinner. The kitchen hadn't changed a bit since the last time I'd sat at the scarred, wooden table. The top, covered in a plaid cloth of green, blue, and red disguised the rough exterior of the table. The yellowed lace curtains, colored by age not grime, hung over the kitchen window and matched all the other curtains in the big, two-story farmhouse. Aunt Grace's cream pitcher collection lined the ledge around the kitchen on a shelf above the cupboards. Perhaps there were some new ones. I couldn't remember for sure. The memory of the Russell kitchen came to mind, tugging my mood down even as I relaxed onto a chair, comfortable with my surroundings.

Little Eb, a skinny ten year old with an untamed cowlick, wanted every detail about our trek across the desert. The way he hung on every word I said reminded me of Richie.

Melancholy settled on me.

Bernice, two years younger than me, preferred to gab on about her high school and the latest heartthrob. A younger image of her older sister, Mae, she looked bored with our news, but her eyes sparkled when we asked after her. Aunt Grace threw out a couple of questions about the activities I'd left behind, when she could get a word in. My brief, non-committal answers satisfied Bernice, and she'd launch into another story about herself.

I tried to listen, show some interest, even if the whole scene hit me like a spectator at an Andy Hardy movie. The concerned glances Aunt Grace slipped in my direction weren't noticed by anyone except me. When Da and Uncle Eb joined us, my cousins finally quieted, so I could tiredly eat dinner.

"I think since tomorrow is Wednesday already,

we'll wait until Friday to take you in to school to get you registered. Then you can start fresh on Monday." Aunt Grace leaned against the sink, wiping her hands on an apron. In the light, her hair matched Da's except brighter. She may have been older, but her skin hadn't weathered or gone ruddy. "After driving a day and half with Hamish, I think you could use a little relax time before getting back into your studies." She kept her gaze trained on me, the corner of her mouth ticked up a bit.

Da's head snapped up, his fork pointed in her direction. "Now, what's that supposed to mean?"

She laughed. "I know how you like to sing those old Irish songs when you're driving. The memories still haunt me from our trip out from Oklahoma as kids. You probably drove the poor girl crazy."

"Ha! That's what you think." He forked another bite of meatloaf. "Claire sings right along with me. We have us quite a time." He chomped triumphantly and nodded his head. "Tell her, Claire."

Their love of teasing each other lifted my spirits, so I joined in, and slyly winked at Aunt Grace. "You've heard the saying, if you can't beat 'em, join 'em?"

Her laughter rang as she dodged the napkin my father threw.

"Is this how it's going to be around here? Both of you ganging up on me all the time?"

"You might as well get use to it." Uncle Eb's long face didn't look away from his food as he spoke. He rarely smiled, but his slow drawl held mirth. "Bernice and Grace give me no peace."

"You reap what you sow in this life," Aunt Grace philosophized as she cleared the table.

Bernice stood to help her momma and snickered, "I guess Mae should've listened to that one."

"Don't get smart, Bea," Uncle Eb corrected her.

"I'm not. We're all family here."

"How's that, with Mae?" Da pushed back from the table.

I doubted my father knew what Bernice meant. I'd spent enough time with Mae, who was my age, one summer to know exactly what they were talking about. She had attempted to include me in on her frolics in the barn, as she liked to call them, but I hadn't been as boy crazy as my cousin back then. I'd walked in on her and the young men she entertained there more than once. Da wouldn't have been too pleased to know about the education I acquired that summer.

"Mae's married, Ham." Grace spoke with her back to us as she scraped plates. "She has a beautiful baby girl now."

"Who'd she marry, and why's this the first time we've heard about it?" He fingered a cigarette he'd rolled earlier while he dug for his lighter.

I kicked him under the table.

"Hey. What was that for?" He sat up straighter, clueless.

Little Eb giggled, and Bernice thumped her brother on the head.

Aunt Grace turned around, dirty plate in one hand, fork in the other. "I swear, Ham, you're as dense as a pig being fattened up for market. The marriage was a hurry-up affair. Not under circumstances which would allow for a proper invitation."

Da's lighter paused, flame flickering, cigarette hanging from his mouth. "Ohhh…"

"She married one of the fly boys at the aeronautics school who was here during the war. He was in the last class, never got into the action. But he stayed on. Got himself a job as a mechanic over in San Jacinto. That's where they're living now."

"I can't wait to see the baby." I hoisted up to join in the cleaning. My legs protested. "What's her name?"

"Ida Louise, and she's a peach." Aunt Grace took one look at me and threw her dishrag in the sink. "Let's get you settled in while Bea and Eb finish the kitchen. I'll tell you all about her."

"I could get her settled in." My cousin reached for an excuse to be relieved of kitchen duty.

"Thank you kindly, Bea, however, I'll take care of Claire while you finish the kitchen. Then back to the books."

My aunt put an arm around me and guided me companionably to the den turned bedroom. "She's the cutest little thing. And real smart, too. We'll take a day trip over there after you're all settled in, maybe next weekend, unless Mae comes here first. She doesn't stay gone from us for too long at a time." She chuckled, pleased.

"Good." I slipped an arm around her waist, affectionately, but also with weariness.

"You look bone-tired, young lady. I think you'd keel over if I took my arm from your shoulders."

My feet dragged with each step, her observation probably close to true.

"You should've spoken up. You didn't have to keep sitting there, talking."

"Sure I did."

We'd reached my new bedroom. The door swung

open with a creak and the glow of the table lamp across the pink flowered quilt whispered an invitation. "It's perfect." I immediately kicked off my shoes and padded on the braided rug to the bed. "This quilt is lovely."

"Oh, that old thing?"

"You made it, didn't you?" I plopped onto the bed and fanned my arms across the material, feeling the comfort a worn, handmade quilt offers.

"Years ago." Aunt Grace sat beside me, her hands folded in her lap. "If there's anything you need to talk about, you know, you can't talk about with a father, I'm here for you."

Her voice, so low and sweet, touched me. I had to offer her some sort of explanation for our sudden decision to move back to California. She wouldn't consider our temporary arrangement an imposition. I could see in her wrinkled brow and down-turned mouth a worry I needed to address.

"There is a man…was a man I loved." The words choked me. The two-day drive full of car problems along with Da's Irish tunes had managed to keep emotions at bay. Talking about Benjamin raked up feelings and clogged my throat like the dust from raking leaves. "It didn't work out."

She pulled me close, tucked my head beneath her chin, and rubbed in circles around my back. "Ah, hon, sometimes men can be cruel."

"He isn't, Aunt Grace." I lifted my head and gazed into her caring face. "He had…obligations."

Her brows pinched together in a question, but I had no desire to satisfy her curiosity. I'd reasoned the unfairness of my plight for two days, even while belting out Irish folk songs. There was nothing more to debate or discuss. I'd put distance between us physically, and in order to get the same distance emotionally, I had to stop giving voice to my pain.

I patted Aunt Grace's back and gently extricated myself from her embrace. "I'm fine." I stood and scanned my temporary room. "This is more than a bedroom, what with the couch and desk." A faded brown couch was flush against the wall under the window, and the mahogany roll top desk stood in the corner. "You'll miss the use of this room, won't you?"

My aunt shook her head and rose. She studied my face for a moment, lips pursed, but decided to follow the change of subject. "No, we won't. I've got another desk upstairs, and I moved everything we needed into it. Anything else we did in here can happen elsewhere." She smiled. "You have a good place to study, to get away from the kids when you want. Speaking of which, I better check to see if they got back to the books."

"Aunt Grace?"

She paused in the doorway.

The words wouldn't come, so I crossed the short distance between us and hugged her.

"You're welcome, sweetie." She kissed the top of my head. "Sleep tight."

I closed the door behind her, blocking out the sounds from the kitchen. The silence wrapped around me as I sank down on the quilted bed, so tired my body collapsed against the softness, and my eyes closed before my head hit the pillow. This old, comfortable place would allow me to start new. I would immerse my mind in studies and throw myself into chores around the farm, leaving body and soul no time or energy for thoughts of Benjamin.

And there he was again.

I jiggled my head to shake him loose and opened my eyes. Above me was the pink ceiling. Aunt Grace hadn't changed the color in probably twenty years. The farm and her pink ceiling were the last things I cared about a few months ago. Now, I felt protected under the roof of this old farm, comforted knowing nothing here had changed. The ground beneath me and the routine around me would afford a solid base to find my new direction, nurtured like the chickens and fruit trees. I smiled at the thought even as a tear escaped the corner of my eye. I swallowed hard. The last tear.

****

I slept late on Wednesday, took my coffee to the front porch, and sat on the steps. Fatigue and the dark last night had blinded me to the bright flowers lining the walkway from the fence to the porch. In the light of day, pansies sparkled yellow, red, and purple. The last time I stayed at the farm, blue morning glory flowers had lined the walkway. Melancholy, my constant companion, rubbed my shoulders when I remembered Benjamin's eyes had reminded me of those blue morning glory flowers the first time I'd seen him. I shrugged off the feeling and declared pansies were the better flower. No memories there.

Without my two cousins around, the day passed quietly. I helped Aunt Grace cook, garden, and mend some of Little Eb's shirts. She didn't press me for more details of our sudden appearance. Her news of all the happenings in Hemet since my last stay entertained us. In turn, I related tales of the talent contest and my favorite movies.

I slept late again on Thursday, and on Friday, Aunt

Grace drove me to school where I enrolled in East Meadow High.

Uncle Eb steered my father to an olive tree farm close to the mountains east of us. After two days of picking olives, he decided being a security guard hadn't been so bad after all. Da decided his full time days of harvesting crops might be at an end. Monday morning, he planned to drive into Hemet to apply for a job at the Lake Hemet Water Company.

Unpacking, storing our few belongings, and getting our clothes washed and ironed filled most of the weekend. When I needed a break, I would wander outside to reacquaint myself with the farm. Uncle Eb grew oranges, but Aunt Grace grew a host of other things for the family's use. The only vegetables left in the garden hid under the rich, dark earth. The remainder of the potatoes could be dug up, but the parsnips and carrots would go another month at least. Fruits and vegetables harvested earlier could be found lining the walls of her extensive pantry, canned for use until harvesting came again.

I enjoyed digging up the potatoes. Shunning the gloves my aunt offered, I relished getting my fingers into the soil. Those potatoes nestled under the earth, like I nestled into the farm, until ready to come up for light. Bernice showed me how to feed the chickens and remove eggs out from under them without getting my fingers bloodied by a mad hen. Her technique didn't work for me. I'd discovered singing soothed the jittery cluckers.

Sunday evening, I accidentally wandered onto what would become my favorite spot on the farm. After dinner, dishes washed and dried, Bernice and Da sat down to checkers. Uncle Eb and Little Eb listened to the radio, waiting their turn to take on the winner while my aunt settled nearby with her needlepoint. I took a sweater hanging from a row of hooks by the back door and ambled up the rise to the barn. Although the temperature was mild, probably no cooler than Phoenix, the lush green surroundings with the view of the mountains compared to the desert, tricked my mind and put a pleasant chill on my bare arms. I intended to walk toward the San Jacinto Mountains east of the farm.

My relatives' property didn't lie exactly in the foothills, but close enough if you walked eastward, the ground took a gentle upward slope. The barn sat on the highest point. Other than machinery that I guessed had something to do with planting and picking, only wilderness spanned the land from the barn to the mountains. The orchards grew from the house west and south.

I walked the path through Aunt Grace's garden then up the rise to the barn. As I passed the corner of the sturdy, red structure, I paused to take in the view. From my vantage point, I could look slightly back and down on the white farmhouse, the light from the windows now brighter than the setting sun. In front of me, a meadow stretched to bushes, trees, and finally mountains in vibrant hues of green and gold, with a sprinkling of gray and brown. The peaks touched the sky, held the blue to the earth.

I allowed myself to think of Benjamin. What was he doing at this very moment? Had he and Susan rushed to the Justice of the Peace for a civil ceremony? Would he be settling down after dinner with his new bride, asking after her, thinking about the child they would share in a few months? I took a deep breath to smooth the ragged edges I dragged myself across. I had vowed not to speak about Benjamin. What good could come from giving voice to my inner misery? But I couldn't control where my mind wandered.

Resigned, I relaxed, and my gaze fell from the mountains to the ground beneath my feet. Stretching out a yard or so to my right, a tapestry in shades of green beckoned. Mother Nature had created a carpet of moss dotted with clover. I collapsed onto the soft blanket of variegated textures and leaned against the barn. My fingertips skimmed over velvety moss and ruffled clover. Benjamin existed a world away from this new life. I hugged my knees to my chest. Thinking about him while surrounded by the majesty of meadows giving rise to mountains took the sting out. Even if I'd left him behind, I could allow my mind to revisit him occasionally here.

Chapter Fifteen
Old Friends

The next few months were filled with activity at school or on the farm. If not happy, I at least enjoyed excelling at my schoolwork and exhausting myself with chores. The holidays came, which gave Aunt Grace the opportunity to teach me how to bake cookies and candy. Winter melted into spring.

When I needed a quiet moment of solitude, I would retreat to the back corner of the barn to feed my eyes with the beauty and let my heart linger over memories, memories more like scenes from a movie than reality. I took no interest in any of the boys at school or the men I encountered on the farm. No man caught my eye, until spring break when I visited my cousin in San Jacinto.

San Jacinto Drug and Fountain was the best thing the one street town had going. I scooped a bite of ice cream from my root beer float. Foam dripped from the spoon and the icy treat nipped at my teeth. The solemn manner of the druggist who doubled as the soda jerk suited me, leaving me to enjoy my float while reading a movie magazine from the stack at the end of the counter. A glass window spanned the entire front of the store, which sported cherry red stools and a white lunch counter. The bright, cheery atmosphere along with the sweet treats lifted my spirits without any effort on my part.

The sleepy, farming town of San Jacinto lay thirty-five miles north of Hemet, surrounded mostly by dairy farms. Cousin Mae, her mechanic husband, and darling baby girl lived a block over from Main Street. Uncle Eb had driven me from Hemet to spend the week of spring break with my cousins, and I'd acquired a taste for the floats my second day there. Each afternoon, as Mae napped with the baby, I'd take a walk and end up at the fountain for the sweet treat.

As I sucked in my cheeks at the first cold bite, I glanced out the window, and nearly choked at the sight of the man strolling by. When his gaze met mine, he stopped in his tracks. I froze like the ice cream. Only when Arnold pushed through the door, the bell jingling with his entrance, did I swallow.

"Claire! What the hell are you doing in San Jacinto?" He strode across the checkered tiled floor as he boomed out his greeting.

"I…I…would ask you the same question." I leaned back from him as he wedged himself between me and the next stool.

He sat and leaned into my space, one arm on the counter, the other hooked in his jean pocket. "I live here, at least for the time being. You should know that."

I briefly wondered if his dazzling smile and movie star looks had wowed the local farm girls in the valley. They didn't work on me. "Well, I don't. I thought you went to live on your uncle's farm in Minnesota."

"I'm on the farm, all right, but my uncle's farm in California. Here in the hopping community of San Jacinto." He touched my back. "Damn, it's good to see you."

I jerked, breaking contact with his fingertips, which

instantly erased his smile. "I'm not experiencing the same pleasure," I spat out between clenched teeth. "You caused me a world of trouble. I've a mind to knock you off that stool." I dropped my spoon into the root beer float then doubled my fists in front of his face. "Get the hell out of here and out of my life."

He raised his hands, palms out in defense. "Whoa, Claire. What trouble? I got banished to farmsville. How much more trouble could I have caused you than I caused myself?"

"Farmsville? This is the social capital of the world compared to where *I* ended up." I brought one fist closer to his face. "Don't play stupid with me."

He flinched, his forehead wrinkled. "I don't know what you're talking about. Were you sent here, too?"

His clueless expression convinced me he really didn't know what happened to me. I slowly lowered my fists, but continued to glower. "Go away, Arnold."

"My parents sent me here a couple of days after the cops took me home. I didn't get a chance to talk to anyone."

The anger firing my mood didn't diminish with his ignorance of how the mess he set in motion ended. "Just go away." I picked up the spoon, and jabbed at my ice cream in frustration. How absolutely unimaginable I ended up living within miles of him. I stared into the float glass and fumed.

He slumped on the stool, elbows on the counter, and his head in hands. "You don't know how much I've regretted what happened. I wrote you ten letters of apology, but tore them up every time without mailing."

I clenched my jaw, darted him a frown, and remained silent.

His hands dropped to the counter. "Please, tell me what trouble I brought on you, Claire. I saw you drive off with the lady. Is that what you mean? Where did she take you? What happened?"

My glare met his puzzled expression. "You honestly don't know?"

"I heard something from Laura's brother, you'd left Phoenix. That's all. He works in Yuma and doesn't have much to say about the kids back home."

I pushed the float away, and stared at the counter for a moment, not sure if I wanted to tell him anything. My chest ached with anger while my temples throbbed.

"Just tell me, Claire. Then I'll go away."

With a sideways glance through narrowed eyes, I studied him. He ran a hand through his hair. I couldn't help notice the muscles rippling in his bicep, more pronounced no doubt due to farm labor. His mouth tugged down at the corners, and his dark lashed, green eyes were mournfully smoky.

"Claire," he whispered a plea.

"I was taken from my father, from my home. They put me in an institution for troubled girls."

"Ah, hell." He leaned toward me. "Ah, hell, Claire."

My mood didn't mellow with his obvious discomfort.

Good. Let the remorse eat at him.

"Now, go away," I said, punctuating each word between clenched teeth.

He ignored my attitude and continued on like two old friends catching up on the news. "How did you end up in San Jacinto? Where's your father?"

I huffed a sigh. "I'm visiting a cousin this week.

Da and I live in Hemet now."

"So, after you got out of…that place, you and your dad moved to Hemet?" He stated as much as I'd let him know.

"Yes, now go away."

"You need something, Arnold?" The druggist sauntered up, ready to sell another float.

I whirled around on the stool and popped off. "Okay, you stay. I'm leaving."

Arnold declined the druggist's question as I strode toward the door. He made it out behind me before the jingling of the bell silenced.

"Wait, Claire."

I strode briskly, but his long legs outstretched my stride, and he appeared beside me. After a half a block, I resigned myself to not being able to out-walk him. "Don't you understand, I want nothing to do with you?" I slowed and glanced at our reflection in the dime store window.

"I do. I understand, but if you knew how I didn't mean anything to happen to you…all I ever wanted was you. Not to hurt you."

I stopped and turned on him. "What about Paulie? What about *her* feelings?"

He shrugged in resignation and frowned. "She kept at me all the time—"

"Oh, it's *her* fault." I sighed disgustedly and stomped away.

He caught my arm. "It's no excuse. I'm not excusing myself, only telling you how I was back then. I didn't do anything she didn't want me to."

I jerked from his grasp.

"Did she say any different?" He persisted.

I wanted to lie, make him squirm some more, but the truth was the truth. "No."

"Then you know I only tried to make you jealous. I know it was stupid. But as far as Paulie…well, I never told her I felt anything for her. I never led her on or made her think she meant anything to me. She knew how I felt about you. You have to believe how sorry I am I hurt her."

I wasn't about to let him know how quickly Paulie recovered from him. Their tryst upset me far more than her first experience with sex had upset her.

"I can't change what I did. But I've had a lot of time to think about it. Give me a chance to show you I've changed."

"You're joking." I snickered.

"What can it hurt? How long are you going to be in town?"

I shook my head and looked into the store window. His back reflected in the glass and blended with the display of children's toys. A child's red wagon intersected his knees and a kite suspended from the ceiling hung over his head. He stood silently beside me, hope radiating like a wall heater. As much as I loved playing with Mae's baby, much of the day I spent alone in boredom. The boredom gave rise to thoughts of Benjamin, which I worked so hard to avoid.

"Two more days."

"We could get together, couldn't we? Maybe I could come visit you at your cousins."

"No." Letting him intrude so far into my present life was out of the question. "It's a small town. We could run into each other again, and I might talk to you." I took a few steps, past the dime store, and left the sidewalk for the gravel of a breezeway between the line of buildings.

He walked easily beside me, frowned, and rubbed his chin. "Do you come here to the soda fountain every day?"

"Most days."

"You didn't finish your float." He nodded back toward the drugstore. "I'd be happy to buy you one tomorrow."

We strolled across the breezeway path, back onto the sidewalk, passing the post office. The least he could do was buy me a float. Or ten. Small payment for his past screw-ups. "If I'm here at the same time tomorrow, I might let you buy me one."

He smiled. "Good. Tomorrow."

"If." I flipped the hair from my neck. "*If* I'm here tomorrow." I turned at the corner to head back to Mae's. "Goodbye, Arnold."

"See you, Claire."

How ridiculous, I chided myself on the short walk back. How ridiculously stupid to even listen to Arnold's lame excuses, to entertain the idea of seeing him again. So what if Paulie hadn't actually been hurt by Arnold? Not deeply anyway. That didn't excuse his actions. Then again, her blasé attitude about the loss of her virginity with a man who had no emotional bond with her shouldn't bother me. But if he hadn't come to my house, made such a scene, I wouldn't have been taken from my father.

I kicked a rock in my path into the street. Oh hell, if it hadn't been the incident with Arnold, the old biddy would've found some other excuse. How lucky for me her sister worked at social services, willing to do her bidding. She had obviously put her sister on alert or my removal wouldn't have been so speedy. I couldn't hold Arnold solely responsible for getting me taken from Da.

He did seem different in some way beyond the obvious physical changes, which were hard to ignore. His smoothly handsome boy-ness had become more rakish. A few strands of his midnight-black hair, now a bit shorter, fell onto his forehead in a sexy kind of mussed fashion. His deep tan, from days outside on the farm, contrasted with his crystal green eyes. And he filled out his jeans and work shirt better than I remembered. Beyond physical manliness, his manner had matured, had mellowed.

Here in San Jacinto, we were both removed from all the ties, all the connections. But I'd brought my anger with me. Arnold was only a small part of the anger, even if I did want to direct it all at him. Life could have gone on after my stay at Good Shepherd. Paulie wasn't hurt; Benjamin loved me. The real reason my life had imploded, my world spun out of control, was the loss of Benjamin.

I swallowed hard.

I missed Phoenix. No matter how much I told myself otherwise, I couldn't get my heart around Hemet enough to make this home.

Like him or not, Arnold connected me to my real home.

****

The next afternoon, I edged past the brick wall to the large window of San Jacinto Drug and Fountain, but peeked in before entering. Arnold sat at the counter, talking to the druggist. He looked comfortable, and the druggist appeared interested in the conversation. My head told me to walk away, and I nearly did, but Arnold glanced up before I could get my feet to move.

He smiled, waved, and finished what he was saying as he rose and strode to the door before I'd taken a step. "There you are." His smile was wide as he held the door open. "Guess you got hungry for a root beer float."

"I can't stay long."

"Ah, Claire. Long enough for a float anyway." He extended an arm and directed me toward the counter. "Have a seat. Let's have two of your best root beer floats, Harry."

I settled on the same stool as the day before. The druggist still looked solemn, but apparently knew Arnold well enough to be on a first name basis.

Arnold rested his elbows on the counter then canted in my direction. "So, who's your cousin? I might know him."

"Her." I folded my hands in my lap. "Mae Reynolds. Her husband is Jess—"

"The mechanic? Jess Reynolds?"

"Yes. You know him?"

"Everyone knows everyone in this town. He's a great guy. Had him fix my breaks last month." He tapped the counter. "Small world. At least in San Jacinto it is."

His mood showed on his face and projected in the tone of his voice. I didn't mirror his joy. My reservations clouded the shine. I'd dreamed of Paulie the night before, no doubt brought on by encountering Arnold, and slept fitfully. I woke wondering if a connection to the home I missed would hamper establishing Hemet as my new home.

The root beer floats arrived. Today, there were two

cherries on the top with double the amount of whipped cream. I glanced up at Harry, but he'd already turned back to the druggist area. Arnold had some influence with him I guessed.

"Thanks, Harry." Arnold called to his back and was answered with a nod. "How do you like Hemet?"

"It's okay. Greener than Phoenix anyway." I ate the cherries with a healthy spoonful of whipped cream.

"How's school?"

I shrugged. "How's school for you?"

"I'm doing okay."

We talked like this for a while, comparing notes on our respective high schools. Both schools could've fit inside the grounds of North High in Phoenix. Arnold did most of the talking. I couldn't shake the doldrums from my dream. I didn't want to breach the fence of reservation I'd formed to hold him in place, and my stubbornness helped with my resolve.

"Glad to be out soon," he said. "Didn't exactly turn out the way I thought my last year would turn out, but hey, things work out."

I hadn't reconciled my life to that point yet. Surrounded by a loving family had taken some of the sting out of leaving Phoenix and all of my dreams, although, I still didn't know exactly how my life would work out. I hadn't found a way out of the vacuum created by losing Benjamin.

We ate a bite in silence.

"It wasn't so easy making friends with the chip on my shoulder I carried here." He took another bite. "But hell, I got over that and charmed my way into their hearts." He laughed.

I wasn't sure if he mocked himself or if the old

Arnold had reared his head.

"Are you going back to Phoenix?" I asked.

A corner of his mouth threatened to smile. "I was."

"Was?"

"Maybe I should hang around longer." He licked his spoon, cocked a brow. "Consider my options here. Or in Hemet."

"Arnold—"

He flashed a smile and took a quick drink of root beer from his straw. "Have you milked a cow yet?"

"It's a citrus farm. You milk cows?"

"Oh, you haven't lived until you milk a cow." He laughed. "I've squirted myself in the face and damn near been kicked in the head."

I laughed with him. The vision of Arnold under a cow, squirting milk in his face, cracked my cold reserve. "That sounds a little more serious than being pecked by chickens when I steal their eggs."

He held his right hand out, palm side down. "Nearly healed, but as you can see, I'm not much good at stealing eggs." We laughed. "Luckily, I don't have to get the eggs very often."

"I've learned to slip them out without a hitch. Those ladies are fond of Frank Sinatra songs."

"Wouldn't work for me. If I sang in the hen house, there'd be chickens squawking and feathers flying everywhere."

I chuckled. "Oh, Arnold."

He stared into my face, a familiar dreaminess in his eyes. "You still have the prettiest smile ever, Claire."

The last spoonful of creamy root beer stuck in my throat. I had relaxed with our easy conversation until he'd turned the dialogue into flattery. Old emotions rose as I swallowed the dessert with his compliment. I stared into my empty glass. "Don't flirt with me, Arnold."

"I'm not flirting."

"Oh, please."

"Since when is telling a woman she's pretty when it's the honest truth, flirting?"

"Since it's *you* telling *me*."

He wiped his mouth with the paper napkin then stuffed it into his empty glass. Leaning on the counter, he rotated on the stool until he faced me, his legs dangerously close to mine.

"The way I figure our situation is this—we're both a long ways from home. I've been here a lot longer than you have and still don't have any close friends, so I'm guessing you don't either. If we can forget the bad stuff in our history, we could be pretty good friends again. Something we could both use."

"Friends?"

"Friends."

I sighed and narrowed my eyes in doubt.

"I won't compliment you anymore, if that's the problem. I didn't realize my natural observant nature and willingness to share those observations are liabilities. I guess I can try to tamp it down." He tipped his head in resignation, lifted his hands in the air, and teased with a half-smile. "You'll slice a piece of my better side off, but far be it from me to—"

"Okay, okay." I laughed. "I've had enough of your better side for today. I need to get back." I stood.

"So soon?" He jumped up. "We could take a walk around the square of grass and trees they call a park. You really should see where they hold their outdoor concerts."

"Concerts?"

"I use the term loosely."

I was curious, but my head said to not over do time with him, even if he had declared us friends. "Not today."

"Tonight?"

"No, Mae has plans for us tonight." Dinner and the radio, same as always, but he needn't know.

"Tomorrow?"

"I'm going back to Hemet tomorrow." I took two steps backwards to make my exit.

He took two steps toward me. "When will you be back?"

"I don't know. We might visit some weekend, or I may not get back until school's out."

"I could visit you—in Hemet." When I didn't jump at the offer, he continued. "We had fun today, didn't we? I could sure use a change of scenery. Look around, Claire. Hemet's a metropolis compared to San Jacinto. You could be my tour guide and show me the sights."

"There's really nothing to see, Arnold, except the countryside. Wine country south and the lake in the mountains east of us."

"Then we'll have a picnic or take a hike."

"Well…I suppose some time that might be okay." I couldn't decide right then and there. I needed distance. Another step put me closer to the door.

He took a napkin from the counter and a pen from a glass by the register. "Give me your phone number and general directions to the farm. I'll give you a shout soon."

That night, I wondered if I should've left an

opening for Arnold to squeeze into my life again. He'd broken Paulie's heart, but I knew she'd offered it up even knowing he had feelings for me. He'd been drunk and stupid, and she shouldn't have gone with him. She'd told me he didn't force himself on her. And as much as I'd blamed him for my ending up in the Good Shepherd's Home for Wayward Girls, the old biddy Mrs. Snyder was the real cause of my trouble, not Arnold.

Could we be friends?

I wished I could talk to Paulie. Would she talk to me after all this time? Did she hate me for not saying goodbye, for not telling her where I was going and why? She would know by now why I'd had to leave. Benjamin and Susan's baby would be due in a couple of months.

My chest tightened. The sadness crept out of the darkness, so I grabbed the pillow from under my head, clutched it to my chest as if for protection, and hugging tight, breathing deep, forced visions of the meadows of Hemet into my mind. No, I wasn't ready to speak to Paulie yet. I couldn't. Arnold was a close enough tie, a glimmer of my old life. He was here and created a comfort level. Maybe in a few months, I could call Paulie. I missed her.

****

Two weeks later, the phone call came.

"Claire," my aunt called out while I squatted and weeded the garden.

I stood and wiped the dirt from my hands on my jeans.

"You have a phone call."

I could see the smile on her lips with a question in

her eyes. As I climbed the back porch steps, she held the door open.

"It's a young man," she whispered. "A very polite young man named Arnold."

"Thanks, Aunt Grace."

The phone hung on the wall in the kitchen. My aunt opened a cupboard and straightened dishes as I picked up the receiver hanging from the phone base.

"Hello, Arnold."

"Hi, Claire. Out playing in the dirt, huh?"

"Weeding. How are you?"

"Great now." His voice cracked with joy. "I wanted to know if you'd like to go to a play next weekend."

"A play? Where?"

"Hemet. My aunt tells me it's a lot of fun. It's called the Ramona Pageant, and it's up in the foothills right outside Hemet. What do you say?"

I wound the phone cord around my finger while I stalled. "Well, I don't know. The Ramona Pageant? Next weekend?" Out of the corner of my eye, I could see my aunt had stopped her unnecessary straightening of dishes. I glanced at her. Her mouth had opened in quiet exclamation as she nodded her head. "I-I suppose I could go."

"Great! I'll pick you up at two o'clock on Saturday. The play is outdoors. We sit in the grass so you know. I'll bring blankets and whatever else we might need. This is swell, Claire."

"All right, Arnold. See you then." A play, outdoors? I couldn't help but feel a lift in spirits as I hung the receiver back on the hook.

Aunt Grace clapped her hands together. "You have

a date?"

"Not exactly." I went to the sink for a drink of water.

She dipped her chin and frowned with obvious skepticism. "What would you call it then? And who is this young man?"

I filled the glass with water from the tap. "I'm going to a play with an old friend." I sipped before continuing. "Arnold is from Phoenix."

Grace put a hand to her cheek. "Now, he can't be coming from Phoenix to take you to see the Ramona Pageant."

I laughed. "No. He lives in San Jacinto right now. You know the play?"

"Yes, it's pert nearly the only play around. But he's in San Jacinto? I think we need to have some milk and cookies while you tell me all about this new development." She opened cupboards and removed plates, glasses, and cookies.

While we dunked chocolate chip cookies in milk, I explained about running into Arnold while visiting Mae. She didn't know about him because I'd not included him in what little I'd told her about our reason for leaving Phoenix.

"A friend is all he ever was to me, and all he ever will be, Aunt Grace, so don't smile at me like that." I could read her mind. It was far too soon to find someone to make me forget Benjamin. But Arnold made me laugh, distracted me from my constant state of melancholy, and since I already knew him took little effort to engage in friendship. It didn't hurt he seemed changed, more mature.

She patted my arm. "Am I so easy to read?"

"Like a book."

"Shame on me."

We laughed. "Tell me about the play."

"Oh, the Ramona Pageant." She put her hand to her heart, a serene expression on her face, as she stared into the air above her head. "I went years ago."

Aunt Grace had a romantic side I hadn't seen before. "Years ago?" I prompted, bringing her back to earth.

"Oh, dear, yes, the pageant. They've been performing this play every year since some time in the early twenties. It's up in the hills in the Ramona Bowl. Absolutely beautiful." She absently smoothed the tablecloth in front of her, her face sweet with memory. "You sit in the grass on the hills, and below you, hundreds of actors, singers, dancers, and horsemen act out the story of love."

"Hundreds? Horsemen?" I stopped dunking to listen. "That must be some stage."

"The hills, the rocks, the meadow—the earth is the stage." Aunt Grace gestured with her hands swooping through the air.

"It sounds amazing." Having never seen live actors perform, I found myself excited with the prospect of a play. The only doubt was if I'd make a mistake going with Arnold, even though his sincerity about our friendship rang honest.

"Oh, it's wonderful. The story is about Ramona and her Indian hero, Alessandro. Eb and I had such a wonderful time at the play. And so romantic," she sighed.

"Why Aunt Grace, is there another side to Uncle Eb I haven't seen?"

"Oh, lordy," she laughed. "The *play* was romantic, not Eb." She stood, picked up our dishes, and winked. "You'll have a great time."

"The play sounds like fun. But it's not a date." I pushed the chair from the table. "I'm going to finish the weeding before dinner."

Doubt and anticipation shared equal time in my thoughts as I leisurely plucked weeds. I stared off into the hills as much as I tended the garden. A play with hundreds of actors, dancers, singers, and horses was hard to imagine, but thrilled me when I conjured such an image. An afternoon with Arnold, improved and resurrected friend, boggled my mind just as much.

Chapter Sixteen
Her Nice Young Man

Ben relaxed back on the front porch, resting against the step above him. A beer sat between his legs, and he smoked, blowing circles into a cloudless sky. Through the open kitchen window, he could hear his mother hum a familiar tune as she cooked potato and egg drop soup. He needed to shower off the plaster dust caking his arms and hair, but his energy level was low, and all he wanted to do was sit.

Today had been one of those days. Claire had been on his mind almost constantly. The job hadn't required any concentration and allowed his mind to wander. And it wandered to the usual when left on its own.

By now, she should've written or called Paulie. She might never want to see him again, but Claire and his sister were so close. His own pain was unending, leaving no room to worry about anyone else who missed her. Yet, he knew Paulie did, too.

He took a drink of his now tepid beer. It might as well be water. Everything seemed tasteless anymore. Dull. That's what life was without her.

If only he knew where she was, he'd run to her.

He flicked his half-smoked cigarette into the dirt. "Son of a bitch, why did it turn out this way?" The regret clawed at his chest and choked the air from his lungs as it always did when he thought about that day.

If only he'd spoken to Susan first. "If only, if only. *Damn* it."

He could wait. Claire had to reach out to Paulie eventually. He wouldn't give up, move on, or…live…until he found her again.

****

The porch swing creaked as I rocked back and forward, my toes inside loafers pushing against the wooden slats, cardigan and purse in my jean-clad lap. I swung easily while waiting for Arnold. I happily anticipated the play, but the thought of seeing him didn't affect me one way or the other. If he had matured as he appeared, then having him as a friend to do something with occasionally would be a nice change to my regular routine. I couldn't bring myself to go out with anyone yet, to get interested in any of the boys at school or in town. Still, I had to move on. Arnold could ease me back into a social life. And with him thirty-five miles away, the frequency would not be so often as to crowd me.

Cotton ball clouds dotted the horizon of an otherwise bright blue sky. I could see the road from San Jacinto, and as I gazed in that direction, a car approached, standing out against the white cloud touching the road. The gray car was the same one I remembered from the last day I'd seen Arnold.

"I'll be leaving now," I called out so Aunt Grace could hear me.

She opened the door with Bernice pushing out from behind her.

Arnold stopped in front of the fence, hopped out of his car, and waved. He let himself through the gate with a smile as he made his way merrily along the walk. His handsome face, now filled out like a man, reminded me more of the movie idol Tyrone Power than when I'd first met him in Phoenix. Bernice sighed so loud I thought she might swoon. Even Aunt Grace fluttered her eye lashes in admiration. Amused, I had to admit, his charisma was hard to ignore.

"Good afternoon, ladies." He stopped at the bottom of the steps and held out a hand to my aunt. "You must be Claire's Aunt Grace. I'm Arnold. Nice to meet you, Mrs. Brighton."

I was pleasantly surprised. The Phoenix Arnold could hardly say two words to an adult he knew, much less a stranger.

Aunt Grace took his hand. "Yes, I am, young man. Nice to meet you, Arnold." Bernice fidgeted beside her. "And this is my daughter, Bernice."

"Your daughter? You don't look old enough to have a daughter who must certainly be in high school." He shook Bernice's hand.

"Now, Arnold. No need to pour water on my wheel." Aunt Grace laughed.

He smiled and winked at me. "Only a little." Extricating his hand from my cousin, he offered it to me. "Shall we go?"

I gave my aunt a quick peck on the cheek. "See you later."

We descended the steps holding hands, but once on the walk, I freed my fingers to arrange the purse on my shoulder. His grasp, comfortable and familiar, bothered me. Wary of the new Arnold, I fought the spark of attraction threatening to melt my resolve to keep him at arm's length.

His face remained neutral when I avoided his

touch. I blushed at my vanity. He'd promised friendship, and I was so self-absorbed to think his friendly physical contact suspicious.

"It's great to see you again," he said and opened the passenger door for me.

"Should be fun," I answered, and slid into the car.

He trotted around the back, flung open his door, and hopped in. "My aunt says it's a great play."

"So did mine."

He started the car, waving to Aunt Grace and Bernice still standing on the porch before turning the car around in front of the barn and off the property. Back on the road, we headed toward the mountains.

"They're nice people. Where's your dad?"

"He and Uncle Eb took some machinery into town to get fixed. Why do you ask?"

"Does he know you're on a date with me?"

"We aren't on a date." I shook my head, but he chose to ignore my response, and gazed in his rear view mirror. "I told him I was going to see the play, and yes, with you."

"He was okay with it?"

"Because you landed me in Good Shepherd's?"

"Ah, Claire."

I hoped he worried about how much my father knew. Some residual anger hung over my head like a tiny gray cloud. I cursed to myself. The excitement of seeing the play, Aunt Grace's delight and exuberance, and Arnold's new self had obscured my lingering discomfort. Until now.

"Claire—"

"By the time I got out and talked to Paulie, your complicity didn't really matter. Da knew you'd been at the house. The report didn't name you, but said a boy had visited me without an adult present. I was found in my bedclothes and an…altercation had occurred which disturbed the neighbors. I told Da you came by, and we got into an argument. He knew the old biddy was looking for an excuse to cause us trouble. My landlady was to blame. She had her sister who worked at Social Services on alert." Now I was glad I hadn't told my father all of the details, even if today ended up being the only time I saw Arnold. I would've told Da eventually, but once I'd heard the truth from Paulie, telling him the details had seemed pointless.

"So, I'm forgiven?"

"We're going to a play together, Arnold. I'm working on the rest of it. Don't push your luck. And it's not a date."

"Claire—"

I draped the sweater across my lap, folded my arms at my waist, and jutted my chin out. "In fact, I'm prepared to pay for my ticket."

"Now you're going too far."

His firmness surprised me.

"This is my treat. Give me a chance, Claire."

I turned on him. "A chance for what?"

"To make it up to you for my bad behavior. To be your…friend again." He frowned, smiled, and turned his gaze back to the road.

"Friends?"

"Sure." He ticked his head side to side as if to end his agreement with a maybe.

Second thoughts about his sincerity inched uncomfortably between us like an uninvited passenger in the front seat. First he called it a date, and now his hesitation concerning our relationship hung in the air.

"Arnold, are you sure you're okay with this? I'm not looking for anything except friendship, and with our history—"

"Let's just have fun, Claire." He winked and flashed his gorgeous, movie star smile. "This sounds like quite a production. Can you imagine horses in a play?"

I put my nagging misgivings aside, and we swapped notes on our aunts' descriptions of the Ramona Pageant as we drove. He was easy to talk to, and his enthusiasm as high-pitched as mine. The reservations faded, and my mood elevated the higher we drove up the mountain.

Wildflowers in shades of red, yellow, and violet sprang up along the roadside. Cool air blew in the open windows.

"We should see the parking area anytime now." He rounded a curve and spotted the sign. "There it is."

He slowed. The car bumped onto a dirt road directed by an elderly man waving a blue flag. Arnold wheeled into the parking spot he signaled us to. He turned off the engine, canted toward me, and slid his arm along the back of the seat.

"I've got a blanket and snacks in the trunk."

"You thought of snacks?"

"Yep." He shook his head. "No. They're my aunt's idea." His fingers touched my hair.

I scooted toward the door, the gesture more familiar than I wanted. "Let's go find a good spot."

We followed the crowd out of the parking field and into the trees. He carried the blanket and a thermos of iced tea while I toted the sack of snacks. As we cleared a stand of trees, we came into a clearing. There were rocks and boulders on one edge, a small hill to one side, and various bushes and plants in another area. A roughly terraced hillside provided seating in a semi-circle at one end of the clearing. We agreed on a spot halfway up, off-center. The mountain air was cool when we got out of the car, but the sun and the climb up to our seating had me heated.

"I think I'll have some cold tea right now," I told Arnold after we sat on the blanket.

People chattered around us and the general feeling of celebration pervaded the air. I drank tea and couldn't help but catch the carefree attitude.

"You look sparkly." Arnold canted toward me, his eyes as green as the backdrop of trees bordering the immense natural stage.

I laughed. "Sparkly?"

"Yeah, you're all bright and glowing, or something. Happy."

I crossed my legs and rested back against the grassy slope. "It's a lovely day." I took a sip of tea. "And your aunt makes good tea."

He leaned against the slope next to me, stared into my eyes, and a smile curved his lips. He held my gaze, and I did glow with a day shared between two old friends. The bad taste Arnold had left in my mouth from the last time I'd seen him in Phoenix washed away with his aunt's tea.

A commotion below us, followed by a hush falling across the crowd, drew our attention. The pageant was about to begin.

The sun grows weak earlier in the hills than the flatlands of the farm. By the final act, we had pulled the blanket over our legs and scooted together, sharing our bodies' warmth. I leaned against Arnold, my eyes teary with emotion. The love between Ramona, a Spanish-American orphan girl, and Alessandro, a Native American, tugged at my heart, and somehow intermingled with my own heritage and motherless childhood. I sniffed. Arnold's arm encircled my shoulders. When the horse disappeared into the trees and the last word was spoken, the hills came alive with applause and cheers. We rose to our feet and joined in the crowd's vocal appreciation.

I threw my hands to my chest as we faced each other. "Oh, my gosh. That was wonderful!"

He brushed a lone tear from my cheek. "Do you always cry when you enjoy something?"

"How could you not cry?" I shoved him and laughed.

He put his fingers under my chin. "Women."

We gazed at each other while his thumb gently rubbed below my lip. A breeze caught my hair, and I hugged my sweater around me. His face grew near. My heart thumped hard, and I backed away. "We didn't even touch the snacks your aunt sent with you." I picked up the paper sack, opened the bag, and peeked inside. "Chocolate chip cookies! And?" I lifted out something else wrapped in paper.

Arnold sighed and took the bundle from me. "Cheese crackers. Aunt Irma makes them." He held one to my lips. "Try one. They're damn good."

I took a bite from the cracker he held. "Mmm. She makes these?" He nodded and slipped the rest of the cracker in my mouth. I didn't miss the touch of his fingers on my lip. "Now I'm hungry."

"Let's go back to the car. It'll be warmer, and we'll have our snack before we head back."

We chattered about the play while we strolled back to his car. But my thoughts lingered on the hill, cuddled next to Arnold, and his touch on my face. He'd gotten closer than I wanted. I drew in a deep, calming breath as we settled onto the front seat.

"I'll pour us tea," I offered. "I'll have a cookie and a cracker, or two, I think." I patted the area between us. "Spread the feast out here."

"You should try out for the play next year," Arnold said between bites of cookie.

Caught off guard, the cracker in my hand stopped halfway to my open mouth. My starry-eyed fascination with acting had ended when my future shone bright with Benjamin. I'd not thought about going down that path again.

He chuckled. "You should. You might even get the part of Ramona."

"Oh…really?" I popped the cracker into my mouth, chewing thoughtfully. "I suppose they do have try-outs, don't they?"

"It's theater. They must have tryouts."

I took a chocolate chip cookie from the seat and twirled it around in my hand. "I suppose we'll be here next year." Da had been put on permanently at the water plant. We'd move into town once I graduated. Then I'd find a job. Hemet would become home. I had resigned myself to this future, but not with all my heart.

"I'm probably going to stay, too."

I stopped twirling and swung my gaze from the cookie to Arnold. "You are?"

"My uncle doesn't have any children. He's hinted

around about me staying on, becoming a farmer."

"Won't you miss Phoenix?"

"Not anymore." His arm stretched across the back of the seat. I could feel the heat of his skin without being touched.

"What was it you called San Jacinto? Farmsville? Only quite a bit more derogatory," I reminded him.

"I like to kid around. Besides, I couldn't miss seeing you in the Ramona Pageant next year." His comment was casual; a bite of cookie followed without a glance.

"You can't count on that."

"I think I can. Anyway, I'll need a job once I graduate, and if I stay, someday take over my uncle's farm…wouldn't be such a bad opportunity."

Picturing farmer Arnold stretched my imagination. "How's your mother going to feel? You staying?"

"Hard to say."

The car next to us kicked up dust turning around and drew my attention outside. "Oh, gosh, Arnold. We're about the last ones left." I dropped the cookie on the paper and wrapped the leftovers. "I need to get back to the farm."

"What's the hurry? This is nice up here in the hills."

"I've had a great time, but I told Aunt Grace I'd be home after the play. And she knows when it ended, so we better get going."

He hesitated, then drew his arm leisurely from the back of the seat, and grazed my shoulder. "I wish we could talk all night. You're so easy to talk to." He smiled. "It's been grand."

I'd had a good time, too. It was the most fun I'd

had with someone my own age since leaving Phoenix. "Grand," I agreed. "But we can't talk all night. You've got such a long drive back to San Jacinto. I'll worry about you driving in the dark."

"You will?" He leaned his long frame across the seat and came so near his chocolate chip breath bathed me.

My heart kicked up a notch, yet I held my ground. "Of…of course, I will. That's what friends do—worry about each other."

His smile faltered for an instant, but he quickly recovered. "That's my Claire." He kissed my cheek and pulled around, grabbing the steering wheel. "Okay, then, let's get you back to the farm and Aunt Grace."

The kiss came so quick, his retreat even quicker, I chose to ignore what might have been a breach of our friends-only status. Perhaps I was just overly sensitive to Arnold's tendency to be physical. I did want to give our friendship a chance.

We'd missed a good deal of the traffic while we talked and ate cookies. Light, enjoyable conversation filled the time on the trip back to farm country at the base of the mountains. Arnold's tales of learning to work with dairy cows kept me laughing. I listened between his words about his big-city-man status at the small high school. He didn't use the phrase, of course, but he'd obviously settled comfortably there. As much as he thought farming would be a joke, he viewed his decided future seriously. I'd found the students in my farming community high school to be more mature, more grounded. Perhaps he'd benefited from the move here.

"You surprise me, Arnold. You've changed."

"I did? How?"

"Wanting to be a farmer for one. And you're more serious about, oh, things."

"Hell, Claire. Don't make me sound so dull."

"No, not dull."

We'd reached the farm.

He turned off the engine and regarded me with soft, emerald green eyes. "So, are you pleased with the new me or…what?"

Probably more of the 'what,' yet I couldn't be totally sure what the 'what' meant, so I answered, "Pleased." For some reason, his stare unnerved me. I had to remind myself this was my old chum Arnold. I opened the door. "Thank you, again. I really had a great time."

He touched my arm. "I did, too, Claire. I'm glad all is forgiven and we—" He jerked his hand back and glanced beyond me out the window, and waved. His heavy sigh filled the confines of the car.

I followed his wave to see my aunt on the porch, her arm vigorously cutting through the air. She stepped down and motioned us to come toward her. I opened the door and barely got outside the car before she called out.

"Tell your young man not to hurry away."

My instinct was to protest her label, but I could set her straight later. "Why, Aunt Grace?"

We met halfway along the walk. On either side, pansies nodded their heads with the light breeze as dusk settled on them.

"It's dinner time, hon. We can't send Arnold off on a long drive with an empty stomach." She peered at him. "By the time you get home, you'll miss the evening meal." She stepped between us and looped her arms through ours, forcing us to form a tight knit unit as we avoided traipsing over the pansies.

Arnold craned around her to wink at me. "You're very thoughtful, Mrs. Brighton, but I better call my aunt in case she's held dinner for me. Although, I'm sure she won't mind one less mouth at the dinner table."

"That's a thoughtful thing to do, and you call me Grace, please."

I peered around my aunt. "I thought you said your relatives didn't have children."

"They don't. Anyone working on the farm joins us for dinner."

My aunt released the hold on us as we climbed the steps. "What's your family name?"

"Smith," he answered her as he held the door open for us. "Martin and Irma Smith."

She stopped and canted toward him. "They own the big dairy farm on the east side of San Jacinto."

"Yes, that's them. You know them?"

"We've met." Aunt Grace's eyes twinkled. "They're fine people." She beamed. "You go use the phone in the kitchen while Claire and I set the table in the dining room."

When Arnold peeled off toward the kitchen, and we continued into the dining room, I turned on her. "Aunt Grace, I really don't think you needed to ask him for dinner. And why on earth are we eating in the dining room?"

"Of course, he needs to have some dinner. That's only polite." She opened the dining hutch and chose a blue patterned tablecloth with matching napkins. "Get the dishes from the bottom shelf." She unfurled the cloth with a swooping motion, floating to land perfectly on the long, cherry wood table.

I stooped in front of the matching hutch to take out plain, white china dishes. I hadn't seen these before.

"And when we have Sunday dinner guests, we eat in the dining room. I would imagine Arnold is used to Sunday dinner at the proper table."

He might be used to Sunday dinner in the dining room, but this family ate every meal at the scarred wooden table in the kitchen. I stood gaping, plates in hand, unable to tamp down her apparent joy before Arnold appeared in the doorway.

"Can I help you with those?" He lifted the dishes from my hands.

Rolling my eyes, I set my jaw, and got the good silverware from a drawer of the hutch.

He again emptied my hands. "Now, you'll have to tell me the proper side for the spoons and forks, Grace. I never can get it right."

In wonder, I watched my aunt and *my young man* set the table, laughing together like old friends. I marveled at how the scene contrasted with another lifetime when we knew each other. The two Arnolds held a space in time, as far from each other as the sun is from the earth. And yet, I couldn't look at him—not even this new Arnold—without thoughts of Benjamin. As soon as his face crossed my mind, the warmth in the room chilled.

"Everyone should pile in soon." Aunt Grace couldn't have smiled any wider. "I'll go check on the roast and make the gravy. You two young people have a seat in the living room and wait for the rest of the family to arrive."

"I thought we had a good time today," he said as he sat on the sofa. I took the chair.

I couldn't tell him that even as I enjoyed his company, thoughts of Benjamin would crowd between us from time to time. As much as I tried to forget my old life, something he would say or do would bring back a memory. How long would it take for me to move on?

Little Eb clambered in the front door and thankfully interrupted the moment. "I'm starving," he called as he stomped into the hallway.

"You're *hungry*," Aunt Grace shouted back. "Little waifs on city street corners are starving. Now go wash up. Claire's young man is eating with us, you rascal."

Arnold canted toward me, slid his hand from the couch arm to the arm of my chair, and flashed a flirtatious smile. "That's the second time she's called me your young man."

"It would appear Aunt Grace is smitten with you." I could hear the sarcasm in my voice.

He laughed so charmingly I had to smile.

"Ah, Claire."

"You know you've always charmed the ladies, and now I'd say you've expanded to include young and old alike."

He drew both his hands to his chest as if clutching his heart. "You wound me." He put a hand on my knee.

I looked at the hand lightly caressing my jeans, then into dancing green eyes. How easily he reverted in his efforts to seduce me. I nearly wanted to toy with him. Amusing as it would be, I no longer had the taste for such games. I opened my mouth to put him back in place, but he most certainly read my intentions and changed directions.

Returning his hands to his own lap, he said, "I can't wait to see you in the Ramona Pageant." He leaned forward, elbows on his knees, and gazed up from under dark lashes. "I think fate brought us back together."

His words hung in the air, and I didn't know whether to suck them in or blow them away. "I didn't say I'd try out for the play."

Voices at the front door heralded the arrival of Uncle Eb and Da and brought Arnold to his feet.

"Whose car is out front?" Bernice's shrill voice joined them as the door slammed again.

"We have company, but not 'til everyone is presentable." Aunt Grace ordered everyone to wash up before we were able to greet them.

"I think I'll see if I can help," I said, rising from the chair.

My aunt emerged from the kitchen. "You can help me get the food to the table, Claire, while Little Eb and Arnold take a seat."

A breather from Arnold's subtle flirting would give me a chance to clear my head. My yo-yo emotions, one moment drawn up by his flattery and the next repelled, put my common sense in question.

"Did you have a good time at the pageant?" Aunt Grace asked as we transferred food from pans to bowls.

"It was everything you said and more."

"You'll have to tell me all about it tomorrow." She handed me a ladle for the gravy. "And sitting next to such a nice young man must've been so romantic."

"Not really. We're just friends, Aunt Grace."

"Of course you are, hon." She sliced the roast in

slow, even strokes. "But if it should become something else, you couldn't do better than the Smith family in these parts." She crossed the knife and serving fork along the edge of the platter. "They're some of the most industrious, civic-minded folks in all of the San Jacinto Valley."

"Aunt Grace—"

"I'm merely saying, if a gal had a mind for settling down, Arnold Smith, with all his handsome looks, social skills, good manners, and fine family lineage would be a mighty fine catch. Now, let's get on with a lovely Sunday evening dinner."

****

I snuggled the quilt up to my chin and closed my eyes, however, my body wouldn't give in to sleep. The day had been eventful and confusing, and had dredged up old memories while creating new ones. I wished I could lie next to Paulie, talk out my feelings, and ease my mind. A romantic play, a new and improved Arnold, my aunt's admiration for him and his family, and a perfectly enjoyable family dinner had left me wide-eyed with pleasure. I needed to talk out loud to get a grip on what it all meant.

Family dinners at the Russells' had been some of the best times of my life. And here, tonight, I'd had a most enjoyable family dinner of my own. Da had made us laugh more than once. Arnold had fit right in.

Was this what I needed to move on?

I punched the pillow, huffed, and rolled to my stomach. Had we ended up here at the same time for that reason? Was it really fate, like Arnold said? It was as if I'd been hot and uncomfortable when he came along like a cool breeze. Or had the breeziness of his words fooled me? My doubts swirled. I'd never doubted Benjamin's words.

So what!

My life and his had taken different paths.

He's moved on.

I buried my face in the pillow, exhausted from trying to reason out this turn of events. Maybe tomorrow I'd be more clearheaded. There was time tomorrow, and days ahead. May Day activities would fill the upcoming week and weekend without Arnold's striking green eyes and movie star smile to distract me. He'd already committed to the activities at his school in San Jacinto.

Only four weeks remained until graduation. Uncle Eb had gotten me an interview at the Parks and Rec Department in Hemet thanks to his donations of citrus for their summer programs each year. If I got the job, Da and I would move into Hemet and our own home in early June. I'd truly start a new life, meet new people, and leave Phoenix and Benjamin behind.

I yawned raggedly. Benjamin had a baby and wife. I would have a career and a new life.

I'd get used to it.

I had to.

Chapter Seventeen
The Truth Comes Out

May Day festivities consumed the schools and town of Hemet for four days with the finale of the parade and fireworks on Saturday. My school had a float in the parade. Each day after school, I worked on the decorations. Bernice and I worked side by side, which was the most time we'd spent together since my arrival. She was young, silly, and had her own set of friends, so we rarely found a reason to spend time together.

Sunday dawned overcast and balmy. By the time we arrived home from church, a steady rain drenched the farm. I'd barely removed my wet shoes and folded the umbrella when the phone rang.

"I'll get it." I volunteered as everyone else had already moved toward the stairs to change out of their Sunday clothes.

Arnold's breathy voice responded to my hello. "Ah, Claire. Nice to have you greet me."

"Hey, Arnold." I pulled a chair from the table to sit by the wall phone.

"I wish I could've gotten over to see you this weekend."

"It's been busy. May Day is quite the thing in the valley, isn't it?"

"There was no way I could get out of any of it."

His voice softened. "I've missed you."

The week had flown by. I hadn't had time to miss anyone, not even the usual people back in Phoenix. I viewed the development as a milestone, a hint of my healing. But I didn't want him missing me. Not in the way I guessed he meant. I hadn't concluded anything about Arnold except we were easy together. Whatever came of our friendship would have to happen slowly. For anyone to take my heart right now would be a difficult task; the last thief hadn't returned it yet.

Without a like response from me, he continued. "I think next weekend we should check out the lake up in the hills by Hemet. My aunt has offered to pack us a picnic lunch on Saturday. What do you say?"

"Saturday? I'm not sure." I wound the phone cord around my finger and tried to decide if I wanted to see him again so soon.

"Unless you'd like to come back here and meet my family. Aunt Irma wants me to have you over, but I thought a picnic by a lake would be a better way to spend the day. I can put her off until after school is out, I think."

Meet his family. *Oh, hell. Wouldn't that tickle Aunt Grace?* "Does she insist on meeting all of your friends?" If I had to keep reminding him we were friends, I'd grow weary with the situation. Maybe this wouldn't work.

"As a matter of fact, she does. I'm like a coddled only child now, you know."

My neck grew warm with embarrassment, and I was glad he couldn't witness my display. When would I be able to trust our friendship? "I should check with Aunt Grace and make sure I can get away on Saturday."

"What about Saturday?" She walked into the kitchen, having changed into a flowered housedress and everyday shoes. The decorative hair clips in the sides of her bun had been replaced with bobby pins.

I covered the mouthpiece with my hand and whispered, "I'll talk to you in a minute."

"Did I hear your aunt? Say hello."

"Arnold says hello." I rolled my eyes at my aunt.

Her face crinkled with a smile. "You tell Arnold hello and ask when we can see him again. And give my best to his family."

"She says hello and to give her best to your family."

"Are they getting rain there, too?" She'd planted herself next to me, hands folded at her waist.

Arnold laughed in my ear. "I heard her. Tell her yes, and my aunt is happy her garden is getting a good soil soaking."

I sighed. "He said yes."

Again he laughed. "You didn't tell her all of it."

I countered with a stall response. "I'll call you back in a day or two after I talk to Aunt Grace." My gaze scanned the floor beneath my feet, avoiding her eyes.

"Ask her right now so we can make our plans."

I glanced at her, a mistake.

"Now, what is it you need to ask me, Claire?" She tilted her head and smiled.

I considered handing her the phone. "Arnold wants to go on a picnic Saturday, and I told him I had to see if I could get away. You mentioned some canning or mending, didn't you?" My attempt at subtly letting her know I preferred to think about the invitation turned out to be *too* subtle.

"Oh heavens, if I did, I've forgotten. A picnic? That would be lovely, wouldn't it? You should drive up to the lake."

"I heard her. Grand! I'll be there around eleven."

****

Saturday morning, I awoke in a funk. Benjamin had filled my dreams, and they left me feeling lonely like the moment immediately after a comforting hug you wish wouldn't end. Even the aromas of coffee and bacon that filtered through the cobwebs of sleep didn't brighten my blues. I gave up staring at the pink ceiling and slid out of bed to draw back the curtain on the window. The new sun weaved through the old oak, and deposited splotches of light on my green nightgown. A dull gray bird jerked his head this way and that from a near branch, calling out a tune. A melody came to mind, and I let the curtain fall back across the window as I hummed to alleviate my weariness.

I slid into jeans and a blouse, but left my feet bare. Aunt Grace was in her usual early morning, cheerful mood. I managed to smile, declined food, and carried my coffee to the vegetable garden. I'd have to perk up or be terrible company for Arnold's picnic plans.

The cool earth hadn't accepted the sun yet. I dug in my toes and walked between the rows of greens, stopping to pick a stray weed or to check for ripeness. By the time I'd walked two rows and drank half a cup of coffee, my chest had relaxed. I breathed deeply the fresh air that swooped down from the hills, and turned my face upward with closed eyes. The early sun gently warmed my cheeks and eyelids.

If Aunt Grace hadn't hovered when Arnold had asked to see me, my day would've been spent lazing around the farm. My answer could've been delayed and more than likely would've been no. But how could I move on if I didn't force myself off the farm? I practiced a smile, decided there was truth in the expression, and returned to the house to get ready for the picnic.

****

"There's nothing like milking cows to get your day started," Arnold cracked on our drive into the mountains.

"Even on a Saturday morning?"

"Cows don't know Saturday from Wednesday. They don't take weekends off."

"And you want to be a dairy farmer?"

"Everyone takes turns. I volunteered this morning since I needed to get on the road and wouldn't be back until…whenever I get back." He winked. "You look downright beautiful this morning, Claire. Not sure I've ever seen you with your hair fixed up like that."

I'd swept my hair off my neck and secured the twist with some of my aunt's combs. "Just keeping cool. Supposed to be a warm one today."

He glanced at my bare legs below the tan shorts. "And I'm glad."

I wanted to tell him to keep his eyes on the road, although the compliment had a positive effect on my mood. Any cautionary comment might've led to more flirting. Changing the subject, I asked, "What would you do today, if we weren't on our way to the lake for a picnic?"

"Wishing I was on the way to the lake for a picnic with you." He smiled, pleased with his own cleverness.

"No, really. If you didn't know I was in Hemet.

What would you be doing?"

"There are some guys from school I might see. But that would be later in the day or evening. I might go into town after chores, get a soda, see who I run into."

"No girls you visit?" It slipped out, conversation always so easy with him, and I chided myself for giving him the opening.

"Are you interested in my sex life, Claire?"

"I don't believe I said anything about sex. I merely wondered if you have a girlfriend. You usually do."

"There are girls." He glanced at me, with a glint in his eyes and a quirk of a smile. "'Course, there's been a bar I've set, and no one here has been able to meet the height."

I tipped my chin up and turned toward the passing scenery. "Well, then, I guess you'll have to start prowling the streets of Hemet and expand your horizons." I leaned out from my seat as if searching beyond the confines of the car. "Do you know how to get to the lake?"

He chuckled. "Aunt Irma said there are signs."

I stayed clear of more personal questions, and we watched for those signs, commenting on the scenery. He went over the menu his aunt had packed, and I told him what Aunt Grace had insisted on adding to the meal. We had enough food to see us through the whole weekend. Thankfully, Arnold didn't mentioned Phoenix or our lives there. We spoke as if our friendship began in California, which led me to believe he wanted me to forget any bad history we'd had. And as for me, I needed not to be reminded about my past life—good or bad.

We turned off the main highway and onto a dirt

road. The lake soon came into view with ribbons of silver glinting off the nearly still surface of the water. The bright blue sky shunned all clouds, so we found a grassy spot in the shade. I spread the blanket while Arnold toted the feast from the car.

"I'm not hungry yet. Let's dip our toes in the water," I suggested.

"I guess we should've brought swimsuits," he said when we made our way down to the lake's edge.

"The thought never occurred to me."

"We could always go skinny dipping."

"Ha. You're a real jokester today."

"We could. Haven't you ever skinny dipped with friends?"

Now he wants to be friends. "No, I haven't."

"There's nothing like swimming nude in a lake."

I slipped out of my sandals and waded gingerly in to my ankles. "Oh, gosh, it's cold. There's no way you could swim in this water."

"Is that a dare?" He'd sat on a rock and took off his loafers and socks.

I wiggled my toes on the pebbly, sand bottom. Goose bumps riddled my calves and, when I waded in a few more inches, spread to my knees and thighs. "No, it's not a dare."

"I'd be willing, if it would get you in, too." He rolled his jeans to his knees.

Annoyance threatened to ruin a beautiful day. "Forget it, Arnold."

He waded in beside me. "Damn. I thought maybe you wanted to see me naked. Friends can see friends naked." His arm snaked around my waist.

I slipped out of his embrace and bent to pick up a

shiny, orange rock. "I can't say any of my friends have seen me naked, and you certainly won't either." Taking a few steps away, I bent to retrieve a speckled gray stone.

"Hey, I'm teasing. No need to run from me. I thought we were sharing a friendly joke."

His idea of verbal sparring didn't amuse me, not on this level anyway. I took the light in his eyes to be the thought of my nakedness, not the fun of joking around. His hands were held out, palms up. Was I judging him wrongly again?

He dropped his hands and glanced away from me. "Are you a rock collector?" He scanned the river bottom around his feet.

"No, but there are some pretty ones—almost like gems the way they sparkle in the water."

"Here's a great one." He lifted a fist-sized rock and extended the blue-tinted prize like a peace offering.

For the next half-hour we strolled along the shore, chose rocks and pebbles then discarded the ones too common. This part of the lake seemed to be reserved for our entertainment only, except for a few ducks who shared the water at a distance. The sun beat down strong while the cold water drew us in to our knees. We settled on the most colorful six rocks before heading back to the blanket.

"I'll put them between the pansies along the walkway to the porch," I set them on a corner of the blanket. "Now, I'm starving for a ham sandwich."

"You're not starving. Little waifs on city street corners are starving," he corrected me.

We laughed, remembering Aunt Grace's reaction to cousin Eb's declaration. I'd heard the same exchange many times over, but was surprised Arnold recalled their banter.

I took the wrapping from two sandwiches and put them on paper plates. "Oh, great—your aunt's iced tea." I poured two glasses.

"Let me have some of your aunt's potato salad." He took the bowl from my hands. "When are the try-outs for Ramona?"

"Mmm." I took a bite of sandwich. "I wouldn't know."

"You haven't checked yet?" He heaped potato salad on his plate.

I shook my head. "No."

"This potato salad is great. Tell Grace for me, okay?" He tapped my knee. "You're going to try out, aren't you?"

"Oh, I don't know." I gazed out on the lake, listened to a bird chirping over our heads, and wondered. The idea had some appeal when he'd first suggested getting involved the day of the pageant. I'd not thought of trying out since. "Probably not."

"Hell, Claire, why not? You're a better actress than the gal who played her."

"Oh, how would you know?"

"I just know."

His gaze flicked over me so quickly I barely registered the action.

"You have movie star written all over you. *All* over you."

I took the last bite of sandwich. "The movies and the theater haven't come to mind in a long time, Arnold." I dismissed the idea with a wave of my hand. "Doesn't really interest me anymore."

"I don't believe it."

"You've changed since you've been in California, and maybe I've changed, too." I folded the paper plate and shoved it in the trash sack. "I'm happy being with family, feeling settled down. I don't need the stage anymore." The feeling settled part had a way to go, although the desire was strong.

"The stage needs you."

"It'll never know, now will it?" I laughed. "More potato salad?"

"I'm full." He added to the garbage sack then raised his arms in a stretch, uttered a noise of contentment, and reclined. "Sure as hell is nice up here." He patted the blanket next to him. "I see a yellow bird of some sort up in the tree."

I stretched out beside him and brought my hands under my neck to support my head and keep combs from digging into my scalp. "Oh, look, there's another one on the branch over. So pretty. I know nothing about birds."

"Me either."

We were quiet for a few moments. One of the yellow birds called and the other answered. A high breeze rustled the most upper parts of the trees with a sound so low we wouldn't have heard had we been speaking. The silence was soothing. I relaxed my shoulders, and my back melted into the blanket. No human sounds existed. We could've been the only two people in the world.

Arnold rose up on one elbow and looked down on me. He whispered, "We're the only two people in the world."

"I was just thinking that," I whispered back.

"Are you sure you don't want to go skinny dipping?" He chuckled, but his eyes were smoky.

I smirked and gave him a slit-eyed stare.

His hand went under my head. "Take out the clips so you'll be more comfortable."

He had them out before I could protest then leaned over and fanned out my hair on the blanket around my head.

"Lovely."

His gaze lingered on my face, drifted down my neck, and paused at the top button of my blouse and what lie beneath. His heat radiated.

"Arnold, don't." My words brought his stare back to my face.

"Don't what, Claire?"

"Don't think what you're thinking." I brought my hands forward and rested them lightly on my chest. "Don't ruin this day."

"I could make this day perfect."

"For whom?" I sniffed and made a movement to sit.

He stopped me with a palm slid under my hand to my breast as his mouth covered mine.

I pushed at his chest, but his weight was too much for me to move, so I wrenched my head sideways. "Stop, damn it." I shoved his hand from my breast. "Let me up."

"Just wait a minute, Claire." His hips and chest leaned against me.

My heart beat with rapid thumps. "Get the hell off me."

"Claire, please. Lie still and listen for once."

"Do you want me to scream?" I squirmed with

more effort. "I will. I'll scream."

"There's no one around, and there's no need. I'll ease up, if you'll calm down."

I stopped my useless squirming, clenched my teeth, and glared. "What?"

He didn't relax his weight against me. His lips curved in a slight smile as he stared into my face.

"Say the hell what you want to say and then let me up."

"Okay. You and me. I don't know why you've fought what we could've had for all these months. This is how it should be. Don't you see how we ended up here, together, for a reason? I need you. You need me."

"Arnold—" I foolishly moved to sit.

"You said you'd listen."

I gave up struggling. "Okay. Get it over with." My heart wouldn't give up the hammering, but I heaved a sigh and forced calmness to prevail.

"You never took me seriously, Claire. You were the only girl at North High who didn't want me. Now, here, it's different. I'm going to be set here with the farm, and we could make a good life. You said you're happy here, happy to be settled down."

"We're nothing more than friends. How many different ways and times can I say it? We are not—"

"Friends, lovers, whatever the hell you want to call it, Claire, it's me and you."

A touch of panic prickled my neck. "Arnold—"

"I know you have feelings for me. I've never known why you've fought them. Back in Phoenix, yeah, I was kind of a punk and you saw that. But we were still friends until I ruined it. You said it yourself, I'm different. You have to admit we've been good together lately." His leg slid over mine and rested on my upper thigh. His gaze fell to where he'd made contact as he inched up higher and used his knee to rub between my legs. "We fit together in so many ways."

A slow, burning anger trumped my panic. "We do not fit any which way!" I wriggled, attempted to break his grasp, and lifted my free leg to kick him.

He dropped closer still, his chest against mine, and with one of his hands, caught hold of my leg.

"Stop it, Claire." The whine of his voice took me back to the Arnold of Phoenix. "You act like I'm trying to hurt you."

My mouth fell open in amazement. The slow burn erupted as my pulse kicked up. "You're holding me down, forcing yourself on me." I shoved him with my free hand.

"I wouldn't hurt you. I want to please you. God, Claire, I love you. I want to marry you."

"Marry?" I choked on the word.

He slid the hand on my leg along my hip until he reached my fingers and brought my hand to his chest. "I would've proposed proper like if you hadn't taken on this attitude, but yes. I'm asking you to marry me."

"Attitude? And stop doing that with your knee."

He rubbed his knee once more between my legs then pulled back. "Marry me, Claire. We'll have a good life on the farm." He grazed his lips across mine; his knee edged up higher on my thigh again. "God, I want you so much, Claire. We don't have to wait until we're married."

"Marry you? That's not what you really want." I jerked my hand from his grasp and slapped at his face with all the force I could muster given the bad angle.

338

His head barely moved with the impact. He frowned, peered into my face, and as I geared up for another slap, he drew away, and released me. I scrambled to my feet, backed off the blanket, and stumbled on a rock. He sat up, his legs crossed with his elbows on his knees.

I huffed with anger while he sat dejectedly. When he didn't look at me, didn't speak, I heaved a deep breath and my heart settled down. He rubbed at his eyes then returned to leaning his elbows on his knees. His stillness bothered me. I stepped beside him, but he paid me no attention. Lowering down, I mimicked his cross-legged position, and sat beside him. I'd not treated his marriage proposal with much respect, but he'd not offered it in a respectful manner.

"Who the hell you saving it for, Claire?" His voice, low and edgy, drifted into the silence surrounding us.

"Perhaps you'd better take me home."

He slowly turned his head and met my glare with misty eyes. "Why won't you let me love you?"

"You make it hard, Arnold." How could I be angry and still have pity for his bumbling attempts?

"I don't get it. I've offered you marriage, love. And I'd be a good lover, Claire. A damn good lover."

Pity evaporated. "That's really your purpose, isn't it?"

"I've known you a long time, Claire. I know you're no cold fish. And I've felt you get hot under my touch. More than once. You stop yourself every damn time. So, tell me. Who you saving it for?"

I dropped my gaze to the blanket and shook my head. The threat of tears choked me. Benjamin's smile, his lips, his kisses flooded my mind.

"Who? I want to know who." He thumped his

palms against his knees.

I swallowed hard, forcing the emotion deep inside and faced his searing expression. "I'm just not ready."

His eyes narrowed. "Can't be that son of a bitch Ben Russell, can it? If it was Russell, you wouldn't be here now, would you?"

I jumped at his supposition. "I…I—"

He grabbed my arms and stood, pulling me with him. "It is, isn't it?" He spat the accusation.

"No." I tugged my arms from his hands. "No, that would be stupid. He's a married man with a baby." I bent and shoved food back into the picnic basket, avoiding his eyes. "Take me home, Arnold Smith." I turned my back on him and set the remnants from lunch off the blanket.

"Married? Baby? Who the hell are you talking about?" He came closer behind me. "I meant the Ben Russell in Phoenix."

I straightened and glared. "I know who you meant."

His puzzlement, the frown, the blank look in his eyes, slowly morphed into surprise. He opened his mouth, but closed it again and averted his eyes away from me. He shook his head.

"What?" I whispered the question.

When he looked at me, he set his jaw, but remained silent.

He knew something, and I shied away from wanting to hear whatever he could tell me. "Take me home." I reached for the basket, but he clasped my arm and whirled me around.

"Where the hell did you get a crazy notion Ben Russell is married?"

I froze. He teased me, cruelly. I stared into his face, and couldn't trust my voice to answer.

"It's him. You're saving it for Russell. And he doesn't give a rip about you."

"I…I'm not. But…but I couldn't anyway. I tell you he's married with a baby." I jerked out of his grasp. "You haven't been home. You don't know."

A hint of sympathy crossed his face, no more than a leaf fluttering over our heads. He narrowed his eyes, the keeper of undisclosed knowledge. "I talk to Jimmy every few weeks."

"Jimmy? Jimmy who?"

"Laura's brother. We talk." He nodded his head like the victor. "What'd the asshole Russell do? Tell you he was getting married to get you off his back?"

"I don't know what you're talking about." My head pounded.

He yanked the blanket up and glared at me. "If he cared about you, like I do, he'd be here. *Here.* He knows where you are, but have you seen him? Hell no!"

My face and neck were so hot I thought I'd faint. Tears burned my eyes, and I choked them back so that I could barely swallow.

"Russell doesn't have a kid. And I can sure as hell tell you, he's not married."

Chapter Eighteen
Going Her Way

The ride out of the mountains gave me a taste of what hell must be like. We didn't speak. Arnold tried, at first, but I kept my gaze glued to the scene out the passenger side window. Not that I saw anything.

He finally gave up.

Without looking, I could sense his mood. I rolled down the window to let the thick, rancid air of anger escape. The struggle to hold in tears had given me an enormous headache. But I'd be damned if I'd allow Arnold to see me cry. I couldn't be sure what tales he'd feed to Jimmy in Phoenix. My humiliation and sorrow wouldn't be one of them.

Confusion over what he'd said about Benjamin made me palpably sick until my head spun. Visions of Benjamin taunted me. I pinched my eyes tight and breathed deep in an effort to rid my mind of him. *Later*, I told myself. Later, alone, I could mull over every word he'd spoken and make sense of why. Anger kept the tears at bay and the sorrow tucked away for now.

Was Arnold lying?

He wanted what he couldn't have. I'd always been the one woman who didn't swoon over him, who wanted nothing more than friendship. And in his perceived defeat, he'd always lashed out to hurt me. Today, he'd hurt me far more than he ever had and yet,

I had a sense he was hurting, too. I chanced a glance. His jaw was clenched as he stared out the window.

"I should've kept my mouth shut," he said without looking at me. "I could've let you think Russell was taken. Played it sweet." He met my gaze, the corners of his mouth turned downward. He wiped at his eyes and turned back to the road. "But when you're close to me, I go a little crazy."

I couldn't speak. My head pounded, and my thoughts jumped helter-skelter, not knowing what was real and what was a lie.

"If…if Russell was out of the picture, would I have a chance, Claire? Would you consider marrying me? I can wait, Claire, if I have a chance."

The farm came into sight. Relief flooded me and so nearly did my sorrow. I closed my eyes on impending tears.

Swallow. Breathe.

And he jerked to a stop by the front gate.

The dust hadn't settled when I grabbed the handle of the car door with one hand while clutching Grace's dishes and my things with the other.

His hand closed around my arm. "Claire."

I didn't look at him. "I…I don't know right now." It was all I could manage.

His hand dropped away, and as I slammed the car door, he said something I couldn't hear.

I entered the gate without glancing back as his angry tires kicked up gravel when he turned around.

Aunt Grace opened the screen door, puzzlement on her face. I gritted my teeth and prepared for the questions.

"Is everything all right, Claire?" She took the

dishes from me.

I avoided the concern on her face by watching my toes cross over the threshold. "Fine."

"Arnold looked like he was in a hurry to get out of here. Was my potato salad so bad?" She closed the door behind us. "And, I must say, you look rather upset. Did you two have an argument?"

That explanation would do. "Yes, we did. I'm not sure we'll see each other anymore." I inched toward my room.

"Oh, hon, I'm sorry to hear that. Is there anything I can do?"

I moved away from her, but managed a quick smile to hopefully rest her concerns. "Thank you, Aunt Grace, no. This is better anyway, what with school winding down and graduation activities and all." I wanted to run to my room and throw myself down in tears.

"Well, maybe over the summer you two can make up and be friends again. Don't let this get you down."

"Maybe you're right." I opened the bedroom door. "I'm awfully tired, so I think I'll take a nap, if you don't need me for anything."

"Heavens no, Claire. You rest."

I barely closed the door behind me before the dam broke. I fell onto my bed, face smashed into the quilt, and sobbed. Mindless sobbing. When I'd finally let out all the tears I'd held in since Arnold crushed my world, I rolled into a fetal position and changed to slow, soft crying.

Benjamin knew where I was? Arnold had said so. He'd told Laura's brother. Laura would've told Paulie. If only I'd called Paulie.

Why hadn't Paulie called me?

My crying stopped. I sniffed. Unless Arnold had given Jimmy precise directions or the names of my aunt and uncle, Paulie and Benjamin wouldn't know exactly where I was. Couldn't they have found a way through Jimmy to Arnold then me? Oh God, it was all so convoluted and confusing. My tears renewed.

I ruined my friendship with Paulie, and Benjamin never really loved me.

My mind wandered as if browsing a photo album. Snapshots of Benjamin from the first time I'd set eyes on him to the last sad moments. He'd said he loved me and always would. He'd said I was honey on white bread.

I uncurled and sat up. The room had darkened with the onset of dusk. I stared into the watery dimness, seeing Benjamin's eyes. They were honest, full of emotion and truth. His voice, his words came back to me and they didn't lie.

But he didn't try to find me.

I needed to know why.

With a jerky breath, at last cried out, I lifted the pillow to my face and dried the last of the wetness away. Somewhat calmed, I could hear the noises beyond my door. The muffled sounds told me dinner would soon be on the table.

Calling Paulie was an option quickly dismissed. If she would even talk to me, calling her to get to her brother would only be a slap in her face. And I wanted to make amends, if possible, with her. When we finally spoke, the conversation had to be about us.

Calling Benjamin wouldn't do either. If what had been between us had been a lie, I wanted to see his face when he explained. And calling him and not Paulie would be another slap in her face. Maybe she'd allow me that, and maybe not. The only friendship I might be able to salvage would be hers. Benjamin apparently was lost to me, but he could sure as hell tell me to my face why.

I stood and straightened my bed with a surge of energy fueled by anger. Two weeks until graduation then I'd have my answer.

I eased my bedroom door open and scanned the hall. Empty. Stepping out as noiselessly as the old tomcat who had the run of the house, I went into the bathroom and locked the door behind me. The image reflected from the mirror clearly had a bad case of the epizoody. I splashed cold water on my face. The splotchy skin and puffy eyes remained. Rummaging in the drawer presented a tin of face powder left over from Mae's days at home. A few puffs helped dull the shiny nose and blend the splotches. I combed my hair. That would have to do.

Back in the hall, I headed for the kitchen. Tonight, I'd answer Aunt Grace and Da about what I wanted for graduation. A bus ticket and a few days in Phoenix. I would tell them it would be two gifts in one—for me and for Paulie; a surprise reunion and a short vacation for me before I started work. And those few days would be no vacation for Benjamin.

****

"That sorry, damned, pissant bastard!" Ben flung clothes into a small duffle bag.

Davie appeared in the doorway of the room he once shared with his brother. "Sure as hell hope you aren't talking about me."

346

He zipped the bag roughly and caught a T-shirt in the zipper. "Damn it!" He jerked the closure to free the cloth.

"Whoa, Ben. Where are you going?"

"I'm…what are you doing here?"

"Glad to see you, too. Barb and I just rolled back into town. We were up in Payson camping and stopped by for a free meal. There's nothing to eat in our cupboards at home." He sat on his old bed. "Getting married and moving out of Mom's has a down side." He laughed, but when Ben glared at him, he continued. "You want to calm down and tell me what's going on?"

Ben hefted his bag off the bed. "I found out where Claire is." He scanned around the room.

"Claire? Where?"

He patted his pockets, checking for keys, cigarettes, and lighter. "California. Little town called Hemet."

"And how did you find out, and who's a pissant?"

He dropped his bag on the floor, shook a cigarette from his pack, and offered one to Davie.

He waved a hand at Ben. "Nope. I'm quitting. The smoke makes Barb nauseous."

"Hell, you a daddy." He shook his head. "Hard to believe." He took a drag off the cigarette, glanced away from his brother to the bag on the floor, and the momentary distraction faded as quickly as the smoke in the air. "Shit. I've got to get out of here."

"Tell me what's going on."

"Last week, I went to Yuma to check on the crews we have working there. One of the guys is Laura's brother. I overheard a conversation and didn't pay much attention until I heard Claire's name. Then I got an earful. Seems the son of a bitch, little jerk Arnold Smith lives not far from her and has taken up with her again."

Davie was silent a moment as he shoved his hands in his pockets. "How the hell could that happen?"

"Jimmy said Arnold told him she'd followed him there."

His brother's frown was disbelieving. "And Jimmy is Laura's brother? Why wouldn't Laura know? If she'd known then Paulie would know and then—"

"He's on the permanent Yuma crew. Has been for months. And I don't know what the hell his relationship is with his family, but I'd say they don't talk much." He sank down on the bed. "He's...he's a bastard like his friend Arnold Smith."

"Do you think Claire would follow him the day after...after the Susan thing?"

Ben took a long, slow drag on his cigarette. He concentrated on flicking his ashes into the ashtray on the floor. "I can't believe it, Davie. I know she was hurt, we both were."

His brother's hands came out of his pockets, and he scooted to the edge of the bed. "If Jimmy knows anything about the goings on here, he knows you're not married to Susan."

He cleared his throat. "I thought of that."

"No one would even know you ever thought you were the father." His brother cocked his head and frowned.

"I tried to tell her. As soon as Susan set me straight, I drove like hell to Claire's, but she was already gone." He buried his head in his hands, the cigarette dangerously close to his hair.

Davie took the cigarette from his fingers, stubbed it out in the ashtray, and tapped him on the knee. "Knowing you drove her away must've been eating at you something fierce."

Ben stilled. It's all he thought about. He'd give anything to turn the clock back and do it differently.

"Maybe, if you'd told Paulie…"

"Maybe what? At first, I was embarrassed and crazy with hurt. What a fool I was proposing to Susan. And then to run to Claire and find her gone near killed me. Besides, Susan asked me to keep a lid on it until she decided what to do."

"But Paulie—"

"Yeah, I know. Paulie was hurt by Claire not telling her goodbye. I thought I had to respect Susan's request. A woman in her condition…anyway, I figured as soon as she gave me the green light, I'd tell Paulie. Then, some time passed and the pipsqueak seemed okay and…hell, I don't know. We didn't know how to find Claire anyway. I kept hoping she'd be back."

"Maybe if Paulie had known and told Laura, if somehow Laura's brother had carried tales home…"

"What the hell, Davie?" He raked a hand through his hair. "That's not how it played out. There're a whole lot of what ifs. If I'd waited to tell Claire until *after* I talked to Susan. If I'd told Paulie. If if *if*." He rubbed his temples.

"And Laura's brother knows where she is?"

Davie's statement redirected Ben's thoughts. He jumped up and grabbed his bag. "I'm going to Hemet to find her."

"Where in Hemet? Do you know?"

"Not exactly. I squeezed Arnold's phone number

out of Jimmy, but every time I've called he's conveniently not available. The lady who answers the phone, probably his aunt, is like a damn caretaker. First time I called, she asked who was calling. The little pissant won't come to the phone. I told the aunt what I was after, just directions to a mutual friend, and she claims she doesn't know. No telling what the hell the lying little bastard told her."

"So, how you going to find her?"

"I'll figure that out when I get there. It's not that big a city. I'll cover every damned inch of the town. Someone will know where a beauty like Claire is."

"What about Arnold? What if—"

"I don't believe she'd take up with him. Not the way Jimmy says." He set his jaw, eyes narrowed. "I don't believe it."

"If she followed him there, Ben, you've got to be ready for anything."

"I need her to know the truth."

"She may be all settled down now."

"School just let out. She's barely out of high school. She might be…hooked up with him but…not married. She can't be married." He swung his bag over his shoulder. "I'm going to find her, Davie."

She can't possibly be in love with that bastard Arnold. I'll find her, lay out the whole messy misunderstanding.

I love her. And she just has to still love me.
****

My arms hung over the edge of the bed as I flipped the pages of a movie magazine, not really seeing the pictures. I'd been thinking about Benjamin. Tomorrow, at last, I'd board the bus. I couldn't comprehend what

350

his reaction would be, but my anger would see me through the confrontation. My anger could possibly be for naught, if the one scenario I'd replayed several times, the only one that made any sense to me, explained why he'd let me believe he had married— Susan refused to marry him. Could a woman possibly say no in her condition? She might. Benjamin would still stand by her. He'd never turn his back on his responsibility. And what kind of life would that be for us? Benjamin would want me to move on and find another who could be there for me one hundred percent.

If Benjamin hadn't married Susan, baby or not, the glimmer of hope existed.

"Claire?" Aunt Grace tapped on my bedroom door. "You have a phone call."

I closed the movie magazine, slid off the bed, and padded to the door in bare feet. "Who is it?" I asked as I opened the door.

Her eyes sparkled even as she checked her smile. "Arnold."

We hadn't spoken since the picnic. The last two weeks of school had been hectic, filled with graduation celebrations and my plans for the trip to Phoenix. I'd slept fitfully and eaten little, my stomach in a constant roil. I'd thought of Arnold at times, when roaming around my relatives' farm and imagining a life like this permanently. It wasn't an altogether unattractive proposition. He'd offered me marriage and lustful love. But I didn't love him.

And I had to take care of unresolved emotions.

The thought of reuniting with Paulie was both sweet and unnerving. Her anger would certainly be lashed upon me for leaving without saying goodbye and for not contacting her since uprooting from Phoenix. Prickles of anxiety crept up my neck like ants marching en masse. I wanted her friendship back, if even on a long distance basis.

Truth be told, most of my thoughts were bent on Benjamin.

"Thanks, Aunt Grace."

She hung back discreetly as I went to the kitchen to take the call. I sat in the chair below the wall phone.

"Hello, Arnold."

"Hi, Claire. Good to hear your voice." He sounded happy. I could imagine his sparkling green eyes.

I played with the phone cord. "It's nice to hear from you." My tone was for my aunt's benefit. Polite.

"Is it, Claire?" His happiness clouded with a serious tone.

Tightness in my shoulders and stomach told me more time from Arnold was needed. I let go the phone cord and sighed deeply. "Arnold—"

"I hoped if I gave it a couple of weeks, you might talk to me."

"I never said I wouldn't talk to you."

A moment of silence, a heartbeat, the old clock over the stove ticked once, twice. He cleared his throat and lightened his voice. "How did graduation go?"

Relief came with a different topic. "It was okay. I think Da had more fun with it than I did."

"My parents came out for it. They left yesterday."

"Oh, Arnold, that's great."

"Yes and no. It was great to see them, but my mother expected me to go back with them."

"Oh, dear."

"She got okay with it before they left." A scraping

noise sounded like he adjusted the receiver or changed ears. "My uncle officially announced he wants me to run the farm eventually." I could hear the pride in his voice. "There were tears. Well, you know how women are when they're happy and sad all at once."

"As a matter of fact, I do. Congratulations, Arnold."

"What now for you, Claire?"

"Um, well, I have a job starting in about three weeks."

A heavy breath of relief translated over the line. "You're staying. That's grand."

I could almost see the smile on his face.

"And then?"

"Da and I are moving into Hemet. We'll look for a place as soon as—"

"I mean with us." He paused. When I didn't respond, he continued tentatively. "Can I see you…in a couple of days?"

Although he hadn't been completely out of my thoughts, as of yet, I had no idea if or where he fit in my life. "We can talk about that when I get back."

"Get back?" It sounded as if he'd bolted from whatever position he'd been in. "Where are you going?"

"I'm using my graduation gift, a bus ticket to Phoenix." An intake of breath sounded in my ear. "To visit Paulie," I added. I didn't need any confrontation about Benjamin.

"To visit Paulie." His skeptical tone vibrated over the line.

"Yes. I leave tomorrow." I hoped my voice was light, yet final. No room for discussion.

Footsteps echoed over the line as if he paced. "That should make all the Russells happy."

His vocal sneer grated. "It's a surprise, Arnold. For Paulie. And it needs to *stay* a surprise." My warning to keep this news from Jimmy didn't need to be spelled out.

"Then let me see you off."

I wanted to hang up the phone. My head was too full of thoughts, my heart too mixed up with emotions to spar with him today. "That's too far for you to come just to watch me get on a bus."

"No it's not. Not too far to see you, Claire." His voice pleaded. "I want to see you again."

But I didn't want to see him. Not yet. "It's early."

"You don't know early. I get up with the cows, remember?"

"Da is going to take me. He's looking forward to it."

"Please, Claire." The scraping noises again, a chair sliding as he sat down. "I've done nothing but think about the last words we spoke. I don't want you going off to Phoenix with that in your head. Let me meet you, have a friendly conversation, keep you company."

"I—"

"Please, Claire." His voice was smoky emotion.

I'd never traveled alone and the purpose of this trip would have my nerves frayed. Da was all I needed. Arnold's presence would be an intrusion. "I'm sorry, Arnold. I'd prefer to wait for the bus alone."

The silence on the other end of the line made me think he'd hung up, but then he huffed and his voice came so low, I strained to hear him.

"Come back to me, Claire."

"It's just a visit. And Da is here. Of course I'll be back." Not the words he wanted to hear, but I couldn't give him what he wanted. "Goodbye, Arnold."

He hung up without responding.

The back door into the kitchen closed as I hung up the phone. "You talking to Paulie? I thought it was a surprise." My father set his lunch pail on the counter.

"No, I was talking to Arnold. He offered to take me to the bus station."

"Hey, gal, I thought I was going to see you off." Da took his hat off and leaned against the sink.

"Of course I told him no. My first trip alone? You have to be the one to take me." I patted his ruddy cheek.

Da twirled his brown fedora between his hands. He'd taken to wearing one since we'd moved here. I thought he looked quite dashing when he tipped it back slightly on his head. Right then, he looked worried.

I threw my arms around his neck and kissed his cheek. "Don't miss me, Da. I'll only be gone a few days. And when I get back, we'll start house hunting."

"You know, well, I worry about you, gal. You was upset when we left Phoenix, and it was 'cause of Ben Russell. You might not've told your old man all of it, but I'm smart enough to figure some things out on my own. Now, if you go see Paulie, well, you're going to see Ben."

"Oh, that's ancient history." I waved my hand in the air and dismissed his concern with a great deal more aloofness than I felt. "I'm totally over what happened back then."

He regarded me with one eye squinting like Popeye. My theatrics weren't always successful with my father.

I put my hands on his shoulders. "I'm okay, Da. I can't wait to see Paulie." I shook his shoulders. "And take a trip by myself on the bus." I punched his arm and giggled. "My first trip all alone. An adventure."

He set his hat on his head. "You be careful." He frowned in his listen-to-your-father way. "Don't be talking to strangers, and always carry your belongings with you when you get off the bus for breaks or at any stops they make. You hear?"

"Promise. Now, get out of here and get washed up for dinner." I shooed him with my hands. "And when you see Aunt Grace pacing the hallway, tell her to come on back in the kitchen so we can start cooking."

He pecked my cheek. "Love you, gal."

"Love you more."

****

I waved as my father backed away from the curb. My eyes filled with tears, and the smile dripped from my face as soon as he was out of sight. I collapsed onto the green, wooden bench in front of the drug store to wait for the bus. My cola, sitting under the bench in the shade, would go warm if I didn't drink it soon. I retrieved the bottle and sipped, the carbonation clearing my throat of swallowed tears.

For two weeks, I'd sleepwalked through the final days of school, endured the happiness around me, and fought with bouts of anger and anxiety. Now, this close to leaving to face not only Benjamin, but Paulie, my legs had a notion to run. My gaze wandered aimlessly around me. People on the sidewalk blurred. Patrons moved in and out of the drugstore. Cars on the street and…

Arnold drove into the Hemet Drug and Sundries

parking lot. My focus cleared with a start when he parked and got out. He smiled, waving, as he strode toward me. His smile was as bright as the morning sun. The anger that sprang from my center was as hot as the same sun.

"Hey, Claire."

My bottom stayed glued to the bench and the cola bottle in my hand was in danger of breaking from my tight grip. "What are you doing here?"

He stood awkwardly next to the bench, stared at me, and tapped his fingers on his thighs.

"What?" I managed through clenched teeth. "Answer me."

"You look really great. Can I tell you that?"

My legs surged as if shot with energy and I sprang from the bench. "No you can't. Why can't you give me space? You know how annoying it is, how unattractive it is when you pester me like this?"

"Pester?" He shifted his shoulders, shuffled his feet. "I…I only wished I'd called you sooner. If I'd known you were leaving…" He let the words hang in the air between us, open-ended, the meaning vague.

My emotions played a tug of war. Angry versus flattered. Arnold stared at me, his green eyes smoky with emotion, and his words came back, "*If Russell was out of the picture, would I have a chance, Claire?…I can wait…*"

I didn't want him here, not now. His persistence annoyed and confused me. I could stay in Hemet and be married, loved. Yet, I couldn't let it pass, couldn't accept Benjamin didn't care.

"*If he cared about you, he'd be here.*"

I had to find out. I gazed into Arnold's eyes and

heard his voice in my head again. "*I'll wait*."

A Greyhound bus roared to the curb, angled front in. I glanced at my watch. Another twenty minutes until scheduled departure.

I collapsed onto the bench. "I'll be back in a few days." I crossed my ankles and sipped the cola.

He sat on the bench. "And we can—"

"We'll talk."

I had no idea what would come of my visit to Phoenix. Arnold would be waiting and, hopefully, my head and heart would be in agreement.

He touched my arm. "Well, that's something."

****

Ben slowed to the posted speed limit as he entered the city limits of Hemet. He'd driven all night, stopping briefly at a rest stop to sleep for a couple of hours. But he didn't feel tired. An edgy alertness, enriched by a thermos of strong coffee, kept him awake. On his drive, he'd devised a plan of attack for the city. He'd drive the main street and take stock of the size of the town and the direction of urban versus farmland. If he had to drive to every farm around Hemet, he would. First, he'd ask directions to the high school. A town the size of Hemet would probably have only one. School was out for the students, but he hoped there would be office personnel still working. If he struck out there, he'd find the shopping area and talk to the sales ladies. Check out the movie theaters. Maybe the Chamber of Commerce would know about someone new who'd moved to their relatives' farm. He'd cover every square mile if he had to.

The first street sign he came to read Main Street. He passed the red brick post office and an impressive city hall glaring white in the sun. He gazed ahead to what looked like a few office buildings, some store fronts, and a few blocks up, a Greyhound bus parked at the curb.

****

Arnold pulled a small, black box from his pocket. "Here."

I gulped, surprised and hesitant to take it from his hand.

"I wanted you to have something to remind you of me while you're gone." He set it in my hand. "Take it. It's only a little something."

Speechless, I opened the box. A sliver chain lay against the black satin. I lifted the delicate bracelet. The sun glinted off the links. A wave like nausea floated through my stomach. This was exactly what I didn't want while thoughts of facing Benjamin drenched me in emotion.

"Oh, Arnold. I wish you hadn't."

"Well, I did." He chuckled. "I don't want you to forget me while you're in Phoenix. Maybe when you look at this around your wrist, well, you'll remember I'm hanging around here, waiting for you. Here, let me put it on."

He lifted my hand, but I pulled away. His brow wrinkled and the sun left his face.

"I can't do this, Arnold. It's beautiful, but your timing…I thought we'd talk when I got back. Didn't we agree?"

"It's not a ring, Claire."

No, it wasn't, but it felt like an attachment, a promise. I set the cola bottle on the ground, stood, and avoided his longing gaze. A few passengers milled about the sidewalk. If only the driver would call us to board.

A couple stood beside the door of the bus preparing to leave. A cream-colored dress hugged the woman's slim frame, and her feet sported matching cream pumps. The man, in suit and tie, tipped his fedora back on his head as he leaned down to kiss her. She put one hand to her hat and tipped her head up, wrapped her free hand around his neck and lifted one leg daintily behind her. The gentleman held her face between his hands for a moment before he helped her up the steps of the bus. He backed up and waved. When he passed by me, I could see his blue eyes glistening.

Benjamin's eyes were bluer, the color of...

I lifted my suitcase.

Arnold stood close behind me. "Claire," he whispered.

A tear found its way from deep inside, and trickled onto my cheek.

He touched my shoulder.

I gazed up the street, the world a blur. A blue blur. The color moved in the street, grabbed me, and startled me so my heart jumped to my throat.

That car looks like Lady Blue.

****

Ben decided to drive the length of Main Street, before choosing where to stop and make conversation, find out the location of the high school and any other information he could glean that might lead to Claire.

As he approached the Greyhound, a couple saying their goodbye caught his notice. Her posture was sweetly sensual, one foot lifted, her back arched to meet the kiss. He was reminded of his goodbye to Claire, her sweet lips, the bitterness of tears. Watching the couple kiss, overwhelmed him with thoughts of Claire. He could almost taste her.

His chest contracted, a fist of remorse gripped his heart. He had to find her, explain, and wrench her from Arnold, if he could.

He cleared his throat of raw emotion as his gaze drifted from the couple now separated to a young woman standing with a suitcase in hand.

Something about the way she held herself reminded him...

She flipped the hair from her neck. And his heart flipped in his chest.

****

The blue car slowed, nearly came to a stop in the street, then picked up speed. I dropped the suitcase and threw my hands to my mouth. My head spun as the car sped toward me.

Benjamin nosed Lady Blue into the curb and jumped out before the engine noise died. He ran, but came to an abrupt stop in front of me. I'd not moved; my hands still covered my mouth, another tear traced the path of the last and pooled on my fingertips.

Arnold shuffled behind me; his thighs brushed the backs of my legs, and his hand touched the small of my back.

"Russell." The name was no more than a growl in his throat.

Benjamin's gaze bounced between me and Arnold several times; anger glazed his eyes, until he focused on me. He studied my hands and a slight smile twitched his lips as he set his blue gaze on mine.

"Claire? Are you okay? You're crying." He darted

a sneer above my head, directed at Arnold.

I sucked in further tears, wiped my cheeks, and nodded. "What are you doing here, Benjamin?" When I said his name out loud, to his face, reality rushed over me.

Benjamin was *here*.

My heart pummeled. I squinted and stared, not quite believing my eyes.

"Boarding," the bus driver called out.

"I found you." His words gushed, his eyes wide as if he didn't believe it either.

"Found me?" My hands slid from my face. *Found me*. I thought my head might burst trying to make sense of this. "Why? What are you doing here?"

"I'm…" The roar of the bus engine sent a swirl of hot air around us. Benjamin glanced at the suitcase on the sidewalk beside me. "Where are you going?"

"What do you care, Russell?" Arnold moved from behind me. "You think you can just mosey into town and start stirring up trouble. You can't expect Claire to answer your questions without explaining yourself. Who the hell do you—"

Benjamin stepped forward, nearly toe to toe with Arnold, his fists clenched at his sides. "And who the hell do you think you are saying anything to me? I'll talk to Claire without your butting in, so back the hell up."

"Stop." I stretched my arm out between them.

Arnold glared at Benjamin, the vessels in his neck bulging. Benjamin's fists had come up to his waist and his biceps strained against the rolled up sleeves of his shirt.

"Please, stop." I pushed my outstretched arm

against Arnold, his muscles pulsed, but he slid his gaze from Benjamin to me. "Arnold!" Pushing harder, I shoved him toward the bench. "Will you wait while I speak to Benjamin a moment?"

"All aboard, this bus is leaving." The bus driver stood on the steps and leaned out to call late passengers.

"You need to leave, Claire," Arnold ordered. "You'll miss your bus."

"I know, but…" I glanced over my shoulder at Benjamin.

Arnold followed my direction, his cheeks flushed, and he whipped his glare back on me, eyes narrowed. "You said you were going to see Paulie, right?"

"Yes…"

"Then get on the bus."

I pushed him farther, until his legs touched the bench. "Stay here. Sit down. I have to talk to him."

"No, Claire. You don't."

The bus driver shut the door.

"Get on the bus," he urged.

My hands dropped from his chest, and I lowered my head. "I can't." My head nearly touched his chest as my eyes filled with tears again.

He took my chin and raised it less than gently. "If you do this, if you defy me and listen to his excuses, give him this chance, then our chances are over. This moment, right now, is your decision. And it seals the deal one way or the other. I won't wait for you."

The bus roared, reversed, and pulled away from the curb.

That was a chance I had to take.

"I'm sorry, Arnold." Even if Benjamin couldn't allay my fears, couldn't be mine forever, my life wouldn't be determined in a split second. I couldn't live my future with what ifs.

"You don't know what you're doing. No one will ever be as good for you as I could've been. You'll be sorry." He roughly dropped his fingers from my chin, turned, and strode away. And stopped. He looked over his shoulder, his eyes squinting from some inner emotion and not the sun. "And when that son of a bitch Russell lies to you again, you'll know how to crawl back to me."

His parting words stung. My tears fell freely, his back a watery vision as he climbed into his car and squealed from my life.

I shoved my palms against my eyes, as if to dam the flow and took a deep breath.

"Claire."

I choked a sob, and my heart raced at the sound of Benjamin's voice.

Hands I'd been yearning to feel touched my shoulders, so gently.

"Claire," he whispered and guided me to face him. "Are your tears for Arnold?"

Fear gripped me. The moment to face Benjamin had been thrust upon me before I was ready, prepared, and I couldn't speak.

He huffed. "Are they?" His voice firmed with a hint of anger.

The throbbing pulse in my ears nearly blocked his words. I shook my head.

He brought my hands to his lips, kissed my fingertips, then pressed my palms to his chest.

From the touch of his lips, a tremble traveled my arms and shook deep inside me. I couldn't speak. Heat fired my entire body as if I'd been numb since the moment we parted, and, now, I could feel again.

He scoured my face with his gaze. "I've found you, Claire. I can't believe I've found you."

Benjamin driving back into my life, the touch of his lips on my fingers, and the beat of his heart beneath my hands took my breath away. I couldn't find the air to speak.

"Claire, honey. Tell me. I've found you in time, haven't I?" He grasped at my hands so tight the pulse in his wrist beat against mine. "Does Arnold mean so much to you?"

"No," I choked out. "Not so much."

"Then, what's going on? Where were you going?"

"To find...to find out why..." I swallowed away more tears. "To Phoenix."

He drew me closer.

I tensed, unsure of myself, or more pointedly of him. "Are you married to Susan?"

"No, Claire—"

The breath caught in my throat. I reared back, but his hands continued to grip mine. "You didn't marry her?" I thought my chest would burst with tension. "You told me you were marrying her. I left because you told me." I tried to pull away, but he held tight.

"No." He closed the distance I'd created. "I didn't lie to you, Claire," he whispered. "It wasn't my baby."

"What? Not yours?"

"No. Susan was already pregnant before...before we...met."

My head whirled as if I'd stepped off a merry-go-round. "But...but...you said—"

"Ruth told me she was pregnant. I didn't know

there'd been another man, and I didn't talk to Susan before I told you. I wanted to tell you first. Needed to. You were the most important part of my life."

Tears spilled down my face. My legs trembled. "Why did you let me go?"

He drew me close, our hands intertwined between us on our chests. "I went to your house to tell you the moment I found out. You were gone. You'd left me."

"I didn't leave you." I dipped my head under his chin. "I didn't leave you because I wanted to," I whispered. "Why didn't you come sooner?"

He kissed my cheek through my hair. "I only found out where you were days ago."

"Only days?" I stared into his eyes and saw a mirror of my misery.

"Don't you think I would've been here, if I'd known where you were?"

"I…I thought you would—"

"I can't live without you. I've been miserable." His eyes filled with tears. "I love you, Claire."

A sob escaped, my knees gave, and I collapsed. He caught me around the waist with one arm, holding tight, and his other hand reached under my hair, caressing my neck.

"Oh, Benjamin."

A deep breath filled his lungs, his chest expanded against me, and the beating of his heart melded with mine. He swallowed, his eyes glistening. "Am I too late, Claire?"

"Too late?"

"Can you still love me, now, after what I've put you through?"

Giddiness welled up and pushed the fear from deep

in my chest. "I never stopped loving you. I couldn't." The beginning of a smile toyed with my lips. "I tried, but it was useless."

"Then marry me, Claire. I beg you."

"You don't need to beg." My mouth touched his, and I whispered the words across his lips. "I love you, Benjamin."

His lips parted, and he drank my confession of love as if after a long drought. His kiss filled my head so there was no room for thought, and my body existed only to hold him and be held. Time ceased until he finally drew away. My eyes opened to a brighter sun.

Benjamin released me, skirted around me, and lifted my suitcase from the sidewalk. "You're coming to Phoenix, but not on the bus." His free hand wrapped around mine. "First, we'll talk to your father."

"Oh, Benjamin." The impact of his words blew over me and elevated me as much as if a strong wind had lifted me from the earth. I floated beside him to Lady Blue and slid onto the seat.

The engine came awake with the turn of the key. Benjamin sat tall behind the wheel. "Life starts right now for us, Claire."

And I would finally be home, forever, with Benjamin.

The Beginning

Check out more titles from Brenda Whiteside and The Wild Rose Press, Inc. including…

AMANDA IN THE SUMMER

Three generations of women…and the secret that strengthens their love.

A line of women, all named Amanda, stretches back for generations. Each with her hopes, her joys, her pain—each pouring out her heart in correspondence with a dear family friend who shares their lives, understands their loves, and joins in their sorrows.

But within the correspondence lies a secret. And as the youngest of the Amandas retraces the journey through the years—beginning in postwar America and following through to modern day—the letters reveal, layer by layer, the Amandas who came before her. Soon, the truths and lies hidden in the letters lead her down a path of self-discovery that forges a bond between her past and future.

A word about the author...

Brenda spends most of her time writing stories of discovery and love. The rest of her time is spent tending vegetables on the small family farm she shares with her husband, son, daughter-in-law, and granddaughter. Together, they've embraced an age-old lifestyle that has been mostly lost in the United States — multiple generations living under one roof, who share the workload, follow their individual dreams, and reap the benefits of combined talents.

Although she didn't start out to write romance, she's found all good stories involve complicated human relationships. And love is the most complicated of all. She's also found no matter a person's age, a new discovery is right around every corner. Whether humorous or serious, historical or suspense, all her books revolve around those two facts.

~*~

Visit Brenda at
www.brendawhiteside.com
www.facebook.com/BrendaWhitesideAuthor
Twitter: https://twitter.com/#!/brendawhitesid2

~*~

She blogs on the 9th and 24th of every month at
http://rosesofprose.blogspot.com
She also blogs about writing and prairie life at
http://brendawhiteside.blogspot.com/